D0722932

PR
6003
U26

52257

Bullett, Gerald William

The jury

LIBRARY
SOLANO COMMUNITY COLLEGE
P. O. BOX 246
SUISUN CITY, CALIFORNIA 94585
(707) 864-7000

A Garland Series

FIFTY CLASSICS

OF

CRIME FICTION

1900-1950

*Edited with
prefaces by*

**Jacques Barzun
and
Wendell Hertig Taylor**

THE JURY

Gerald Bullett

LIBRARY
SOLANO COMMUNITY COLLEGE
P. O. BOX 246
SUISUN CITY, CALIFORNIA 94585
(707) 864-7000

Garland Publishing, Inc., New York & London

1976

A list of all the titles in the FIFTY CLASSICS OF CRIME FICTION is included at the end of this volume.

This edition published by arrangement with A. D. Peters & Co.

Introduction Copyright © 1976 by Jacques Barzun and Wendell H. Taylor.

All Rights Reserved

Library of Congress Cataloging in Publication Data

Bullett, Gerald William, 1894-1958.
    The jury.

    (Fifty classics of crime fiction, 1900-1950 ; 7)
    Reprint of the 1935 ed. published by J. M. Dent,
London.
    I. Title. II. Series.
PZ3.B874Ju15 [PR6003.U26] 823'.9'12   75-44960
ISBN 0-8240-2356-0

Printed in the United States of America

PZ
3
B874
Ju 5

52257

Preface

There are no trial scenes in Sherlock Holmes. He had little interest in a case except as a problem to be solved, and after him most other unofficial detectives have felt as he did. Dr. Priestley, who often provided the police with evidence, never felt the urge to appear as an expert witness, a role which he could have sustained and which was obviously ideal—indeed compulsory—for Dr. Thorndyke, the first and greatest of "scientific" detectives. In more recent work, the final trial scene has sometimes become a ritual, as in Erle Stanley Gardner, where Perry Mason's legal ingenuity and aggressiveness practically demand a courtroom showdown for the not always guiltless client. (See No. 19.)

In all such scenes the jury is usually of small interest to the reader, compared with the examination of witnesses and the speeches of opposing counsel. Yet in a handful of crime stories the jury does play a real part—for instance at the beginning of Sayers' *Strong Poison* (No. 43). But suppose an author wanted to make the jury the center of interest: how should this be done? Making the trial—which, it goes without saying, must be a trial for murder—constitute the entire book, as in Frances Hart's admirable *Bellamy Trial* (1927) will not quite do, for then the feelings and "reactions" of the defendant, the witnesses, and the audience are likely to supplant those of the jury. No, the only way the jury can become a collective protagonist is to extend its fictional existence beyond the trial, both before and after the courtroom proceedings; the author must "study" this twelve-headed creature and let us into the secret of its lives and loves, so that we may become involved in its opinions and behavior when it is cut off from the world and deliberates. The verdict is the high point of such a study, and it must be painstakingly prepared.

Eden Phillpotts in *The Jury* (1927) achieved an early success in this difficult genre. He even managed, though working with fairly simple minds in rural surroundings, to produce quite naturally a surprise ending. Much later, Raymond Postgate in *Verdict of Twelve* (1940) gave a masterly account of the effects of evidence on the diverse minds of the defendant's "peers." But it is to Gerald Bullett that one must award the palm for a story of truly heroic proportions. Published in 1935, the work still seemed to the author, seven years later, a model not yet improved on. It remains such to this day.

No detail is spared in the account of the trial of Roderick Strood for the murder of his wife, and the reader is left convinced that only in one of the scholarly volumes of the *Notable British Trials* series could he find an equally rich panorama of characters in conflict. Yet the whole thing—examination of witnesses included—goes by with a smoothness belying its length. At the end, not only has the reader got to know each juror like his own neighbor, but he has also come to appreciate an important legal and moral axiom: that being proved guilty of one kind of crime does not imply being guilty of another.

J.B.—W.H.T.

Gerald Bullett (1893-1958) was educated at Cambridge, after work in a bank and early attempts at writing. In addition to poetry and fiction, including several tales of crime, he produced works of biography and books for children. His *Collected Poems* were published in 1959.

TO
**FRERE REEVES
IN FRIENDSHIP**

CONTENTS

CHARACTERS

Mark Perryman: *journalist*
Daphne Strood: *wife of Roderick Strood*
Roderick Strood: *architect*
*Lucy Prynne: *unmarried*
Mrs Prynne: *Lucy's mother*
Brian Goodeve: *literary novice*
*James Bayfield: *stationer*
Gladys Bayfield: *his wife*
Ernie & Dolly: *their children*
Edward Seagrave: *acquainted with Lucy Prynne*
*Charles Underhay: *Civil Service*
Betty Underhay: *his daughter*
Elisabeth Andersch: *pianist*
*Clare Cranshaw: *widow*
*Reginald Forth: *retired soldier*
*Oliver Brackett: *auctioneer*
Molly Brackett: *his wife*
Tucker: *the Stroods' butler*
Mrs Tucker: *their cook*
*Roger Coates: *city clerk*
Gertie Coates: *his wife*
Vincent & Marjorie: *their children*
A. J. K. Simpson: *writer on popular science*
*Lionel Bonaker: *a friend of Simpson's*

Mr Cradock: *Strood's partner*
*Cyril Gaskin: *expectant father*
Stella: *his sister-in-law*
*Blanche Izeley: *wife of Paul*
Janet Ensworth: *acquainted with Blanche Izeley*
*Sidney Nywood: *builder and undertaker*
Flo Nywood: *his wife*
*Arthur Cheed: *garage proprietor*
Nellie Cheed: *his wife*
The Reverend Mr Strood: *Roderick Strood's father*
Sir John Buckhorn: *Attorney-General*
Gregory Tufnell: *his junior*
Leonard Bolton: *police officer*
Antony Harcombe: *a K.C.*
Mr Justice Sarum: *presiding*
Ernest Nix: *detective*
Alfred Oscar House: *barman*
Dr Cartwright: *general practitioner*
Cyrus Hartman Lampetter: *pathologist*
Ronald Young: *Mr Harcombe's junior*
Mrs Henstroke: *Roger Coates's mother-in-law*
Sarah: *servant to Strood senior*

* *Member of the jury*

PART ONE

THE TWELVE CONVERGING

§ 1

CONVERSATION IN SOHO

ON an April evening not many years ago a man sat in the upper room of a Soho restaurant, waiting for the arrival of his guest. She was not yet unduly late, and Mark Perryman was not impatient. He was a man approaching thirty-five who picked up a precarious living in Fleet Street. He had lived through many excitements, and at his present advanced age he liked to think of himself as imperturbable, but he would not have denied that his mind was pleasantly warmed by the prospect of an evening with Roderick Strood's wife. The Stroods were old friends; he had dined at their house the very evening before, and had been surprised and amused to hear Daphne say, with an engaging candour which her husband gave every sign of enjoying: 'Why don't you take me to dinner some evening, Mark? No, not with Roderick. Just you and I.' Only Daphne, he reflected, could do a thing like that and get away with it, by virtue of a quality rarer than beauty, and, when allied to beauty, irresistible. With this thought the sense

13

of her was so vivid in his mind that he became
suddenly impatient for her coming; and to pass the
time he beckoned the waiter and ordered a cocktail. As he raised the glass to his lips he caught
sight of Daphne poised in the doorway and looking
for him. He waved a hand; she saw him and
came forward, greeting him with an air of pleased
surprise, as though he were the last person she had
expected to see and the one she had most wanted
to see.

'Hullo, Mark! How nice of you to come!
May I sit here?' She looked round. 'I like this
place.' She was a child at a party, taking it for
granted that Mark himself had designed everything for her pleasure, even to the mural decorations
of a public restaurant.

'Foolish, but not revolting,' said Mark.

She sat smiling at him, peeling off her gloves.
'Do you mean me?'

'I might have meant you,' said Mark. 'You
are probably foolish, and I don't find you revolting.
But what I really meant was this room, with its
arcadian nonsense. I don't hold with it, but there
are worse forms of humbug. The flowers. The
shepherdesses.' He waved his hands at the walls.
'What are you going to drink?' The waiter was
discreetly hovering.

'Do I want a cocktail or don't I?' asked Daphne.

'You do,' said Mark. 'Possibly two. Possibly
three.'

'Madame will per'aps like a cocktail *à la maison*,' suggested the waiter. 'A secret of the 'ouse. Very beautiful.'

'And then,' said Mark, 'we'll take the table d'hôte, do you think?'

'Yes,' agreed Daphne. 'And we'll take it slowly, shall we? How long can you spare for me of your busy life, Mark?'

'My dear Daphne! If the devotion of a lifetime is of any use to you . . .'

She laughed. 'Good!' They studied the menu, and, eager to be rid of him, set themselves to answer the waiter's catechism. When that was over Daphne gave a sigh of relief, and seeing a small secret light that shone and faded in her eyes, a visiting gleam of mystery, Mark felt his pulse quicken with expectation.

'And now?' he said.

She looked across at him with challenge. 'And now what?'

He had meant 'And now for the secret!' But daunted by her look he made haste to repudiate that meaning. 'And now,' he repeated, 'tell me what you think of everything.'

'Everything?'

'Life. The world. The modern girl.'

Her smile was perfunctory. It faded quickly. 'Why have you never married, Mark?'

He grinned. 'The more I see of marriage, the better I like my monastic cell.'

15

'And not so monastic either, I dare say,' remarked
Daphne, with mischievous humour. 'But you
haven't answered my question. Why have you
never married?'

'Nine out of ten of the married couples I know
wish they were single,' said Mark. 'It's not
encouraging, is it?'

'And what about the tenth?'

He considered for a moment. 'Well, you and
Roderick can be the tenth, if you like. You're
the conspicuously lucky ones of my acquaintance.'

'Are we? Now isn't that nice!' Daphne
sounded dangerous. 'Rod and I as a model
couple. That's very good indeed. You've known
Rod a long time, Mark. Longer even than I have.
But perhaps you don't realize how much he's
changed. For two years now he's made me very
unhappy.'

Mark was surprised, but not so much surprised
as he pretended to be. He had not expected this
piece of information, and was wary of taking it at
its face value. But nothing nowadays surprised
him very much. 'Really? How's that? I always
supposed that you and Rod . . . Here's that
confounded waiter again.'

The waiter continued to interrupt the conversation from time to time, but the food was pleasant,
the wine exquisite, the ritual soothing; and the
presence of other diners, each pair or group a self-
contained neighbouring world, added to the quality

of the hour. It's like a planetarium, thought Mark Perryman. It's like the constituents of the atom. It's like . . . but Daphne was telling her story, and the buzz of discreet voices about him provided a running accompaniment to that recital. The human orchestra, he said to himself. Violin concerto, with the soloist in great form. He despised these captions, but could not stop inventing them. On the whole he was enjoying his evening. He wearied of many things: boredom lay perpetually in wait for him. But he never wearied of receiving the confidences of attractive young women, and he never betrayed a confidence. It suited his humour to take a cynical view of himself, but he was ingenuous enough to believe that there was something about him that made people tell him the story of their lives on the shortest acquaintance. It flattered him to be trusted, and it was a point of vanity to be worthy of the trust. He got more kick out of keeping a secret, he would explain, than others got out of gossip. He was a practised listener and seldom went unthanked for the advice he professed not to give.

'Mark, I want to ask your advice,' said Daphne. 'You're such a wise egg.'

'Yes, aren't I?' said Mark. 'Go ahead.'

She went ahead. And, while he listened, the figure of Roderick Strood moved about in his reverie, a dark, stiff, precise figure, long-faced,

17

square-jawed, taciturn. The face of a hanging judge, thought Mark; but he repented of the phrase, remembering how the eyes could twinkle, the severe mouth relax. And if he was a judge of anything it was not of his fellow-men but rather of the houses they lived in, for he spent his days devising such things, paying far more attention, Mark imagined, to the utilities than to the aesthetics of the matter. Mark, himself of a more mercurial temperament, liked him for his limitations as much as for his qualities—because they *are* his qualities, thought the journalist. He was sensitive and conservative and nowadays (Mark recalled livelier times) unambitious. Nature, in designing him, had failed to provide him with the means of emotional expression, and though he could enjoy a joke he was fundamentally unhumorous in grain, thought Mark. But his massive integrity, the loyalty of his affections, sprang from something more vital than respect for conventional standards, though he had that too. As Daphne talked on, lowering her voice, exclaiming, pausing, making eyes of wonder and gestures of pride, looking now indignant and now distressed and always lovely in her small sleek velvet-skinned fashion, Mark Perryman's quick fancy pictured the scenes she sketched for him. Going home in a taxi after the party: Daphne angrily silent, Roderick unmoved and indifferent. The bedroom quarrel, with Daphne in tears (a disturbing sight, thought Mark) and Roderick

coldly reasonable, distant, stupid. And what was
it all about? That, it appeared, had been precisely
Roderick's reiterated question; and Daphne had
not been slow to answer it. In anger she had a
wonderful flow of language. He had spent too
much time flirting with that notorious red-headed
girl. Everyone had noticed it. Everyone was
talking about it. He had danced three times in
succession with someone else. He had neglected
his wife. He had drunk too much champagne and
made stupid jokes. She, Daphne, had been ashamed
of him. Mark's wonder grew big as he listened,
and it moved him to his one indiscretion. Did
Daphne really mean that poor old Roderick was
running after another woman?

'No such luck!' said Daphne bitterly. Mark's
eyebrows invited an explanation. Instead of offering one she smiled and said: 'Oh, Mark! What
an idea! Staid old Rod running after a woman!'

'Then what precisely is the trouble?'

'He wants me to be a good girl and just stay
put. He takes me for granted. He forgets I 'm
there. It 's not good enough, Mark.'

'No,' said Mark thoughtfully. 'I see that.' He
waited for more, knowing by instinct that something more important than these trivial domestic
rumpuses was to come.

'Besides,' remarked Daphne, after a moment's
silence, 'I expect you 'll think it very dreadful of
me, but I 've fallen in love.'

Mark tried to look surprised. 'Really?'

'Yes, really.'

'Do I know the gentleman?'

'I mustn't tell you who it is,' said Daphne. 'That wouldn't be fair. Let's call him X, shall we?'

'I shall be delighted to call him X,' said Mark, 'if you think he won't resent the liberty.'

Daphne dimpled. 'How absurd you are! No, but this is serious, Mark. It's really no laughing matter. He's Roddy's friend as well. That makes it more difficult. He was taking me home from the theatre one night. In a taxi, you know.'

'Oh, I know,' assented Mark. 'I know what these taxis are. And then?'

'Well, suddenly he was kissing me.'

'I see. And you?' His manner was oddly neutral. No one but he could have said whether the question was sympathetic, ironical, or amused. Perhaps it was all three at once.

'What do you mean?' asked Daphne, a dangerous gleam appearing suddenly in her eyes.

'I mean, how did you take it? Were you surprised, indignant, or what?'

He observed her closely, and the tender absent smile that played about her lips was a sufficient answer.

'It was the most wonderful thing that had ever happened to me,' said Daphne. 'And that's what

I want your advice about. You know Rod and
you know me. I can't let him down, can I? But
then, it seems to me he's let me down. He has,
hasn't he? I mean he's so casual, and moody, and
all that. He doesn't want me any more, and . . .
X does. X wants me to go away with him and
have a divorce and everything.'

'But he hasn't got any money,' said Mark.
'I see the difficulty.'

'What makes you say that? Do you know
who X is?'

'Haven't the least idea.'

'Then why do you say he hasn't got any money?'

'Well, has he?'

'Not very much. But he will have, in time.'

'Yes, when his father dies,' agreed Mark. 'But
his father may live another fifteen years. Have
you considered that?'

'Mark!' She stared in anger. 'Then you *do*
know who it is!'

'My dearest Daphne, I know nothing of the
kind. I'm merely helping you to tell your story.
It's not exactly a new story, you know, and one
can't help being familiar with the general outline.
When is this Heidelberg trip going to happen?
Next month, isn't it?'

'You make the most surprising leaps,' said
Daphne. 'But you're right again. You know
now why I want Rod to make his sentimental
pilgrimage without me. At home we can keep our

distance, we need never be alone together. But a holiday *à deux* is a very different matter. Never out of each other's sight. It would be merely hell. It's really Heidelberg that's brought things to a head for me.'

'And Heidelberg may solve the whole problem,' suggested Mark. 'When you get away from each other, things will fall into perspective and . . .'

'But I don't like the idea of Rod being on his own like that,' said Daphne, following her own thoughts. 'I wish *you* could go with him, Mark.' She became suddenly excited. 'Yes, that would be splendid. Why didn't we think of that last night? Will you, Mark? Will you?'

Mark shook his head. 'An impecunious journalist . . .' he began. But realizing in time that an avowal of poverty would come ill from host to guest, he abandoned his sentence and plunged back into the middle of things. 'Let's get back to the point. You and Master X. You're really in love with each other?'

She nodded.

'You're lovers?'

'Of course not.' Her cheeks were suddenly scarlet.

'Why not?'

'Is that your advice?' she asked frigidly.

'In effect, yes. Or it would be, if it weren't my strict rule never to give advice. If all you want is an adolescent romance, a tragic renunciation, and something to be wistful about in your middle age, I 've nothing to say. But if there 's more to it than that, why not try it out, put it to the test?'

'Behind Rod's back? Is that your idea of honour?'

'It 's my idea of common sense. Of course if you think it would be kinder, kinder to Rod I mean, you could consult Rod first. I'm sure he'd be interested in the project.'

'What a cynic you are!'

She had often called him a cynic, but this time there was real reproach in her voice. He glanced at her in momentary contrition. How pretty she is, he thought. How pretty and how . . . But he couldn't find the word he wanted, and his thought, swerving at the check, rode off on another tack. It would be quite fun to go to Heidelberg with old Rod. I wonder if it could be managed.

§ 2

MARK LOOKS ON

ON the banks of the Neckar the chestnut trees were in full bloom, and, though he had known it well in other days, Heidelberg was now agreeably strange to Roderick Strood. Strange, yet sufficiently familiar to induce a pang of recognition in a heart he had supposed to be moribund. Arriving on a Tuesday afternoon he observed the brightness in the air, the pink and green of the trees, the flowing sunlight of the river; but he greeted these things with a dyspeptic eye, and feigned to ignore that hint of waking interest in his heart. For many months now he had been in a state of anger with his universe. Life had denied him what he wanted, and he was resolved to refuse all substitutes in the shape of this accidental, this incidental, this impersonal beauty. But he considered himself to be a matter-of-fact person, was a great believer in reason and common sense, and he had come away for a change of scene, not because he believed in its efficacy but because it was recognized as the sensible thing to do. He took his medicine mechanically, without believing in its power to cure him. And his thoughts had turned towards Heidelberg for no better reason than that he had spent a student's year there eighteen years ago.

A happy year? Yes, happy for two reasons. Every year that had passed before his marriage now seemed to have been a period of freedom and bliss; and in those days the supreme happiness, though not achieved, was always just round the corner. At twenty a man looks forward with expectancy: at thirty-five he looks backward with regret. With such thoughts vaguely in mind he allowed himself to be driven across the bridge to the other side of the river, and thence to the Gasthaus zur Hirschgasse. At sight of the familiar place he experienced the momentary illusion of being back in the past, but his companion, Mark Perryman, was there to remind him of sober reality. In a general way he was glad of Mark's company, but at the moment the fellow struck a jarring note. He was not sorry when Mark declined to turn out, after their early evening meal, to accompany him to the Stadthalle, where Beethoven was to be played: he went alone, leaving Mark engaged on a piece of journalism. 'I'd like to come,' said Mark, 'but I feel like writing this stuff before it goes cold on me. I'm always in my shop, you must remember.' So in the luminous evening Roderick Strood walked back across the bridge. He noted again the beauty of the chestnuts, and said to himself: 'How futile it all is! And why am I going to this concert?' . . . Twelve hours later, looking on that scene with new eyes, he found a poignant meaning in its beauty, a

meaning, a revelation, and a promise. In the
interval he had heard some music and had a night
of broken sleep, but Mark Perryman found difficulty in believing that these things alone had
caused so great a change in his friend. On the
way out from England Strood had been an un-
responsive companion, shut up in himself, moody
to the point of moroseness. He had taken obscure
offence at the sight of Cologne; the voyage up
the Rhine had bored him almost beyond bearing
('Why the hell did we come this way?' he asked
bitterly); and the arrival at Heidelberg, after so
much tribulation, had seemed to give him no
pleasure. Mark had never seen him so obviously
out of sorts before: he could only conclude that
Daphne had confessed her desire for divorce and
that poor Roderick, knowing himself bereaved of
her love, was in process of making terms with
despair. And now, suddenly, he was friendly, gay,
young again. What magic was there in Heidelberg
that could work such a change? Roderick was so
obliging as to tell him everything—everything
essential—in one unguarded sentence.

'Has it ever occurred to you, Mark, that there 's
something rather insipid about Englishwomen?'

So that 's how it is, said Mark to himself. 'I 've
noticed,' he answered, 'that after living in Bedford-
shire, the mountainous regions of Wales seem
singularly agreeable.'

Roderick stared gravely, but his thoughts were

elsewhere. 'There was a young pianist at that concert the other night. She played some sonatas.'

'Good?' asked Mark.

'Marvellous, I thought. I don't pretend to be a judge, but she seems to me to be in the very first class.'

The young pianist's name was Elisabeth Andersch. By the most miraculous chance Roderick had observed her, the very morning after the concert, strolling by the riverside. He had introduced himself.

'Did you, indeed!' said Mark, raising his eyebrows in admiration. 'You young chaps don't lose much time, I must say. Did she call the police?'

'I suppose,' said Roderick, 'it *does* sound an audacious thing to do. But luckily I didn't think of that at the time. It was my one chance and I took it.'

'What did you say?' asked Mark. 'You paid a formal German tribute to her performance, and remarked, apropos of nothing in particular: *Ich war zu Heidelberg Student*. Was that it?'

Roderick's tolerant smile could not quite conceal his surprise. 'You seem to know all about it.'

'Far from it,' said Mark modestly. 'I'm only a learner.'

The silence that followed was so protracted that Mark began to fear that his banter had been ill received. But when at last Roderick spoke again

27

it was made clear not only that he had taken it all
in good part but that he was translated to a paradise
far beyond reach of humour.

'Look here, Mark. This is the most important
thing that has ever happened to me.'

Mark was sobered by the avowal. He looked
sympathetic, but answered nothing. What a trite
situation, he thought. 'Life is so flagrant a copy
of fiction, isn't it?' he remarked. 'And not the
best fiction either.'

Roderick was not attending. 'I 've been waiting
for this all my life,' he said, in a voice at once shy
and defiant.

'Are you seeing her again?' asked Mark, feeling
oddly at a loss for anything better to say.

Roderick looked at his watch. 'In half an
hour. You 'll forgive my running away, my dear
fellow?'

Only seven days of the holiday remained, Roderick
being due back in London at the end of May.
Mark had hoped to renew old times by having
with his friend some of those tremendous conversations, so dear to young men, in which the
nature of things is endlessly and excitingly
explored. As fellow-undergraduates they had
dedicated many a glorious hour to that pursuit.
And there was indeed no dearth of conversation
during this holiday: the thing resolved itself into
one enormous rambling discussion of love and
marriage, with special reference to Daphne Strood

and Elisabeth Andersch. Mark felt his own position to be one of exquisite delicacy. Being in Daphne's confidence, he found it irksome to be prevented, by a point of honour, from assuring his friend that all would be well, and that Daphne, so far from being distressed, would sigh with relief to be rid of an unwanted husband. All that hints could do, he did: beyond that, nothing would have persuaded him to go. Roderick had reached the point of believing that his passion for Daphne had never been the real thing; he was for ever explaining his marriage away; but he seemed unable, without more help than Mark was willing to give him, to leap to the idea that Daphne might be in the same state of mind about himself. He conceded the possibility that she might be generous, but he could not believe that she would release him without hesitation or distress. He was tortured by indecision, whether and when to tell her of this wonderful thing that had transfigured his life. For that this new passion was the real thing he couldn't for a moment doubt: he was as ingenuous about it as a schoolboy. Fräulein Andersch, by a coincidence in which it was impossible not to see the hand of a benign providence, was on the point of going to England, where she intended to give a series of recitals; and there was no reason in the world why the affair should not prosper. No reason except Daphne.

'And as for Daphne,' said Mark, 'she may take

the whole thing more quietly than you fear.   There may be aspects of Daphne's character that even *you* don't understand, Rod.'

'And that *you* do, I suppose?' bantered Roderick.

Mark grinned. He came, moreover, within measurable distance of blushing. 'I wouldn't make such a bold claim as that. But it's perhaps not so preposterous a notion as it seems.   Onlookers see most of the game, if my copybooks are to be believed.'

'So you think I ought to tell her?' asked Roderick.

Mark shook his head, smiling. 'I never give advice.'

Roderick said no more. His mind followed, wincingly, a new train of thought, and for a moment he was back again, a small child, in the Vicarage orchard, clutching desperately at his father's hand.

§ 3

LUCY PRYNNE

BOARDING, at King's Cross, the train that was to carry her safely to the North-London suburb where she lived with Poor Mother, Lucy Prynne was quite unaware of the connexion, which time would make apparent, between herself and the Roderick Stroods. She had much to think about; but now, the tension of the day being relaxed, she was not so much thinking as watching the random thoughts drift in and out of her mind. She was small and slim, and dressed with a neat homeliness, an absence of enterprise, that was part of her character. She sat very upright in her corner, with her back to the engine to avoid the flying smuts, and her glance rested incuriously, even blankly, on the familiar metropolitan landscape that moved past her. Her face, except for its city pallor, had all the qualities that make for prettiness; and, if it was not in fact pretty, that was because the vigilant spirit within her, the unconscious censor of her impulses, would not have it so. Cold blue eyes, a small straight unaggressive nose, delicate eyebrows set high on a fair brow, and a clear skin upon which her thirty-one years had made scarcely a mark, these were advantages which many a woman of her age might have envied her, and many a man might have observed with quickening interest. But the total effect was neutral rather than alluring, rather an absence of noticeable blemishes than the positive attraction of womanly bloom; and the small tight-shut mouth hinted at severity, gave her the air of being always afraid that some unauthorized person was about to speak to her.

Nearly twenty years had passed since Lucy Prynne had first tightened her lips against the world, and against the rebel within her that was secret even from herself; and it now made part of the habitual expression of her face in repose. Nearly twenty years, for she could not have been more than eleven when, with her father and brothers, but leaving Poor Mother unaccountably at home, she had spent that odd momentous fortnight at Netherclift-next-the-Sea. She remembered the queer name of the place, and she remembered, was not likely to forget, the very surprising surprise that Father had had in store for her. They took possession of their little bungalow on a Friday evening, and next morning at breakfast Father said, suddenly: 'Lucy my love, there's a new auntie coming to see us to-day. Won't that be nice?' Father had large drooping moustaches and bushy eyebrows. When he smiled he exposed a gold tooth, and the nostrils of his blunt nose dilated in a manner that made him seem unexpectedly fierce. Lucy had never quite got used to him, so incalculable were his humours; and she was puzzled that he should single her out to be the special recipient of this piece of news when, as she could see from their faces, it was equally news to Reggie and Tom, who were both her seniors. But obediently, timidly, she returned smile for smile, and when at teatime the new auntie drove up in a cab from the station, whence Father had escorted her, she as obediently kissed the velvet cheek offered her, and said, repeating her drill: 'Good afternoon, Aunt Lena.' Aunt Lena was as plump and vivacious as Mother was slim, gentle, apathetic. Her vivacity was rather unnerving after Mother's quiet ways, and her trick of never addressing children except in the third person was one that kept Lucy always at a distance, though the boys, who took everything as it came, voted her a decent sort. 'I wonder if Lucy would like sixpence to buy sweeties with,' Aunt Lena would remark; and it took the child a long while to realize that this form of inquiry demanded an answer from herself. Aunt Lena shared Lucy's bedroom during the whole of the fortnight: a circumstance that afterwards gave the girl much food for puzzled thought. During the day Father had eyes for no one else. He and Aunt Lena went for long walks together every day, leaving the three children to their own devices.

Lucy did not mind that at all; she got on well enough with her brothers and could play most of their games. When they were tired of the beach and the cliffs, they wandered inland, down winding country lanes and through fields of standing corn. To children born and bred in the suburbs it was heavenly to be made free of such a paradise of fields and farms and far horizons, to breathe the rich country scents (even the smell of pigs was rapture to Lucy's nostrils), to lie in the lee of hedges watching the sky float past and filling all one's senses with the drowse of high summer. Why must Reggie spoil it all? But to Lucy it seemed not Reggie himself that did it, but something in the nature of things, something unspeakably horrible that lay concealed under the smile of the day. Reggie caught sight of a young rabbit and gave chase. The small creature quivered in his grasp, and with a queer grin, before anyone had time to think, he swung it carelessly by its hind legs and dashed its head against the post of a five-bar gate. Seeing the rabbit hang limp, the boy dropped it with a cocky excited laugh. His eyes, glittering with pleasure, stared boldly; but behind their glitter, behind their staring defiance, they were furtive and ashamed. After a moment of speechless horror Tom broke out into loud schoolboyish protests. But Lucy took three steps towards the dead animal, then turned away, turned her back on the boys, and began vomiting. The shameful secret kept all three of them silent on the way back to the bungalow, and when, within sight of the door, Reggie broke the silence by saying 'Are you going to sneak, young Lucy?' she could answer him only with a glance of pure misery. No one, she knew, would ever understand what had made her be sick: both Reggie and Tom supposed it to have been the sight of the rabbit with blood trickling from eyes and mouth. She was glad when the holiday came to an end and they went back to Mother. They had said good-bye to Aunt Lena, but naturally she came into the conversation. It was Lucy herself, at the tea-table that first day home, who mentioned her.

'Aunt Lena gave us all half a crown, Mummy.'

'How kind of her!' said Mrs Prynne. Lucy

was suddenly aware of something strange existing between her father and her mother, of something queer in the quality of her mother's pause before she added with a kind of breathless quiet: 'And who is Aunt Lena, my dear?'

'Aunt Lena,' said Tom, 'that's our new auntie, Mum. You never told us about her.'

Mrs Prynne had so far avoided her husband's eyes, but now she looked at him, and so did Lucy.

'Ah,' said he, jauntily, meeting her question with a look that was like a sneer, 'you haven't met her, Mary. A charming woman. Isn't she, boys?' After a deliberate pause he added, without shifting his gaze: 'She shared little Lucy's bedroom.'

He stared his wife out of countenance. She flushed a little, and her glance dropped. 'That was very clever of you, Reginald,' she said tonelessly.

Watching her father's face, Lucy was reminded sharply of Reggie's look when he felt the rabbit hanging limp from his hand. The same glitter, the same twist of the lips. And in that moment her childhood came to an end; and summer, she half-knew, would never be the same again. Whatever immediately happened between husband and wife happened behind the scenes. Nothing more was said at the time, and it was not till some months later that the final rupture came, that bewildering day when the three children were summoned to

Father's study and commanded to choose which of
their parents they would live with. Father, in his
morning coat and white stock, straddled across the
hearthrug, stroking his buttocks with an alternating
movement as though trying to rub the fire's warmth
into them. His head was held at a proud angle;
his eyebrows and moustaches had never seemed so
prominent, his eyes never so big and darkly shining.
Mother, big with her fourth child, sat in a chair
near the window, her hands folded in her lap, her
eyes turned fixedly away from the room. She did
not look up when her children, after respectfully
tapping on the door, filed in. She made no sign
when Reggie and Tom, warmed by their father's
ferocious geniality, and perhaps not fully understanding the import of their choice, elected to go
away with him and live in a fine new house.

'Aha!' cried Father, rubbing his hands together.
'We'll have a jolly time, lads. You see if we
don't. And now . . . what says little Lucy?' He
brought the full power of those shining orbs to
bear upon his daughter. His confidence was overwhelming, and for a moment she could not take her
eyes off him. But something, whether a faint sound
or something less palpable, broke the spell, and she
turned, frightened and alone, to her mother for
guidance. Mrs Prynne's posture had changed:
one hand covered her eyes, the other lay twitching
upon the arm of the chair. The child looked from
one parent to the other.

'Well?' demanded Father. 'Speak up for your-self, ducky.'

Lucy spoke at last. 'I want to stay with Mother,' she said . . . and ran stumbling into the arms outstretched to receive her.

The young woman in the train did not recall these scenes, but they were deeply scored in a hidden part of her mind. She was thinking or dreaming now of more immediate things: of the day's events, the fat important woman who had come in to order an evening dress, the new designs, Brenda's earache, the ever-so-comical story told by one of the girls, and the sly insolence of the window-cleaner. Her happening to know Brenda Willing-don had been a piece of good fortune; for who else would have given her her chance as a designer? And without that chance how would she have sup-ported Poor Mother? When her parents separated by private agreement, kind Mr Brown, Father's solicitor, had drawn up a document which safe-guarded, so he said, the rights of both parties. Mrs Prynne, humiliated and spiritless, the kind of woman that attracts persecution and is not sur-prised when it comes, put her name to this instru-ment without protest. Thirty shillings a week did not seem much for a woman and two children to live on, but kind Mr Brown, that sympathetic friend of the family, seemed to think it quite a nice little sum, and she was too desperately weary to argue about it. For that weariness Lucy had paid, and was still paying, with no help from her absent father or her equally absent brothers, whom she never saw. She had exhibited a decided talent for drawing, and after the break with Father she cultivated this talent assiduously, with her mother's languid and absent-minded approval. Being nurse-maid to her new little brother, however, left her little time, out of school hours, for drawing. Besides, there was housework to do. Mother was slow in recovering from her confinement: in fact it might be said that she never recovered, for even now, so many years after the event, she was forced to spend the greater part of her life lying down.

All things considered, Lucy might have been expected to feel relief at her little brother's prema-ture death; but in fact she grieved more tumultu-ously than the mother herself, who accepted the calamity with the same drooping misery, the same maddening resignation, as she brought to every-thing. Even the incorrigibly loyal Lucy some-times caught herself wishing that Mother would rouse herself a little, though she would have held it blasphemy to speak the wish out loud. Leaving school at fourteen, by the kindness of a neighbour she was able to attend art-classes for a few months; but she couldn't keep it up, so difficult was it to fit in with her other duties, and especially the duty of sitting with Mother in the evenings. As soon as Lucy began earning money, Mr Brown was instructed to pay Mrs Prynne ten shillings a week less, although the value of the pound had depreciated. Lucy said couldn't they go to a magistrate and show him their precious agreement and get their rights; but Mother said she'd rather not be mixed up in any unpleasantness with Father, and of course Mother knew best. It hurt her to hear Father so much as mentioned, and Lucy acquired a nervous dread of seeing her mother wince at the mere approach of the subject. Yet after all one had to be a little practical, so Lucy secretly wrote to Father herself, sending the letter to Mr Brown's office to be forwarded. It was what she thought of as a very strong letter, but apparently it had not achieved its purpose of frightening Father, for it evoked no reply. Lucy wished afterwards that she had put things differently and appealed to his Better Self, but this regret was only half sincere, for she could not think of her father as anything but vicious and cruel, just as she could not think of her mother as anything but a martyred saint. Yes, one had to be a little practical, and Lucy did her best, taking and losing one job after another, till here she was (secure at last, she believed), earning three pounds ten with Brenda Willingdon, the *Madame Brenda* of the shop-sign.

The first stop was Finsbury Park, and at Finsbury Park she made ready to leave the carriage and get into another one; for everybody got out except the man in the far corner opposite, and at first it looked as though no one was going to get in. But in the nick of time two women arrived to relieve her anxiety, and the journey proceeded without further event. Arriving at her home-station, she set her face towards Mother and moved to that destination with a swift gliding motion, looking neither to right nor left, except when, crossing a road, she had to give heed to the traffic. By the time she reached her house—and hers it was, for it was rented in her name, lest Father should interfere—she had her latchkey ready to hand. She entered with habitual swiftness and care, shut the door quietly, and removed her hat and coat and gloves. Clutching her leather handbag under her left arm she approached the sitting-room door and tapped gently. A low response from within assured her that Mother was awake. Soundlessly the door-handle turned under her hand.

'Well, Mother? I'm back.'

'Good evening, dear. You're a little late this evening, aren't you?'

Mrs Prynne lay in a long chair by the window that overlooked a gravel path and a bed containing five small rose-trees. The room was small, and in Lucy's estimation cosy. She was a capable designer of woman's dresses, but her notions of art did not extend to wallpapers. She was, however, conscious of the stuffy smell, and it was on the tip of her tongue to ask her mother why she didn't have a window open. A fire was burning in the grate, somewhat at odds with the sunlight streaming in through the window. Some knitting lay on the table at Mrs Prynne's side; but Lucy could not resist the impression that her mother had sat all day with idle hands, waiting for her return. If Lucy's face had been lined and plump and submissive, instead of smooth and pale and timidly resolute, the resemblance between the two women would have been striking. And it was almost with her mother's voice that Lucy asked her accustomed question.

'Have you had a good day, Mother?'

'Quite nice, dear. A touch of my sciatica again, but I must expect that.'

'Poor Mother!' murmured Lucy. And to herself she said: How brave Mother is!

'But it's very nice to see you back, dear. Did you manage to get the library book changed?'

'Oh, not today, Mother,' cried Lucy in great discomfort. 'It's tomorrow the boy comes round. I thought I told you.'

'Very likely you did, Lucy.' Mrs Prynne sighed deeply. 'My memory's not what it used to be. And I'm sure you've more important things to think about than my library book.'

Feeling herself vaguely at fault, Lucy went to the sideboard drawer and got out a white linen tablecloth. She began laying the table for the evening meal.

'Has Mrs Baker been looking after you properly,

Mother?' Mrs Baker was under contract to look in from time to time, in case Mrs Prynne should be suddenly taken worse. 'Did she cook you a nice lunch?'

'I really forget, dear. Yes, I think so. Have you seen your letter?'

'A letter for *me*?' said Lucy in surprise.

'It came this afternoon. I put it on the mantelpiece for you.'

Lucy finished laying the table before looking at her letter, and before opening and reading it she scraped the potatoes and put them on the gas-ring to boil. The handwriting was strange to her. Strange and interesting, and even a little exciting. She read with startled eyes: Dear Miss Prynne, I wonder if there is any hope of your being at the Literary Society meeting tomorrow (Thursday) evening, when I, alas, am to give my little effort on 'The Religion of Wordsworth'? I am dreading the ordeal of a public appearance, and I cannot tell you how much I should appreciate the moral support of your presence in the audience. I so much enjoyed our little talk three weeks ago, and I only wished it could have been longer. If you *are* able to spare the time, and would not be too bored, perhaps you would allow me the pleasure of escorting you home after the meeting. With kind regards, believe me, yours very sincerely, Edward O. Seagrave.

Lucy folded the letter and restored it to its envelope, conscious of her mother's anxiety to know all about it, and oddly (unreasonably, she felt) resolved to say nothing. All men were bad at heart. All men were potentially Father. All, except perhaps Mr Seagrave, who was somehow different. Mr Seagrave taught in the Congregational Sunday School and was an active member of the Congregational Literary Society. Lucy could not manage to get to chapel every Sunday, and she had only been once to a meeting of the Literary Society. It was on that one solitary occasion, three weeks ago, that Mr Seagrave had advanced from a bowing acquaintanceship to something that might have been the beginning of a friendship, had friendship with a man, and with so intellectual a man, been conceivable. He was old-fashioned in manner, even a little pompous; but his sincerity was manifest, and Lucy, on the strength of ten minutes halting conversation about books, mostly books she had never read, was inclined to suspect him of a secret shyness. Stooping, eager, intent, he had something gnomish about him that was at once attractive and a little comical. It would certainly be interesting to meet him again. And of course there was Wordsworth too.

But how could she leave Mother? How could she even broach the question? So that she might think unobserved she went into the scullery, on the pretext of seeing whether the potatoes were done, and stayed there until driven back by the fear of her mother's impatience. Not till the meal was nearly over, and Mother supplied with her cup of chocolate, did she venture to remark:

'It's the Literary Society tonight.'

Mother received the information in silence.

'And someone's reading a paper on Wordsworth,' said Lucy, desperately.

'Indeed?'

'I expect it will be very interesting,' added the girl, with a forced lightness of tone. 'I've always wanted to know about Wordsworth. You know, Mother. The poet.'

'It's a long time since I read any poetry, dear,' said Mrs Prynne, with a hint of reproach.

The subject seemed dead. But after a long pause Lucy was horrified to hear herself say, in a trembling voice: 'Mother, would you mind very much if I went to the meeting tonight? I could be in by ten at latest.'

Blushing, she met her mother's glance, but dropped her eyes quickly at sight of that strange sad smile.

'I *had* rather looked forward to seeing something of my daughter tonight,' confessed Mrs Prynne, with gentle resignation. 'But if you *want* to leave Mother, Mother won't stand in your way, dear. You know that.'

'Oh, it doesn't matter,' answered Lucy quickly. To hide her disappointment she gathered the used plates into a pile and carried them into the scullery. There she stayed for a moment, bent over the sink.

And presently the picture of Mr Seagrave faded from her mind, and she found herself looking, with fear and hatred, into the dark commanding eyes of Father.

§ 4

ANOTHER MAN'S WIFE

STARING into his shaving-mirror Brian Goodeve said to himself: 'It is impossible that she should love me.' But his blood, quickened with desire, made nothing of that specious argument. His was not, whatever he might think or feign to think, an ill-favoured face. It was young, pale, a little gaunt; and the chin, even when newly shaved, lived in the dark aura of the beard he so despairingly battled with. Occasionally, too, his flesh had a raw look; occasionally a pimple appeared; and these disasters, timed (it seemed) to occur whenever a meeting with Daphne was in prospect, were capable of sapping his courage and of precipitating a mood of bitter self-depreciation. Yet personal beauty was not, he told himself, the chief attraction that a woman desired in her lover; and when Daphne was with him his fears would always vanish out of mind in the tumult of his emotions; she, and she only, had the power to make him forget himself. Moreover, however impossible it might appear to cool reflection, she had given signs of love which not even he could explain to his disadvantage. That she, a thing enskied and sainted, a being of such exquisite delicacy, should give her heart to an impecunious and socially inexperienced young man like himself was impossible; but it was true. So sensitive was he about his respectable but undistinguished antecedents that he winced from making comparison, even in his secret mind, between himself and her in that particular respect; but, whether he confessed it or not, his passion was greatly augmented by gratitude to her for not minding that he was the son of a Midlandshire tradesman, while she . . . But of Daphne's origins he had made no question, taking it for granted that they were rich and strange and of an impeccable gentility. With an awkward, a too eager honesty, he had blurted out all the truth about himself: that he had come to London to seek his fortune, fortified by nothing but his ardent literary aspirations and an allowance of a hundred and fifty a year from his father. And she had received the dreadful secret without turning a hair, telling him that he was very lucky and how she wished she could write poetry too. But she had done more than that: she had introduced him to a man who knew a man who knew an editor, and from this editor, from time to time, he picked up little jobs of reviewing. In his gratitude to Daphne, which had preluded this consuming flame of love,

he couldn't quite forget, however, that it was Strood
who had first taken notice of him, had liked his
poems (several of which had appeared in the
weeklies), and encouraged Daphne to ask him to
the house.

He couldn't forget that, much as he wished to.
For some weeks now he had declined all her invitations to dinner, insisting that they should meet
either in his own rooms or on neutral ground.

'Darling, how sweet of you!' she said, mocking
him. 'One of these days I shall hear you saying
to Rod: Sir, my feelings for your wife make it
impossible that I, as a man of honour, should continue to avail myself of your hospitality. . . . Is
that the idea?'

Brian laughed. 'Something like that,' he admitted. 'Don't you feel the difficulty yourself?'

She ignored the question. 'So old-world of you,
Brian. We 've changed all that. . . . And if you
say *Plus ça change*, I shall scream.'

'It 's the inevitable comment,' said Brian.
'Hackneyed, but true.'

'It 's not true. People are more sensible nowadays than they were in our fathers' time. I don't
say jealousy has ceased to exist——'

'Don't you, Daphne?' said Brian. 'I thought
you did.'

'I don't say anything so absurd as that,' Daphne
went on, quelling him with a look. 'But it *is* true
that we 're getting more civilized. More tolerant

47

and less possessive. Married people are beginning
to learn the logic of freedom.'
'All the freedom *I* want,' said Brian, 'is the
freedom to be married to you.'
'Foolish one!' she murmured fondly. 'You'd
soon get over that if you *were* married to me.'
She waited for his repudiation of this blasphemy,
and did not wait in vain. 'But, you know,' she
warned him teasingly, 'to me you're a mere child.
I'm older than you.'
'By precisely ten months and three days,' said
Brian. 'I've told you——'
'So you have, darling,' agreed Daphne, 'but I
don't mind hearing it again.'
Fragments of conversation such as these floated
through his mind as he stood in front of the shaving-
mirror and lathered his offending face. A thousand
small remembered moments—enshrining a trick of
speech, a tone of voice, a word, a look, a gesture,
the way she peeled her gloves off, the way she
turned her head at a question, the enchanting
asymmetry of her lips when she began to smile—
these things made up the sum of her in his mind.
But she was not the mere sum of her qualities, as
he well knew: she was a living spirit and she loved
him. Tremendous, impossible, undeniable fact!
By loving him she made him life-size who had
always been too ready to believe himself insigni-
ficant, ineffectual (ineffectual in action, that is: for
behind all his self-depreciation lived the calm con-

viction that somewhere in the depths of his being there was a Shakespeare, only waiting for release); had imparted a new virility to his step, a new clearness and candour to his eye, a new confidence to be seen in the very poise of his head. He even wielded his razor more expertly, for no better reason than that Daphne had declared she loved him.

It was six o'clock (Greenwich time) on a bright cool evening during the last week of May. On the waters of the Neckar, in a little dinghy painted a bright blue, Roderick Strood and Elisabeth Andersch drifted on the golden tide of their dream. In the moment when Roderick shipped his oars and leaned forward to look more deeply into the eyes of his companion, Daphne refolded and re-enveloped a letter she had been reading, Brian Goodeve dipped his razor in hot water, and Mr James Bayfield, of Peckham Rye, told Ernie to shut the shop-door. Expectation ran like fire in Brian's veins. All day he had tried to ignore the thought consuming him; the hope, the all-but-knowledge, that Daphne, visiting him in his rooms this evening, would give him at last that which hitherto, through some fine-drawn scruple, she had withheld. He contemplated the prospect of that ultimate intimacy with a rapture more than half mystical, the tumult in his blood being, by promise of fulfilment, held in the leash of awed adoration. Having completed his toilet he cleansed and stropped the razor, washed the brush, screwed the top on the tube of shaving cream, and put everything back in its place, lingering over every operation with an almost finicking care, so that the time might seem to pass more quickly. That this deliberating tidiness was no part of his ordinary habit was shown, all too clearly, in the general disorder of the bedroom. The appearance of the place struck sudden panic in him, and with a controlled frenzy he set about putting things straight. Nothing he could do, however, would avail to make his apartments seem elegant to the eye of a woman accustomed to comfort. He knew bitterly that the place must seem to her fastidiousness little better than squalid. His two rooms ('with kitchenette,' as the advertisement had said) were as drab as the district in which they were situated. The walls of the sitting-room he had stripped of their pink cabbage-roses and covered with a cream distemper, but the bedroom retained a wall-paper which seemed, by the mere fact that he hadn't positively died of it, to accuse him of tastelessness. A decent Van Gogh reproduction over the sitting-room fire-place, a bit of gaily coloured pottery on top of the bookcase, a few well-sprung easy chairs, and a carpet costing, say, twenty-five pounds, these would have made all the difference between unromantic bareness and bright bohemian poverty. Brian looked about him with discontent. But the discontent was a matter rather of habit than conviction. Daphne had seen the place often enough and accepted it. If her private reaction had been one of distaste, no hint of any such thing had appeared in her manner. Which only shows, said Brian to himself, what breeding can do for a woman. He got into his accustomed chair, picked up a book, and set himself to forget the storm of expectation in his heart. Daphne looked up at him from every page.

Soon he abandoned the pretence of reading and gave himself up to anticipating the sweet, impulsive, passionate things he would say to her. But when she came in fact, he could at first say nothing at all. The sight of her struck him dumb, and every nerve in his body tingled with delight when she lent herself indulgently to his embrace. Indulgently: and he was enchanted; content, now he had her in his sight, to be patient, to wait until she, throwing aside her languor as she had thrown aside her cloak, should give herself, with him, to the love that he felt to be hovering above them, making their hearts one. But when, preceding him into the sitting-room, she half-turned to him again, with the full light of that glowing evening on her face, he saw with a shock that something had happened. Instead of giving voice to the thought, he tried cunningly to ignore it, and quickly, as if to cut off her escape, he said: 'Darling, this is marvellous. The beginning of the world.'

He would have seized her again, but she evaded

51

his arms, saying: 'Let me sit down for a bit.
I'm tired.'

'Didn't you have a taxi?'

'Yes.' She looked at him half-defiantly. 'But
it's quite possible to be tired even after a taxi-ride.'

He refrained from answering, lest he should be
betrayed into tears and be shamed in her sight
for ever.

Noticing his silence, she glanced at him in a way
that was almost furtive. 'Brian, I hope you're
not going to mind too much.'

With dry lips he asked: 'What do you mean?'
But what she meant was already in his mind, a
hideous fear awaiting the seal of her word.

'I mean I want you to be sensible, my dear,' she
said. 'I've had a letter from Roderick,' she went
on, in a cold voice. 'It seems he's picked up a
young woman in Germany, if you please.'

Brian stared blankly. 'What's that got to do
with us?'

Daphne gave no sign of having heard the question.
'It's the letter of a child, a romantic schoolboy.
He actually talks of marrying her. If you ever
heard of such a thing?'

Brian jumped out of his chair. 'But Daphne!
Darling! What could be better? You'll divorce
him and we can get married. Why—don't you
see! It's the very best thing that could have
happened.'

He came towards her with outstretched hands.

She turned her head away with a gesture of impatience.

'Please, Brian! I'm not in the mood for sentimentalities.'

The room spun round him. 'What did you say, Daphne?'

'If you and Roderick imagine that I'm going to be pushed aside like that, you're mistaken, both of you. The first pretty face he sees, and I'm superseded.'

'Did you say *sentimentalities?*' asked Brian. His voice was hard.

'Besides,' she went on, 'there's Roderick to be thought of. I'm very fond of Roderick. I can't let him fall into a trap like that. Of course if he really loved this woman, and if she were a really nice woman, I wouldn't stand in his way for a moment.'

'And isn't she a nice woman?' asked Brian dangerously. 'What makes you think so?'

'No nice woman tries to steal another woman's husband,' retorted Daphne, her voice rising. After a tense silence her demeanour suddenly changed. 'Poor Roderick!' she said, with a smile. 'He's never looked at another woman in his life. We've been married nearly eight years now and I know my Roderick. He's very simple really, in spite of his brains. Musician he calls her. He would, the poor darling. She's probably some little piece out of the chorus.'

53

Brian waited, in a kind of trance, for her speech to end. Then he said, with mechanical precision: 'Was it last week or the week before?'

Daphne became aware of him. She seemed almost surprised to see that he was still there. 'What are you talking about, Brian?'

'You told me,' said Brian, 'how glad you would be if Roderick could find happiness with some other girl, a happiness, you said, such as you had found with me. Was it last week or the week before?'

Daphne's eyes flashed with anger. She rose from her chair. 'If you want to score debating points I'll go, before we start quarrelling.'

'Sit down! Sit down!' Seeing a gleam of alarm in her angry eyes, he realized, with sudden shame, that he was shouting at her, threatening. 'Oh, God!' he cried, and flung himself into a chair, burying his face in his hands. He heard her voice as from a great distance.

'I'm sorry, Brian. Sorry.' Her hands stroked his hair. 'Don't take it like that, Brian. You'll make yourself ill.' She sat on the arm of the chair and rocked his head on her breast, as though he had been indeed the baby he now seemed to be.

He looked up: ashamed of his exhibition, but obscurely comforted, and ready to clutch at hope. He put an arm round her unresisting shoulders and pleaded for her love. And while he did so some part of him stood aside, a detached but contemptuous spectator. If she refuses me now, after I 've humbled myself, I shan't be able to go on living.

She disengaged herself from his embrace and moved away. 'No, no,' she said. 'It 's useless to talk of that now, Brian. Can't you see, it 's not the time for it.'

'Then you don't love me after all? Is that it?' He knew that his persistence was stupid, that his weakness was alienating her affections still further from him. But he couldn't leave the thing alone: some demon in his brain drove him on to encompass his own destruction. 'You love Roderick? Is that it?'

The compassion went out of her eyes. 'Of course I love Roderick,' she said coldly. 'Roderick is my husband.'

Then damn and blast Roderick, said Brian in his heart.

'And even if I didn't love him,' remarked Daphne, reaching for her gloves, 'it would be my duty to save him from that little foreign tart.'

§ 5

MR BAYFIELD AT HOME

HAVING told Ernie to shut the shop-door, and having watched to see that he did it properly (for he did not trust this son of his), Mr James Bayfield counted the day's takings, locked up the cash, and sauntered into the parlour. He was tired after the day's work, but he owed it to his dignity to saunter, and saunter he did: it was a gesture, unconscious or only half-conscious, of independence, a way of reminding himself that his soul was his own, and that being in his middle fifties, and having to sell tobacco, stationery, newspapers, gum, string, two-penny novelettes, chocolates, boiled sweets, nougat, liquorice all-sorts, bachelor-buttons, and the rest of it, were facts that did not dismay him, and don't you make any mistake about that. The parlour was a small overcrowded room, full of heavy furniture upholstered in red plush. It was inadequately lit by a window that looked out upon a narrow asphalted side-passage shut in by the high blind wall of the next house. Mr Bayfield and his neighbours worked hard and late to keep the owner of this rabbit-warren in comfort and comparative idleness; if they had been organized in squads and driven to work with whips they could hardly have done more for him; but Mr Bayfield

for one was so far from thinking of himself as a
slave that any attempt to set him free would have
seemed to him a dangerous innovation. Mr Bayfield's fireside chair was placed with its back to this
window, so that Mr Bayfield could read in comfort,
for he was known as a great reader; and the rest
of the family managed as best they could and saw
no injustice in the arrangement, making the most
of the dim light that filtered through the frosted
pane set in the door intervening between themselves
and the shop. Despite its deficiencies Mr Bayfield
entered the parlour with an air of satisfaction and
even of self-satisfaction. Trade had been brisk
today; besides his regular customers, many strangers
had dropped in for a packet of ten, or an ounce of
this or that; there had been quite a run on the
evening papers; and the Tottenham murder had
provided him with a great deal of very agreeable
conversation. To say that he was looking forward
to his evening would be an overstatement, for he
gave the matter no conscious thought; but the fact
that he was now for a few hours a free man, and
the fact that he would use his freedom in a manner
prescribed by his daily routine, this double fact, a
paradox but not a contradiction, undoubtedly gave
colour and quality to this moment of release, and
imparted good temper to the voice in which he
remarked on the absence of his wife. 'Hullo,
where's Mother?' The room was empty; the
words fell on no ears but his own. But he did

not mind that, for the sound of his own voice was always a pleasure to him, and he was in the habit of offering himself, a willing and appreciative audience, a kind of running commentary on the moving picture of life. Customers often caught him at it, and were seldom tempted to laugh, for it was somehow all part of his character, and Mr Bayfield's opinion of that had proved infectious to all but a negligible few. The table was covered with a soiled white cloth which had grown old in the service of the Bayfields, and crocks had been set out for the evening meal. Four places had been laid. 'What's this mean?' asked Mr Bayfield. 'Who's coming?' In his heart he hoped it might be Dolly, who was turning out such a credit to him. 'Time she came to see her old Dad,' he said. But observing that the preparations were incomplete—for where was the bread, where were the teacups, the jam, the pot of pickles?—a spasm of indignation moved in him and he went over to the inner door, opened it quickly, and called 'Mother! You coming, Mother?' A distant cry reassured him, but he could not refrain from retorting: 'Shop's been shut these *ten* minutes.' He went to his accustomed chair and sat down, remarking, again aloud, that it was a good job he was a patient man. His patience, however, was not overstrained; for within three minutes Mrs Bayfield came into the room, bearing on a tray all the articles whose absence had caused him disquiet.

'I was out in the garden,' said Mrs Bayfield, flattering with this designation the small square patch of ground whose diagonal accommodated two posts and a nine-foot length of clothes-line. 'It's my belief there's a shower coming.' The pocket of her apron still bulged with clothes-pegs, for she knew Jim didn't like being kept waiting for his food, and so had not spared a moment in which to rid herself of them. 'I've got a pair of nice kippers for you tonight,' she said.

'Ah!' returned Mr Bayfield. '*And* I can do with 'em.' He grunted a little as he took off his boots. 'Where are my slippers, Glad?'

'Where they always are,' said Mrs Bayfield. But she left the table, nevertheless, to get them for him from under his own chair. Scenting his impatience she had been prepared to propitiate him, and equally prepared, if need arose, to answer sharpness with sharpness; but the hint of sharpness that had inadvertently slipped out was due not to irritation but to a momentary surprise that was almost confusion. After being Mother for a quarter of a century or more, it always made her 'feel funny' to be reminded that she had received another name, Gladys, in holy baptism. It made her in fact feel girlish, you and me together, quite like old times; and since to feel girlish at her age was foolish, and perhaps not quite proper, the effect of it all was disturbing and confusing, so that you didn't hardly know where you were.

'Ah!' said Mr Bayfield, receiving his slippers, and slowly, with the effect of much dignity, putting his feet into them. He nodded at the table. 'Who's coming?'

Mrs Bayfield was an unremarkable woman, the sort of woman you could meet three times and fail to recognize at the fourth meeting. Nor would she have taken offence at this failure. She had never made the mistake of regarding herself as of much importance. Mr Bayfield, she thought, had importance enough for two; and there wasn't really room for any more of it in the house when he was at home. She was content to have it so. She did not share her husband's view of himself, but she did not resent his having it, and during her thirty years of marriage had learned unconsciously to allow for it in all her calculations. If this was wisdom in her it was an instinctive wisdom, which she was not aware of possessing. Indeed she was unaware of much that went on, within her and without. She neither enjoyed her married life nor disliked it: she took it for granted, and it had never for one moment occurred to her that things could be different. She was of medium height and stocky figure, with black wispy hair and a rather square face. Spectacles combined with her thin sharp nose to give her a slightly owlish appearance, but the suggestion was not strong enough to make her memorable. In earlier years Mr Bayfield had sometimes caught himself feeling weary of seeing her about the place, and wishing for a change, but temptation had never synchronized with opportunity, so instead of being unfaithful he had been querulous and sarcastic. But all that was over and forgotten, and nowadays, at his age, change was the last thing he wanted. It was not, precisely, that the two liked each other better: it was rather that they had learned how to avoid occasions for conflict, had elaborated a technique for living in the same house and sharing the same bed without often noticing that the other was there. Mrs Bayfield regarded her husband as something inevitable and unalterable, like the weather. And Mr Bayfield had got used to his wife just as he had got used to his corns.

'Who 's coming?' echoed Mrs Bayfield. 'Who but our Dolly?' she asked rhetorically.

Mr. Bayfield sat up in his chair, and his eyes protruded with something that threatened to be indignation. 'Indeed? First I 've heard of it. Why wasn't I told?'

'Because you were in the doubleyou when the card arrived,' answered Mrs Bayfield. 'And because I didn't think to tell you when you came back to serve.'

'What card?' demanded Mr Bayfield.

'Dolly's card, to be sure. Postcard it was. Sech a pretty picture of the little girls with their hockey-bats. Hopes to be along about nine o'clock, she says, and stay the night. And she says not to wait supper.'

'Very kind of her,' said Mr Bayfield, with heavy irony. 'Nine o'clock indeed! What a time to come! Serve her right if we was all in bed.'

'Go to bed if you want to, dear. Feeling tired?'

'It 'd teach her a lesson,' continued Mr Bayfield, who had not heard the remark. 'I should be sorry if any daughter of mine was to turn into one of these *modern* girls we read about. After I 've pinched and saved to give her a good education like I have.'

Mrs Bayfield handed him his tea, and just as he liked it, a dark brown brew, with three lumps of sugar to take the edge off. She had no remark to offer about Dolly's education, was unmoved by his complacency and undismayed by his forebodings. Dolly, a clever and industrious child, had made quite a habit of winning scholarships; and now, at twenty-three, she was teaching in a secondary school with every apparent success, thus compensating her parents for the loss of Agnes, their eldest, who had married beneath her, and not a moment too soon. Mr Bayfield felt it his duty to find fault with his children to their faces, and think well of them, if he could, only behind their backs; in no other way could a family be controlled. And he failed to see any significance in the fact that Dolly, the least scolded, had turned out a Credit, while her sister Agnes had been a Disgrace, and her young brother Ernie, though conscientiously cuffed from time to time, was already in process of becoming a Worry.

'And where 's Ernie got to?' asked Mr Bayfield. 'Doesn't milord want any supper tonight? You 're too soft with that boy, Mother.'

'A pair of nice kippers these are,' said Mrs Bayfield, putting the plate in front of him. 'Eat them while they 're hot. It 'll do you good, I 'm sure. . . . Ah, that 'll be Ernie, I expect.'

Making too much noise, as he always did, Ernie flung himself into the room. He was nineteen and beginning to feel his age: a slim, strong, pasty-faced youth, with a curve in the lips that suggested cunning, and a boldness of eye that suggested insolence. The movements of his limbs were coltish, awkward, vigorous, provoking in his father a reluctant admiration and a resentful envy The stream of life in this young man was too copious: it made Mr Bayfield's seem the merest trickle.

'And what 's been keeping you, my boy?' asked Mr Bayfield. 'Punctuality, they say, is the polite-ness of princes.' Fortified by a mouthful or two of kipper, he was growing more genial.

'Had to go down the road,' said Ernie. He did not explain the nature of the compulsion, but his manner betrayed his consciousness of what his father suspected: that there was a girl in the case. And why the hell shouldn't there be? said Ernie to himself. 'Looks to me as though that fellow 'll swing. What d' you think, Dad? Say, Mum, give us a cup of tea.'

'D' you mean the Tottenham business?' Mr Bayfield swallowed hastily, and took a gulp of tea.

'You sit down, Ernie,' said Mrs Bayfield, 'and then you shall have your cup of tea. You oughta been here before, as well you know.'

'Oh, don't go on at the boy, Mother.' Mr Bayfield cleared his throat, and the noise somehow suggested a royal proclamation. 'I had a bit of an argument with one of the customers about that case. I passed the remark, same as you, Ernie, that things looked pretty black against the prisoner. Shouldn't care to be in his shoes, I said. Customer says, I 'm afraid you 're right, Mr Bayfield, he says. And as for shoes, he says, I shouldn't like to be in the jury's shoes either. That 's right, I says, time 's money nowadays, and once you get on a case like that there 's no knowing how long they 'll keep you at it. I didn't mean that, says the customer. What I meant was I shouldn't like the job of condemning a fellow-creature to the gallows. Do *you* believe in hanging 'em, Mr Bayfield? he says.'

'A nice subject for the supper-table, I must say,' remarked Mrs Bayfield, in a tone of banter.

'You can't deny a murder makes good reading, Mum,' said Ernie, teasing her.

'Would you like to be at one?' asked his mother.

'Depends where I was sitting,' said Ernie. 'Not in the dock I wouldn't.' He laughed, relishing his smartness.

'So I said, What else can you do with 'em?'
Mr Bayfield continued his narration. 'A murderer's a murderer after all.'

Mrs Bayfield gave a shudder of distaste. 'I should
think so indeed. Hanging's too good for some of
them. They ought to be done to as they did.'

'I'm not sure you're not right, Mother,' said
Mr Bayfield approvingly.

'Well, this Tottenham chap,' remarked Ernie,
'seems to have done the job with a hairbrush, by
all accounts. Take a bit of doing with a hairbrush, I should say. But I'd like to see you
having a try, Mum. Expecting a visitor?' he
added, noticing the fourth place set at table.

'Your sister Dolly is paying us a call,' said Mr
Bayfield, with humorous grandeur. 'If she can
get away from her numerous engagements.'

Ernie acknowledged the information with a
grunt, and instantly became aware of his mother's
eyes fixed penetratingly upon him.

'It's a long time since we saw our Dolly,' she
remarked pointedly.

'Yes,' agreed Ernie. 'Matter of fact, I've got
a date tonight. So unless she looks sharp I shall
miss her.'

'Can't you put it off for once?' pleaded Mrs
Bayfield.

Ernie shook his head, flushing. 'Imposs.'

'The pictures again, may I ask?' said his father,
with ponderous humour.

To avoid further inquisition Ernie stuffed a piece of bread and cheese into his mouth and washed it down with tea. He got up, scraping his chair on the ground as he pushed it away from him. 'Well, so long, folks!' Aware that his hunger was still unsatisfied, he glanced involuntarily at his father's now empty plate. 'Enjoy your kippers, Dad?'

Before Mr Bayfield could have replied, Ernie was out of the room. But Mr Bayfield, having missed the point of the question, had no intention of replying except with a bare acknowledgment of the unexpected courtesy. He glanced at his watch. It still wanted twenty minutes of nine o'clock. Time for a nap before Dolly arrived: she was sure to be later than she had said. He was secretly excited by the prospect of her visit, but at the moment he felt weary and drowsy. While Mother began clearing the dirty things from the table, Mr Bayfield removed his teeth, placed them in a wooden cigarette-box which he kept on a shelf at his elbow for that purpose (he was a man of method and had a place for everything), and leaned back in his chair with a contented sigh. Sleep, however, was warded off by a small quivering anxiety lest he should be caught by Dolly unawares; and when, some forty minutes later, the front-door bell rang, his eyes opened with a start and his hand groped hurriedly for the wooden box.

§ 6

EDWARD PERSEVERES

So Lucy Prynne, instead of hearing Mr Edward Seagrave's paper on 'The Religion of Wordsworth,' spent the evening sitting with her mother. They sat for the most part in silence; for, like the Bayfields, like the Stroods, these two had long ago exhausted all possible sources of conversation between them; except on matters they could not or would not broach, they knew each other's minds and could hope for nothing fresh. From time to time, however, Mrs Prynne would ask a question or make an observation. 'And what did you do today, dear?' she would say. Or, 'We had a nice little shower this afternoon. Quite a little shower we had. Did you see anything of it in town, dear?' And Lucy would obediently provide a suitable answer. All this was usual enough, perfectly in accordance with the routine of their life together. But though outwardly much the same, this evening was different from previous evenings because Lucy herself was different. Her answers were given more at random than usual, and she was obliged to make an effort to control her impatience. No outward sign betrayed her; her 'Yes, Mother,' and 'No, Mother,' fell as gently as ever from her lips; but in her heart she was saying quite other things. I'm thirty-one, and I shall never escape. Other girls are mothers long before thirty-one: I shall never be a mother. Soon I shall be forty, and Mother will be sixty-nine. And I shall never know about Wordsworth and all the things Mr Seagrave knows about.

'You're very quiet tonight, dear.'

'Am I, Mother?'

'You're not feeling ill, are you?'

'No, of course not.' Habitually truthful, Lucy realized too late that had she pretended to be suffering from a headache she could have put an end to the evening by going to bed. She added half-heartedly: 'A little tired perhaps. Brenda keeps us at it, you know. Not that it's her fault: the work's got to be done.'

'Did you have a proper lunch?' asked Mrs Prynne.

Lucy began to be surprised by the catechism. How thoughtful Mother is, she told herself reproachfully. But in fact this manifestation of solicitude was a little unusual, and she did not wholeheartedly welcome it.

She disposed almost briskly of the question about her lunch and retired again into her private dream. Had she been less deeply immersed in it she might have been surprised at her novel state of mind. For this active, this almost passionate discontent was a new experience; or if not quite without precedent it was something which had not troubled her for a long time now. With the ways and means of livelihood to worry her, she had found it easy not to think overmuch about herself; and a few hours ago she would have asked nothing better than that tomorrow should be as much like today as possible, since to be safe was everything. She would have found it strange, had she paused to reflect, that a letter could have made all this difference, could have so definitely disturbed her peace. And a letter from someone whom she hardly knew.

'Why don't you get your sewing, dear?'

'Oh . . . I don't know. I don't feel much like sewing tonight.'

'I'm sure,' said Mrs Prynne, cheerfully, 'I couldn't sit still with my hands in my lap.'

'Couldn't you, Mother?'

Mrs Prynne looked sharply across at her daughter, as though suspecting irony. But Lucy had answered without malice and even without thought; for she was busy with other things. She was thinking of a school reader which contained two or three poems by Mr Seagrave's Wordsworth. There were *We are Seven*, something called (she fancied) *The Idiot Boy*, and a poem about dancing with the daffodils. Perhaps there were others: she wondered if the book were still in the house, feeling sure that Mr Seagrave would be interested to hear about it. She half-smiled at the thought, but the memory of tonight's disappointment came suddenly back, and a pang of resentful misery seized hold of her.

'I think I shall go to bed, Mother, if you don't mind.'

Mrs Prynne glanced at the clock, pursing her lips. Half-past nine.

'Very well, dear. I suppose I must go too.'

'Oh, must you, Mother?' cried the girl remorsefully.

'I 'd rather you saw me upstairs, dear. One of these days I shall turn giddy on those stairs, and then I shan't trouble you any more.'

'Oh, Mother! What a dreadful thing to say!' Tears stood in Lucy's eyes, and she was ready to give up the idea of going to bed early. But Mrs Prynne was already raising herself in her chair. Lucy ran to help her. What a brute I am, she thought. And Mother is so brave.

Twenty minutes later, when Mother and her bravery had been at last put to bed, Lucy opened the arms of her spirit to embrace the best hours of the day. Life held for her no greater pleasure than the pleasure of going to bed early with 'a nice book'. Having kissed her mother good night, she went to her own little room and stood for a moment pondering the problem of the nice book, with tantalizing memories of that school reader still haunting her. She wanted something that would take her mind off herself. All Lucy's reading was done either in bed or in the train, for nowhere else was she free from incessant interruption. And even now, in her musings, she was interrupted.

Was that, or wasn't it, a knock at the front door? If so, it was the discreetest knocking that ever fell on mortal ears. With self-effacing politeness it seemed to be apologizing for the fact that, by its very nature, it could not avoid calling attention to itself. If only there were such a thing as a noiseless noise, it seemed to say, that is the kind of noise I should be. It was like a modest cough, or a hesitating murmured word. But this very gentleness doubled its effect for Lucy. It fell on her heart like a thunderclap, and the wildest fancy flashed across her mind. With an instinct to secrecy she ran quietly downstairs, and, against all precedent, quite unthinking of the dangers to which normally she was so much alive, she quietly, almost conspiratorially, unbolted the door.

'Oh, good evening,' he said. 'I 'm afraid . . .'

She did not pretend to be surprised that it was Edward Seagrave. That he should come was utterly unexpected, fantastic, incredible; but the knocking had announced him to her, and she would have been astonished had it proved to be anyone else.

'Oh,' she said breathlessly. 'Oh, good evening.'

'I 'm afraid, Miss Prynne . . . forgive this very late call . . .'

Her shyness seemed to rebuke him, and she knew it. Even with his stoop he was a tall man; and even though his years were perhaps nearer forty than thirty he seemed very young at this moment. His confusion, his respectfulness, his fear of offending, all this was suddenly as real to her as the touch of the night air on her face. And a strange warmth, like a gathering wave, moved in her breast.

'Won't you come in for a minute?' she said, in her cold, polite, rather husky voice.

'Thank you, no. No, I mustn't do that. I just came to inquire . . .'

He hesitated. And after a silence she said, helping him out: 'Yes?'

'Not seeing you at the meeting, I thought perhaps . . . Of course,' he broke off hastily to add, 'I had no right to *expect* you at the meeting. You'll think me very presumptuous . . .'

In her sympathy with his confusion her own vanished. Suddenly she knew that she was very happy. 'But do come in for a minute,' she said. 'And you shall tell me about it.'

She opened the door wide, and as an afterthought switched on the light in the little hall. He stepped timidly across the threshold, and took up his stand just inside the door, which she quietly shut.

'I won't keep you,' he stammered. 'I mustn't stay. I only wanted to say . . .'

She faced him meekly and gravely, forbearing to invite him into the sitting-room, knowing that in his eyes the situation would compromise her and fill him with self-reproach. She was wise and old and serenely careless of the conventions. She was everything that she was not.

'. . . to say, to inquire,' he went on, 'if you were quite well. You 'll think it strange of me, but I felt I couldn't go to bed without seeing you.'

Though the implications of this added nothing to what he had already told her without words, she found herself blushing a little, and was constrained to counter with a question: 'Did you have a good meeting?'

'Very nice indeed,' he said. 'Everybody was most kind.'

'I wish I could have been there. I should have been *so* interested.' She wondered whether she should tell him about the school reader. But it seemed hardly the time and place for that. 'I was terribly disappointed I couldn't come.'

He looked at her eagerly, courage returning. 'Were you really?'

'And it was *so* kind of you to write.'

'Oh, no,' he said, with manifest surprise. 'Not kind at all.'

'Did you read your paper?' she asked. 'Or just, I mean, speak it?'

'Oh, I had a manuscript.' He touched the breast pocket of his coat. 'I couldn't have managed without that.'

'I suppose . . .' began Lucy. She broke off and tried again. 'It 's a lot to ask, but I wondered if I might, well, borrow it to read.'

The effect of this simple request astonished Lucy. For a moment Mr Seagrave seemed struck dumb, and a vast childish joy began dancing in his face.

'Really?' he stammered. 'That's wonderful of you.' He snatched the manuscript from his pocket and thrust it into her hand, too eager for ceremony. She thanked him, and there seemed no more to be said.

'Well, good night,' he said, holding out his hand. 'So kind of you.'

'Thank you for coming,' murmured Lucy politely. Fearing lest that sounded too formal she added quickly, with a laugh: 'I shan't need to write to you now, shall I?'

In retrospect it sounded an ungracious speech, but Mr Seagrave did not interpret it so. 'To write to me?' He stared in sheer beatific wonder. 'Were you going to write to me?'

'To answer your letter, you know,' she explained. His face fell a little. 'Ah, yes. I'd forgotten.'

Seeing his crestfallen look she said: 'But of course I shall have to write to you about this paper. I won't keep it too long.'

Standing on the doorstep he stared at his boots, seeming unable to go. She waited, nervous now, and wishing him gone. The excitement of this strange interview was already inducing a reaction. If he stayed much longer he would spoil everything. If he said anything more he would brush the bloom off an unspoken enchantment that the warm hour held. Go, go, her heart said to him,

74

and leave me to find my bearings in this brave new world.

At last he looked up, and said: 'I simply had to see you.'

'Had you?'

There was another silence.

'Good night.'

'Good night.'

She shut the door on him almost too quickly, and locked fast in her dream moved towards the foot of the stairs.

'Lucy!'

'Oh!' cried Lucy. Her heart leaped into her throat. 'How you frightened me, Mother!'

Mrs Prynne stood at the stairhead, a lean, watchful figure wrapped in a dressing-gown.

'Who ever was it, Lucy? And at this time of night?'

Mother. This was the real world. The other had been only a dream. As she raised her eyes to meet that inquisitory gaze, a thought, gone as soon as come, flashed into and out of her mind: If Mother were to lose her balance . . .

§ 7

CHARLES AND BETTY

THERE was something about the little Essex town
that made it irresistible to Charles and Betty
Underhay. So, having inquired of a friendly
policeman, they parked the two-seater in the space
between church and market square that seemed to
have been set apart by Providence for that purpose,
and got out to explore.

'I like the look of your town,' said Charles.

'I thought you would,' said Betty.

They exchanged a look of mutual understanding,
and for Charles the moment had a rounded perfection like that of eternity itself. Betty was six,
Charles forty years older. Each lived in a private
world which the other could never enter; each
brought to the other an inviolable aloneness; yet
at moments like this, when something beyond word
or thought flashed between them, the illusion of
sharing was not to be denied. Betty had, and
could have, no doubts of its reality, no doubts and
no formulated thought; but Charles was haunted
by the fear that for all his watchfulness, his earnest,
incessant contemplation of his child, he would
never understand her as her mother had understood, never make up to her for the loss of that
mother. He felt himself, in his dealings with

76

Betty, to be slow, plodding, conscientious, where Catherine had been wise and gay; by much intellectual puffing and blowing he came somewhat short of conclusions which Catherine would have reached in an intuitive flash. As a parent, he thought, he had nothing to recommend him but his devotion, his resolve, at whatever cost, even the cost of self-effacement, to do the best he could for the child. A middle-aged man, of sedentary, bookish habits, content with his routine, and cherishing no ambitions outside his official life as a Civil Servant, what sort of a companion was he, he asked himself, for a little girl of six? Catherine had been only thirty-four when she died, six months ago, and young for her years. If Betty had been a boy, it would perhaps have been a different matter, and his inaptness for parental responsibility of less account. He did not, however, wish that Betty had been a boy; did not wish her in any single respect different from the rather dumpy, silent, stolid-looking child she was. But he knew at least enough of her to know that this appearance of stolidity was deceptive; and it was a delight to him, and an agony, that sometimes it was as if Catherine herself looked for a moment out of her daughter's eyes.

The sunlit square was full of bustle and noise, for by a piece of great good fortune (as Charles conceived) it was market day. The two rows of shops adjacent to the square were each enclosed by a railed-in pavement; and to these railings a score or two of cattle were haltered. Their broad buttocks and swishing tails drew the eyes of the two visitors; their occasional mooing and stamping dominated all other sounds. For the rest, the paved square was filled with pens containing pigs, sheep, calves, in groups of six or seven; and behind one of the pens, on a contrivance that looked to Betty like a step-ladder, stood a red-faced gentleman in a bowler hat, barking with great rapidity. 'What is he doing?' asked Betty, but so quietly that her father took no notice. The man in the bowler hat seemed excited and even angry, and it puzzled Betty that the people surrounding and watching him were apparently quite unmoved by his performance. They stared and stared, and every now and again some one of them gave him a curt nod, and whenever this happened she noticed that he pitched his voice on a new note and continued his noises with renewed vigour. From this spectacle her glance strayed to a very small calf tied up near its dam, the only one in the row. Near its dam, but not near enough; for her udders were dripping milk, and at intervals she roared lustily. Betty looked away, and found a moment's distraction in watching nine extremely pleasant little pigs busy at the dugs of their obliging parent. But her mind returned all too soon to the calf, and her glance involuntarily followed. The soft wet nose, the comical ears, the large oily eyes that expressed nothing in the world but a disarming innocence, the body scarcely bigger than a dog's, and the long spindly shanks—in happier circumstances she could have stared at this calf for ever. But he was tied by the neck to the railing, and couldn't get at his mother, for all his shy capering.

'Do you like the market?' asked Charles, smiling down at her.

Betty fixed her eyes on the ground. 'Not very much.'

'Don't you?' cried he, in great surprise. 'Well I never!' He suffered a pang of disappointment; for a moment the day was dark about him, and a sense of his blundering inadequacy made him almost despair. Mingling with that sense was impatience. What on earth's the matter with the child? But instantly controlling himself, he forced cheerfulness again into his voice. 'Well, what would you like to do now, eh?'

'The toys,' murmured Betty.

'Toys? What toys?'

'There's a shop,' explained Betty. And she added, in the oddly grown-up way she sometimes had: 'Shall I show you where it is?'

It was not the first time they had visited this town. They had passed through it in the car almost precisely a year ago. Catherine had been with them then, and Catherine and Betty had got out at a certain shop, where they had spent rather less than five minutes looking round. 'Inspection

79

invited: you will not be asked to buy'—it was that
kind of shop. It was because Charles had com-
pletely forgotten the place, and because Betty had
wanted to come again, that he called it *her* town.
'Don't you remember,' she had said, 'that day
Mummy and us . . .' For at last they had got
over their shyness of mentioning Catherine; or
perhaps it was only that Charles had learned to hide
his wincing reluctance at the subject. In reply to
the inevitable questions he had done violence to his
stern veracity and told the traditional story about
going to live with Jesus in heaven. He himself
had no belief in it, and he was sometimes afflicted
by the suspicion that Betty saw through his benevolent pretence, though from time to time, in conversation, she had amplified it with fancies of
her own.

And now here they were again at the Arts and
Crafts Shop, and Charles was mercifully spared any
recollection of his former sight of the place. It
was here, at this corner, that Catherine had asked
him to stop the car; but on that tour she had made
a similar request several times, and anyhow he had
a bad memory for places. Betty was too much
accustomed to this peculiarity in her father to feel
any surprise at it now. That he should have com-
pletely forgotten what she remembered so vividly
did not for a moment engage her thought. Her
mind was filled with a picture of that past. The
shop-window was full of bright junk, copper and

brass and pottery, and something called 'peasant-work'. There were also moral maxims hand-lettered on pieces of cardboard, such as *See it through and see through it*, and *Count your blessings and they multiply*. But inside, as Betty remembered, there was a back room devoted to toys. They were toys of quite unearthly fascination: dogs, horses, men, camels, all the creatures of the farm-yard and all the creatures of the Ark carved in a white soft wood and dabbed each with a significant spot of bright colour. No two were alike; each was a creation embodying the thought of its maker. The Ark, too, had a character all its own. It was somehow better than any doll's house Betty had seen, better even than any other ship; and the whole scene became part of the pleasant furniture of her mind. Since that day she had looked at it a thousand times, at the group of animals on their way up the broad plank that led into the Ark, at Mr and Mrs Noah standing stiffly in the fore-ground waiting till all were safely in, and particu-larly at the giraffe and the donkey. The giraffe seemed to have lost his place in the queue and to be quite unconcerned about it. He stood outside the Ark, with his tail to the others and his long neck stretching towards the Ark's window, through which was thrust the friendly head of the donkey. The two were in conversation, Betty supposed; and the thought of that conversation going on and on, that moment of time caught and held, gave her, whenever she remembered it, a deep though obscure satisfaction. And now she was on the point of seeing it again, not in fancy as she had so often seen it, but in solid and delicious fact.

'Is this your toyshop? Would you like us to go inside?' asked Charles humbly, after they had stared for some seconds at the windowful of assorted quaintness.

'Yes,' said Betty.

He looked down at her, trying to read her mind. But for its solemnity her plump little face was almost expressionless. He could not for the life of him decide whether or not she was happy in the prospect of going inside.

'We'll see if they've got any toys, shall we?' said Charles, grasping her hand and moving towards the door. 'Though it doesn't look quite like a toyshop to me,' he added.

Betty was held in a trance of expectation. His warning fell on deaf ears, and she did not answer him. And for the moment he paid her no further attention, for as soon as they were in the shop a pale lily of a girl came floating towards him with a nice shop-smile on her face.

'You would like to look round?' she asked.

'We want to look at the toys,' explained Charles, with a somewhat self-conscious air of humour.

'Toys?' The shop-smile became tinged with sincerity as the young woman glanced at Betty.

Then it vanished altogether, to be succeeded by a frowning effort to remember something. 'I 'm not sure that we have any,' said the young woman vaguely. 'But perhaps you 'd like to look round?'

'We were here this time last year,' said Charles. 'And my instructions are,' he continued, with a facetiousness of phrase for which he despised himself (but he was too shy to say 'my little girl tells me'), 'my instructions are that you then had a large number of toys on sale. A whole room full of them, I fancy.'

'Ah, yes, I expect we did,' said the young woman warmly. She seemed delighted to agree with him. 'I wasn't here then, but my friend will know.' She retired to the back of the shop and held a shouted conversation with an invisible but not inaudible female. On her return she explained that the toy-room was now used for a display of glass and china.

Charles glanced helplessly at his daughter. Her expression, or lack of expression, had not changed.

'And the toys?' he said. 'They 're gone, are they?'

'Well,' said the young woman, with a laugh, 'I don't expect they were sold. I dare say they 're about somewhere. Put away, you know. We 've an attic where we stow our lumber. Such a glory-hole!'

'Well, Betty?' Charles gave her a little dig,

wishing she would speak up for herself. 'Would you like to go and hunt for them?'

Betty shook her head.

'Wouldn't you?' said the young woman coaxingly. 'I'll show you the way if you like. We'll hunt together.'

But the donkey and the giraffe were no longer in conversation. Betty shook her head again. 'No, thank you,' she said politely. She could not, however, manage a smile. Suddenly she remembered Catherine and began dragging at her father's hand towards the door. . . . And time, with unhurrying, undeviating flow, carried him on towards his meeting with Roderick Strood, Lucy Prynne, James Bayfield, the excellent Bonaker, and some others. The crime was not yet conceived that was to bring together this diversity of souls.

§ 8

RODERICK AND ELISABETH

BUT how could he be happy? The cottage he had found for Elisabeth at Frendham was everything that could be desired. The surroundings were perfect, and the distance from town was not excessive. But how could Roderick Strood be happy in it while the bitter problem of Daphne remained unresolved? He tried to remember a time when

he had been in love with Daphne, but it was too
long ago, if indeed it had ever happened at all. He
was confident that he had never felt about Daphne
as he now felt about Elisabeth Andersch. How
young he had been in those days, how ignorant of
himself, how much the dupe of biological forces,
how ingenuously ready to believe that the first
woman he kissed was the one woman! The whole
business, he now thought, had been a piece of half-
wilful self - deception, the sentimentalizing of a
commonplace need. The marvellous affinity between himself and Daphne had existed only in his
imagination, for in all the years that had followed
they had never really learned to understand each
other. They had lost their illusion of love without finding anything to put in its place. This was
how he saw the matter now. He was not so simple
as to suppose that Daphne had greatly changed,
and it puzzled and exasperated him that qualities
and mannerisms that he had once found charming
should now be merely irritating. Could he have
looked at her through Mark Perryman's eyes he
would have seen a sleek, admiration-loving, but
undeniably seductive young woman; through Brian
Goodeve's he would have seen and adored a creature
of infinite mystery and magical beauty. His Daphne
was as different from these as these were from each
other; and the real Daphne was different from them
all. That occasional pout of hers, which Mark
found amusing, was to Roderick an intolerable

affectation of childishness; that social manner, which drew tears of admiration from Brian when in his solitude he recalled it, seemed to Roderick both mechanical and pretentious. There was, to his mind, a metallic hardness and glitter about this woman he had married.

If that had been all, there would have been no problem. But it was very far from all. For Daphne was Daphne, the first woman in his life. He did not want her, and did not believe she wanted him except for her pride's sake; but the idea of hurting her was painful to him, and now he caught himself perpetually wondering, with a wincing conscience, how she was getting on. In some way he could not have defined, he felt that he had a more than legal responsibility for her. If she was unhappy—and she certainly was—he was ready to believe that it was his fault. He was ready to believe it, and she was more than ready to impress it upon him. During the few days he had spent at home after returning from Heidelberg, things had been said that would never be forgotten while he or she was alive to remember them. He had stated his position at first with studied calm, and then with a display of emotion which he now blushed to recall; he had begged for patience, friendship, understanding—but above all for patience. 'How can I say whether it's permanent or not?' he said. 'I'm simply lost in it. It possesses me.'

'I see,' answered Daphne, with frigid anger.
'Your wife means nothing to you. The first pretty
face you see——'

'My dear Daphne, why repeat that nonsense?
I 've seen hundreds of pretty faces since I married
you.'

'Well, what do you want me to do? Do you
want me to divorce you?'

When he admitted that divorce was in his mind,
she began, with a kind of deadly deliberation, un-
packing all her store of bitterness. As he listened,
the world grew ugly and obscene, and all human
life a squalid confusion of lechery and greed. Outwardly he met anger with anger, bitterness with
bitterness; but in his heart, during that nightmare
interview, there was nothing but misery and pain.
He was hurt and humiliated by the vileness she
heaped upon him, bewildered by her reckless hatred;
but mingling with those emotions, and surviving
them, was pity for her desperate condition, and
the thought came, never to leave him again at
peace: She wasn't like this before. This is what
I 've done to her. He would not in quieter
moments accept that verdict: he argued cogently
against it and found himself not guilty. But the
fear lurked in his mind, the sense of a spiritual
responsibility for Daphne was always ready to leap
out upon him from the dark corner to which he
had dismissed it. Yet here he was, with Elisabeth; here he was in the paradise that Elisabeth

made for him. The very grass of these lovely hills was greener for her sake. The noble contours of that heavenly horizon were an aspect of her; the sky was filled with her light; she was as various as life itself. These boyish sentiments gushed in his heart at sight of her, but he knew better, had learned better, than to put them into words. When he said to himself, sentimentally, that she was the woman he had always dreamed of, he went wide of the truth; for she was a new world to him, and a world beyond imagining. She seemed to belong to no nation and to conform to no type. She was dark and slim, with a beauty that was austere to the point of coldness; and despite the young perfection of her body, the rose-petal smoothness of her face, sometimes, even though she gave herself with a dark abandonment, he felt that she might be a thousand years old, a woman of legend, remote and unearthly, always listening to a music beyond mortal hearing.

'I don't really know you at all, do I?' he said.

She smiled. 'How could you know me better?' What the smile meant was more than he would ever know. Was it irony or tenderness? Or a compound of both? Even her tenderness had a quality strangely impersonal; and though she was generous in love, and utterly innocent of coquetry, he knew that there was some part of her personality, some part where the mystery of her self resided, that was for ever beyond his possession. It mad-

dened and delighted him to be always moving
forward to a goal which he could never reach.

'Will you marry me, Elisabeth?'

'You would have two wives?' she asked.

His brow clouded a little. 'I'm assuming that
that difficulty could be adjusted. My wife will
divorce me as soon as she realizes that I'm serious.
It's the only logical thing to do.'

'And will she do what is logical, Roderick?'

The sound of his name on her lips never failed
to cause him a pang of pleasure. They conversed
always in German, which he spoke with ease; and
this 'Roderick' was the only comparatively English
word she often had occasion to pronounce. He
began, now, to answer her question, beginning
with a somewhat elaborate analysis of Daphne's
emotional reactions to this new situation . . . but
he very soon realized that Elisabeth was listening
rather to his voice than to his words.

'You're not listening,' he accused her.

'Am I not?'

'And you haven't answered my question either.
Will you marry me when I'm free?'

She shrugged her shoulders. 'Perhaps. . . .
But no. You are not yet out of prison. It is
early to talk of what prison you shall be confined in
next. And I think marriage is not for us.'

'But surely?' he protested. 'We love each
other. And so . . .' He broke off, suddenly shy
of speech. Yet after a silence, which she showed

89

no sign of breaking, he forced himself to ask: 'You do love me, don't you?'

She sat down at her piano, the piano which, obsequious to her wishes, a famous London firm had 'put unreservedly at her disposal' and been glad of the chance. She began playing, improvising: then, as if his words had only just reached her, she let her hands fall to her lap and turned to look at him.

'Do I love you? What does that mean? We have loved, yes. We shall love again perhaps. But certainly we shall love again. Love will take us. The moment comes and passes. But I can't make words about love. Love isn't words: it is something that happens.'

'It happens,' agreed Roderick. 'And it *has* happened. It's here, with us, isn't it? It's taken possession of us.'

She shook her head, and her smile was more than ever remote. 'I am your friend. That goes on. But this love, it is a storm. It comes and it is gone. And then perhaps it comes again. Meanwhile, we are friends. Isn't that so?'

He was puzzled. 'Well, I don't see what better basis there could be for marriage, do you?'

'Now I shall play to you,' she said.

This she had often said to him, and now, for the first time, the words were not quite welcome. There was more to be said, and her playing would be an evasion. But the opening chords persuaded him otherwise. The world crumpled at a touch of her fingers; all senses were lost in listening; the personal was pared away and the naked spirit stepped into a region of pure light. It was a region without form, and void of anything but this vital element; and in the void, as it were of the very light itself, a new world of unimaginable beauty was in process of building, a flowering pattern of melody clear and cool and confident, a discourse reasonable and sensual in mode, but in essence a continuum transcending reason and sense, an affirmation of the absolute. Fulfilled of all desire, brimming over with an inexhaustible satisfaction, it was calm and joyous, orderly and inevitable, untroubled by passion. Its order was the outward sign of a celestial economy; its joy was the joy of perfect statement; it was itself the reality that it affirmed.

For some moments after the music ceased he remained contemplating the thing it created, and it was with a deep involuntary sigh that he came back at last to his body sitting in a chair, surrounded by the four walls of a room, imprisoned in a network of material relations, himself a mere tangle in the vaster tangle of time and space. Thought, which had been so divinely suspended, began stirring again; and he wondered, idly, whether this choice of Haydn had been Elisabeth's answer, deliberate or intuitive, to his urgent tedious practicalities. Or had she played the first thing that came into her mind, in order to escape from him into her own country? While Roderick was framing this question, Mark Perryman, in a telephone call-box near the Strand, heard the operator ask him for ninepence. It was six o'clock, but the day was still hot, and Mark was sweating copiously after five minutes' confinement in this place. He pressed a sixpenny-piece into the slot, and three pennies into the larger slot, and waited with that air of dogged resolve which telephoning from a call-box makes inevitable.

Roderick, resenting the interruption, picked up the receiver. 'Who? Yes. Speaking. Oh, is that Mark?' He listened for two minutes. What he heard did not please him, but he put a good face on it. 'No, not tonight. Absolutely impossible, tell her. What reason? Any reason in the world. The truth if you like. I might manage tomorrow. All right, I *will* manage tomorrow. Very good of you, Mark—sorry you 've been dragged into it. Oh, of course. Naturally . . . I 'll ring you up from the office. . . . Good-bye.' Roderick looked at Elisabeth with unhappy eyes. 'A message from my wife.'

'Yes?'

'It wasn't she herself speaking. We communicate through a friend. She preferred it so.'

'And is she in a logical mood?' asked Elisabeth, lightly.

'She wants to see me.'

'But naturally!'

'She thinks we must meet and talk things over. And come, as she says, to an understanding. She even suggested that I should go there tonight.'

'Go there? Where is that?'

'Go home. She must have known I couldn't do that at a moment's notice.'

Elisabeth smiled, and the effect of the smile was to make him wonder if he was being quite sincere. 'You mustn't be angry with her,' she said. 'Perhaps she is not so very wise, eh?'

Roderick made a wry face. 'Anyhow I 've had to promise to meet her tomorrow.'

'Yes?'

'Will you forgive me if I 'm not able to get down to see you tomorrow? You do understand?'

She faced him steadily. 'My poor anxious friend, do not apologize to me. It is the only thing that makes me angry. You are very fond of your logical wife. It is a habit perhaps, but never mind, you are fond of her. Perhaps you 'll make up your quarrel and then you 'll be a good husband again. Why not?'

He stared ruefully, disconcerted by her coolness. 'A funny question for you to ask. Doesn't it matter to you? It matters a lot to me.'

'What are you afraid of, Roderick?' she asked, almost coaxingly.

'Afraid?'

'Yes, you 're afraid. Afraid of your conscience.

93

Afraid that your wife will be so unhappy that you
must go back to her. Isn't that it?'

He evaded her glance. It was painful to his
vanity to be so easily read, but he was half-glad,
none the less, to be spared the burden and humilia-
tion of laying bare his quivering conscience to this
cool, kind gaze.

'I shall be with you again on Thursday, you
know,' he said suddenly, after a silence.

'Yes?' she answered. No irony was ever
kindlier. 'And if not Thursday, some other day.
Next week. Next month. I shall be glad when
·ou come. And if you don't come at all I shan't
ᴠe angry.'

He realized, with a spasm of indignation, that
he was being treated like a child. But indignation
was short-lived, for indeed he had not for thirty
years felt so much a child, so helpless and bewildered.

§ 9

MR BAYFIELD IS DISTURBED

THE front-door bell rang, and Mr Bayfield, starting
out of his nap, made haste to get his denture into
position before rising to greet Dolly. She did not
visit home so often nowadays, and a man with a
smart young daughter has to think of his appearance a bit, or she's apt to consider herself a cut

above him. He stood in an expectant attitude in front of the empty fire-place, while Mrs Bayfield went to answer the door. But he listened in vain for the sound of Dolly's high-pitched voice and refined articulation. What was going on? The suspicion that it was not Dolly after all, that he had had all his trouble for nothing, that perhaps Dolly wouldn't come this evening in spite of her promise, provoked in him an emotion that expressed itself as indignation. Here he was, the head of the family, a respectable hard-working tradesman; and nothing went right unless he saw to it himself. In some obscure fashion he felt that it would be his wife's fault, and his son Ernie's, and the world in general's, if Dolly failed to put in an appearance. That it would be Dolly's fault, too, went without saying, young people nowadays being all alike, even the best of them; no consideration for a father's feelings, no common gratitude; slave you do and slave you may, and what thanks do you get? That was what Mr Bayfield wanted to know. But what he wanted to know even more immediately was what Gladys was doing at the door so long. If the girl's come, bring her in. If she's not come, shut the door and let me have my nap out in peace.

He was on the point of explosion when the sound of the door being shut eased the tension of the moment. But his irritation was renewed at sight of Mrs Bayfield. Dingy and forlorn, she stood looking at him, with fear in her bespectacled eyes. Her accustomed serenity had vanished.

'Well, I must say——' began Mr Bayfield, not knowing in the least what he must say, knowing only that he was a much-tried man. For it was plain that Dolly had not come.

His wife interrupted him. 'It 's Dolly,' she said.

'What d' you mean, it 's Dolly?' he asked angrily. But he saw that she had a paper crumpled in her hand. 'D' you mean she 's not coming?'

'An accident,' said Mrs Bayfield. 'She 's in hospital.'

'There!' shouted Mr Bayfield. 'What did I tell you!' Meaningless words: he had told her nothing. Dolly in hospital. He snatched the telegram out of her hand, and read it. 'Them blasted cars ought not to be allowed.'

'Oh, do be quiet, Jim! It 's *Dolly*, I tell you. And us standing here,' she added, suddenly coming to life.

The appeal sobered him a little. 'Get your hat on then. Where are my boots?'

'And I 'm all untidy,' said Mrs Bayfield, hurrying into the passage.

As he lugged on his boots—he was a man who had never taken to shoes—he heard her moving about the bedroom above. 'Take her an hour to get ready,' he grumbled. But he remembered, with a sort of surprise, that Dolly was her daughter as well as his; and the thought invested the drab

96

woman with a new quality, so that he was suddenly impatient to see her again; but when, three minutes later, he met her at the bottom of the stairs, something made him avert his eyes. 'Come on, do!' he said. His right arm moved blindly round her bony shoulders and for a moment rested there.

That moment passed quickly, and the mood with it. Mr Bayfield lapsed into peevish annoyance with all the inconsiderate circumstances that were forcing him to break his routine. Surely a man had a right to a quiet half-hour after his supper? Yet here he was, being forced to an untimely exertion of his heavy, unalert limbs. It was astonishing how people *would* get in his way, and infuriating that they should be so cheerful about it. Boarding the tram was like a sick dream, everybody moving with the most fantastic deliberation, as though resolved to delay Mr Bayfield as much as possible. At intervals throughout the journey he felt compelled to mutter at his wife: 'Some people don't seem to know what time is.' Not once, however, did she answer him: a fact that heightened his sense of grievance. Dolly had plucked him from his chair and was dragging him across London, but his thoughts were not of Dolly, by some trick they managed to avoid Dolly, until the sight of the hospital sent them swarming back to her. Somewhere in this building . . . it was hardly credible. Mrs Bayfield was suddenly in command and Mr Bayfield in confusion. Have you, can you, accident, yes, it's my daughter. The man at the door was serenely helpful, wafting them on. And then ask again. They asked again, and the nurse said Follow me. Like Jesus Christ, thought Mr Bayfield, and good shepherds came into his fantasy, and Christmas bells, and robins in the snow. And all the while he was getting nearer the moment when he must see Dolly.

All his truculence was now gone. He was awed into a feeling of insignificance by the atmosphere of this strange new world. It was like being in church, yet unlike it as well, for the quiet of this place has a sinister quality, clean, bare, cold. And now the ward-sister had possession of them: he and Gladys stood before her like a pair of shabby school-children, downcast and docile, listening respectfully while she spoke of Dolly's accident and Dolly's condition. The patient had just re-gained consciousness. They might see her, if they wished, for three seconds, no longer: she must not be expected to talk.

'Is she . . .?' said Mr Bayfield. 'I mean, will she . . .?'

'She has everything on her side,' said the ward-sister. 'We're going to give her a nice sleep.'

So they went and looked at the death-pale stranger that Dolly had become. She smiled at them with her eyes, though her mouth was misshapen with pain. Dolly's mother stared while she could: Mr Bayfield glanced in dismay from one to the other, startled to see a sudden beauty dawn in his wife's faded face. 'You 're going to have a nice sleep,' he heard her say, but he was already groping his way back to the door, and in a moment Gladys was with him again, and asking questions of the sister.

'Here 's the young man himself,' said the sister. 'He can tell you more than I can.'

Mr Bayfield turned to confront a tall youth who carried his arm in a sling and his head in a bandage. 'Huh!' he said. 'What 's he got to do with it?'

'Oh,' stammered the young man breathlessly, 'are you Mr and Mrs Bayfield? I 'm so . . . I 'm so . . . How 's Dorothy now? I hope . . .'

'Dorothy?' echoed Mr Bayfield. 'If it 's my daughter you mean . . .'

Mrs Bayfield intervened. 'Are you George? She was asking about you.'

'Who was asking about him?' said Mr Bayfield.

'Be quiet, Jim.' He was quiet.

'You see,' explained the young man, 'we were in the crash together. I was taking her for a run in the car, and I crashed. Like a fool, though it wasn't really my fault. It 's no good saying I 'm sorry. Worst of it is, I 'm hardly hurt at all, and Dorothy . . .'

Mr Bayfield resented this George, resented his youth, his air of breeding, his making free with the name of Dorothy. If he *must* use a familiar name, why not the name that was truly hers, and

99

not this stuck-up, superior-sounding 'Dorothy'? Taking her for a run in the car, was he! And what, Mr Bayfield asked himself darkly, were his intentions?

'Taking her for a run, if you please,' remarked Mr Bayfield, when they had regained the street. 'Nothing about bringing her to see us.'

Mrs Bayfield did not answer for a moment. She seemed to be lost in thought. When she did speak it was to say: 'Save your coppers, Father. We shall want 'em for the telephone.'

'Telephone?' he echoed vaguely.

'Yes,' she said. 'I 've got the number safe and sound.' She gave him a bleak smile and added: 'In my bag.'

§ 10

THREE AT TABLE

HAD Mrs Cranshaw been told that before the year was out she would be sitting at the same table with so small a tradesman as Mr Bayfield of Peckham, she would have been incredulous, mystified, and indignant—in that order. But no prophet arrived to disturb the serenity of this golden Sunday afternoon in July. Mrs Cranshaw reclined in a hammock under the largest of her cedars and took pleasure in the smooth green of the lawn that stretched at her feet. Her white stone house, with its civil proportions, its good sense and unobtrusive dignity, had this afternoon, she thought, almost the brilliance of an Italian villa. The faint wistfulness induced by the memory of Italian holidays rather enriched than impoverished the enjoyment of her moment. Mrs Cranshaw was not a woman much given to wistfulness. She had no anxieties, material or spiritual, and no lack of interest in the everyday incidents of a life that to outsiders must have seemed tame and colourless. She exchanged afternoon calls with 'some nice people'; she owned one of the half-dozen beautiful houses left in a suburb largely over-run by rows of red brick; she was fond of gardening and spent much time stridently instructing the aged. man nominally in charge of that department; and she approached her fortieth year with equanimity. Every day, when she looked in her glass, she saw a dark-haired, dark-eyed, and still comely woman, and, though she was the least bit stouter than she could have wished, it seldom occurred to her to question that Time would treat her like a gentleman. 'If anything were to happen to my husband,' she had once remarked to the Vicar's wife, 'I should keep a dog and live very quietly.' And, five years ago now, something *had* happened to her husband, something into the nature of which she did not too curiously inquire, well assured that having died solvent, and been buried according to the rites of the Church of England, he had gone to the place prepared—by an Anglican Saviour—for the reception of English gentlemen. Though only to be expected at his age, it was sad that he had had to go, poor dear man; but she was in no hurry to join him. At this moment her cup of contentment was brimming over. She had paid her respects to God by attending morning service at Saint Andrew's; she had had an excellent lunch, and knew that in the fullness of time the comfortable maternal Millerby, one of the few 'treasures' left in domestic service, would bring tea and cream-cakes on a tray; and the day had reached that point of ripe perfection at which it seems inconceivable that the cosmic arrangements are not entirely of the best. A hammock, a patch of shade on a sunlit lawn, and the dead body of Sir Peter Chezil just discovered in the library: what more could a middle-aged lady ask of life? Clare Cranshaw asked nothing more, unless . . . at times . . . something that neither marriage nor luxurious widowhood had brought her—some intimate glory, compact of earth and fire, that even a detective novel could not give.

Not even a detective novel, and not even Major Forth, though her meeting with that gentleman was to have momentous consequences for her. Major Forth, late of India, was enjoying a rather different kind of widowhood some six or seven miles southwest of Mrs Cranshaw's house. His memsahib, being (alas) something less than pukka, had dis-

covered to him, ten years ago now, a preference
for a junior officer of his own mess. She had paid
for the indiscretion with the loss of husband and
children, and here was Major Forth, at fifty-nine,
tolerated by Evangeline and Edgar, and managed
by a hard-faced housekeeper, living a life of spiritual
isolation in Kensington. At the club, where the
greater part of his time was spent, he was always
ready to talk of old times, but not always able to
find a listener. He walked in the Gardens every
Sunday. He was punctual in his attendance at
what he still liked to call church-parade. He often
regretted his retirement from the service, and sometimes, in moments of exceptional wisdom, he even
regretted that he had come into the old man's money
—for what was the use of it to him, what purpose
did it serve but to keep him idle and discontented
when he might have been busy and important?
As Mrs Cranshaw, turning the pages of her novel,
decided that the French maid could not possibly
be an accomplice, the evidence against her being
so pointed, Major Forth spared a passing glance
for the statue of Physical Energy and wished himself a younger man. It was Muriel who had made
him old, he said to himself bitterly; and because of
Muriel he would never trust woman again. But
catching sight of a squirrel, which sat with bright
listening eyes at the foot of a tree, he was surprised
into sudden pleasure, felt like a boy again, and the
novel thought visited him that perhaps after all

there had been excuses for Muriel's perfidy. If Mrs Cranshaw had chanced to be walking in the Gardens that afternoon . . . but Mrs Cranshaw was busy following another false trail laid by the ingenious author.

Next to the soldier, and next but one to the widow, at that conference-table of the future, would sit Oliver Brackett, whose foxy-red face and yapping recitative were endeared by familiarity to all those of his neighbours who frequented the local sale-room. Oliver had been born and bred to auctioneering, stepping into his father's shoes as a young man. He was young no longer, nor yet old: a man of substance, with a wife already grey-haired, and two sons, one of school-leaving age. Everyone knew him for a brisk business man: no one guessed, not even his wife, that there was a secret in his life. This Sunday afternoon, while Major Forth strode along in Kensington Gardens, and Mrs Cranshaw swung gently in a hammock, pushing at the ground with her neatly shod little foot, Oliver Brackett was enjoying a fantasy of his own making. The morning he had spent on the golf-course, breaking the Sabbath with certain godless neighbours. During lunch he had listened, a little absently, to Molly's conversation, which, being so often pent-up (she was much alone), was apt to flow at full tide on such occasions. And after lunch, with the expressed intention of having forty winks, he had retired to the little sitting-room in which we now find him. But Mr Brackett led a double life, and his forty winks was a mere fiction. That he was a great reader was no secret from Molly: indeed it was one of her grievances. But the nature of his reading was a matter with which she did not think to concern herself. Mr Brackett, an addict of the stage, possessed a large collection of dramatic literature, old and new, picked up in all sorts of odd places, from the second-hand shops of Charing Cross Road to the dusty corners of his own sale-room. In the course of his business great quantities of unregarded books passed through his hands, to be sold, for the most part, in bundles of fifty or so at a few shillings a bundle. No one knew (except his clerk, who thought it a dull form of eccentricity) that nothing in the shape of a play ever got into those bundles; that for years Mr Brackett had made a practice of putting all such volumes into a separate lot, and buying them himself at his own auction. Good or bad, old or new, it was all one to Mr Brackett so long as it was a play, and so long as it contained a part or two in which he could see himself as an actor. For an actor was what he dreamed of being. It was nothing so practical as an ambition: it was a form of daydreaming, hidden from the world by an invincible shyness. In his heart he had no doubt at all that he could have done wonders on the stage; and in his fancy, every Sunday afternoon, those wonders were achieved, amid tumultuous applause. His auctioneering itself was a dramatic performance, the only one that the fates had allowed him; and, though he often wearied of the part, he was sustained by a secret pleasure in the fact that the people who came to watch and listen could not see through his make-believe to the real person behind it. He had small acquaintance with literature in general, and no taste for it; but his knowledge of the English drama, though haphazard, was extensive. Sitting at ease in his large leather chair, he spent this afternoon strutting and posturing and mouthing in the character of Webster's Brachiano; and so it was that his wife, when she came to call him to tea, found him with a book in his lap and a gleam in his wide-open eyes. The gleam vanished at sight of her, to be replaced by a look of embarrassment.

'There you go again,' she said, in half-humorous reproach. 'You come in to have your forty winks, and you 've been at your blessed books all the time, *I 'll* be bound!'

She had said precisely that more often than he could count. Nearly every Sunday she said it.

MARK : DAPHNE : ROGER COATES

MARK : DAPHNE : ROGER COATES

EMERGING from the telephone-box after giving
Daphne's message to Roderick, Mark Perryman
took a handkerchief from his pocket and began
mopping his face and ears. He heaved a sigh of
discontent, wishing that his two friends could have
contrived to quarrel and part without his help.
There was Roderick, away in the country, staging
a full-dress romance in a cottage surrounded by
green fields and wooded hills. There was Daphne,
amid the comfort of her well-staffed house in
Merrion Square, building high tragedy out of a
commonplace situation; and here was he, Mark
Perryman, sweating like a pig in the blazing heat
of the Strand. And now, having spoken to
Roderick, he must communicate his answer to
Daphne. The telephone-box was at his elbow,
waiting to be re-entered. Mark had two pennies
in his hand, and Daphne's number was on the
tip of his tongue, but he turned away and sauntered
undecidedly in the direction of Kingsway. At this
moment he had little stomach for a conversation
with Daphne. But that was only half the truth.
When he remembered the new Daphne that this
situation had called into being he was repelled and
wanted to avoid her. But the thought of her purely

personal quality lit a flame in him, and he was exasperated to feel that his status in this affair obliged him to behave like a perfect gentleman. His uncensored thoughts were wanton enough to make him chafe under that tedious obligation. He greeted these thoughts with a grin, taking what pleasure he could in playing the part of sardonic spectator of himself; and with the same grin he noted that his feet were carrying him rather rapidly —far too rapidly for so hot an evening—in the direction of Merrion Square. To take a taxi or a bus would have committed him too definitely to a course of action he was pretending not to have decided on: it was better to drift, and so to escape responsibility for the fact that at half-past seven he found himself at the door of the Stroods' house.

'Good evening, Tucker. Is Mrs Strood at home?'

Tucker greeted him with a cheerful smile: a small, snub - nosed man who had never quite lost his sense of good luck in having survived the war. He had been batman to Mark himself for nine fantastic months in France, and now formed part of a man-and-wife employed by the Stroods on Mark's introduction. With the air of pleased surprise that was habitual in him he conducted Mark to the drawing-room and said he would tell madam. The trenches were homelier, thought Mark, glancing round at the modernist interior he had seen so often before. But not, he added, so comfortable. He sat down in a chair whose eccentric design was justified by the exquisite tact with which it received and supported him. It was a smart room, the latest thing, and clearly Daphne's choice; but so smart, thought Mark, so infernally well-bred, that it might have been designed for the express purpose of making a plain man feel small. Mark wasn't precisely a plain man, but he felt small none the less. A place like this calls for dress-clothes, he said resentfully, and at that moment Daphne appeared. She appeared noiselessly, grace-fully. He met her in the middle of the room and took her hand. For a moment he felt that he was on a stage with her, in a fashionable West-end play. Enter Lady Constance, exquisitely gowned. There are signs of nervous strain in her face. She moves centre to greet Henry. She gives him her hand. He stands stiffly before her, with questions in his eyes. . . . But that sense of theatricality vanished. And it was as if the room itself vanished, leaving only Daphne. For Daphne at least was vivid and real enough, vivid, real, and infernally desirable. What more does Roderick want? But he knew the question for a foolish one.

'Well?' said Daphne quickly. 'What does he say?'

'Tonight's impossible. He'll come tomorrow.'

'Tonight's impossible, is it?' she echoed. 'Pray, why?'

Mark grew hot and uncomfortable under her

cool accusing gaze. 'How do I know, my dear?'
He shrugged his shoulders.

'Where is he?' demanded Daphne.

Underneath this cool sophisticated exterior she
is a purely primitive woman, said Mark to himself.
She is civilized only in so far as it suits her. Civilization is just something to wear: in anger, in love,
she would cast it off without thought, without
scruple. In love, if she loved, she would be a
savage . . . and what a savage!

After a feverish moment he found an answer.
'What does it matter? The point is that he will
come to see you tomorrow. And then you can
talk the whole thing over.'

'I see,' said Daphne. 'He is with that woman.
Why do you try to make a fool of me, Mark?'

'I thought it was understood,' said Mark,
ignoring the question, 'that you were not to
interfere with each other.'

'Am *I* interfering?' she asked quickly.

'It was understood,' said Mark, easily, 'that
you 'd know nothing of each other's movements
for a while, so that you 'd both have time to see
things in a proper perspective. That 's why I was
appointed go-between, wasn't it? You must remember that I didn't ask for the appointment.'

Daphne moved three paces towards the window.
There was a distant look in her eyes, an odd smile
on her lips. 'It 's funny,' she said at length. She
turned to face him again. 'You don't seem to

understand things at all, Mark. I quite thought
you would understand, but you don't, do you?'

He felt like a man cheated of his wages. Hitherto Daphne had never failed to say, from time to
time: 'You're so understanding, Mark. It's such
a comfort to talk to you.' And such words had
never failed to give him a double pleasure: the
pleasure of caressed vanity, and the pleasure of
observing and deriding that same vanity.

'What don't I understand?' he asked.

Leaving him derelict in the middle of the room,
she moved over to the empty fire-place and stood
staring down into it as though in hope of conjuring
a flame into existence. 'I thought you were *my*
friend, as well as Roderick's.'

'You know I am,' said Mark, addressing her
back. It was a lovely back too, its cream and
ivory luxuriously in contrast with the black gown
environing it.

'You only see his side. You take his part all
the time. You think I want to hold him against
his will.' Mark was silent, and suddenly she
wheeled round upon him with a kind of eagerness.
'And there, Mark,' she said primly, 'you're quite
mistaken. I wouldn't for the world stand in the
way of his happiness. I'm a great believer in
people being free. A *great* believer. And when
a marriage becomes tiresome to either husband or
wife it's time it came to an end. Otherwise it's
a mere mockery, a sham.' The thought of these

sham marriages seemed to move Daphne to high
indignation. 'I know what you think, Mark, and
you needn't suppose I don't. You think all women
are jealous and possessive, and you think I 'm like
all the rest. But I 'm not. I think jealousy 's
hateful and unreasonable, always have thought so.
This isn't a question of jealousy. If you don't see
that, it shows that what I said just now was true:
you don't understand. You don't understand what
marriage is, what a bond it is, living together and
sharing everything. That 's something beyond you.
I 'm not thinking of myself: I 'm thinking of poor
Rod. He can't just walk out like this. It 's un-
manly and unfair. He 's got his duty to think of,
hasn't he, the same as other men? What would
happen if everyone behaved in that irresponsible
way? We 've built up a life together, Rod and I.
For years we 've been building up a life together.
And now he tries to pull it all down in a moment.
If you think that 's right you 've got very strange
notions. But you 're a bachelor: there are things
in life you simply don't know about. It 's not the
fact of his leaving me: it 's the way it 's done, the
lack of consideration, lack of common decency.
He 's always been free to go when he chose. He
knows that well enough. I 've told him a hundred
times. We can part and be friends, I 've said.
Nothing need stop our being friends. Time and
again I 've told him that. But I never supposed
he could behave really *shabbily*, Mark. That 's

what hurts so much. It 's dreadful to see someone one 's fond of behave *shabbily*. Even you will admit that. If he had found someone who 'd be as faithful to him as I 've been, someone I could trust to make him happy, I wouldn't raise a finger to keep him. I wouldn't think of myself. I 'd let him go gladly, even though my heart were breaking. And I 'd be grateful to the woman, yes, grateful, for making him happy. And now he 's gone off to this foreign chorus-girl, or whatever she is, with not a thought of me, and all that 's been between us. And he won't even come and quietly talk things over. He treats me like a stranger and an enemy.'

Mark bowed his head under her spate of words. The spell of her sensual charm was abruptly broken. He was no longer aware of her ripe lips and large deep eyes and soft animal grace: he was aware only of the tortuously twisting mind, intent on deceiving itself. His gorge rose at sight of so gross a feast of irony: he had looked for more romantic fare.

'But are you sure this young woman can't make Rod happy?' he asked nervously.

'Jealousy is something quite foreign to my nature,' went on Daphne. Her eyes assumed the fixed look of a victim of toothache engaged in denying the reality of pain. 'I can't let Roderick spoil his life like this. It wouldn't be kind or right.'

'She isn't a chorus girl, you know,' said Mark.

'She's a pianist. Rather a distinguished one, I understand.'

'Do you know, Mark, I sometimes wonder if poor Rod is quite sane. All this is so unlike him. That he should refuse to come and talk things over . . .'

'But he hasn't refused, my dear Daphne. On the contrary, he's promised. He's coming tomorrow.'

'He can't even leave that woman for a single night to come and see his wife. He's not himself: that's what it is. He's just being taken advantage of by an unscrupulous adventuress.' Daphne turned on him suddenly. 'And you stand there and tell me to be patient and let it all go on. You want me to *desert* Roderick, just when he needs me most.'

'I want,' retorted Mark, with a rather laboured jocularity, 'nothing of the kind. I want you to stop talking and come out to dinner with me and drink a bottle of wine. It'll do you good.'

'I don't want to be done good,' said Daphne.

He was silent for a while, silent and baffled. Watching her out of the corner of his eye he saw her tiredness, her desolation, her writhing vanity, and something like anger took possession of him. He was angry with himself, angry with Roderick, angry with the civilization that makes liars of us all (a good phrase, he thought: I must remember it). And angry, most of all, with Daphne herself for being so impregnably shut up in her ego, so cut off from all contact with reality. That she had turned her back on him again was suddenly more than he could put up with. His fear of her, his fear of himself, vanished. He seized her by the shoulders and jerked her round none too gently. Willy-nilly she fell into his arms and he kissed her mouth hungrily. She shut her eyes and submitted. He looked down at her, puzzled rather than exalted, though excitement ran in his veins. With eyes still closed she offered her mouth again, but even in the tumult of his senses he was visited by the nightmare conviction that it was Roderick she kissed. Roderick, Roderick, there was no getting away from the fellow. He experienced a moment's sick hatred of Roderick, followed by a spasm of self-disgust.

He quickly released her, retaining, for politeness' sake, only a hand.

'What did we do that for?' she asked coldly. She had the air of coming out of a trance.

He was obscurely grateful for that 'we,' but pride made him repudiate it. 'You mean, why did *I* do it. Because you 're a beautiful woman and I 'm a man.'

She examined his face curiously. 'You 're not in love with me?'

Lay not that flattering unction to your soul, he thought . . . and mocked himself for being always the literary journalist. For answer he shrugged

his shoulders. 'Yes, I suppose so. In a fashion.'
Hypocrisy is infectious. Clearly I 'm not in love
with her.

'I don't think I understand. You 're Rod's
friend, aren't you?'

'I don't expect you to understand,' said Mark
savagely. 'You live in a mist and understand
nothing. Nothing.' She did not answer. 'Moreover,' he added, 'I rather think I was lying. I 'm
not in love with you. And I 've no intention of
trying to seduce you.'

'Why did you kiss me like that?' she asked,
flushing.

'Not a very sensible question, Daphne.' He
affected lightness. But in fact it was a question
he couldn't answer. Why had he kissed her? An
impulse to shake her out of herself had begun it,
and simple male desire had done the rest. He
looked at the hypothesis squarely enough and
thought that on the whole it would do. But who
cares, anyhow? The moment was passed, the
passion side-tracked by tedious self-analysis. A
dreary conclusion, but since that momentary flicker
of feeling was to be smothered in talk, let talk be
given its head and made to carry him safely back
to the *status quo*. 'We 've been friends a long time,
haven't we, Daphne? No, that 's not the opening gambit of a sentimental appeal. We 've been
friends a long time, and in the nature of the case
it wasn't possible for me to think of you in what

is so oddly called "that way". Roderick was a
very good reason why one's thoughts should keep
at a sober pace. And in fact it never occurred to
me to want to make love to you. Quite a speech,
isn't it?'

She smiled: a welcome sight. 'Yes, isn't it!
Go on.'

'Our relationship was comfortable and settled.
But this business of you and Rod has changed
you, made you like a stranger, with all a stranger's
mysterious attraction. It made you distant with
me, and it's easier to leap across a distance than
to advance from ordinary easygoing friendship to
love-making. Now there's a nice tidy explanation
for you. I shall probably work it up into a little
article,' he added maliciously. 'Borderline Friend-
ships, or Should Wives be Kissed? It ought to
be worth ten guineas to me at least.'

'How absurd you are!' She looked at him in
almost her old way.

'And now let's go and have a meal,' he said
quickly. His pleasure in seeing her restored made
him almost happy for a moment, and there was
disinterested satisfaction in the thought that his
self-exhibition had at least distracted her from herself for five minutes. 'Go and powder your nose,
if you must, while I phone for a taxi.'

He went to open the door for her, but before he
reached it it was opened from the other side by
Tucker. Tucker did his best to look like the perfect

butler, but in the presence of Mark his performance was never quite convincing: humanity kept breaking in. Standing stiffly in the doorway, and looking with formal respect towards his mistress, he said: 'Would you wish me to bring in the cocktails, madam?'

Daphne was surprised by the interruption. 'Yes, Tucker, do.'

Tucker was not yet satisfied. 'And when,' he asked, almost furtively, with an embarrassed sense of Mark's genial eye upon him, 'when will madam take her egg?'

'I shall not be in to dinner,' she answered quickly.

'Very good, madam.' The door closed behind Tucker.

'What's this about an egg?' asked Mark. 'Was that to have been your dinner?'

'If you must know, Mark, it was.'

'An egg,' repeated Mark. 'A nice nourishing lightly boiled egg. And two thin slices of bread and butter perhaps? Or would that have been too gross?'

'Food chokes me,' said Daphne, going to the door. 'Drink your cocktail, Mark, and mine too. I'll be ready in two minutes.'

While Daphne was getting ready to go out to dinner with Mark Perryman, a family party of four persons emerged from an underground station into the noise and sunshine of Oxford Street.

Young Vincent was the first to reach the pavement, though his sister Marjorie was a good second: these two, in the posture of impatient adolescence, stood at the stairhead waiting for their parents to join them. 'Where do we go next, I wonder?' asked Vincent Coates, rather contemptuously. He was fresh from his first shave and it seemed unlikely that the evening's outing would prove to be worth his while. 'Don't know,' said Marjorie. She called: 'Which way, Dad?' She did not address the question to her mother, for Mr Coates was in command, and it was important that he should be kept in a good temper. Mrs Coates, for the same reason, was careful to keep a pace or two behind her husband: Roger was so sensitive, and it would spoil his evening if he were allowed to notice that she, having a four years' advantage of him, and less fat to carry about, was untroubled either by the weather or by these few stairs. Forty-five 's no age for a man, but poor Roger 's as touchy about it as a woman. 'All right, all right!' answered Mr Coates, confronting his daughter at last. 'There 's no such hurry, is there? We haven't got a train to catch? Where 's Vincent?' Vincent, at his elbow, said: 'Here I am, Dad. Where now?' Mr Coates looked round for his wife. 'Come along, Mother.' With his family collected, he stood for a moment taking his bearings. 'There!' he said at last, in a tone of great decision. 'That 's our way. Now come along. Keep close to me, all of you.' He shepherded his flock across the road, and with a demeanour blending irritation and pride led them, by stages, to his objective. It was Mother's birthday, and Father had contrived this delightful surprise, a Supper in Soho. A colleague at the office had told him of a restaurant that was good, not too expensive if you chose your dishes carefully, and really quite respectable. 'Well, here we are then,' said Mr Coates triumphantly. 'A bit bohemian, you know. But people are more broad-minded than they used to be.' He glanced round at wife and children; then, with an air of saying 'No, don't thank me now!', marched at their head into the restaurant, the door of which was held open by a bowing and brilliant commissionaire. He knew, none better, that it was very kind of him to be giving his family such a treat, and that gratitude could be reasonably expected. But his bearing was regal, his smile lofty. 'So long as you're pleased,' that smile seemed to declare, 'we'll say no more about it.'

Mark Perryman saw Mr Coates without observing him. He had eyes only for Daphne, and he was at some pains to avoid looking directly even at her, curious though he was to know whether she was aware of the intention behind his choice of a restaurant. In the taxi she had said: 'Where are you taking me, Mark?' But he had evaded the question by talking quickly of something else. And, now, his choice of a table was even more

pointed, and it seemed hardly possible that she
was so far gone in egoistic isolation that she could
not see the point. One particular table, and no
other, would content him: his guest was not
consulted.

'You 'll have a cocktail now, won't you?' he
said, meeting her eyes squarely, and searching them.
Her glance drooped, and he added, meaningfully:
'They have rather a good mixture of their own
here. A secret of the 'ouse, as Georges calls it, if
you remember?'

She smiled self-consciously. 'Let 's have that
then, shall we?'

Mark gave the order. 'Well, here we are again,
Daphne, surrounded by the arcadian wall-paper.'
She smiled again, but offered no remark. 'By the
way, what became of that young man of yours?
You 've never told me the end of that love-story,
have you?'

Mr Roger Coates was examining the wine-list.
His manner with the waiter was half-lordly, half-
conspiratorial. He indicated his choice with his
forefinger.

'*Oui, m'sieur,*' said the waiter, lowering his voice
to a discreet whisper. 'A bottle of Number 57.'

'H'm. Half a bottle,' corrected Mr Coates.
He met the eyes of his family. 'In honour of
Mother,' he explained gaily.

'Oh, don't get wine for *me*, Roger,' said Mrs
Coates. 'You know I never touch it.'

'Come, just a drop,' said Mr Coates. 'I insist. You don't have a birthday every day. You children would like some ginger-pop, I expect, eh? Yes, garsong, two stone gingers. I haven't quite forgotten my young days,' he declared, searching Vincent's face for the reflection of the indulgent parent he felt himself to be. 'I know what boys like.' But Vincent was looking elsewhere: for a moment, across the room, his scowling glance encountered Daphne's absent stare. Nothing had been said about a theatre, and seeing that it was already past eight the boy decided that no theatre was in prospect.

'It wasn't exactly a love-story,' said Daphne. 'Too one-sided for that.' Her glance wandered from Vincent's face, and suddenly, incredibly, there he was, Brian, watching her from the doorway with burning eyes.

'Really?' Mark could not keep irony out of his voice, and did not try very hard. 'Yet I seem to remember your saying——'

Daphne looked down at her plate. 'What I said was mostly nonsense. Anyhow, that's all over.' Brian looked more than a little mad. What was he doing there? She wondered if he intended to make a scene. So like him to do that, she thought, with a little shiver.

'You've dismissed him?'

She did not answer.

'And did he take his dismissal like a gentleman?'

The waiter arrived with the cocktails. At last she dared to look up. That monitory melodramatic figure had vanished.

She faced Mark with a smile. 'Of course, Mark. What else was there for him to do, poor lamb?'

§ 12

BONAKER UNCHANGED

As he heaved his suitcase into the rack, and arranged his sheaf of newspapers on the carriage-seat, Simpson was still thinking of the problem that had exercised him at breakfast, the problem which, with quite a sense of guilt, he had carefully concealed from sister Eleanor. It troubled and angered him to think how troubled and angry Eleanor would be if she had known what was drawing him away from her to spend a few days in London. As a psychologist he could have stated the case in terms of the current materialistic mysticism, as a biologist he could find no fault with his intentions, as a student of astro-physics he realized that his and Eleanor's domestic happiness was of negligible account in the sum of sublunary events, and not even the most severe moralist would have conceded Eleanor's right to resent the idea of her brother's marrying. There had been women in his life before—well, naturally, for he was within sight of his fortieth year—and Eleanor, though she had not been definitely told of these affairs, must have assumed, in a general way, that he had what she would perhaps have called an empirical as well as a theoretical knowledge of sex. But so long as he did not make a fool of himself, so long as he did nothing that threatened to disturb their pleasant quiet intellectual life together, she was the last person to complain, and he remained untroubled by any twinges of conscience. But for months now his thoughts had turned with ever-increasing urgency and frequency in the direction of marriage. Gilian wanted children, and he himself wanted Gilian to a degree that he had never experienced before. He wanted her from January to December, not for occasional honeymoons (these, contrary to all precedent, had increased rather than diminished his 'fixation' upon her); and he wanted—this was the most disquieting feature of his plight—he wanted no one else. When by some misadventure he heard the refrain of a popular song:

> I'm tired of being fickle,
>   I'm longing to be true,
> I want someone to love me,
>   And someone must be you,
> I want you for my baby, dear,
>   And no one else will do,

he recognized, with a shock of dismay followed by a grin of self-ridicule, that in these lines his own state of mind was described with a frightful accuracy. It was a sobering thought, but far from likely to have a sobering effect on Eleanor. And if Eleanor had been his wife he could hardly have felt more responsible to her, more guilty at the thought of leaving her. This sense of guilt, he thought ruefully, was positively mediaeval; but calling it names did not frighten it away.

It said much for Eleanor that he should be haunted by a sense of her calm penetrating scrutiny even now, half an hour after having said good-bye to her at the door of their home, and notwithstanding that every revolution of the wheels took him nearer to Gilian. He was not, however, afraid of Eleanor. He was afraid of hurting her, and afraid of the boredom which she had the power to inflict on him. To escape that presence and that boredom he took a newspaper from the top of his pile and opened it. From the mass of close print his own name was the first thing to reach his eye. 'Mr. A. J. K. Simpson, the well-known scientific writer . . .' Something he had written was quoted, apropos of something else. His spirit purred within him. He was too intelligent to suppose that this kind of importance was important, but the momentary pleasure, the caressing of his vanity, lightened his humour and seduced him from his circling thoughts of Eleanor and Gilian, Gilian and Eleanor. Simpson had a journalist's knowledge of everything, but it was in popular science that he specialized. He had the knack, so much valued by editors, of inducing in the minds of ordinary intelligent inquisitive citizens the illusion that they came within a hundred miles of understanding Einstein. He discussed the chemistry of food and the variation of species; if there was a comet in the calendar, or an eclipse of this or that, he was ready with his stuff six weeks in advance. He expounded Freud, interpreted Marx, and had sharp things to say about Eddington's religious musings. He waxed ironical at the suggestion, made by a distinguished mathematician, that God was primarily a mathematician, and was discreet enough not to publish his own secret conviction, which was that God might be more usefully envisaged as a kind of journalist. In short, he turned out a commodity that was much in demand, and made a modest living at it. And when he remembered his humble parentage, his very middle-class schooling, and the narrow suburban environment from which he had emerged, he felt obscurely grateful to his stars, found something romantic (though his sophistication forbade the thought) in the contrast between what would have been reasonably predicted of him as a boy and what he had in fact become. He had dreamed of being the kind of person that he now was, at a time when it had seemed even to himself a fantastic improbability. This work, this position in the world, this freedom from the limitations and snobberies of class, this was what he had wanted; and by an astonishing coincidence this was what he had got.

This morning, however, he was thinking not of his past but of his future; and it was therefore with the sensation of being flung to a great height, or being snatched out of a deep dream, that, glancing over his paper, he perceived a fragment of his past sitting opposite him. For twenty minutes he had had the carriage to himself—and no wonder, since the train stopped at seven stations in a fifty-mile run—but at the last stopping-place someone had got in. He had been vaguely aware of a dark, long-faced, square-jawed man in blue serge and a stiff white collar; and a bowler hat, strange flower of fantasy, had hovered on the fringe of his consciousness; but now, in this second glance, these particulars were lost in the plain incredible fact that here was Bonaker.

'Excuse me,' said Simpson. Twenty-five years is a long time, and one must be cautious. 'Didn't you once live at Broad Green?'

'Well, yes, I did.' Bonaker looked at him half-suspiciously. Then recognition dawned in his face and he shot out a large lean hand. 'Simpson!'

'How extraordinary!' said Simpson, shaking hands. The powerful illusion of having rediscovered a lost epoch kept him silent for a moment. He looked shyly away, savouring the miracle. To be thirteen again, to be back in that boy's skin and living in that boy's senses, the boy that was

127

buried in himself! For here was Bonaker, unchanged except for his ridiculous accoutrements. 'Last time I saw you,' remarked Simpson, 'you were wearing an Eton collar.'

A gleam of humour shone in Bonaker's eyes, but his long saturnine face moved scarcely a muscle. 'H'm!' he said, and in so precisely the old way as to make Simpson cry out (but in the secrecy of his mind only): He hasn't changed a bit. He's only a boy still, dressed up, pretending. What a preposterous hat!

After another pause Simpson spoke again.

'It's twenty-two years,' he said, almost breathlessly.

Bonaker made a silent calculation. 'You're right. It's just that.'

'Do you remember . . .' began Simpson.

He himself remembered so much. Pictures of that time crowded upon him, and again and again he came back to the fact, which he found so deliciously reassuring, that Bonaker had not changed. Slightly battered, a wrinkle here and there, teeth not so good, but otherwise the same. He had always been sombre, shrewd, matter-of-fact, inclined to taciturnity; had always had that odd lanky square-cut build and that steady penetrating look. His eyes were the same dark brown with a touch of green, his hair still black, sleek, and well-ordered. There had always been that suggestion of gauntness about him. He had an air of detachment, but it

was not a dreamer's detachment. Good-natured
he was, but you wouldn't have called him genial.
An odd, logical sort of chap, unhumorous, yet good
company because of his dry way, and certainly no
prig. His very lack of temperament made him
somehow rather funny. These boyish judgements
could still, thought Simpson, be sustained. But
on the heels of that reflection came a memory somewhat at variance with the fancy picture he was
building up of a reserved, common-sensible, self-
contained spirit: of that day when he and Prescott
had sat in class whispering and giggling together
about nothing in particular, and a little screwed-up
note had come sailing across from Bonaker, a few
desks distant: 'Dear Sim, What are you and Prescott
saying about me? Yrs sincerely, L. Bonaker.
R.S.V.P.' There are grades and varieties in
friendship. Prescott was his chosen companion,
his kindred mind: he and Prescott shared a desk
when they could and considered themselves injured
when they couldn't. With Bonaker he had become
acquainted by the accident of propinquity: Bonaker
lived in a road contiguous to Simpson's ('avenues',
they were called in the newly created suburb of
Broad Green), so it was inevitable that they should
walk to and from school together, twice a day.
At a certain point of the journey they met Mr
Stark, the first assistant master, and on one occasion Mr Stark so far unbent as to say to them,
before striding on his way: 'You boys are as

punctual as Big Ben. I always set my watch by you.' Simpson felt greatly honoured by this condescension, and was puzzled when Bonaker, without the least ill nature, said coolly: 'The funny old fathead!' It was equally inevitable that the two boys should sometimes 'call for' each other in the evening, after their homework was done. Simpson would ring the bell, raise his school cap to Mrs Bonaker, and say: 'Please, can Bonaker come out?' That was at the very beginning of the friendship; for one day, after Bonaker's mother had got used to finding young Simpson on her doorstep, she countered his formula with waggery: 'I 've got two in the house. Which one would you like?' Thereafter he asked politely for 'Lionel', though it cost him a great effort. Bonaker, when he called for Simpson, had no such difficulties to overcome; for Eleanor, the studious serious Eleanor who (ten years his senior) stood to Simpson *in loco matris*, had no time for joking with schoolboys. The meeting achieved, the two would go at once into the fields: fields none the worse, in their estimation, for being neighboured by new houses, and all the better, some of them, for having stacks of bricks or piles of planks lying about. And there were still, after all, trees to climb, and large ponds on which a decent-sized plank could be navigated. There was home-made cricket, there were tadpoles, and there were numerous games of pretence which at this distance from school (they

guessed, with good reason, that their school con-
temporaries would hold these pursuits to be soppy
and babyish) could be played with complete safety
and with solemn satisfaction. They wasted no time
in considering what they should do. Decisions
were instant and spontaneous: what one proposed,
the other seldom failed to agree to. This kind of
thing happened two or three evenings a week during
the first summer of the acquaintanceship. Yet,
back within the precincts of school, it was Prescott
that Simpson sought out, Prescott he confided in;
and Bonaker, without the least resentment, discreetly followed his own devices. And though the
official leisure was severely limited, a break in
morning school and a break in the afternoon, in
practice there was no lack of social intercourse.
Discipline was strict only in intention, and, among
many lessons, the chief thing Simpson learned at
his day-school was the art of surreptitious note-
passing and of conversing unobserved under the
very nose of the master. As a supplement to the
official time-table of lessons, Simpson and Prescott
drew up a time-table of their own, showing what
subjects they proposed to discuss together at what
hours. It was not in nature that they should keep
to the programme, but it was fun drawing it up,
and it never occurred to either of them that it
constituted a shattering criticism of Mr Stark's
history teaching, for example, that while he wrote
dates and sentences on the blackboard, and referred

them to this page or that, they proposed to make, *sotto voce*, a systematic inquiry into questions they were supposed not to be interested in. Religion, psychical research, the possibility of reaching the moon: such things were meat and drink to Prescott and Simpson. But Bonaker was not like that. Bonaker would discover America with you any fine evening of the week, but when it came to disquisition at large, or to arguments about one's origin and destiny, you couldn't have got a word out of him. Quite unruffled he would have said 'Yes' or 'No' or would have put the whole question aside with a non-committal grunt and got on with the job: whether it was playing cricket, pretending to be a pirate, or merely walking to school, there was always a job to be got on with, and Bonaker got on with it. Simpson knew this without testing it, without thinking about it: it never occurred to him to talk to Bonaker as he talked with Prescott. His instinct had been sound in that. Now, a quarter of a century later, he was more apt to blunder, to attempt the impossible.

'Do you remember . . .' The most heartening conversations in the world begin with this phrase. But Simpson ought to have known better than to expect a riot of reminiscence from Bonaker. Bonaker said Yes he remembered, but Simpson was not encouraged to proceed with his litany of remembered episodes, episodes which, like Bonaker himself, had for him the surpassing value that anything

must have, however trivial, which seems to restore
to a man some part of his lost life. He wanted to
recall to Bonaker's mind the fight he and Bonaker
had had with Netherwood, the great boaster; but
instead of that he began asking the usual questions.
Yes, Bonaker was married. Yes, he had children:
three of them. Yes, he lived in London. What
was he doing in these parts? He was here on
business: had several people to see on business.

He belonged to a firm that supplied sanitary
plumbing requisites. How right, how exquisitely
right, thought Simpson. A traveller in water-
closets! What a good, solid, sensible way of
earning one's bread: prosaic, necessary, dignified,
and just like old Bonaker. 'How did you get on
in the war?' he asked. But it was another fight
he was thinking of, the fight with Netherwood
which had been fought twenty-three years ago in
the brickfields of Broad Green. He could hardly
listen to Bonaker's answer, so deeply was he immersed in the past. A foreigner in effect, this
Netherwood: he went to another school, a cads'
school. He attached himself to Bonaker and
Simpson one evening when they were having some
cricket practice. Without invitation he began
fielding; without invitation he said he'd show
them how to bowl; and presently, as a matter of
right, he took possession of the bat and remarked
that he didn't mind having a whack himself.
Simpson was resentful but polite; Bonaker was

Bonaker, silent and inscrutable. Finally, having knocked his young friends all over the field, Netherwood relinquished the bat with a laugh and said: 'I'm Netherwood. You've heard of me.'

'No, we haven't,' said Simpson.

'Oh, haven't you!' Netherwood gave him an ugly look. 'I go to Farringay School. I go by train every day.'

Simpson held his peace. Bonaker said: 'Do you?'

'Yes, I jolly well do. It's a better school than yours, you little sops.'

'How long were you at our school?' asked Bonaker.

Netherwood stared, divided between wrath and perplexity. 'Whadjou talking about? I never went to your school. My father knew better.'

'Then how do you know yours is better than ours?' asked Bonaker. 'I mean, if you haven't been to ours,' he added, with an air of genuinely seeking information.

Netherwood thought he was being got at. 'All right,' he said. 'I'll fight you. What d'you say?' He peeled off his jacket and rolled up his sleeves.

'Mind you don't catch cold,' said Bonaker.

The answer to that was a vicious slap on the face. Bonaker, without exciting himself, stepped back and removed his jacket. Simpson began following suit, but his friend said No, he'd see to this himself. 'You stand by and see fair play, Sim.' And so they went at it. It was a fight not according to the Queensberry rules, being a kind of cross between boxing and catch-as-catch-can. Bonaker got decidedly the worst of it: he was badly knocked about, and Netherwood celebrated his triumph by sitting astride the chest of the vanquished, and forcing his arms into the posture of crucifixion.

'Which school's better now?' demanded Netherwood, with a sneer.

For a while Bonaker was too short of breath to achieve an answer. The question was repeated. Sundry promises of torture were made.

'I don't know,' gasped Bonaker at length.

The victor interpreted this answer as a sign of weakening morale. 'Oh, you don't know, don't you? Why don't you know, eh?'

'Because I've only been to one of them,' said Bonaker.

While Netherwood spent half a second devising his revenge Simpson intervened. He felt he had been inactive too long. 'Get off him, you swine! Get off him, and quick.' He brandished a cricket stump, and Netherwood, jumping up, gave ground. Bonaker, too, was now on his legs again; but it was against their code to set upon the alien unless he showed further fight. Instead of doing that he walked away, whistling a tune, trying not to look as though he feared pursuit.

'Does it hurt much, Bon?' The reference was

to Bonaker's right eye, which was closed and discoloured.

Beyond shrugging his shoulders, Bonaker took no notice of the question. And, after a thoughtful silence, 'I wonder which really *is* the better school,' he said.

§ 13

FLEET-STREET RENDEZVOUS

THE morning after that second visit to Soho, three men woke with the thought of Daphne uppermost in their minds. One suffered a pang of nervous sickness in the thought that today he would be obliged to see her; one with fresh appetite resumed a bitter feast, eating his own heart out because she was not for him; the third, before rolling out of bed, played for a moment with the question whether or not he should contrive to see her today. Roderick rose stealthily and left Elisabeth sleeping. He hardly dared to glance at her, for he knew, and she knew, that today's interview with Daphne held danger for them: he doubted, and he knew that she doubted, whether he had resolution enough to stand out against the demands of Daphne's pride and desolation. His mind assured him again and again that he was fully justified in leaving his wife, that he was only acting on principles which they had both affirmed, that to resume a loveless marriage

would be merely the wanton sacrifice of himself
and Elisabeth on the altar of Daphne's vanity. But
a small voice out of the past, which he was in
danger of mistaking for the voice of conscience,
insisted on urging him towards this sacrifice, regard-
less of consequences. It's my duty to make Daphne
happy. But one can't make another person happy
unless one is happy oneself. Besides, I don't want
her, and to pretend I do would be disgusting, an
outrage. But is it true I don't want her? At this
last question he wavered. In his heart he knew
that eight years of marriage, even of a marriage
that was largely unsatisfactory, had bound him to
Daphne with bonds of habit that were indistinguish-
able from affection. He knew that she was no
longer sexually interesting to him; and he knew,
too well, that this was by no means the result of
any diminution or sublimation of his own sexuality.
These three facts remained to confront him whenever he could escape for a moment from the more
immediate, the overwhelming fact, that he was in
love with Elisabeth Andersch. He took them to
the office with him this Wednesday morning, and
sat at his desk staring at them moodily. He felt
that it was essential to get his attitude defined, his
policy planned, before seeing Daphne.

'Well, Roderick my boy?'

'Hullo?' said Roderick. 'Good morning.' It
was Cradock, his venerable senior partner. The
two liked and admired each other up to a point.

Beyond that point—but it was Roderick's resolve that they should never go beyond that point, for he was well aware that outside the sphere of their common professional interests most of his convictions would seem to Cradock wrong-headed and pernicious. Certain questions that still agitated Roderick had been settled for Cradock for half a century and would never be reopened. On all matters of conduct and religious belief his mind was rigid, and he had no difficulty in averting his eyes from anything that challenged the faith of his fathers. He lived in a small universe of unshakable certitudes, and it would have disturbed and even angered him had he supposed Roderick to be anything but the right-thinking young fellow he took him for. In Cradock's philosophy a fellow was either a gentleman or a cad, and he had no doubts of Roderick.

'Well, Roderick, they 've given us the new court.'

Roderick looked vague. 'The new court?' Then he remembered. 'By Jove, you 've pulled it off? Congratulations.'

'Come,' said Cradock heartily, 'it 's *your* work, my boy. Well, you 've got something now to keep you happy for a time.'

Roderick grinned. 'Busy, anyhow.'

'Same thing,' said Cradock, with a wave of the hand, and went back to his own room.

Something in that, thought Roderick, trite though it is. Where but to think is to be full of sorrows. Don't stop to think. Even in love don't stop to think. Corrosive stuff, thought: it eats happiness away. He saw the undergraduates moving about that new court of his. What will they learn there? Not the difference between right and wrong. Nobody knows that—except Cradock, of course, and poor old Dad. For at last it came up into consciousness, the lurking thought of his father and all that his father stood for. A gentle old man with a cure of souls. Was that true or was it mere sentimentality? An old man pottering about his vicarage garden in Somerset, with a kind word for everyone (even the dissenters), a skilful hand with bees, an expert knowledge of roses, and a bland simplicity (or was it cunning?) in face of modern scepticism. An old man, full of good works, who even now, at an advanced age and with a curate to rely on, insisted on keeping in touch with the village, shaking his head sadly over the tipplers, rebuking the uncharitable, visiting the bedridden, smiling benignly on the 'young men and maidens', and comforting the dying with false promises of resurrection. It was all very pretty and idyllic, and Roderick could not resist the conviction that his father was a kind of saint; but had it any bearing on his problem? Would it indeed darken his father's last days on earth if Roderick, the apple of his eye, was proved rotten at core? Would it indeed darken his days, or would he only pretend that it did—pretend,

that is, to himself? It was difficult to know what
to believe, and to put an end to his speculation
Roderick touched the buzzer on his desk, and the
demure young woman who typed his letters for
him came gliding into the room, note-book in hand.

'Oh, Miss Stephens! Good morning. Could
you ask them to get Mr Perryman at the *Evening
Sun*? Put him through here.'

He turned over the letters on his desk while
Miss Stephens spoke into the telephone. When
she put up the receiver he cleared his throat and
said: 'Dear Sir . . .' What was Elisabeth doing
at this moment? And what was Daphne doing
and thinking? Tonight he must see her and they
would have a tremendous discussion. Discussion?
What was there to discuss? He would feel like a
defaulting debtor, asking to be let off. 'It isn't
that I don't love you,' he'd say. 'It's simply . . .'
For he had to keep on saying that. He couldn't
bring himself to tell her point-blank that his love
was dead, and, worse than dead, a dream in which
he no longer believed and by which he felt himself to have been unfairly trapped. He couldn't
tell her this. Perhaps because he was squeamish,
a moral coward; perhaps because it wasn't the whole
truth. Then what was the truth, and how could
it be found? The feeling of the moment was the
only convincing truth, and in that there was no
stability. Anything rather than give up Elisabeth.
Anything rather than go on hurting Daphne.

Miss Stephens was still waiting. 'Dear Sir . . .' repeated Roderick guiltily.

The telephone-bell rang. 'That will be your call,' said Miss Stephens.

She gathered up her note-book and was fading out of his presence, but at the door she was called back. Roderick snatched up a document and thrust it towards her. 'Hullo, Mark. . . . They 'll want this in the drawing-office, Miss Stephens. . . . Yes, Roderick here.' He listened to Mark's voice and then said: 'Make it half-past, can you? All right. What a chap you are for pubs, Mark!'

Most mornings, between twelve and one, Mark Perryman and others of his profession were to be found gathered round the bar of their chosen Fleet Street pub, discussing life and death and the many books they would write had they but world enough and time. From ten till noon, in the offices of the *Evening Sun*, he concocted obsequious anonymous paragraphs about newspaper celebrities; from four till six or seven he sat in a building on the other side of the Street, writing for the *Morning Echo*, under the pseudonym of Peter Punctilio, a daily column of derision, choosing for his butts precisely that cant and hypocrisy which the *Morning Echo* was so zealous to conserve. But from noon till late afternoon he took his ease, consorting with his peers. Roderick Strood, though he would have hotly repudiated the suggestion that he disapproved of men meeting in bars, was never quite at his ease in these surroundings. It was a foreign country to him, and the scene of much criminal waste of time, to say nothing of money. To Mark, on the other hand, it was England, Home, and Beauty; and unless his guest was a woman he seldom thought of appointing any other rendezvous. It was here that, at Daphne's request, seconded by Roderick, he had some few months ago made Brian Goodeve's acquaintance; and it was here that he was to meet Roderick himself this morning.

Brian was not forgetting all that. He was remembering it with peculiar bitterness. Perryman had done him a kindness. Roderick had done him a kindness. Daphne . . . Daphne had opened the door of paradise and then slammed it in his face. A rotten cheap metaphor, said Brian, and just like me. I 'm rotten and cheap, that 's why she treats me like this. If I 'd got any guts she 'd never have dared. I 'm soft and easy and she was laughing at me all the time. When I kissed her she was laughing that first time: when I kissed her that first time she was thinking what a young sop. But it 's a quaint experience she said to be necking with a bootmaker's son, such a nice smell of leather, and how he trembles, how his eyes bulge, how lovely I am, aren't I, darling? Nice to feel my body so soft in your arms, isn't it, darling? And you so tame and modest and not taking liberties like that chauffeur. But then he was a man wasn't he, shouted Brian in his mind, taking his part in the dialogue. He was a man, not a lovesick baby. He was a man, he yelled, and by now this fictitious chauffeur was real to him: he had a little close-clipped moustache and stained teeth; his eyes were red and full of lechery; he was grinning like a fox at his woman, saying nothing, grinning, grinning, while his lascivious fingers unhurriedly seized her. He was a man and knew how to treat you, didn't he, my lovely Daphne? And now it's Perryman, he's your fancy. Sitting so sleek in Soho restaurant with downcast eye demure. And when he'd fed you did he bed you, did he rape you, did he pluck you, did he pluck his beauteous bird, his flower of the night? And you insatiate lay like Messalina, great whore of all the world. Is that Marlowe, is it Ford, is it one of those boisterous boys, dear? No it's me, it's mine. It's my pent heart unvialling its gall. By God, I know how Shakespeare felt, by God I do, by God! Shakespeare, you should be living at this hour. I'm your man, I'm your brother, I have a soul like yours. And she, what is she but a filthy drab, soft and white, soft and warm, soft fleshing clouds enclose the pyramid in streets of Soho cavernously cool. God, I'm raving, I'm ranting, I'm spouting! My sperm is a trickle of words. I'm a minor poet, I'm a muckheap, I'm nothing. She knows I'm nothing. She's made me nothing. I won't go on living. Won't I? You bet I will. But some shall die, not I, not I. Perryman, for one. Perry-

man, you should be dying at this hour. Sweet
Perryman, merry Perryman, I would have speech
with thee, dear love.

She has driven me mad, said Brian, as he pushed
his way into Perryman's favourite tavern. I am
a very foolish fond young man. I watch myself
going mad. I wallow in filth, she is stripped bare,
she is foul, my great heart cracks and reason is
o'erthrown. The vile quality of his emotion convicted him of greatness. Yes, he was great: he
couldn't but know it. He was a giant among
pigmies and he suffered like a giant. He would
stalk into the middle of the stage and there die,
superbly, with the spotlight on his tragic face.
No, she would cry, you mustn't, Brian, you
mustn't; I can't bear it. Too late, light heart,
too late. I am dead. I am noble in death.
Dead, he's dead, and I have killed him. Never
look upon his like again. Away, Perryman, I
hate you. This white body is dedicate to a dream
. . . He saw Perryman and Strood standing together at the bar, and the flow of phrases stopped
abruptly. He was an ordinary young man, diffident, pimpled, humbly waiting for a nod of
recognition.

'Hullo, Goodeve,' said Perryman. 'What'll
you have?'

Brian smiled nervously. 'Hullo . . . perhaps
. . . bitter, I think. Thanks awfully.' Perryman ordered a pint. 'Oh no, half a pint, please.

Thanks very much.' Well, paramour, are you her perryman?

'What are you doing nowadays?' asked Roderick. 'Haven't seen you for a long time.'

'Oh, the usual things,' said Brian. 'Bits of verse, and a few short notices.'

'You ought to get down to something big,' remarked Perryman paternally. 'Why aren't you writing a novel? Everybody else is.'

'Are *you*?' asked Roderick. He was weary of this place and this talk. He wanted to hear news of Daphne.

'Not I,' said Perryman. 'I know better. But everyone under thirty is. Men, women, and children.' He noticed Roderick's glazed eye. 'Come along, Rod. We must be moving along. Bye, Goodeve. . . .' He steered Roderick out into the street. 'We'll have a bit of lunch. I know a quiet place.'

Roderick, striding along by his side, wondered why poor old Mark couldn't have met him at that quiet place instead of requiring of him this ritual drinking-act. 'Well, out with it, Mark,' he said. 'You've seen her?'

'Daphne?' said Mark. 'Daphne's gone away.'

'Gone away. What on earth . . .? I thought she said . . .'

'Yes, she said she must see you. Now she says she won't see you. She's gone away.'

'Where?'

'That,' said Mark, 'is supposed to be a secret.'
'Very likely.' Roderick was impatient. 'Where
has she gone?'

'She said I wasn't to tell you.'

'Did she? All right. But I don't want to know
what she said. I want to know where she's gone.'

'Here we are,' said Mark. He pushed open the
door of his quiet restaurant. Roderick followed.
They sought and found a table for two. 'Steak-
and-kidney pudding. Humble but delicious. It's
positively *de luxe* here. What do you say?'

'Yes, yes,' said Roderick. 'Anything you like.'

Mark smiled. 'Not exactly graceful, as from
guest to host. But never mind. Now look here,
Rod. Are you *sure* you want to know where
Daphne is?'

'Obviously. I've got to know. What the
devil's she playing at? It's childish.'

'You left her. She's left you. That's the
idea. And now, why not let well alone and wait
till you're asked for?'

'How can I? Don't you see, I'm responsible
for her.'

'You mean in law? Her debts and so on?'

Roderick shrugged his shoulders. 'Well, yes.'
But that was not what had been in his mind, and
Mark knew it. 'She told you not to tell me,
did she?'

'She did,' said Mark. 'And she'll be profoundly disappointed if . . . if what, Roddy?'

'If you betray her confidence?'

'Wrong,' said Mark. 'She 'll be profoundly disappointed if I don't betray her confidence. Or, at all events, if you don't find out from someone where she is.'

Roderick looked uncomfortable. 'I see what you mean. But I don't think you understand Daphne.'

'She agrees with you there,' answered Mark with a sigh.

'You rather misjudge her, old chap. Daphne is very unhappy, you know. This business has upset her.'

'Really?' said Mark. 'I hadn't thought of that.' As he met Roderick's troubled glance he had to admit that his irony was a trifle heavy. 'So you want the address, do you?'

Roderick nodded.

'She kindly wrote it down for me. Somewhere on the coast of Somerset.'

'Widdicot?' asked Roderick.

Mark had found the slip of paper. 'You 're a wizard, Rod. No hiding anything from you. What made you think of Widdicot?'

'The last time we spent a holiday at Widdicot,' said Roderick slowly, 'we hired a car and drove over to Budleigh Parva.'

Mark waited for more. Roderick's manner excited his curiosity. 'Really? I don't know Budleigh Parva. Never heard of it.'

'It's where my reverend father lives,' explained Roderick. 'He's been vicar there for about fifty years.'

§ 14

GOOD MAN AND TRUE

CYRIL GASKIN, even at thirty-five, still had moments of regret that his mother had not named him Michael or Patrick, so that the world at large might the more readily see him—as he saw himself— trailing clouds of Celtic Twilight. His maternal grandmother had been at least half-Irish, and it was from her, they said, that he had inherited his curly black hair, his blue eyes, his carefree, laughing style. He knew—how could he help knowing—that he had 'a way with him', and if ever he was tempted to lose confidence in his famous charm, the thought of that grandmother, whom he had never seen, brought to his eye a sparkle that few women could resist. 'If I weren't such a scrupulous chap,' he would sometimes say, with a sigh half-wistful but wholly self-appreciative . . . As for his father's line, there was neither doubt nor evidence that Gaskin was merely an anglicized version of Gasquin, and that the logical volatile French, as well as the whimsical volatile Irish, had contributed to the unique blend of him. Such an inheritance was a responsibility as well as an asset: only a man of sound principles could be safely trusted with it. There was little Stella now, his nineteen-year-old sister-in-law, a dear child whose full red lips and large eyes and soft peach-bloom complexion were, to a man advancing towards high summer, a rather poignant reminder of springtime joy. That was the worst of being so sensitive. Perhaps Agnes herself had looked something like that at Stella's age, ten years ago. But he doubted it. Be that as it might (a favourite phrase), it was a great comfort to have so charming a creature to share his vigil with him. For there she sat, in the arm-chair in which he had tenderly placed her, while upstairs, on the second floor, poor Agnes lay in labour with his first child. The anxious husband paced up and down the room, occasionally pausing to glance, with an almost more than brotherly solicitude, at his young companion in anxiety. In distress she was prettier than ever: very unusual that, he thought, generally quite the other way round. Prettier than ever, and she adored him. You could not blame her for that, and Cyril in fact did not blame her. It was all very natural, almost inevitable. A man mature in judgement yet still young, a man of boundless good nature, do anything for anyone, and . . . well, one isn't conceited, but it 's no use pretending that one 's altogether repulsive to look at, is it? And then, on the other side, a young and loving heart, not quite understood at home perhaps, a wee bit lonely in this big world, missing the favourite sister and glad—one might almost say, like the poet, surprised with joy—to have found a brother. They had always been pals; pleasant chaff and alluring dimples had never been wanting in their friendship; and Agnes's state of health during the last few weeks of pregnancy had brought them still closer to each other. Stella's sympathy had been a great solace to him, and now, in this supreme hour of trial, he appreciated it more keenly than ever. Moreover, the Stella he had been accustomed to think of as a little girl (and of course he still thought of her so, how else?) was fast growing into a lovely woman; and (one must be honest, mustn't one?) that sort of thing, that new shyness, that swelling bosom, that hint of sweet agitation in the heart of innocence, well, it does make a difference and what's the use of denying it? It was precisely this difference that made Cyril congratulate himself and Stella that he was the man he was. Come, little sister, we must be sensible, mustn't we? There, there, let's have a jolly laugh. That's what he'd say. Then there'd be a long, gentle understanding kiss, a little stroking and fondling . . . well, naturally: anything short of that would be sheer unkindness. And . . . no more tears, darling. We've something that no one can take from us, haven't we. We'll play the game, eh? Straight bat. At this point in his fantasy Cyril paused to thank God that she had fallen into the hands of a man of honour.

'. . . someone to share my vigil,' he said lovingly. And at the word 'vigil' his smile became braver, became tragic. He was a knight of old time suffering for his lady. She little knew how much he suffered. 'It's this waiting, Stella. This suspense. This . . . this . . . *silence*. Eight hours now it's been going on. And to me it seems like eight years.'

Stella, in his best arm-chair, sat in a posture strangely unrestful. Turning eyes of wonder towards him, she answered in a low meek voice. 'Yes?'

'A son, Stella, think of that. Think what it must be to have a son. A new life, and part of oneself. Part of one's very essence. And to think that this wonderful experience may be mine at any moment now! But it's still in the balance. This waiting is the most dreadful part of the whole business.'

'Is it?' asked Stella. 'Still, one can always talk.'

'Talk!' He echoed her with gentle derision. 'What good is talk? How can one talk when at this very moment, Stella, in this very house, the great drama is being enacted that is to make me a father! But you're right. One mustn't give way to one's feelings. Tell me, what have you been doing with yourself lately? Tennis? Theatricals?'

She made no answer, but sat staring at her thoughts. So he came nearer and laid a caressing hand on her shoulder. 'What are you thinking about, little star?'

She looked up at him wanly. 'Does it matter?'

'It matters if it makes you unhappy, darling. It matters very much . . . to me.'

Her shoulder slipped from under his hand as she altered her position in the chair. 'I don't know what you mean. I'm thinking of Agnes. What else could I be thinking of?'

'Agnes?' he said. 'Yes, Agnes. We mustn't forget *her*.' What else, indeed, could the poor child think of but Agnes? The point of honour. The sword, as it were, between. But he couldn't resist probing further. 'And what,' he said, in a low sad tone, '*what* were you thinking about Agnes?'

As though nervous of his hovering presence, perhaps untrustful of herself so near the arms of temptation, she got out of her chair and moved away. Then faced about and stared at him. 'Really, Cyril, you're rather extraordinary, aren't you?'

So, ah so, it was coming at last! 'Am I?' he said. 'Not really, Stella. I'm really a very ordinary sort of chap. It's just an idea you've got about me. An idea. An ideal.' He moved towards her with arms ready to shelter her, and a manly shoulder against which she might hide her confusion. Loyal little sister. A shame that she should be so bewildered and unhappy.

'Yes, you are,' said Stella with emphatic decision. 'Quite extraordinary. I believe you've quite forgotten that Agnes is having a baby——'

'My *dear*!' he broke in. 'How *could* I forget! It makes it so much more difficult, I know. This moment of all moments. You and I, and Agnes having a baby.'

'—and that her life is in danger,' finished Stella obstinately.

'Yes, yes,' said Cyril. He smiled a strange sad smile, like a martyr forgiving his persecutors. 'It's terrible. Only you, dear, can understand what this ordeal means to me. I tell you, Stella, I'm simply worn out with it.'

'Are you?' Her eyes gleamed. 'Poor Cyril! Thoughtless of Agnes to put such a strain on you.'

He went on, unhearing. The theme drew him irresistibly. 'Yes, my dear. No one knows what I've been through these last few days . . .'

'Don't they?' said Stella, widening her wide eyes. 'Well, it's not for want of telling, is it?'

He heard that, and was puzzled. The dialogue was taking an unexpected turn. She was doubtless distraught, not quite herself, talking at random in her brave resolve to be loyal to Agnes. Ah, little bird, you have nothing to fear. No need for this iron control. No need for dissembling. Your secret is safe with me. Think of me, darling, not of Agnes. Think how I've suffered, be sorry for me, celibate all these weeks, anxious, thinking of my child and of poor Agnes. Come and be comforted, come and comfort, give me your lips . . .

a kiss of kindness, pure kindness—what could be lovelier, what could be purer?—let the tears come, let the tears gush out. . . .

There was a tap at the door. Stella opened it. What was all this? Ah, the doctor! 'Doctor,' he stammered, 'is it . . .?'

Yes, it was all over. It was all right. A boy.

'May we see her?' asked Stella, clutching the doctor's hand.

'Him, Stella,' said Cyril, gently correcting her. 'It's a boy. Didn't you hear?' My son. My firstborn.

Cyril Gaskin was happy. And with good reason. A new Cyril Gaskin had entered the world of men.

§ 15

RODERICK AND DAPHNE

MARK may be right up to a point, said Roderick, back in his office. But he over-simplifies everything—the journalist's trick. Daphne running away to make me run after her. Well, supposing she is? And suppose she *does* dramatize her suffering and make the most of it, that doesn't prove she's not suffering. And, so, it doesn't let *me* out. In the train that evening, on the way to Widdicot, he resumed the argument, telling himself that there was, whether one liked it or not, a sort of identity between himself and Daphne. That phrase about being one flesh was not entirely meaningless, though it was rather in the spirit than in the flesh that people got so damnably united. He felt in his bones that he would never really get away from her so long as they both lived. It 's the sharing that does it, he said. Sex is nothing— or at least it 's only one thing, and it passes. But the sharing, having house and purse in common, eating together, being tired together, or amused or bored or excited, even quarrelling and gradually learning how to avoid quarrels—good or bad, lively or dull, intimacy or habit, it was all one, and it was marriage: not the legal fiction or the mystic self-dedication, but the inconvenient reality that came of continuous living together. Roderick both soothed and terrified himself with these reflections, for while they provided moral support to the craven impulse that urged him to surrender, they also, by the same token, threatened to betray his new love and cheat him of his heart's desire. At moments he suspected himself of the subtlest form of hypo-crisy, the deceiving oneself into the belief that to submit to the so-called inevitable is the true part of wisdom. And at such moments he clung frenziedly to the fact of Elisabeth. It was Elisa-beth that he wanted. In her love, in her life, in her very flesh, he was fulfilled. She 's all I want, he said, and the rest is lies. . . . Then why am I in this train? he cried in a sort of terror. What idiot weakness is driving me to Daphne, to listen, to talk, to let myself be spiritually blackmailed, to be betrayed into a pious treachery? Nevertheless he winced at the thought of the alternative policy, the ruthless but perhaps less cruel policy, of calling her bluff, leaving her alone to her anger and misery. Now he faced the fact that bluff it was, this running away, this refusal to see him; and now, a moment later, that fact seemed dubious indeed. Perhaps her image of him was really dead, killed by his own act. And to think that was to feel that Daphne herself was in some sense dead, and so to be beset by memories of happy times together. And though he knew that memory too is a deceiver, with a strong sentimental bias, he could not but lend himself to the deception. His past was himself, and Daphne was part of his past. To cut her out of himself was a piece of surgery he lacked the nerve to perform. Yet perform it he must, or be for ever something less than a man.

He had sent a telegram, and there was Daphne on the platform to meet him. He was astonished to see her. It had seemed inconceivable that she would feel friendly enough to come. Relieved of its misgiving, his heart gave a bound. Often he had thought: If only Daphne were someone else, so that I could talk to her quite frankly about all this, man to man! And now . . . was it possible . . .? He stepped out of the train and went towards her. But she, after one glance of recognition, one oddly neutral glance, turned her head away and awaited him with apparent apathy. 'Hullo,' he said, tentatively. 'Hullo,' she answered. She did not look at him again. She stood aside so that he might give his ticket to the collector and precede her out of the station.

'So you're staying at Mrs Hewitt's again,' remarked Roderick, when they reached the road together.

'Yes,' said Daphne. 'I asked Mark not to tell you.'

He stole a glance at her profile. 'Why did you do that?'

'Do you want a meal?' she asked.

'No, I had one on the train.'

She seemed to hesitate. He noticed that her glance rested for a moment on the suitcase that he carried.

'I'd better put this thing in the cloakroom here, hadn't I?' he suggested. He felt awkward and guilty. 'And see about a room somewhere,' he explained, in an agony of discomfort.

'Yes,' she said. 'No doubt the hotel will have room.'

'Oh, sure to.' He spoke hurriedly. He was doubly at a loss. Desperately afraid of saying the wrong thing, he blurted out: 'Well, perhaps it would be more sense to go to the hotel straight away?' He waited in vain for her answer. 'Would it?' What a feeble idiot I am, he thought. No guts. No decision. Crawling down here like a beaten dog, to ask for another beating.

Her blank face offering no help, he went back into the station and got rid of the suitcase, returning two minutes later to find her still standing in precisely the same attitude of rigid inattention.

He came and stood at her elbow. 'Well, shall we go and walk by the sea?'

'Just as you like,' said Daphne politely.

'Well, I mean, if we are to have a talk,' he explained, blunderingly. 'After all,' he added, in a tone grown suddenly angry, 'you said you wanted to talk.'

But the anger was superficial: underneath it was mere misery. Without more words they began walking at a brisk pace, and no sooner were his legs in motion than Roderick began to feel his burden less heavy. But the soothing of his ruffled nerves brought a new burden. In the earliest days of his marriage walking had been among the chief of the pleasures shared with Daphne, and for an instant of time he was able to cheat himself into believing that the old easy taken-for-granted comradeship was restored to life again. These moments, contradicted at every other step by his sense of fact, added to this experience a poignancy which he was afraid to recognize. These two mortal spirits, enclosed together in the heart of a lovely summer, and walking side by side at an easy, swinging pace, were yet divided and at odds, each suffering a solitary confinement. When they came within sight of the sea, that sudden amplitude, that large sane horizon, offered Roderick a moment's escape, from himself and from Daphne. But, alas, the beauty of the sea put him in mind of Elisabeth, and that it should do so made him feel guilty. The crystal of the evening was shattered, and he glanced stealthily at Daphne's shut face. He saw nothing there that Brian Goodeve, that Mark Perryman, had seen. And his heart sank into despair. If only I could look on her with desire, he thought. But I can't. It's Elisabeth I want.

They had been walking, along the cliffs, for what seemed a long time, without exchanging a word; and even now he could not bring himself to begin making words, more words, of the plight in which they found themselves. It's utterly commonplace, nothing the least unusual about it. And God knows we've talked enough. Too much. Though peace had taken flight from the summer evening, silence remained, and he entertained a vague fond hope that silence, if only it were given time, might heal them as no words could do; might bring them magically into a state of serene, passionless harmony. Refusing to engage itself with the tedious problem, which was indeed no problem at all, but a plain deadlock, his tired mind wandered off once more in contemplation of sea and sky and the random dreams that their strangely personal presence set moving in him; so that it was almost with the effect of waking that he became again sharply aware of Daphne.

For she came to a sudden standstill and said: 'I think I shall sit down.'

The announcement sounded so much like an accusation that he could find no answer. Frowning, confused, he watched her sit down, and then followed her example.

'We *are* having a nice talk, aren't we?' said Daphne, with aggressive loudness.

He met her sudden stare with raised eyebrows and deprecating face. 'I 'm ready enough to talk, if there 's anything to say. That 's what I 've come for, isn't it?'

'Well, what are we going to do about everything? We can't go on like this: that 's evident. Are you going to send me hotel bills or something? I 'm sure that will be very nice.'

Ah, thought Roderick, so it 's beginning. The same chattering recrimination.

'One thing I 've made up my mind about,' said Daphne. 'I won't have any of your money.'

'That 's hardly reasonable, is it?' He spoke in the carefully level voice of an exasperation too profound for utterance.

'I won't take your money,' she repeated.

'Then what are you going to live on?' he asked.

'That 's my own business. I won't have any money from *you*. I 'm not a kept woman, to be pensioned off.'

'I see,' said Roderick. He saw. He recognized the tactics and almost, in his extreme bitterness, admired them. Already, against all reason, he felt mean, because he no longer wanted to live with his wife; and now a more vulgar kind of meanness was to be forced upon him; he was to be put in the position of a defaulting husband, a man who leaves his wife without money, so that she must fend for herself and excite the world's indignation against him. 'That's what I call hitting below the belt.'

They lapsed into silence again, and sat staring at the sea. Daphne's violence had spent itself. But it had done its work. Before her outburst he had felt melancholy and bewildered, the victim, with her, of a disaster he could have neither foreseen nor averted. But he was not to escape like that. Her voice, her very posture, accused him. He alone was responsible. He had done it all, and done it with the sole purpose of wounding her love and dragging her pride in the dust. This, he felt, was what her bitter speech had told him. But glancing again at her averted profile he saw that she was quietly weeping. The sight of that small puckered face made his heart turn over. Resentment died in him. Knowing that he risked rebuff, he put out a hand and touched her drooping shoulder.

'Don't do that,' he said. 'It's not worth it.'

She turned and leaned against him, like a child

wanting to hide its tears and to be comforted. Frightful, he thought, that people have to hurt each other like this.

'We 'll find a way out,' he said, holding her. For now they were indeed two children confronted by an impersonal calamity. But on the heels of that thought came the fear: Have I said too much? Have I surrendered?

She lifted a tear-stained face. 'Oh, Rod, I hate us not being friends.'

'I know,' he answered.

She scrutinized him with knitted, childish brows. '*Can't* we be friends? Can't we save *something* out of this smash?'

'If only we can,' he said eagerly, 'it will be wonderful. You know how it is with me. If somehow you could bring yourself not to mind too much.'

She was silent for a moment, staring at the ground. 'I think perhaps I could, if you would help me. When your telegram came I thought anything might be possible. I even thought that you could have us both, me and . . . her. But when you came you seemed so strange, so shut away, that I went all ugly again. I didn't, you know, mean everything I said—it just came out of me.'

He was a little dazed. A miracle was happening, the remote, impossible thing he had so fondly prayed for. 'Let 's forget all that. We 've both

said things we didn't mean.' But is that true?
he asked himself.

After a pause she spoke again. 'Is she *very*
important to you?'

Say no, say no, urged his weakness. It's
easiest to say no. But if I say no, he argued, it
will be a lie, and it will lose me all I 've been
fighting for.

He said: 'Yes. I won't pretend otherwise. But
you 're important too.'

He half expected an outburst of emotion, but
she took the avowal calmly, resignedly. 'Yes,
she 's very important to you. I must face that.
But I 've sometimes wondered, the last day or two,
if it 's worth quarrelling about. People have got
to be free, haven't they? No one has the right
to interfere.'

He had the impression that she was repeating
a lesson she had taught herself. But he said
nothing, waiting for her to go on.

'If you want a divorce, and not to see me any
more,' she said presently, 'well, you must have it.
That 's obvious.'

Resisting his impulse to repudiate the project,
he answered carefully: 'And if I don't want a
divorce, and yet do want to go on seeing . . . her.
What then?'

'Well, why not?' She forced a smile. 'You 'd
better have your own way, Rod. Anything to put
an end to this everlasting talking about it.'

His release from darkness was like a new birth. But something of shame mingled with his gratitude. He felt that he had stood out for unreasonable terms and had got them. His victory made him feel shy and a little mean. Now that the point was won he longed to distract Daphne's attention from it and to make her happy, happier than she had ever been.

'You 're very generous,' he mumbled.

'I 'm very hungry,' said Daphne. 'In fact I 'm starving.'

'My dear child! When did you last have a meal?'

She grinned penitently. 'I had a little lunch.'

'Good God, and it 's nearly half-past eight.' He jumped up and helped her to her feet. 'Come on, we 'll feed. I 've had nothing since five myself.'

'We can't ask Mrs Hewitt to prepare food at this time of night,' said Daphne.

'We 'll feed at the hotel. And . . . I suppose they 'll collect my bag from the station, if I ask them?' A momentary embarrassment revisited him.

'Yes,' agreed Daphne, without much conviction. 'Of course,' she added, with careful neutrality, 'you *could* stay the night at Mrs Hewitt's.'

'Well, yes,' said Roderick. 'Why not?'

'I 've brought Mrs Tucker with me. Tucker 's looking after the house at home.'

Roderick did not answer for a moment. He was in the grip of a sudden misgiving. It was good to be friends again, very good. But the lamentable fact remained that he wanted Elisabeth, and the prospect of seeing her again seemed somehow to have receded. Victory? Yes, Daphne had conceded everything: no man could ask more. But what that victory was worth remained to be seen. Ungenerous fears, he thought: Daphne's too good for me. He held out his hand to her with a laugh, and they broke into a run together.

§ 16

SPIRITUAL MATTERS

Despite all its agitations and disappointments, Elisabeth Andersch had enjoyed her English summer. She had rested much, soothed by the odd charm and tranquillity of this foreign countryside; she had walked much, both with Roderick and alone; and her occasional recitals in London, and in those other towns of England where music may be heard, had enhanced her professional reputation. And now, with September well advanced, she found in herself an unusual reluctance to move on, to proceed with the next part of her programme, which was America. The warm days were over, the beechwoods changing colour. At dusk, and an hour before dusk, the air had a tang more rich and subtle than the blended fragrances of summer:

the flow of time was like the slow movement of the
Seventh Symphony. She was resolved yet reluctant. The episode of Roderick must be left unfinished. He had delighted her, and she knew
herself to be permanently enriched by his extrava-
gant adoration, as one may be by a piece of literature
or the sight of a new country; but the book had
been snatched out of her hand before she had done
justice to it. After his reconciliation with that so
logical wife of his, his visits to herself had at first
been hurried and infrequent, full of protestations
and apologies; and during the past six weeks, for
the sake of his happiness no less than her own,
she had divided her time between the cottage at
Frendham and a town flat, a flat from whose upper
windows Chelsea Bridge could be seen, and, on
misty autumn mornings, seen much as Whistler
saw it.

Elisabeth's flat was only a little more expensive
than she could well afford, but to Blanche Izeley,
who was owner and tenant of a tiny four-roomed
cottage near Barnes Common, it would have repre-
sented the height of unspiritual luxury. A small,
vivacious woman, with grey in her bobbed hair but
a dancing lightness in her step, Blanche Izeley sped
home this morning after her shopping, carrying
with her a busy world of thought and dream, hunger
and pride. In the foreground of her mind was
displayed, as upon a counter, the frugal but dainty
lunch that she would prepare for herself and Janet.

'Dainty' was one of her favourite words: forced by
the perfidy or ill-fortune of her husband to make
do on next to nothing a week, a sum supplemented
by Janet Ensworth's twenty-five shillings, she had
accustomed herself to a diet that was sparing but
'dainty', both in substance and style. And so far
from admitting defeat or even disaster, she was
conscious of being a person of finer sensibility, of
a more delicate spiritual apprehension, than those
who from habit or appetite consumed their two or
three square meals a day. It was not, she explained,
the gross food, it was the attitude that was harmful.
Attitude indeed was everything. At the moment
Janet's attitudes were causing Mrs Izeley anxiety,
particularly her attitude to Trevor Thaxted. She
herself had met Trevor Thaxted, six months ago,
at dear Nancy's house. He was in search then of
a large bare room that could be used as a studio,
and Blanche, by the happiest chance, had knowledge of just such a place within a stone's throw of
her own cottage. It was quiet, spacious, cheap;
it was precisely what he wanted; and Blanche,
by a friendly conspiracy with the landlady, had
contrived to give the place those Deft Womanly
Touches which make all the difference. Trevor
Thaxted was not only an artist, but a poet too;
not only a poet, but a thinker; and not only a
thinker, but a listener. He was a young man of
independent mind; clever, with much good in him.
But he was a seeker after Truth: not, like Blanche,

its custodian. He needed a guiding hand, and a guiding hand was precisely what Blanche could joyfully supply. Affectionate, unselfish, overflowing with eager vitality, she was ready to wipe away the world's tears, and, with her lucid spiritual theory, smooth out the wrinkles from its puzzled little brow. 'You need the truth: I have it,' said her patient smile. She had been made perfect by suffering; the fires of affliction had purged her of all unwisdom and left her pure gold. Affliction's other name was Paul: Paul who had wearied of listening to the Truth, even from the lips of the pretty young woman he had married; Paul, who was sunk so deep in Mortal Error as to declare, with crude emphasis, that the human body did not exist solely for the purpose of being explained away; Paul who at last, blind to the Immortal Beauty of Real Love as personified in Blanche, and unaccountably preferring the visible illusion to the unseen reality of which he had heard so much, ran off to live a life of quite unspiritual happiness with another woman. Since then, supported only by a sense of her own rectitude, Mrs Izeley had had a hard struggle to live, being compelled to supplement Paul's meagre and unpunctual remittances by typing manuscripts at a shilling a thousand words. She was proud to remember all she had suffered, proud of her courage, proud of her humility, proud of the youthful spirit that shone in her, during these middle years of life, as brightly as when she had

been Trevor's age. It was small wonder that with
so rich a harvest of wisdom she should be apt to
regard her fellow-creatures, one and all, as ignorant
lovable children who, with patience and tact, must
be taught better. Yet she was eager to learn, too.
The knowledge that is to be had from books was
something she knew herself to be somewhat deficient
in, and for that reason she took pleasure in the conversation of the expensively educated Trevor. But
most of all she recognized in him a kindred spirit.
Janet had been holiday-making when Trevor first
took possession of his new studio, and the glad
tidings were conveyed to her in a twelve-page letter
from Blanche. 'It will be very pleasant for me to
have him for a neighbour. We shall have gorgeous
conversations about everything in the world. Though
he is a good deal younger than I am, younger in
years and younger still in experience of life, he has
a brilliant, eager mind. It will do me a lot of
good, there are so few people one can *really* talk
to, and I do hope, dear Janet, that you will manage
to get some reflected benefit from this new friendship of mine. The more *I* get out of it the better
it will be for *you*, dear. And *he* won't be the loser
either, because I feel that he is at a stage when a
good influence will make all the difference to him.
And by a good influence, as you know, dear, I mean
someone who can lead him towards the Truth. . .'
Dear Janet was such a nice simple girl: not clever
or subtle, like Blanche, but wonderfully good and

loyal, with clear wholesome little intuitions, sterling
integrity of character, a ready and docile intelligence, and no intellectual pretensions or poses of
any kind. It was this humility, this willingness
to learn, that Blanche so much valued in her. The
broad fair brow knitted in thought, the quiet alert
attention, the patient endeavour to understand Truth
—what mentor could fail to be touched by these
things? Not Blanche certainly. Her warm heart
grew warmer with every session of sweet silent
listening; she had endless patience, she encouraged
questions, she made every allowance for the girl's
quaint (but really rather delightful) plainness of
mind; she had never had a more ductile pupil.
With Trevor Thaxted it was different; for with
Trevor there was always the clash of opinion, the
sharpening of mind on mind, the gaiety of intellectual battle. Trevor was stubborn in his errors.
And when, as sometimes happened, Blanche's per-
sistent endeavour to wean him from them was
witnessed by the silent Janet (all eyes and ears she
seemed then), his mental agility was somehow
increased, and the speciousness of his arguments
less easy to demonstrate; and before long Blanche
found herself entertaining a definite fear that
Janet's young unformed mind might be infected
by the Wrong Thoughts that figured all too conspicuously in his conversation. And though she
knew, none better, that anything in the shape of
fear was itself a Wrong Thought, that knowledge

failed to have the desired effect. Her anxiety grew.
Trevor was far from being the only potential
source of such infection, for as secretary to the
matron of a large London hospital Janet spent
every working day of her life in an atmosphere
saturated in error, and, perhaps for that reason,
continued to be perplexed by Blanche's dogma
of the essential unreality of sickness and death.
Blanche had therefore a special reason for hoping
that Trevor would gain no ground in Janet's mind.
But for that, she told herself, it would have been
a delightful surprise to see these two getting
together and having a nice friendship. A surprise
it was: for what interest could Trevor have in a
mind so unfurnished and unremarkable as Janet's?
Once or twice, when it chanced that Blanche herself was unavailable, the young man had taken
Janet for a turn round the Common: and once,
dropping in during Blanche's absence, he had been
entertained by Janet to tea. On these occasions,
when she learned of them, Blanche smiled benevolently, with the air of saying that Janet was getting
quite a big girl and beginning to acquire grown-
up behaviour. But secret misgivings came thick
and fast. The thing was absurd, and yet it was
happening: a definite relationship, independent of
herself, had come into existence between her two
friends. Blanche was the last person in the world,
she assured herself, to stand in the way of such a
friendship, unless it was manifestly her duty to do

so. On that point she was firm: no matter what it cost her, she would do her duty. A little thought made it clear to her that Trevor was a Bad Influence. For herself it did not matter: she was impervious to that kind of influence. But Janet was anything but impervious; moreover, it became more and more possible, as the weeks went by, to entertain the impossible idea that Janet was in danger of losing her head: the modest little hedge-sparrow was being dazzled by this bird of bright plumage. Natural enough, though pathetic. But what had put it into Trevor's head to bestow so much attention on the little hedge-sparrow? That was no part of Blanche's plan, and she searched her mind busily for an explanation. It might be that he thought the child wanted taking out of herself; he had once said as much; but such kindness is dangerous, and if misinterpreted by the recipient can become even cruelty. What could he see in her? In her mind and conversation, nothing. Then what else? There was always, of course, Animal Magnetism to be considered. Blanche had learned a great deal about Animal Magnetism from her religious preceptors, and she refreshed her memory from time to time by consulting the relevant passages in their scriptures. To set against that hypothesis there was the somewhat reassuring fact that Janet was not after all so very young, and not precisely beautiful. She had, of course, Beauty in the true sense, but Blanche's experience of Paul had taught her that it was not this True Beauty that men were apt to run after. Her conception of Janet varied with the purposes of the argument. Sometimes she was Just a Young Thing, untouched by experience; sometimes she was a gaunt and placid spinster of twenty-nine: the first was intellectually more gauche, and the second physically less attractive, than Blanche herself had ever been.

The air was fresh this morning, and Mrs Izeley bounced lightly on her way, winged with the thought that Janet, who had a few days' holiday, would be waiting for her return. Entering her little front garden, latchkey held ready between forefinger and thumb, she flashed a shrewd glance at the window of Janet's ground-floor room. Meeting no answer, her glance travelled with appreciation over the whole domestic exterior. She loved her home, every brick of it: it stood in her mind for the stability and solace that she had somehow failed, unaccountably, to find in her personal relationships, but was beginning to find in Janet herself.

'Hullo,' said Janet.

'Ah!' said Blanche. 'So she didn't keep you long today, dear?'

'No,' said Janet.

'I 'm glad. And now you 're away from her—for ten days, is it?—you 'll be yourself again.'

'Aren't I myself?' asked Janet meekly.

'Mental poise,' said Blanche. 'The right

173

atmosphere. Your spirit will be able to bathe in harmony.'

Janet considered for a moment. 'You know, don't you,' she said at length, 'that I quite *like* Matron?'

Blanche laughed—a soft merry peal. 'You funny child! Of course you like her. You see the truth of her. And yet . . . but let's have our lunch.'

'Is it time?' Janet glanced at the clock. 'So it is.' She began laying the cloth.

'No, Janet, let me do it. I've brought some tomatoes for a treat.' She spread out her purchases on the table and invited Janet's admiration. And while Janet admired, Blanche watched. 'You're in one of your starry moods, Janet.'

'Am I?' Janet averted her eyes, then swung away with something like a toss of the head.

'Yes, Janet.' Blanche Izeley spoke with all the emphasis of extreme quietness. 'Am I to know why?'

'What is there to know?' asked Janet. 'Perhaps I was happy. There doesn't need to be a reason, does there?'

'Doesn't there?'

'Anyhow I'm awfully hungry.'

So the reason for Janet's starriness was put on one side while the two women prepared and consumed their meal together. It was not, however, put out of mind. It presided at their feast, constraining them to a silence broken only by remarks of a painfully casual kind.

At last Blanche said, fixing her gaze on Janet with searching love: 'My dear, you are not being quite open with me, are you?'

Janet was silent.

'When one loves, one can't help seeing,' continued the elder woman gently. 'This has been going on for some time, this change in you. You want to shut me out, you want to shut my love out. Now why? What have you to fear?'

Janet made a gesture of protest. 'Nothing. I'm not afraid. I don't understand you, Blanche.'

'I think you do,' said Blanche. 'I've seen you changing, moving away from the Truth. I've seen you and I've watched you. Not pryingly. Never that. But with sympathy, and, yes, with sorrow. It's hard to stand by and see one's friend yielding to Error. But the spirit can only grow in freedom, so how could I interfere? That would have been quite against my principles. You know that, Janet.'

'Yes, I know one must be free,' agreed Janet.

'And now you're giving way to foolish fancies, aren't you, dear? Foolish fancies about Trevor Thaxted.'

Janet flushed. 'Must we discuss Trevor?'

'Ah!' cried Blanche, 'that's not like Janet. That's like some stranger. Janet was always frank and confiding, ready to be healed and helped. What's become of Janet now?'

Janet got up from the table. 'Please don't talk like that. It's so unreal.'

'Listen, Janet. You must listen. It's natural and good that you should like Trevor. I like him too, the *true* Trevor, very much. But to entertain fancies about him, to give yourself up to girlish dreams, that can only lead to unhappiness for us all. You mustn't think because he is kind to you that it is you, you yourself, he's being kind to. He lives in a different world from you, a world where you'd be out of place, dear. Out of place and unhappy. You mustn't be hurt, Janet, if I speak plainly, for it's love that makes me speak. To Trevor, with his cleverness and knowledge, you must seem a mere child, dear. He and I have never let you *feel* that, because we thought it wasn't necessary. But that's only one side of the picture. For all his brains you're nearer the Truth than he is.'

Janet stared. 'You mean,' she said, as if puzzling it out, 'that I'm not good enough for him. And you mean,' she added, 'that he's not good enough for me. . . . Do you know, Blanche, I'd really rather not talk about it.'

'Yes, nearer the Truth,' went on Blanche. 'Much nearer. Trevor is full of mistaken ideas, and very stubborn about them. He mixes with very shallow people, the kind of people my poor mother would have called *fast*, bless her! Yes, indeed, Janet. We must face facts, dear. Trevor has the most

176

unspiritual thoughts, for instance, about what the world calls sex.'

'I don't agree with you,' said Janet.

With quiet deliberation Blanche continued: 'He 'll amuse himself with any pretty woman. He admits it. He 's proud of it.'

'That 's not true,' said Janet.

'So you see what I meant, dear, when I said you don't belong to his world. Thank heaven you don't, for it 's a world of shadows and self-indulgence and discontent.'

She was finished at last. She had said her say, and now stood looking tenderly at Janet, ready to pour the healing balm of her kindness on the wounds that she had felt it her sad duty to inflict. All colour was drained from Janet's face, and she stood motionless, one hand resting lightly on a chairback, her gaze fixed dreamingly on the brightness of the world beyond this cottage window. The pathos of that young eager profile brought tears to Blanche's eyes; and other tears, tears of pride in her own goodness, hastened to join them.

Janet turned her head and looked at Blanche with steady, unsmiling eyes.

'It 's your turn to listen now, Blanche.'

Blanche smiled benevolently. 'I 'm listening.'

'I happen to love Trevor,' said Janet. 'And he happens to love me. We 're going to be married.'

Blanche's eyes widened. She opened her mouth as if to speak, but the sound she emitted was faint and inarticulate. So without a word she turned on her heel and went out of the room, returning, how-ever, two minutes later, with an anxious smile fastened on her face, and carrying in her hand a volume bound in limp black leather. 'Look, Janet.' She opened the book, turning its pages quickly. 'Here it is. The chapter on Animal Magnetism. Read it through quietly to yourself, dear.' She placed the open book on the table, within reach of Janet's hands and eyes. 'Read it, dear,' she repeated. 'I won't disturb you.' And, turning, she tiptoed out of the room, closing the door gently behind her. Trevor. Janet. If I can't lead her back to reason, I shall lose them both.

§ 17

A GENTLEMEN'S AGREEMENT

AT breakfast one morning, at the house in Merrion Square, Daphne remarked to her husband that she wouldn't after all be going to the theatre that evening. Roderick winced at the information but was outwardly unmoved. During these past weeks he had done a good deal of mental wincing, and he had acquired, by constant practice, an extraordinary command of his facial muscles. Having a secret to hide he resorted to this wooden demeanour as his only defence, and that the secret was in fact an

open secret, so far as Daphne was concerned, made
its hiding the more imperative. Living with
Daphne was nowadays very nervous work indeed.
Nothing, he felt, could escape her unwinking
vigilance: it was as if his very thoughts lay exposed
to her. The tumult of their reconciliation had left
them both a little exhausted. Each had brought
to it a mingling of remorse and gratitude; each was
resolved, resolved rather than eager, to make a new
beginning. They renewed their vows of mutual
toleration, though Daphne put Roderick at a moral
disadvantage by making it clear that in no circumstances would she make use of such freedom as she
was allowing to him. Freedom was reaffirmed,
but it was Roderick's freedom only, she herself
having no use for the commodity. She imposed
but one condition: 'Don't let me know anything
about it.' A simple condition, a reasonable request;
and Roderick, feeling a cad to be taking so much
and giving nothing, was quick to pledge himself.
So Roderick studied to deceive, and Daphne studied
to be ignorant. But neither was a very good
student. Daphne, despite herself, grew infinitely
cunning in forcing him to try to account for every
minute of his time; and though, true to his undertaking, he lied and prevaricated with all diligence,
he did it unskilfully, feeling in his bones that he
was failing her, that she did not believe him, that
the situation was an impossible one. Impossible
or not, he struggled to maintain it, lest something

worse should befall. The failure of this compromise would mean the revival of his old dilemma,
and he was as far as ever from being able to
resolve that.

'Not going?' said Roderick. 'But I thought
Mark had fixed it. He's taking you, isn't he?'

'He was. But he isn't. I shall ask him to
find someone else.'

Roderick's face expressed polite concern. His
heart was racing with anxiety. 'Nothing wrong,
is there? Mark hasn't offended you, I mean,
has he?'

Daphne laughed. 'How absurd you are! As
if Mark could offend anyone! No, Rod, I just
don't feel like going out tonight. I thought it
would be nice to have a quiet evening together
for once.'

'An evening together?' said Roderick, helplessly.

'Just you and I.' She smiled winsomely across
the table. 'It's a long time since we had one,
isn't it?'

'Is it?' He felt trapped. The old resentment
began rising in him, but he managed to keep it
out of his voice. 'Not so long really, is it? Last
night . . .'

'Last night we dined with the Savernakes. That's
not my idea of a quiet evening by ourselves.'

'Well, the night before, then?'

'Oh, if you're going to argue——' She shrugged
her shoulders.

'Heaven forbid,' said Roderick. 'But the trouble is, I'm fixed up for tonight. I understood Mark was taking you to a show, and . . . well, I'm fixed up.'

'I see.' She saw too much. 'What are you doing? Anything important?' The question was desperately casual.

'I shall be in about midnight,' said Roderick quickly. 'Now if you go out with Mark——'

'I'm not going out with Mark. Didn't you hear me say so? I suppose you couldn't put off your engagement, whatever it is? And I'm sure I don't want to know what it is, not in the least. You couldn't put it off?'

'But really——'

'I see you don't intend to, so that's all right. I'm sure I shall have a very happy time alone. Very happy indeed.'

'If only you'd listen——'

Daphne smiled. 'Well, I *am* listening. Go ahead.'

Checkmate. He had in fact nothing to say. There was nothing that he dared to say. He was carrying out the terms of an impossible agreement, and the agreement was impossible because there was something in Daphne that was resolved to wreck it, with or without the consent of her conscious will.

'I'm waiting,' said Daphne. Her smile was full of malice. She was enjoying his embarrassment.

The sight of that smile made him cold. She was a stranger: he could feel nothing for her. 'Never mind,' he answered. 'On reflection I find I 've nothing to say.'

A diversion was created by the entry of Mrs Tucker. A lean, straw-coloured woman, her face screwed up into an expression of indomitable anxiety, the expression of one who expects the worst and is not to be put off with anything less.

'You rang, 'um?'

'Yes, Milly. Some more coffee, please. This is cold.'

'Hot enough when I brought it in.' Gathering up the coffee-pot and the milk-jug with an air of resentful resignation, Mrs Tucker made for the door. Before she reached it she was called back.

'Mrs Tucker!' A spasm of fury took hold of Roderick.

'Yes, sir?'

'Are you having the insolence to complain?'

Without answering, the woman went out of the room. Roderick felt himself blushing. His outburst was without precedent, and it was profoundly unlike him. Yet he was glad he had been able for once to throw off his accursed mildness. It was time that woman was taught her place. But as he met Daphne's eye his anger changed to confusion, for he knew, and he thought she knew, that Mrs Tucker had been the excuse rather than the cause of that anger.

'Why don't you get rid of that woman?' he asked irritably.

'And lose Tucker?' said Daphne coldly. 'What should we do without little Tucker?'

'Well, where *is* Tucker, anyhow? It's not her job to serve at table.'

'He's in bed with a temperature, if you must know, darling. New for you to interfere with the servants.'

Roderick stared at his plate like a guilty school-boy. 'Can't have her speaking to you in that tone.'

'Sweet of you, Rod. But it's late in the day, isn't it, for you to start protecting me?' After waiting in vain for an answer she added, with an irony far from subtle: 'It's a man you're meeting tonight, of course?'

He answered in the same spirit. 'That goes without saying, doesn't it?'

'I should ask him to play the piano to you, if I were you,' said Daphne. 'I believe he's rather talented in that way.'

'Really?'

'And no doubt in other ways too.'

He did not answer, and she was content to leave it at that for a moment. But before the silence had had time to establish itself in his mind, she spoke again, and in a different voice.

'Rod, don't let's quarrel any more. Why can't we be friends?'

He smiled a little bitterly. 'I thought you'd made up your mind to prevent our being so.'

'Yes, I deserve that,' she answered, with a chastened air. 'But you know I don't mean all I say.'

He seemed to deprecate the implied apology. 'Oh, let's forget it. Anything in the paper this morning?' Glancing towards the door, he said: 'I wonder why Mrs Tucker always leaves the door open?'

He guessed that Daphne was working up for an emotional reconciliation, and he resolved that he could not, again, lend himself to that self-deception.

'You must make allowances, Rod,' she persisted. 'You will, won't you?'

'Of course,' he said gruffly. He forced a laugh. 'The subject's hardly worth pursuing, is it?'

'But I had rather a special reason for wanting you at home tonight.' She laughed nervously. 'Perhaps you'll think it sentimental, but there it is. I suppose a woman *is* sentimental at a time like this.'

'I don't quite——' he began.

'I think I'm going to have a child,' said Daphne. 'In fact, I know I am.'

Roderick stared. 'Are you sure? Have you seen Cartwright?'

'Yes.'

'Well, I'm damned!' said Roderick. Shocked

into sincerity, he could not conceal his dismay. It was as if he heard the door clang behind him, the jailer's key turned in the lock.

Daphne watched him with quivering lip. 'Is that all you can say?'

'I'm sorry, Daphne,' he said. 'But you must admit it's rather ironical, to put it mildly. Here we've wanted a child for eight years and never had one. And now . . .' He shrugged his shoulders, leaving the rest to her.

'And now you *don't* want one. I see.' Daphne gripped the edge of the table. At that moment, being hurt and frustrated, she wanted nothing so much as to hurt him in return. 'I suppose it's never occurred to you to wonder *why* I haven't conceived before during those eight years?'

A hint of her meaning flashed on him. 'Well? Why?'

'Because I took care to prevent it.'

He got out of his chair. 'You've cheated me.'

'And now,' she added, with frenzied calm, 'I've taken care not to prevent it.'

'Very clever indeed. I congratulate you.'

'But you needn't be afraid,' said Daphne. 'You're free to go when you like. Today if you like. Run off to your pleasures, leaving your wife pregnant. It will be quite a revelation to your friends, won't it? I wonder what Cradock will say. And your father.'

With bent head Roderick moved towards the

door, saying irrelevantly: 'When's that damned coffee coming?'

Mrs Tucker entered at that moment, nearly colliding with him. She entered without noise and deposited her tray on the breakfast-table. Mrs Tucker could be very silent when she chose.

§ 18

HUE AND CRY

At nine o'clock on an evening in October a message for Roderick Strood was broadcast over the ether in the hearing of some millions of his countrymen. It caused anxiety to his friends, and excited a certain degree of curiosity among those of his more casual acquaintances who happened to hear it; but to the overwhelming majority of listeners it meant nothing. Among these latter were Mrs Cranshaw, Oliver Brackett, Roger Coates, Sidney Harrington Nywood, and Arthur Cheed, all of whom took it for granted that the matter was no concern of theirs. For a mistake so inevitable they cannot be blamed.

Sidney H. Nywood, as his billheads described him, had had a tiring day. A bit of luck, in the shape of a funeral, had fallen to him, and the nervous strain of seeing that all went off nicely, and more particularly of making a public appearance in his silk hat and frock coat, made him more than commonly grateful for the peace of his little parlour, the comfort of his arm-chair, the fire in the grate, and the sight of Laddie stretched out at ease on the hearthrug. He had left Flo in the kitchen, busy at her ironing, and now, as his ears told him, she was doing the day's washing-up. There was time for a nap before she joined him at the fireside, and he sat with eyes closed, fragments of thought and dream drifting in and out of his mind. The loud-speaker at his elbow was reading him a lecture on the care of gardens in autumn, but he paid no attention to that. He liked a noise in the room, so long as it wasn't too loud: it was companionable and nice and you weren't obliged to listen. He wasn't listening now: he was thinking, in a disjointed fashion, of the funeral, and Mrs Newky's roof that wanted seeing to, and the drop of stout he'd have when Flo came in, and how Laddie seemed to be smelling a bit more than usual tonight. Flo had funny ideas. She was always at him to give up the undertaking part of the business, and keep to what she called his proper job, that of builder and decorator. But where was the sense of quarrelling with your bread and butter? After all, someone had got to bury people, you couldn't leave 'em lying about, and the more he left it to others the worse it'd be for his balance-sheet at the half-year. That's what came of marrying a refined girl. Not but what she was a good girl, talker or no talker. Undertaking

wasn't everyone's choice. Naturally enough. But
what Sidney H. Nywood most disliked about it was
not the job but the fancy togs. He couldn't get
used to that top-hat. It had served him for ten
years and he still couldn't get used to it, and it
was hard work pretending not to know that some of
the neighbours laughed to see him in it, to see him
looking, as he knew he did, like something out of
a farce. But what the corpse's relatives would say
if he wore anything less customary was more than
he cared to think about. Nevertheless he began
to think about it, and on the tide of that speculation
he was floating away into dreamland, easily and
luxuriously floating away, when something, some
sudden catastrophe, recalled him to wakefulness.
He opened his eyes and looked round in perplexity.
What had happened? Things didn't seem the
same somehow. Ah, yes . . . his brow cleared.
What had happened was silence: the voice of the
loud-speaker had ceased. Not like home at all.
Funny how you got used to a thing. But, mercifully, the silence did not endure. 'There is one
S O S before the news,' said the loud-speaker into
Mr Nywood's ear. 'The name is Strood. Will
Roderick Strood, who left home yesterday evening,
return at once to his house in Merrion Square,
where his wife, Daphne Strood, lies dangerously
ill.' That's better, thought Mr Nywood. If only
I can lose myself for a minute I shall be another
man. Snuggling into his chair again, he closed

his eyes contentedly, to be lulled to sleep by changes
in the Cabinet and rumours of a European war.

Arthur Cheed, on the other hand, who kept a
garage some seven miles east of Mr Nywood's
workshop, always made a point of listening attentively to the news bulletin. As a conscientious
citizen he felt it his duty to take a lively interest in
everything uttered by the voices that haunted the
ether. In a dogged ineffectual way he worried a
great deal about the Versailles Treaty and what
they were doing at Geneva. Having an exceptionally tender heart he wanted to shoot all arma-
ment manufacturers out of hand; for it seemed to
him common sense that if the wicked people in the
world were all killed, only good people would be
left, and we could then make a fresh start. His
hatred of violence was so strong that the mere
thought of it sometimes filled him with a kind of
blood-lust. Now and again he came within an
ace of realizing that his interest in larger things
was due in some measure to the fact that there was
a lamentable dearth in his life of the smaller and
more personal interests that occupied his easygoing, unpolitical neighbours. He and Nellie were
childless, and had lost hope of children. In default
of children they kept two handsome tom-cats. His
was a blue Persian called Henry. Nellie's, a golden
tabby, answered to the name of Silas. Most of
the conversation in that household of two centred
on Silas and Henry; much of it, indeed, was

attributed to them. 'Does Henry like his milk pudding? Yes, he says, got any more, Mother? What a cheeky boy!' This game was Nellie's invention, but Arthur played it with equal relish. 'Silas says Father must go and change his wet clothes. Can't have you catching cold, Father, he says, or where's my milk to come from?' And so on: there was no end to it, and it formed the intellectual substance of a happy marriage. Apart from Nellie, Silas, and Henry, Arthur Cheed had nothing to think about but the fortunes of his business and the mysterious and much-advertised fermentation known as world-politics. On this particular October evening he was in the act of gulping down a third cup of tea (a beverage to which he was much addicted) when his daily dose of international alarm was administered to him. It was followed by football results, but at that point, remembering that young Fred was not so sharp at the job as he might be, he switched off and hurried back to the shop.

Arthur Cheed had not consciously attended to the S O S concerning Roderick Strood. But the name had found safe lodgment in him somewhere, so that when he chanced upon it five days later, in his evening paper, the paragraph in question had more meaning for him than it had for Sidney H. Nywood.

'Look, Nellie. Listen to this. Here's the chap they were asking for over the wireless the other day.'

The inquest on Mrs Daphne Strood, who was

found dead in her bed, was concluded today, when sensational allegations were made by Mildred Tucker, deceased's cook. On the direction of the Coroner, a verdict of wilful murder was returned against. the husband, Roderick Strood, thirty-four, architect. . . .

§ 19

LETTER FROM BUDLEIGH PARVA

MY DEAR BOY,—I have spent this morning in Venns Wood, wondering what I could say to you of all that is in my heart and mind. There are still some green leaves showing, in spite of the season, as though they did not know it was winter. You must bear with me if I ramble too much. I am still dazed from the shock of what you tell me, and cannot collect my thoughts, cannot quite bring myself to believe your dreadful news. You have kept yourself something like a stranger from me for so long, only an occasional visit and nothing said to the purpose, and it is difficult for me to understand how these things can have happened to you. God knows I am not reproaching you, but you must understand how it is with me. I think I am not so quick as I was. Perhaps I was never very quick, or I could have been a better father to you and things would never have come to this. But it is idle to be thinking of that now, when your need is so great. Your faith lost, your marriage dishonoured, those are not small things, but they are small indeed, they are trifles, compared with the cruel blunder that has put you where you are now. And dear Daphne gone—I cannot realize it yet. I dare not begin to grieve for you, for once I began there would be no end to it.

I thank God, and I thank you, that you did not let me hear all this from strangers, from the newspapers. You say the hardest part of your burden was the having to tell me, and you wonder, you say, what I must think of you and whether I can forgive you. Perhaps that last, my dear, was not quite sincere in you. I hope it was not, for it would hurt me very much if I believed you doubted my love at such a time. You wish you could have spared me. You must not wish that. It would have been a mistaken kindness had you tried to shield me from knowledge of your situation. Don't you see that I must be with you now and suffer with you? That is all there is left for me. Not with you in the flesh, for you say that would make your ordeal the harder to bear, and I am ready to believe it. Nevertheless I shall be with you, as God is with you. He is with you, whether you know him or not. Nothing can separate us from the love of God. I do not want to write to you in a language that is alien to your way of thinking, but I cannot be silent on a matter that so deeply

concerns you. For nearly fifty years I have
preached a simple gospel to simple people. It
has served their needs, and I have never thought
it necessary to correct the crude pictures they have
in their minds. Pictures of some sort they must
have. If poor Maggie Boyle chooses to picture
Almighty God as a sentimental busybody, someone rather like her own Vicar with omnipotence
added, I shall only muddle her by trying to put
her right. You remember Mrs Boyle, Roddy—
she's the young woman, not so young now, who
got herself provided with three children, and only
consented to come to church with their father in
time for the fourth to be born in wedlock. A good
soul, in spite of her eccentricities.

But I'm running on, and away from the point.
The other day I was reading about what they call
the New Physics. I know little enough of the
subject, but the writer made one point that struck
me as very suggestive. He said that in the last
century it was the aim and practice of physicists
to make mechanical models of the phenomena they
observed, and that the events in their world, 'the
world of the infinitely little' was the phrase he used,
were such as could be clearly pictured in the mind.
But now, it seems, all that is changed. I expect
this is familiar ground to you. The new world of
the physicist, said this writer, is unimaginable, and
cannot be described except in the language of
mathematics. A foreign language to me, as you

know. You 'll say I am a long time getting to the point, but here it is. You think you 've lost your belief in God, my dear child, because you can no longer take seriously the foolish pictures we Christians have made of him. God is not this and not that; every picture of him is a fiction and a falsification; in his essence he is beyond the utmost reach of thought. I say *he* and *him* for lack of alternative. I should be glad indeed, for your sake, to get away from that misleading, limiting, pictorial phraseology. There 's a saying by a fourteenth-century mystical writer that I have never dared to quote to my congregation. Of God himself can no man think, he says. By love may he be gotten and holden, but by thought never. But forget the *he* and the *him*, Roddy. Forget the Creator and the Judge and all pictures whatsoever. I would almost dare to say—Forget, if it stands in your way, the picture of a Heavenly Father which Our Lord gave us. But of this be persuaded, as I am persuaded: that there is an eternal and living reality in whom we live and move and have our being, and whose being in some sense we share. This has been the central faith and fact of my long life. There is a light beyond our darkness and a purpose that makes music of our confusion—and we, you and I, have some part in both. Hold fast to that and fear nothing.

So here I am, preaching again, though preaching was not what I intended. I had a very kind letter

from a Mr Perryman. It came with yours this
morning, a very great kindness, the touch of a hand
in the dark. He tells me you are to have the best
possible help and advice, which is a great comfort.
You were always a brave child and you will be
brave now. For your own sake and mine you
must not dwell overmuch on past sins and follies,
nor waste your strength in wishing them undone.
You know, as I do, that you are innocent of the
terrible crime they charge you with, and before
long your innocence will be declared to the world.
I am having the telephone installed, to be in touch
with your friend Perryman. I think he is very
fond of you, Roddy. Don't lose heart, my boy.
Do you remember that day in the orchard when
they brought us the news of your dear mother's
accident? You were in your tenth year, I remember. Well, now we are together again, as we
were then. Brothers, shall I say, as well as father
and son. I am an old man, and in the nature of
things it cannot be long before I am called away
from this place. But I know God will not let me
die till you are free again. I have you in my
heart and in my prayers, and God has us both.
For underneath are the everlasting arms.

PART TWO

THE TWELVE LISTENING

§ 20

SPEECH FOR THE CROWN

HAVING been duly sworn in, they filed into the jury-box—Charles Weedon Underhay, Clare Cranshaw, Reginald Forth, George Oliver Brackett, Arthur Cheed, Cyril Enderby Gaskin, Blanche Izeley, Roger Coates, Sidney Harrington Nywood, Lionel Bonaker, Lucy Prynne, and James Bayfield. The most timid among them, Lucy Prynne, sat with averted head for some moments, as though in prayer; but the others could not resist glancing towards the dock. Natural curiosity: they wanted to know what a murderer looked like. And though they themselves were assembled to decide precisely this question, whether the man accused was a murderer or not, there couldn't be much doubt about it—could there?—since he had been already branded as such by a Coroner's court. . . .

AN USHER OF THE COURT: If any one can inform my Lords the King's Justices, the King's Sergeant, or the King's Attorney-General, ere this inquest be taken between our Sovereign Lord the King and the prisoner at the bar, of any treasons, murders, felonies, or misdemeanours, done or committed by the prisoner at the bar, let him come forth, and he shall be heard; for the prisoner now stands at the bar on his deliverance. And all persons who are bound by recognizance to prosecute or give evidence against the prisoner at the bar, let them come forth, prosecute, and give evidence, or they shall forfeit their recognizances. God save the King.

DEPUTY-CLERK OF THE COURT: Roderick William Strood, you are charged on indictment for that you on the 30th day of October in this present year feloniously and wilfully and of your own malice aforethought did kill and murder your wife Daphne Strood. How say you: are you guilty or not guilty?

PRISONER: Not guilty.

DEPUTY-CLERK OF THE COURT: Members of the jury, the prisoner at the bar, Roderick William Strood, is charged in this indictment with the wilful murder of his wife Daphne Strood on the 30th day of October in this present year. Upon this indictment he has been arraigned, and upon arraignment he has pleaded not guilty. Your duty therefore is to inquire whether he be guilty or not guilty, and to hearken to the evidence.

SIR JOHN BUCKHORN, K.C., HIS MAJESTY'S ATTORNEY-GENERAL: May it please your lordship. Members of the jury, the charge against the prisoner, as you have heard, is the gravest of all charges, that of murder. I must now open to you a case which, though its technical features may present some little difficulty, is in its essential character a perfectly straightforward case. It is my duty to put you in possession, link by link, of a chain of evidence which I cannot but believe will prove too strong to be broken. Let me say at once, and I say it without affectation or pretence, that the duty is a peculiarly painful one. All such cases are painful, in the nature of things; but this one, I say, is peculiarly painful, in that the crime in question is imputed, not to some unhappy wretch of criminal habits and low intelligence, but to a man gently nurtured, an educated man, a man of whom, something less than a year ago, it might have been said, would have been said, that he had an unblemished character. He is a professional man, an architect; the material circumstances of his life were easy and comfortable; and you might have supposed that here, if anywhere, was a man who had every reason to be contented with his lot. Yet it is the contention of the Crown that this man, on the 30th of October, at his house in Merrion Square, murdered his wife by poison. The facts, briefly, are these. At about five o'clock on the evening of that day, the deceased woman, Mrs Strood, feeling a little feverish and having for some days suffered from sleeplessness, went to bed. The prisoner had not then returned from his office. He did, however, return, reaching home, as you will hear from Mrs Tucker the cook, at about twenty-five minutes past six. Naturally, he was admitted to his wife's bedroom and had an interview with her. The conversation, in spite of Mrs Strood's low state of health, seems to have occupied something in the neighbourhood of three-quarters of an hour, for it was between seven-twenty and seven-thirty that the prisoner finally emerged from that bedroom. Now Mrs Tucker, at the prisoner's request, had prepared a cup of hot malted milk for her mistress. On her way through the hall with this beverage she was met by the prisoner, who had just come downstairs, and he, the prisoner, gave her further instructions. As you will hear from the lips of Mrs Tucker herself . . . [*summary of Mrs Tucker's evidence omitted*]. Next morning Mrs Strood was discovered to have died in the night. But, members of the jury, there was something else that happened that night. Or, if you like to put it so, there was something else that didn't happen. A few minutes after Mrs Tucker had taken the cup of milk to her mistress, the prisoner left the house. He did not return that night. He did not return next morning. He sent no message. So far as we can ascertain, he manifested no sort of interest in the state of health of his wife, whom, you must remember, he had left ailing and in bed. The next day passes, and there is still no sign of the prisoner, no message, nothing. He is not at his office. His professional partner, as that gentleman himself will tell you, telephoned to the house in Merrion Square to inquire after him. In the evening of that day, the day after the night in which Mrs Strood died, in the evening of that day, before the second news-bulletin was read, an S O S was transmitted from Broadcasting House asking Roderick Strood to return at once to his house, where, as the message put it, 'his wife Daphne Strood lies dangerously ill'. As we know, she was not dangerously ill. She was beyond danger: she was dead. Now the broadcasting of news has become a very familiar feature of our everyday life and at a conservative estimate it must be supposed that at least a million people listened to that S O S in which the name of Roderick Strood was conspicuous. Among that million, or whatever the number may have been, there was a man standing in the bar of an hotel at Southampton, a man who, as we believe, had in his possession a passport made out in the name of Williams, and who had booked a passage to the United States of America on a liner that was due to sail from that port, and did in fact sail at eleven fifty-five that same night. But though the name on the passport was given as Roderick Williams, there is good reason to believe that the man who carried it was Roderick William Strood, the prisoner at the bar. Let me say here, in plain terms, that every point in the case I am putting before you will be spoken to in that witness-box by witnesses that the Crown will call. It would be most improper were I to ask you to accept as proven fact the story that I am putting before you in this opening address. I do not, the

Crown does not, ask you to accept the story as proven: I merely put it before you as the story which, in due and proper form, and with the aid of witnesses, I propose to prove. So far as this point about the passport is concerned, I say frankly we cannot prove absolutely that the prisoner carried this false passport on his person on the evening of October the 31st. But we *can* prove that he was passing as Williams, that he was entered as Williams on the passenger-list; and we can prove that the false passport—which you will have an opportunity of examining for yourselves — was found in his house, among his personal possessions, after his arrest. In point of fact it was found in a collar-box. You may think that an extraordinary place for a passport to be found in. I confess it seems to me a very extraordinary place. These facts will suggest to you—I think it is not going too far to say that they will irresistibly suggest to you—a guilty conscience and a secret flight.

Let me, then, resume the story. The prisoner is standing in the bar of a Southampton hotel when a loud-speaker, the property of the hotel, announces in his hearing that Roderick Strood's wife is lying dangerously ill. Any husband who had his wife's welfare at heart, I will go further and say any man who had his friend's welfare at heart, would on hearing such news hurry to the bedside of the sick person. Roderick Strood, however, did nothing of the kind. That he had intended to sail for America

that night is sufficiently proved by a conjunction
of circumstances, his presence in Southampton, his
passport, his booked passage, his own words to
which a police witness will testify; and the evidence
will show that that intention, that resolution, was
in no degree shaken by the news that his wife, the
woman whom it was his duty to love and protect,
was lying dangerously ill.   But on his way to carry
out that intention he encountered a check.   What
happened, as you will hear, was this.   The prisoner
emerged from the hotel accompanied by a woman,
and preceded by a hotel porter carrying luggage.
The luggage and the woman were handed into a
waiting taxi; the prisoner directed the driver to
drive to the docks, adding the word *Mercatoria*, the
name of the liner, in order to make his destination
quite clear.   He was then accosted by a police
officer in mufti, who asked him if he were not
Mr Roderick Strood.   He replied: 'My name is
Williams.'   The officer then informed him that he
had serious news, whereupon the prisoner said: 'Is
it about my wife?'   Told that his wife was dead,
he exclaimed: 'My God!   I killed her!'   There
followed some conversation between the prisoner
and his woman companion . . . [*further summary
of police evidence omitted*].   You see how all these
incidents that I am putting to you are consistent
with the contention of the Crown, and I believe
that after hearing all the evidence you will decide
that they are not consistent with the theory that

the prisoner is an innocent man. The case does
not rest there, however. Some of you, many of
you, perhaps indeed all of you, must have noticed
a very extraordinary omission in the story I have
so far unfolded. For I have said nothing yet about
the cause of death. I am coming to that now, and
it will take us back to the morning of October
the 31st, when, as you will remember, the un-
fortunate Mrs Strood was found dead in her bed.
Now Mrs Strood was a young and beautiful woman.
And, what is more to the point, she was, as her
physician will tell us, a healthy woman. He will
tell you, further, how he was called to that scene
of death, and how, being at a loss to account for
the sudden catastrophe, and having moreover certain suspicions forced upon him, he considered it
his duty to communicate with the coroner. The
coroner ordered a post-mortem, which was carried
out in the afternoon of the same day. I will not
at this stage ask you to burden your memories with
any technical details. All that side of the case will
have to be gone into with the utmost care and in
very considerable detail, and you, realizing, as I
am sure you all do, the extreme gravity of the issue
(and indeed no issue could be graver), will follow
the medical evidence with close and unremitting
attention. You will hear that death was caused by
chloral poisoning, and you will hear . . . [*summary
of medical evidence omitted*]. The contention of the
Crown is that the fatal dose was administered,

feloniously and wilfully and with malice aforethought, by Strood, the prisoner at the bar. But
when I say fatal dose I must qualify the phrase
with an explanation. It may be that the amount
of chloral actually handled and administered by the
prisoner, if it shall be shown to your satisfaction
that he did handle and administer it, it may be
that that amount would not in itself have been
sufficient to cause death. But if it was administered
by Strood in the full knowledge that other chloral,
or some similar drug, had been or was about to be
taken by the deceased lady, that will overwhelmingly
suggest to you a murderous hope or expectation,
and in the event of death ensuing—and we know
that in this case death did ensue—that will be
murder in fact. As to whether or not the prisoner
knew that a draught had been given by the doctor,
the evidence will leave you in no doubt.

Now a question will arise in your minds, I have
no doubt it has already arisen in your minds, and
the question is this: Supposing, for the sake of
argument, that the prisoner is guilty of this crime,
what can have been his motive for it? As to that,
you will not be left long in doubt, and indeed you
will have already formed a suspicion from what
I have told you. If you ask me what can account
for this apparent change in a man's character, what
can turn a man of respectable life and human
instincts into a cruel and calculating murderer, I
answer that there is one thing and perhaps one

thing only—the force, the overpowering force, of a guilty sexual passion. It is true that the prisoner benefits financially, to the extent of some twelve hundred pounds, by the death of his wife. But because I wish to be perfectly candid with you, because I wish to put before you no argument in which I do not sincerely believe, I will say at once that it is no part of my case to suggest that this murder, if murder it be, was committed for the sake of that twelve hundred pounds. No, the true motive is glaringly obvious. You will hear in evidence that over that happy and prosperous home there had fallen the shadow of a husband's infidelity; that the prisoner for a period of months had been cherishing and indulging a passion for another woman, the very woman in whose company he was seen at Southampton; that he spent the night of October the 30th, when his wife lay dying, in the intimate company of this woman—alone with her, at her flat—and, finally, that this woman was to have been his fellow-passenger—I say his fellow-passenger and for the moment I leave it at that—on the liner that was to carry him to America. The Crown, as my lord would tell you, is under no obligation to prove motive in a case of this kind; but, if you want motive, here is motive enough and more than enough.

Members of the jury, I have given you a very brief outline of the case into which you have to inquire; and now, with the assistance of my learned friends, I shall proceed to call the evidence upon which it rests. You, I know, will bring to the consideration of that evidence the close and careful attention that the gravity of the occasion requires. If, at the conclusion of this hearing, you are able to believe, consistently with the evidence, that the prisoner is innocent of the charge for which he stands indicted, you will not hesitate to say so; if, moreover, your fair and unprejudiced consideration of the evidence leaves you with a reasonable doubt of his guilt, then the prisoner will be entitled to the benefit of that doubt. But if you think the Crown's case has been fairly made out and fairly proved, if you come to the conclusion that the prisoner did indeed, as the Crown contends, commit a cunning and cowardly murder, it will be your solemn duty and obligation to return a verdict of Guilty. I have said that my task is a painful one, but I am very keenly sensible that your task, as members of the jury, is equally painful, equally arduous. You have to rid your minds of all prejudice, whether for or against the prisoner. You have to steel your hearts and do strict justice, according to the evidence, on the issue that is yours to determine. Your duty, when the time comes, will be to give a true and honest verdict, a verdict with the consequences of which you have no legitimate concern. I am confident that you will not flinch from that duty.

§ 21

DETECTIVE-SERGEANT BOLTON

LEONARD BOLTON, examined for the Crown by MR GREGORY TUFNELL.—I am a detective-sergeant. On October the 31st I was at Southampton in pursuance of duties that have nothing to do with this case. In consequence of certain information received by telephone I proceeded to a point a few yards distant from the Zenith Hotel. There I met, by appointment, the person who had laid the information. It was then five minutes past nine.

Do you know the name of that person?—The name given was Ernest Nix.

Did you have some conversation with Nix?—Yes.

I must not ask you what he said, but I will ask you what happened then.—After we had been waiting about half an hour, a porter came out of the hotel with a suitcase in each hand. He hailed a taxi, which pulled up. He put the luggage into the taxi, and stood holding the door open while a man and a woman came out of the hotel and crossed the pavement to the taxi. The woman got in, and the man said something to the taxi-driver.

Is this man you speak of in court at the present moment?—Yes.

You recognize him?—Yes.

So that there may be no doubt in the matter,

will you tell us which among those present you recognize as the man you are now speaking of?—I identify him as the prisoner at the bar.

You have told us that you saw Strood speaking to the taxi-driver. Did you hear what he said?—Yes. He said: 'The docks. The *Mercatoria*.'

Did you then accost him?—Yes. I accosted him and said: 'I believe you are Mr Roderick William Strood?'

What did he answer?—He said: 'My name is Williams. What can I do for you?'

And you then said?—I said: 'Are you not Mr Roderick William Strood, of Merrion Square, London?' He answered: 'Well, suppose I am? I'm afraid I don't remember you.' I said: 'Are you by any chance sailing tonight on the *Mercatoria*?' He answered: 'Yes. What do you want? I'm in a hurry.' I said: 'I'm afraid you'll have to put it off. I have very serious news for you. He answered: 'Serious news! Is it about my wife?' At this point in the conversation he became agitated and began stammering.

And what then?—I told him that Mrs Roderick Strood was dead and that an inquest had been ordered.

Now what did Strood say when you told him that his wife was dead?—He said: 'My God! I killed her!'

The words were: 'My God! I killed her!' You are sure of that?—Yes.

Was that one speech or two? I mean did he say 'My God, I killed her!' in one breath, as it were?—No. He first said: 'My God!' Then after a pause he added: 'I killed her.'

What did you say then?—I said: 'I know nothing about that, Mr Strood. But I think you 'd better come back to London, don't you?' He answered: 'It 's impossible. Was it the sleeping-draught? She 's dead, you say?' I answered: 'Of course you will have to attend the inquest.' He said: 'Very good. When is the next train?'

Did the woman, his companion, take any part in this conversation?—No.

Was she still in the taxi?—No. She remained in the taxi for a few moments, but while we were talking she got out.

Did she make any remark?—She said something to the prisoner in a foreign language.

Do you know what language?—It sounded like German. I did not understand what was said, but I got the impression it was German.

Did the prisoner answer her?—Yes.

Also in German, or in something that you thought was German?—Yes.

You did not understand the actual words, but did you get any impression of the general character of the conversation: whether, for example, it was friendly or angry?—I wouldn't say angry. But it was some kind of dispute, I thought. The prisoner was very agitated.

And the woman?—She spoke quietly, with her hand on his arm.

After that conversation between them, what happened?—She said slowly, in English: 'We have here the automobile. We will go to the railway station, both. It is very simple.' From then on she seemed to take charge of the prisoner. I asked if I might be allowed to share the taxi and she made no objection. We all got into the taxi and were driven to the station. The prisoner seemed dazed. He made no remark except to ask me who I was. When I told him that I was a police officer he made no answer.

Cross-examined for the Defence by Mr Antony Harcombe, K.C.: When you said to the prisoner 'I believe you are Mr Roderick William Strood,' he did not deny knowledge of the name?—He said: 'My name is Williams.'

Yes. I heard you say so in answer to my learned friend. I am now asking you, did he deny knowledge of the name Roderick William Strood?—No.

And he did not, in set terms, deny that he *was* Roderick William Strood?—Not in set terms.

Then the answer is No?—The answer is No.

Do you agree that it would be fair to put it like this: that so soon as he realized that your business was serious he admitted his identity?—No.

Are you telling us that he did not admit his identity?—He was evasive.

The words you gave us are these: 'Well, suppose
I am?' Is not that an admission?—I should have
called it a supposition.

A supposition in form, but an admission in effect?
—A sort of admission.

In fact, an admission?—Yes.

Now you have told my learned friend that on
hearing that the news you were bringing to him
concerned his wife, the prisoner became agitated
and began stammering?—

ATTORNEY-GENERAL [*intervening*]: My learned
friend is mistaken. According to the answers given
by this witness to my learned junior, the prisoner
anticipated the witness's news by asking: 'Is it about
my wife?'

MR HARCOMBE: I apologize to my learned
friend, and stand corrected. [*Continuing cross-
examination*] You have told us, however, that the
prisoner became agitated and began stammering?
—Yes.

By the word 'stammering' you mean that he
was having difficulty with his speech?—I mean
stammering.

What was he trying to say when he was stammering? Have you any idea?—No.

You were listening carefully?—Yes.

Yet you have no idea. How is that?—Because
he was stammering. His words were not clear.

His words were not clear? You mean that he
couldn't get them out properly?—Yes.

His words were impeded by stammering?—Some of his words.

Now when you told him that his wife was dead his agitation increased, did it not?—Yes.

And he said, according to you: 'My God! I killed her.'—Yes.

You are quite sure of those words?—Yes.

You can swear not only to the substance of what he said, but to his actual words?—Yes.

I think you said a moment ago that his words were not clear, that he was stammering?—That was before.

Before what?—Before I told him that his wife was dead.

But the news of his wife's death increased his agitation. That is what you told us just now?—Yes.

Do you now say that after receiving that news he ceased stammering?—He wasn't stammering when he said those particular words.

In fact he had ceased stammering?—Yes.

The man is already agitated. You have told us so. The news of his wife's death increases that agitation. You have told us that too, haven't you?—Yes.

That news at once increases his agitation and gives a crystal clarity to his speech. Is that what you are telling my lord and the jury?—(No answer.)

In your experience, is that the usual effect of agitation?—No.

Are you still convinced that you have made no mistake as to the prisoner's words?—Yes.

Not so much as a syllable?—No.

I am going to put it to you that what the prisoner did in fact say was not 'My God—I killed her!' but (listen carefully) 'My God—so I 've killed her!' Would you agree to that?—No.

You carried the words in your memory?—I committed them to paper.

How soon after the conversation in question did you make notes of it?—Some five or six minutes afterwards.

Why not at once?—I had no opportunity and I did not wish to alarm the prisoner.

You will remember that a moment ago I suggested another form of words that the prisoner might have used?—Yes.

It was nothing like so long as five minutes ago? —No.

Here is pencil and paper. Kindly write down that alternative form of words, to the best of your recollection.

[The witness having complied, the paper was handed to the Judge.]

MR JUSTICE SARUM: The witness has written: 'My God—so I killed her.' I find that this differs in one detail from the words used by learned counsel: 'I killed' instead of 'I 've killed.'

MR HARCOMBE [*continuing cross-examination*]: You

see how easy it is for even an experienced officer to make a mistake?—If you call that a mistake.

You don't deny it was a mistake?—It's not material.

MR JUSTICE SARUM: That is an improper observation, which I am surprised to hear from a witness of your experience. You must confine yourself to answering the questions.

MR HARCOMBE: You have told my learned friend that on your telling Strood that he would have to attend the inquest, he said: 'Very good. When is the next train?' Have I got you right? —Yes.

Does the expression 'Very good' seem to you the kind of expression the prisoner would use?—Yes.

If I suggested to you that he said 'Very well', what would you say?—I have 'Very good' in my notes.

·And your notes are infallible?—They are accurate.

Perhaps you can see no difference between 'Very good' and 'Very well'?—They are different words.

But no other difference? No difference in tone? —Well, they mean the same thing.

So that it wouldn't really matter which way you put it in your notes?—No.

The remarks that you have told us he made to you were made before he had any reason to suppose that you were a police officer?—Yes.

You did not think it necessary to warn him that

his words might be used?—No. As I was not arresting him, I did not think it necessary.

Re-examined for the Crown by the ATTORNEY-GENERAL: You are accustomed to taking notes of conversations?—Yes.

Have you had long experience in that kind of work?—Yes.

About how long?—About twelve years.

In the Force of which you are a member have you a reputation for accuracy?—Yes.

Have you often had to give evidence in criminal cases?—Yes.

Even in cases involving a capital charge?—Several times.

Have you always given your evidence in a manner that satisfied the Court, so far as you are aware?—Yes.

Have you ever been commended on the way your evidence was given?—Many times.

Until you met the prisoner at Southampton on October the 31st had you ever set eyes on him, so far as you know?—No.

Nor heard of him?—I didn't know of his existence.

Had you then, or have you now, any reason to wish harm to the prisoner?—Certainly not.

You are here solely as a matter of duty, and in the interests of justice?—Yes.

In view of the questions put to you by my learned friend, do you wish to modify any of the answers you gave to Mr Tufnell during examination?—No.

Let me see if I have got everything clear. When you addressed the prisoner as Mr Roderick William Strood, he said: 'My name is Williams'?—Yes.

When you said you had serious news for him he said: 'Is it about my wife'?—Yes.

That was before you yourself had mentioned his wife?—Yes.

When you told him Mrs Strood was dead, he said: 'My God! I killed her!'?—Yes.

§ 22

NIX AND OTHERS

ERNEST NIX, examined for the Crown by MR TUFNELL: I am a professional detective. I am employed by a private detective agency. I have no connexion with the police. On October the 20th I received instructions to keep a certain gentleman under observation and to report his movements.

What was the name of this gentleman?—Roderick Strood, of Merrion Square, London.

Is he in court?—Yes.

Do you recognize him?—I recognize him as the prisoner.

From whom were your instructions received? —From Mrs Strood.

MR HARCOMBE: My lord, I object to this witness.

MR JUSTICE SARUM: On what grounds, Mr Harcombe?

MR HARCOMBE: I submit that his evidence is inadmissible. My client is already labouring under a grave disability, in that matters having nothing to do with this case were advertised and misrepresented in another place and subsequently circulated throughout the country by the press.

MR JUSTICE SARUM: On the last point, I agree. I must warn you, members of the jury, that anything any of you may have heard or read about the prisoner outside this court is immaterial to the case now before you, and must be put out of your minds.

MR HARCOMBE: I am sure it is far from the wish or intention of my learned friend to import prejudice into this case; but that, I submit, will be the tendency and effect of the evidence he proposes to call.

MR JUSTICE SARUM: Sir John, it is submitted by learned counsel for the defence that it is my duty to disallow the evidence of this witness. I shall be glad to hear your observations.

ATTORNEY-GENERAL: My lord, with great submission, this is an important and necessary witness for the Crown. His evidence bears directly on the issue.

MR JUSTICE SARUM: It will help me, in view of the objection that has been raised, if I know upon what particular aspect of the case it bears.

ATTORNEY-GENERAL: My lord, on the question of motive in the first place. And, in the second place, on the behaviour of the prisoner on the night of the alleged crime. We—my learned junior and I—are very ready to meet my friend, and to pursue that particular question no further.

MR HARCOMBE: My objection is not to any such question in particular. I have no wish to make a mystery about that question. My objection is to the importation of moral prejudice into this case.

MR JUSTICE SARUM: I will hear the evidence.

MR HARCOMBE: As your lordship pleases.

[Continuing the examination, MR TUFNELL elicited from witness the following statements: that the prisoner had been in the habit, over a period of months, of visiting a flat occupied by an Austrian woman, a pianist, by name Elisabeth Andersch; that the lady lived quite alone, having no resident maid; that on at least two occasions the prisoner was seen to emerge from the flat in the morning, in a furtive manner, having apparently stayed with her all night; that he was with her on the night of October the 30th; that early on the following day he travelled with the woman Andersch by train to Southampton; that the witness, following him there, reported his movements to his (the witness's) employers by telephone; that he (the witness) was subsequently put into touch with Detective-Sergeant Bolton, whom he met by arrangement in Southampton, near the Zenith Hotel, as stated in evidence by Bolton himself; that the woman who was with Strood when he came out of the hotel was this same Elisabeth Andersch. There was no cross-examination of this witness.]

ALFRED OSCAR HOUSE, examined for the Crown by MR TUFNELL.—I am a barman employed at the Zenith Hotel, Southampton. I was on duty on the evening of October the 31st, in what is called the lounge-bar. At about a quarter to nine the prisoner, Roderick Strood, came to my counter and ordered a double brandy. I did not then know his name, but I now recognize him as the prisoner. He had had a meal in the dining-room of the hotel, and I had sent drinks to him by the waiter. Also, I had occasion to enter the dining-room myself and saw that he had a lady with him at dinner. The lady was not with him when he was in the lounge.

You say that the prisoner came to the lounge-bar at about a quarter to nine. How are you able to fix the time?—It might have been a little later or a little earlier. Later if anything, because soon afterwards they started reading the news-bulletin. I mean it started coming over the wireless. That was at nine o'clock.

You have a loud-speaker in the bar?—Yes.

Before the news was read, was there a message broadcast?—Yes.

Will you tell us what that message was, as near as you can remember?—It said for Mr Roderick

222

Strood to go back home because his wife was dangerously ill.

Had you a good view of the prisoner when these words were being broadcast?—Yes. As near as me to you.

Did you notice anything about his demeanour? —Yes. He changed countenance, as you might say.

Do you mean he appeared startled?

MR JUSTICE SARUM: You must not lead the witness. Let him give his evidence in his own words. [*To witness*] What did you mean when you said that the prisoner changed countenance?—He looked done-up, my lord, like as if he 'd had a shock.

MR TUFNELL [*continuing examination*]: Did he make any remark?—No.

Did he appear to listen attentively to the news?— No. He drank off his brandy and went out very quickly.

When he had finished drinking, what did he do with his glass?—He put it down on my counter.

Did you notice any further sign of agitation?— I noticed that his hand was shaking.

The wireless set, I take it, was in good order? I mean, the message was clear and audible?— Quite clear.

And audible? It could be heard by everyone? —All over the room.

You don't think it possible that the prisoner failed to hear it?—Not unless he was deaf.

Cross-examined for the Defence by MR HAR-

COMBE: When you heard that message coming over the wireless for Roderick Strood, you had no idea who Roderick Strood was, had you?—No.

You did not recognize the name?—No.

To the best of your knowledge and belief you had never heard it before?—No.

Were you on duty in the lounge-bar on the evening of the 30th of October, that is the evening before the evening in question?—Yes.

Were you on duty at nine o'clock that evening?—Yes.

Was the wireless turned on?—Well, we always have it on.

Because, I suppose, the customers like to hear the news?—Yes.

Do you remember that an S O S message was broadcast that evening? I am speaking of the evening before Mr Strood came to the hotel?—No, I don't remember.

Well, will you take it from me that there was?—There may have been.

And if there was a message (on October the 30th, that is the date I am speaking of), you, being on duty in the lounge-bar, would have heard it, would you not?—Yes.

But you remember nothing about it?—No. Perhaps I didn't hear it.

But if you had heard it you would be able to give me some particulars of it, wouldn't you?—I might or I might not.

You might not?—I might not remember.

Because you hear so many messages coming over the wireless?—Yes.

And I suppose you pay no particular attention to them as a rule?—Not as a rule.

I wonder what made you pay particular attention to the message for Mr Roderick Strood which you have told us about?—I didn't. Not what I'd call particular attention.

And yet after an interval of several weeks you are able to give us the exact name. How is that? Can you account for that extraordinary feat of memory?—I don't know.

Let me see if I can help you. Did you read in the newspaper any account of the inquest on the late Mrs Strood?—I may have done.

Did you, or did you not?—Yes.

And something was said during that inquest I believe, about this S O S message, and how at the time Mr Strood was in the Zenith Hotel?—Yes.

And then you cast your mind back, did you not, and thought to yourself: 'Why, I was on duty that evening, he may have been in the bar, I may have seen him!'?—Something like that.

And, thinking things over, in the light of what you had read in the newspapers, you thought you recognized the photograph of the prisoner that was printed in the newspapers?—I did recognize it.

And you thought you remembered that he had behaved in a suspicious manner?—Yes.

Now when Mr Strood ordered that double brandy, you did not know who he was, did you?—No.

And when the message came over the wireless for him, you still did not know who he was?—No.

At the time, you noticed nothing odd in his behaviour, did you?—Not at the time. Not exactly.

But thinking it over afterwards, when you had read about the case in the newspapers, and knew how important it was, you remembered that he had seemed agitated. Is that so?—Yes.

One more question. You told my learned friend that Mr Strood 'changed countenance'. Is that an expression you are in the habit of using?—How d' you mean, sir?

Let me put it another way. Do you think it is a proper way to speak?—Well, the gentleman said——

MR JUSTICE SARUM: That is not the question.

MR HARCOMBE: Let me put it another way. Did you hear that expression, 'changed countenance', from someone you felt sure would be careful to speak properly?—Yes.

From whom?—The gentleman who came to see me about this business.

Did he suggest to you that the prisoner 'changed countenance'?—Yes.

And after thinking it over you decided that he had?—Yes.

If I were to tell you that Mr Strood had left the bar before that message came over, would you be surprised?—Yes.

[From other witnesses it was elicited by the Prosecution, and not contested by the Defence, that the names of Elisabeth Andersch and Roderick Williams figured in the passenger-list of the liner due to sail for America at 11.55 p.m. on October the 31st; that Strood was not seen at his office at any time on October the 31st; that Strood booked his passage on October the 31st; and that a passport in the name of Roderick Williams was found in a collar-box in Strood's bedroom, after his arrest. Mrs. Tucker was then called.]

§ 23

MRS TUCKER SPEAKS OUT

MILDRED ALEXANDRA TUCKER, examined by the ATTORNEY-GENERAL.—I was employed as house-keeper and cook-general by the late Mrs Strood, my husband being butler. No other servants were kept. I have been in this situation for three and a half years, and have always given satisfaction. I was comfortable and happy in this situation until the trouble began.

To what trouble are you referring?—The trouble between Mr Strood and my mistress.

You are telling us that there was trouble between them? What kind of trouble?—The usual kind.

I must ask you to be very careful, Mrs Tucker, and to speak only of what you know at first-hand. What you have seen and heard at first-hand is evidence, but what you have imagined or guessed, or what has been told to you by others, that is another thing altogether. You will bear that in mind?—Yes.

Now when you say that there was trouble between your master and mistress, what do you mean?— I mean they quarrelled.

How do you know that?—I heard them with my own ears.

You heard them talking with raised voices and in an angry manner, and you concluded that they were quarrelling. Is that it?—Yes.

Did this happen often?—Several times, once the trouble had begun.

Before then it was a happy household, so far as you could see?—Yes.

When did the change occur?—About May.

How do you fix the date?—It started the night Mr Strood came back from Germany. And that was in May.

It was on the night of his return from Germany that you overheard the first of these angry conversations?—Yes.

Did Mr and Mrs Strood know they were being overheard?—No.

How did it happen that you were within ear-shot?—I was passing down the passage when I heard Mrs Strood scream out something. I ran to the door of the drawing-room, wondering what was to do. I then heard the two of them having words.

The scream was not repeated?—No.

Did you hear what was said?—It was about the other woman.

MR JUSTICE SARUM: You must not say things like that. You are to answer the questions. Learned counsel has asked you if you heard what was said. The proper answer is Yes or No.

MR HARCOMBE: With great respect, my lord, this tittle-tattle from the servants' hall is waste of the court's time.

MR JUSTICE SARUM: That remains to be seen, Mr Harcombe. We must curb our impatience.

MR HARCOMBE: The late Mrs Strood died on October the 30th. Is it necessary to rehearse matrimonial disputes alleged to have taken place five months earlier?

ATTORNEY-GENERAL: In order to spare my learned friend's feelings—it is a pleasure to be able to oblige my learned friend—I will pass over four of those months. [*Continuing examination*] Your late mistress, as you know, and as you have just heard, died on October the 30th. Some ten days or less before that event, did your husband contract an influenza cold?—Yes.

What did you do about that?—I made him keep to his bed.

It was part of his duty to serve at table?—Yes.

And on this particular morning, he being confined to his bed, who was in attendance during breakfast?—I was.

Did anything come to your notice that morning? —Yes.

Concerning what?—Concerning Mr and Mrs Strood.

Will you tell us exactly what happened?—Mrs Strood rang for me during breakfast. When I answered the bell I noticed there was something wrong.

What was wrong?—I had the feeling that there was something wrong because they suddenly stopped talking.

Yes. And then?—Mrs Strood said the coffee was cold and asked me to make some more. They both looked black as thunder.

Never mind that for the moment. What happened when you came back with the coffee?— When I came back with the coffee I heard them talking. Ever so loud they were talking.

You were standing outside the door, with your tray perhaps, just on the point of going in, when you were startled by the sound of raised voices. Is that right?—Yes.

And naturally you waited a moment or two, not knowing quite what to do?—Yes.

The voices were angry?—His was. Devilish, I'd call it.

Did you hear anything of what was being said?—Mrs Strood, she said she was caught.

Mr Justice Sarum: She said she was 'caught'?—Yes, your lordship.

Attorney - General [*continuing examination*]: Those were not Mrs Strood's actual words, were they? Can you give us her actual words?—Well, she told him she was caught.

Can you explain what that means?—She was caught. In the family way.

Do you mean that you heard Mrs Strood tell her husband that she was going to have a baby?—Yes. That's right.

Mr Justice Sarum: But that is not what you said. You said 'caught'.

Attorney-General: It comes to the same thing, my lord. It is a vulgarism in common use.

Mr Justice Sarum: It is new to me, I am happy to say. You have the advantage of me, Sir John.

Attorney-General [*continuing examination*]: Now tell us, Mrs Tucker, how did the prisoner receive this piece of news?—He flew into a temper.

What did he say?—He said: 'Well, I'm damned! You're a dirty cheat!'

You swear to those words?—Yes.

I come now to October the 30th, the day of Mrs Strood's death. At what time did Mrs Strood go to bed that day?—Five o'clock, as near as makes no matter.

And why so early?—She was badly off for sleep and felt very sadly.

MR JUSTICE SARUM: You mean she felt very ill?—Yes, your lordship.

ATTORNEY-GENERAL: 'Very ill' is an expression that needs defining, my lord. [*Continuing examination*] When you say 'very sadly' or 'very ill', do you mean that she was in a state of collapse?—I wouldn't say that.

Did you have to help her to undress?—No.

What did she complain of?—She said she wasn't feeling very well.

So by 'very ill' you mean 'not very well'?—Yes. That's right.

Did you then ring up Dr Cartwright?—Yes.

Did you speak to the doctor himself on the telephone? And did you tell him that Mrs Strood had been suffering from insomnia?—I said she'd been having bad nights.

Now, so that we can get on a little faster, I am going to ask you to tell the story in your own way, and I will not interrupt you with questions unless it is absolutely necessary. What happened after you had spoken to Dr Cartwright?—Well, the next thing was the doctor coming. He was come and gone within the hour, as he lives quite near. He stayed with Mrs Strood about ten minutes and then he went away. When he came downstairs

I asked him was it serious. He says 'No', and I says: 'Poor lady, she can't get any sleep.' 'Well, Mrs Tucker,' he says, 'you and me must get her well again. Now here's her medicine, to help her to sleep. She'll be right as a trivet in the morning.' He gave me a little bottle of medicine, it looked like plain water, and told me to give it her in a glass of water. So I did what he told me and next time I went to make her comfortable I took the glass of water with me and put it on her table.

Her bedside table?—That's right.

You didn't ask her to drink it at once?—No. I knew Mr Strood would be home soon and perhaps there'd be an upset and stop her going to sleep.

And did the prisoner arrive shortly afterwards? —Yes, about six twenty-five. I told him madam wasn't well and was to have a sleeping mixture. He told me to prepare a cup of malted milk for her. Then he went upstairs.

Into which room upstairs did he go?—Madam's bedroom.

He went into Mrs Strood's bedroom?—Yes.

Did he stay long?—He went in at half-past six, because I heard the clock strike in the hall, and he didn't come out again till a quarter-past seven.

Where were you during that time?—Most of the time I was in my kitchen, but after a bit I went into the hall and hung about, waiting for him to come down.

Why did you do that?—I was anxious about madam and wanted her to get some rest.

You didn't think that the prisoner was equally anxious?—Not him.

Before he came downstairs did you hear something?—I heard the bedroom door slam. Then he came down. He was in one of his moods.

One of his moods?—He gave me a black look. I was in the hall, and I had the malted milk with me, ready to take up. He said: 'I think Mrs Strood had better have a biscuit or two as well'. He then took the tray from me and put it down on a little table that stands in the hall while I went back to get the biscuits.

You went back to the kitchen?—Yes.

Leaving the cup of malted milk within reach of the prisoner?—Yes.

How long were you away?—Two or three minutes, as I had to open a parcel of grocery to find the right kind of biscuits.

Mrs Strood favoured a particular kind of biscuits, and there were none in your cupboard. Is that it?—That's right. Digestives were what she fancied, so I had to open the grocery parcel.

After first looking in the cupboard?—Yes.

Did you then return to the hall?—Yes.

Was the prisoner still there?—No.

The tray containing the cup of malted milk remained where he had placed it?—Yes.

And you then, I suppose, took it up to your mistress?—Yes.

Did she eat any of the biscuits?—No. She wouldn't touch them.

Did she drink the malted milk?—Yes.

In your presence?—Yes. I waited till she'd taken every drop.

Did she ask for anything else?—She asked for some more water. Then I saw that the glass was empty.

You are speaking now of the glass of water into which you had poured the sleeping-draught, according to Dr Cartwright's instructions?—Yes.

She asked for some more water?—Yes. She wanted it by her bedside, because when a person's feverish they're always thirsty.

Quite so. Did you make any remark?—She said: 'There was something in it to make me sleep.'

What did you answer?—I said: 'Ah, you're too sharp for me, madam. I wasn't going to say anything about it.' She seemed very drowsy, so I went out of the room.

Was that the last time you saw Mrs Strood alive?—Yes.

While you were with Mrs Strood, did Mr Strood leave the house?—He must have done, as he was gone by the time I came downstairs.

Did he return that night?—No.

He did not return next day?—No.

You heard nothing from him next day? No

inquiry about his wife's health? No communication of any sort or kind?—No.

Cross-examined for the Defence by MR HARCOMBE: I believe, Mrs Tucker, you were deeply devoted to your mistress?—Yes.

In these disputes between husband and wife which you have told us about, you had no doubt at all that she was entirely in the right?—Yes.

You formed the opinion that Mr Strood was being unfaithful to his wife, did you not?—Yes.

And naturally, as a woman, your sympathies were entirely with her?—Yes.

You never liked Mr Strood very much, did you? —I never gave it a thought until he started treating her wrong.

Perhaps you felt *he* didn't like *you*?—He was always rather stuck-up, if that's what you mean.

Whereas Mrs Strood was more friendly in her manner?—Yes. Always the pleasant word.

Did Mr Strood ever lose his temper with you?— He always had his nose up in the air.

That hardly answers my question, does it? I'm asking whether he ever spoke angrily to you?— Not specially. He never spoke to me at all, if he could help it.

Now cast your mind back for a moment to the morning in October when your husband had to stay in bed with a cold, and you were in attendance at the breakfast table. You've just told my learned friend about that, haven't you?—Yes.

You answered your mistress's ring and were instructed by her to bring in some fresh coffee?—Yes.

She said, I believe, that the other coffee was cold?—She may have done.

I think you said so, didn't you?—Yes.

What answer did you make to her?—I don't remember.

Did you say something to this effect: 'It was hot enough when I brought it in'?—I may have done.

And did Mr Strood then become very angry?—I don't remember.

I put it to you that Mr Strood became very angry, and that he called you back and said to you: 'Are you having the insolence to complain?' or something like that. Do you remember that?—I don't know.

Come now: either you remember or you don't. He shouted at you, didn't he?—Yes.

Then you *do* remember?—I do now.

And naturally you resented that, didn't you?—Yes.

It was very disagreeable being so angrily rebuked?—Yes.

And in your mistress's presence too. That made it worse, didn't it?—Yes.

You had never liked Mr Strood much, and after that you liked him still less, I suppose?—Yes.

In fact you hated him from that moment, didn't you?—I wouldn't say that.

Have you a good memory, Mrs Tucker?—I remember what I hear.

You make rather a study of listening at keyholes, don't you?—No.

But you have told my learned friend of more than one occasion when you listened to conversations that weren't meant for your ears?—That was different.

How different?—Because they were shouting at each other.

You don't listen at keyholes but you listen behind closed doors. Is that it?—The door was on the jar.

On all these occasions when you overheard private conversations, you stood listening behind a door, and the door was ajar?—Not always it wasn't. It was shut sometimes.

That made it more difficult for you, didn't it: when the door was shut, I mean?—Yes.

Nevertheless you managed to hear a good deal even then?—Yes.

Did you write down what you heard?—No.

You relied on your memory?—Yes.

Yet you are able to swear to the exact words?—Well, I know what I heard.

Did you tell anyone else about what you 'd heard? —I told my husband.

And you talked it over with him?—Yes.

Several times?—Yes.

Was there any disagreement between you and

your husband on this matter?—Well, we had a few words, if that's what you mean.

Did he question the accuracy of what you told him?—He may have done. Just like a man.

'Just like a man'? What do you mean?—Men are all alike.

Now we will come to the day of Mrs Strood's death. When you were carrying that cup of malted milk through the hall, on your way to the bedroom, Mr Strood, coming down stairs, asked you to fetch some biscuits?—Yes.

The cup of malted milk was on a tray?—Yes.

And in order not to have to carry it back to the kitchen when you went to fetch the biscuits, you placed the tray on a small table that stands in the hall?—Yes.

You placed it on the table in the presence of Mr Strood?—Yes.

In answer to my learned friend you said that Mr Strood took the tray from you and that it was he who placed it on the table?—I don't remember.

You don't remember saying that in evidence, or you don't remember Mr Strood's placing the tray on the table?—Yes, he did. That's right.

But just now you told us that you yourself placed it on the table. Now I don't want to trap you in any way, but this is a point of some importance. You understand the nature of the oath you have taken, to speak the truth and nothing but the truth?—Yes.

That means that if your memory is not clear on any particular point, you must say so, doesn't it?—Yes.

Now are you able to tell my lord and the jury whether it was you or Mr Strood who placed the tray on the hall table?—No.

You can't remember?—No.

But you can remember the exact words of a conversation you overheard some ten days earlier? —Yes.

Let me see if I have got it right. On October the 30th, the last day of your mistress's life, Mr Strood reached home at about half-past six. As soon as he entered the house you went and spoke to him. Is that right?—Yes.

Where was he when you spoke to him?—He was in the hall, hanging up his overcoat.

I see. Did you enter the hall from the kitchen or from the stairs?—The kitchen.

You spoke to Mr Strood?—Yes.

Will you tell the court just what you said, the exact words if you remember them?—Well, I think I said——

You *think*. Aren't you sure?—I know what I told him. But it's difficult to remember the very words.

Yes, it is, isn't it? Well, do your best.—I said: 'Madam has gone to bed, she's not feeling so well.' Or something like that.

'Not feeling so well' or 'Not feeling very well'?

Which was it?—I can't exactly say. It's the same thing.

You don't remember the exact words you used? —No.

But you remember the exact words the prisoner used ten days earlier?—Yes.

Very well. Now about this malted milk. You said: 'Madam has gone to bed, she's not feeling so well' or 'she's not feeling very well.' Did you then say that you were going to prepare a cup of malted milk for her?—Yes.

You had already planned to do so, and you mentioned it to the prisoner?—Yes.

He had said nothing about malted milk, but you mentioned that you were going to prepare some. Is that right?—No.

It isn't right?—He said 'Yes'.

Quite so. You mentioned that you were going to prepare some malted milk, and he said 'Yes'. Is that what you are saying?—Yes.

Now tell me, did your mistress ever suffer from depression?—Yes.

During the last few days of her life, did she seem very unhappy?—Yes.

Did she sometimes not answer when you spoke to her?—Yes.

As though she were thinking of something else? —Yes.

Did she sometimes seem dazed?—Yes.

She did not confide any of her troubles to you?—No.

You became anxious about her?—Yes.

Did she seem tired of life?—In a way.

On the afternoon of October the 30th, when she decided to go to bed, you sent for the doctor?—Yes.

Was that at Mrs Strood's request?—No.

Was it without her knowledge?—Yes.

Why did you send for the doctor without her authority and without telling her that you were doing so?—I thought she would tell me not to.

You had reason to think that she was anxious not to be visited by the doctor?—I thought she didn't want to have him.

You gathered that from her manner?—Yes.

When she told you she was going to bed, did she look ill?—Yes.

Very ill?—She didn't look at all well.

In answer to my lord, you said she was very ill, I think?—I didn't like the looks of her.

And so, being anxious, you rang up the doctor without telling her?—Yes.

Did you tell her afterwards?—No. Not till the doctor came, and it was too late for her to say No.

And afterwards, perhaps for the same reason, you kept it a secret from her that she was to have a sleeping-draught?—Yes.

Because you fancied she might refuse to take it?—Yes. I thought I 'd better humour her, seeing she was so strange.

She was strange in manner?—Yes.

§ 24

MEDICAL EVIDENCE

OLIVER CARTWRIGHT, examined by the ATTORNEY-GENERAL: I am a qualified medical practitioner in general practice. I have attended the deceased woman for minor ailments on several occasions. My relationship with the Stroods was social as well as professional. I was on terms of friendship with them. As her medical man, I was familiar with Mrs Strood's general physical condition, and I had some idea of her medical history. I was called to her by telephone on the afternoon of October the 30th. She was in bed and looking a little flushed, but she said she was perfectly well.

You examined her nevertheless?—I asked her a few questions.

And you found no reason to disagree with her? —I could not agree that she was 'perfectly well'. That was an exuberance of speech. Both pulse and temperature were slightly above normal. But I did not regard her as ill.

Nor as likely to become so?—That is more than anyone can say. I can only say that her condition gave me no sort of anxiety.

How long was it since you had last seen her, I mean in your professional capacity?—She had consulted me on October the 18th. Between then and October the 30th I had not seen her in any capacity.

When she consulted you on October the 18th, did you examine her?—No. It wasn't necessary.

You mean there was nothing seriously the matter with her?—Precisely.

Upon what point did she consult you?—She had reason to think she had conceived.

Did you ask her various questions?—Yes.

And as a result of her answers did you form a definite opinion as to her condition?—I formed the opinion that she was pregnant.

Now, coming back to the later date, October the 30th, did you judge, from the pulse and temperature, that she was feeling some of the effects of pregnancy?—No.

We are speaking now of October the 30th, are we not?—Quite so.

Did Mrs Strood appear to resent your having been sent for?—She seemed a little nettled.

Will you tell us what she said on the point?— When I entered the room she seemed surprised and said: 'Is this a social call?' I laughed and told her that Mrs Tucker had sent for me. She said: 'You've been brought on a fool's errand. Milly is too officious'. Or words to that effect.

Yes. And then?—I then asked her a few professional questions.

She made no further objection?—No.

Did she tell you she was in want of sleep?— Not exactly. I remarked that Mrs Tucker had told me as much and she did not deny it.

Did you tell her she was to have a sleeping-draught?—I did not use that particular phrase, but in effect I told her.

MR JUSTICE SARUM: Can you remember the words you used?—So far as I remember I said: 'We 'll see if we can give you a night's rest'.

MR JUSTICE SARUM: Did she make any answer to that?—I think not.

MR JUSTICE SARUM: Was any further reference made to a sleeping-draught, or to the subject of getting a good night's rest, either by you or by the patient?—Not so far as I remember.

ATTORNEY - GENERAL [*continuing examination*]: When you left her she did not appear to be ill? —Not ill, in the ordinary sense of that term. Merely a little feverish.

Although she made no point of being in want of sleep you decided to give her a draught?—Yes.

Why was that?—From what she had told me on other occasions I believed her to be in a state of psychological stress.

And did you in fact administer a sleeping-draught? —Not in person. I gave it to the housekeeper, Mrs Tucker, with instructions how to administer it.

Of what did the draught consist?—Oscitalin. Two drachms.

Is that an ordinary dose?—Yes.

MR JUSTICE SARUM: Wait a moment. Did you say 'digitalin'?—No, my lord. Oscitalin. A proprietary preparation.

MR JUSTICE SARUM [*to Counsel*]: Osci-talin? The *c* is hard?—ATTORNEY-GENERAL: Yes, my lord. I fancy the name is derived from the Latin *oscitare*.

MR JUSTICE SARUM: Quite so. And [*to witness*] is it, as the name suggests, a soporific?—Yes, my lord. A soporific drug in common use.

MR JUSTICE SARUM: Do you mean that it is supplied to the general public?—No, my lord. I mean it is frequently prescribed by physicians.

ATTORNEY - GENERAL [*continuing examination*]: Were you sent for again next morning?—Yes.

And what did you find?—I arrived at the house at eight o'clock and found my patient dead. She appeared to have been dead for seven or eight hours.

That was a great shock to you?—A very great shock.

Did the appearance of the body give you any clue to the cause of death?—Cardiac and respiratory failure were indicated, but there was nothing distinctive.

MR JUSTICE SARUM: By that phrase we are to understand heart failure and failure in breathing? —Yes, my lord.

MR JUSTICE SARUM: Such indications would be given by any natural death, would they not?—In many cases, my lord. But in some cases, there would be major indications of other causes.

MR JUSTICE SARUM: You must have mercy on my ignorance, but the phrase you employed ('cardiac and respiratory failure,' was it not?) would seem to a lay mind to be synonymous with death itself. It tells us nothing of the causes, does it?—I agree, my lord, that the cause of death is not manifested in those indications. That, if I may say so, was the effect of my answer.

MR JUSTICE SARUM: The question, members of the jury, was: 'Did the appearance of the body give you any clue to the cause of death?' The answer is 'No'.

ATTORNEY - GENERAL [*continuing examination*]: In the circumstances you did not feel justified in giving a certificate?—No.

In consequence of that decision did you ask certain questions of Mrs Tucker?—Yes.

And in view of her answers, and your own uneasiness, did you report the matter at once to the Coroner?—Yes.

Were you present at the post-mortem examination conducted by Dr Lampetter?—Yes.

Cross-examined by MR HARCOMBE: When you saw Mrs Strood on the afternoon of October the 30th, did she seem depressed?—No.

Her manner was normal?—Rather gay, if anything.

Would it be correct to say that she was a little excited?—Perhaps a little.

Even a little hysterical?—I think not.

Had you ever seen her in precisely that state of excitement before?—Yes. She was an excitable person.

What was her temperature-reading?—99·1.

That is definitely above normal, is it not?—Yes.

That symptom, the increased temperature, is sometimes observed in cases of chloral poisoning, is it not?—There was no indication of chloral poisoning.

I am not asking you that, Dr Cartwright. I am putting it to you that a heightened temperature is, or may be, a symptom of chloral poisoning?—Yes.

Thank you. Now I am not suggesting anything more than a possibility, but if that heightened temperature had in fact been caused by a dose of chloral, that dose of chloral, a purely hypothetical dose you will remember, must have been taken not many hours before your arrival on the scene. Is that so?—The times vary greatly.

Yes, but in view of the absence of other symptoms, in this hypothetical case I am putting to you, not many hours?—I agree.

What shall we say: two hours, three hours?— Certainly not more than three hours.

What in your opinion would be a fatal dose?— It varies with the idiosyncrasy of the patient.

Am I right in saying that twenty grains would be a fatal dose in the case of an adult?—It might or might not.

Such a dose has been known to prove fatal, has it not?—Yes.

Now as to this oscitalin prescribed by you. You know the formula for this preparation?—Naturally. Otherwise I should never have prescribed it.

Very well. You will be able to give me the benefit of your knowledge. Am I right in saying that oscitalin contains, among other things, chloral, urethane, and alcohol?—Yes.

And that chloral is in fact the major constituent? —Yes.

You prescribed two drachms?—Yes. That is a very usual dose.

Will you tell my lord and the jury what quantity of chloral would be contained in two drachms of oscitalin?—Fifteen grains.

In effect, therefore, you prescribed fifteen grains of chloral. Wasn't that cutting it rather fine?— Not in the least.

Without any previous knowledge of her reaction to chloral, you felt justified in giving as much as fifteen grains?—It was not the first time I had given her oscitalin.

On what other occasions had you given her oscitalin?—Once only. I think it was in September. She complained of insomnia and she was also suffering from neuritis.

The same dose? Two drachms?—Yes.

And the dose was justified by results?—Yes.

So that on this second occasion, October the 30th, you knew from the success of the September treatment that she could safely take such a dose?—Yes.

But for that precedent you might have hesitated? —It is quite a reasonable dose.

But might you not have hesitated?—I might have done.

Now when you gave what we will call the September dose you had no precedent to guide you, had you? I mean, of course, so far as this patient was concerned?—No.

Yet you did not hesitate?—No. Two drachms is not a dangerous dose.

Never a dangerous dose?—Given sound organs in the patient, never a dangerous dose.

On the soundness of which organ or organs in particular does this safety depend?—The heart.

Are you aware that Mrs Strood's mother died of heart failure?—No.

Yet I think you said you were acquainted with her medical history?—I may have heard the fact mentioned. If so it has escaped my memory.

Now let us return to the oscitalin for a moment. Is it supplied to you in cachets or tablets of a specific uniform dosage?—No. It is in liquid form.

I see. And the dose of two drachms given to Mrs Strood on October the 30th, was it dispensed by yourself?—Yes.

Would you be good enough to describe the process for us?—I measured two drachms, which I diluted to a fluid ounce. The bottle containing this fluid ounce I handed to Mrs Tucker, instructing her to give it to the patient in a tumbler of ordinary drinking water.

The measuring of two liquid drachms is a delicate matter, I take it?—Not exceptionally so. It is a matter of ordinary care.

It is very easy to make a mistake, is it not?—Not at all. I am trained not to make such mistakes.

This is a case in which a small mistake would make all the difference, is it not?—No.

Come, Dr Cartwright. You have admitted that twenty grains of chloral can be a fatal dose, and you have told us that two drachms of oscitalin represents fifteen grains of chloral, have you not? Now that means, if my arithmetic is correct, that if by inadvertence you had dispensed two and two-thirds drachms, instead of two drachms, you would have given a possibly fatal dose. Am I not right?—Yes. But that would not have been a small mistake in dispensing: it would have been a very gross one.

Are you confident that it did not in fact occur?—I am quite confident. The suggestion is outrageous.

Re-examined by the ATTORNEY-GENERAL: You have conceded to my learned friend that chloral poisoning may induce a heightened temperature, such a temperature, in fact, as you found in your patient on the material date?—Yes.

Is heightened temperature a characteristic symptom of such a condition?—No.

What state of temperature is more generally found in such cases?—A subnormal temperature.

Are we to understand that a heightened temperature in such cases is comparatively rare? An exception rather than the rule?—Yes.

Further cross-examination by MR HARCOMBE: Do you agree that Mrs Strood's condition on October the 30th, when you saw her, was consistent with the theory that she had taken chloral within the past three hours?—There was no indication of any such thing.

Will you be good enough to answer the question as it was put?—There would have been other symptoms.

If chloral had been taken something less than half an hour before your arrival, would there have necessarily been symptoms?—No.

And there was nothing on the face of it to contradict such a theory?—No.

Then you *do* agree that Mrs Strood's condition was consistent with the theory, the possibility, that she had taken chloral before your arrival?—If you put it that way, yes.

CYRUS HARTMAN LAMPETTER, examined for the Crown by MR TUFNELL: I am a Doctor of Medicine and a Fellow of the Royal College of Surgeons, and I am a pathologist. On October the 31st I made a post-mortem examination of the body of a woman who was identified, in my presence, as Daphne Strood. Dr Cartwright was present throughout the post-mortem examination. The deceased was five or six weeks advanced in pregnancy. I found no disease, either in the heart or elsewhere. But in various organs I found an aggregate of 19·7 grains of chloral and a smaller quantity of bromide. I also found traces of hyoscyamus and cannabis indica: these are not constituents of oscitalin. In the bladder I found an aggregate of 2·9 grains of uro-chloral acid and glycuronic acid, which are products of the decomposition of chloral. The amount of chloral and of chloral products actually found does not represent the total of the amount that must have been taken. As to the amount taken, it is impossible to be precise; but it is a fair inference that not less than thirty and perhaps as much as forty grains had been taken. In view of these results my opinion is that death was due to chloral poisoning, and that the poison was taken either in one dose or in a series of doses taken all within a short time, say an hour.

[In the course of an exceedingly lengthy cross-examination, by Mr Ronald Young, junior counsel for Defence, witness gave the results of his post-mortem examination in minute detail, specifying the organs examined and the amount found in each. It was put to him repeatedly (a) that his findings could only be approximate, and (b) that the deduction he made from them as to the total amount of chloral taken by deceased was largely in the nature of guess-work; but to neither of these suggestions would he agree. He said that it was impossible to say how soon death ensued after the taking of the fatal dose: it might have been in less than an hour and it might equally well have been three or four hours after. He described in detail the tests he employed for the detection of chloral hydrate in the stomach and other organs and would not agree that there was any appreciable margin of error. He also described, in detail, Vitali's Test, which he had used, with positive results, for the detection of hyoscyamus. The amount of hyoscyamus indicated was minute; it was not a poisonous amount. He said further that though twenty grains of chloral was the minimum fatal dose for an adult, and that much more had been known to be taken without fatal result, the presence of so large a quantity in the stomach and intestines established an overwhelming probability, in the absence of other causes, that this chloral was in fact the cause of death. His attention was called to Dr Cartwright's statement that Mrs Strood had taken chloral on a previous occasion, but negatived the suggestion that this would have produced in the patient some degree of tolerance in respect of the poison. Re-examined, he said that though habitual taking of chloral sometimes produced a degree of tolerance, which was to say a degree of immunity, this was not by any means a necessary result. DR CARTWRIGHT, recalled, said (in answer to MR TUFNELL for the Prosecution) that there was no bromide, no hyoscyamus, and no cannabis indica in the draught he had prepared for Mrs Strood, and that he was unable to account for their presence in the body. He repeated, with much emphasis, that the draught could have contained no more than fifteen grains of chloral. This concluded the evidence for the Prosecution.]

§ 25

MR HARCOMBE ADDRESSES THE JUDGE

MR HARCOMBE: My lord, the case for the Crown having been closed, it is now my duty to submit to your lordship that this is a case which ought not to go to a jury, because upon evidence so scanty and inconclusive no jury could reasonably convict. With great respect I submit that it is your lordship's duty to give a ruling in that sense. I need not remind your lordship that long before this trial began my client was the subject of sensational news, and even more sensational conjecture, throughout the length and breadth of this land, that his behaviour and alleged motives were published to the world, and that before his trial began he was a murderer in the public estimation—in the estimation, my lord, of that public from which this jury has been selected, from which indeed every jury must be selected.

MR JUSTICE SARUM: It is late in the day, Mr Harcombe, to object to the jury.

MR HARCOMBE: My lord, nothing is further from my thought than to object to this jury more than to any other jury that might have been empanelled. I make no question at all that the members of this jury came to the court as free from prejudice as it is humanly possible for people to be who do not possess trained legal minds, and who

255

have never had occasion to acquire the habit of suspending judgement and the ability to weigh evidence. I have been greatly impressed, and subject to correction I hazard the belief that your lordship has been impressed, by the close attention which the jury have given to the evidence my friend has put before them. But my point is that remarks made in another place, by a gentleman dressed in a little brief authority, cannot fail to have coloured the mind of the entire newspaper-reading public to the prejudice of my client. Your lordship will forgive me if I seem to labour a point which is not after all my main point in this submission, but it is a matter on which I feel very strongly. Nobody has ever questioned the rule and tradition of justice, as it is administered in this country, which is that an accused person is presumed innocent until he has been manifestly proved guilty by the evidence for the Prosecution. I submit that in this case that presumption was overlaid, in the minds of the jury, by a prejudice to the contrary.

Mr Justice Sarum: You say that that is not your main point in this submission. I must ask you to come to your main point. If you wish to imply that persons appointed to inquire into the cause of a death are mischievously exceeding their duty when they stray beyond that province, I shall not, so far, disagree with you. But if you are contending that what was said in another place had the necessary effect of making this trial abortive from the start, I cannot agree. Nor could I have agreed, had you offered such a contention at the proper time. You will recall, moreover, that I explicitly warned the jury to put all prejudice from their minds.

MR HARCOMBE: Yes, my lord. And I do not question that so far as lies in their power they have obeyed your lordship's injunction. My point about prejudice is sufficiently made. I will offer no further observations on that head, but will come to my second and main contention, the insufficiency of the evidence. I agree that, if there is sufficient evidence, the overlaying it with prejudice does not affect the case. But here, in my submission, the evidence is manifestly insufficient. It is evidence upon which the jury cannot reasonably convict.

MR JUSTICE SARUM: You are asking me to tell the jury that on the evidence that has been brought they cannot reasonably convict?

MR HARCOMBE: Yes, my lord. I should hardly be going too far if I said that there was no case to answer. I will not, however, say that. In so far as there is a case I am prepared to refute it point by point and to call evidence in proof of that refutation. I am not afraid of the issue. But I say, and I ask your lordship to say, that upon this evidence the prisoner ought not to be required any longer to stand before the bar of judgement, in peril of his life. The story of the Crown is plausible on the surface, but it is no more than plausible: it is

I   257

not convincing and it is a thousand miles from being proved. Much of the evidence has been of a kind that has no bearing, or at least no direct bearing, on the issue, and of a kind calculated to augment the moral prejudice that already existed. A great deal has been made of the prisoner's so-called infidelity to his wife, and to the fact that he intended to visit America in the company of a woman not his wife. From this we are invited to infer that he poisoned his wife by adding chloral, whether in oscitalin or in some other compound, to a cup of malted milk. No evidence of his having done so has been adduced, and it is clear that even if he did so—which he is prepared to deny and eager to deny—it would remain for the Crown to prove murderous intention, since of the 19·7 grains of chloral found by Dr Lampetter at the post-mortem examination, as much as fifteen grains is admitted to have been given medicinally by Dr Cartwright. Allowing a margin for absorption, that leaves some twenty grains or less to be accounted for, and it has been established in this case that twenty grains is not necessarily, or even probably, a fatal dose for an adult. Any one of three other people may have given that other dose — Mrs Tucker, Mrs Tucker's husband, the deceased woman herself. And whoever did it may well have done it innocently, seeing that it was not, in itself, a lethal dose. Not a tittle of evidence has been adduced to show that the prisoner possessed chloral or could have possessed it. Nor has it been so much as suggested that he had any means of knowing that a drug containing chloral had been given, or was about to be given, by order of Dr Cartwright.

MR JUSTICE SARUM: That is all you have to say on this head?

MR HARCOMBE: Yes, my lord.

MR JUSTICE SARUM: It has been submitted by learned counsel, on behalf of the prisoner, that the evidence is so insufficient that it is my duty to withdraw the case from the jury. I have listened to his arguments with attention and I wish to make it perfectly clear that I make no sort of comment on them. What I have now to say is not to be taken as implying that I have formed any opinion whatever on the issue before the court. And what I have to say is that the case must proceed.

§ 26

SPEECH FOR THE DEFENCE

MR HARCOMBE: May it please your lordship. Members of the jury, you have been giving very careful attention to this case, and I am sure that you will listen with equal patience and care to what remains to be said. For it would be indeed grievous and unfair—and I know my friend the Attorney-General will be heartily with me in this—if having patiently heard all that the Crown can urge against the prisoner up to this point, you were to hear with any less care, any less degree of patience, what is to be said in his defence. I do not fear or anticipate any such thing: on the contrary I know that I can rely on your giving me your closest attention. If you do that, I think I shall have no difficulty in convincing you that the case against Roderick William Strood is a very weak case indeed, a flimsy structure of suspicion, conjecture, and false inference. That the case has been very skilfully pieced together, and very skilfully presented, you do not need to be told. But indeed I hardly know whether to admire my learned friend's skill or to marvel at his audacity. He has presented a case that has all the high finish of a piece of well-wrought fiction, and I shall suggest to you, I shall do more than suggest to you, that in fact—though not, of course, in the estimation of my learned friend— it *is* fiction in its general character and especially in the particular conclusion to which it points. Here is the case of a man charged with murder where no murder has been proved to have occurred. Here is a man charged with poisoning his wife with chloral, and no evidence has been offered to show either that he was in possession of chloral or that he had any means of obtaining it. Members of the jury, I say to you not only that the facts before you are insufficient to justify you in returning a verdict against Roderick Strood: I say that they would be insufficient to justify a verdict of murder against anyone. Of course, murder may have been done. I do not deny the possibility. But when we have got the facts, when we have extracted the few definite facts from the agglomeration of prejudice and suspicion and pure fancy which is the case for the Crown, when we have got at those facts, we find, I suggest, that they do not clearly point to murder at all, whether by Strood or anybody else: they are equally consistent with a theory of suicide or a theory of accidental death. You have heard the medical evidence. You have heard that in the opinion of Dr Lampetter, who performed the post-mortem examination, the late Mrs Strood died of chloral poisoning. But even on that point there is an element of doubt. Even if we concede that the chloral was a contributory cause, there may well have been other causes which these medical gentlemen were unable to detect. For all we can know, Mrs Strood may have inherited a subtle and unsuspected form—if you like an all but imperceptible form—of that heart disease of which, as you will hear in evidence later on, her own mother died at the age of fifty-six. So far as the evidence for the Prosecution has revealed, her heart was never, during life, subjected to a searching examination. And if my learned friend asks why we should seek to bring in other causes when, as he might say, there is this fact of the chloral staring us in the face, I answer: Because of the comparatively small amount found in the body, an amount which, as

Dr Lampetter admitted if I understood him aright, has often been taken without fatal results. Let me make myself perfectly clear on this point. I do not say that Mrs Strood positively did not die from chloral poisoning: I say only that there is some doubt in the matter. Dr Lampetter himself—and I speak subject to correction, for nothing is further from my wish than to misrepresent him—Dr Lampetter himself used expressions which to my mind, and I think to any fair mind, implied an element of doubt. He used the word 'probability'——

ATTORNEY - GENERAL: 'Overwhelming probability' was the expression used.

MR HARCOMBE: I am obliged to my learned friend. 'Overwhelming probability.' But you, members of the jury, will not, I hope, allow your judgment to be overwhelmed by mere probabilities: the thing must be established for you beyond all reasonable doubt before you will be justified in returning a verdict against my client. You and I are not medical men, and ninety-nine times out of a hundred we are humbly prepared to defer to the opinion of an expert, and if that expert speaks of a 'probability', or of an 'overwhelming probability', well, we take a chance, we give him the benefit of the doubt. Ninety-nine times out of a hundred, I say, we can do this, and not regret it. But this is the hundredth time. A man stands in peril of his life, on a charge of murder. You cannot take chances in such a matter: it would lie heavily on your consciences for evermore, if you did. You cannot take chances, and if there is any doubt in the matter, it is the accused man, not the expert witness, that is entitled to have the benefit of it. That, as my lord will tell you, is the law; and that is the obligation placed upon you.

That is one weakness in the case against Roderick Strood. But it is not the only one and it is not the most serious one. In cases of alleged murder by poisoning it is customary for the Prosecution to bring forward evidence called 'tracing possession' —that is, tracing into the possession of the accused person the poison with which the murder is said to have been committed. In this case no such evidence has been called—not a shred of it, not a hint of it. On that point there is nothing in this case beyond what I venture to describe as an unsupported hypothesis. The Crown seeks to persuade you that chloral and hyoscyamus were introduced by Strood into the malted milk that Mrs Tucker left within his reach when she returned to the kitchen to fetch biscuits. You will remember Mrs Tucker in the witness-box, and if ever there was an unreliable witness, if ever there was a witness as cram-full of malice as an egg is full of meat, that witness is Mrs Tucker. You noticed perhaps, not only her malice, but the very grave discrepancy in her evidence. First she said that Mr Strood took the tray from her and placed it on the hall-table; later she said that she herself placed it on the table; then she tried to brazen it out that her first version was accurate; and finally she confessed that she didn't know, she couldn't remember. And this is the chief witness for the Crown! That is one specimen of Mrs Tucker's accuracy. Here is another, and I want you to pay particular attention to these points, remembering that a man's life depends on your coming to a just view of this evidence. Answering the learned Attorney-General, Mrs Tucker said: 'He told me to prepare a cup of malted milk for her.' But in cross-examination she admitted that the mention of malted milk came in the first place from herself, not from the prisoner, and that the prisoner merely assented to her suggestion—I can put it higher than that and say her plain statement —that malted milk was to be prepared. You will see the significance of that. It means that the prisoner did not contrive, and could not have foreseen, that this beverage, or any other beverage, was to be sent upstairs to his wife. So much for Mrs Tucker! It is on the word of this woman that the whole case rests—or if not the whole case, certainly the vital crux of the case. Such as it is, the crux of the case. Take away Mrs Tucker's evidence and what have you left? Nothing worth a second glance. Now Mrs Tucker makes no secret of her dislike of the prisoner, though she did attempt to withhold the fact that he had had occasion to rebuke her for insolence to her mistress. And the scraps of dialogue she served up to us—

fruit of her industrious eavesdropping—what are they worth, what do they amount to? Are you not convinced, in your own minds, that whatever Mrs Tucker may have heard pass between her master and mistress, it has been so twisted and distorted by her memory, so coloured by her dislike of Mr Strood, that what she heard bears very little relation to what she thinks and says she heard? I do not say that Mrs Tucker is dishonest; I do not suggest that she has come to this court with the deliberate intention of bearing false witness against an innocent man; but I do suggest that she is, however honest and well-meaning, a dangerous woman, a woman with an imperfect sense of fact, a woman easily duped by her own fancies and quick to translate mere suspicion and conjecture into terms of positive assertion. She gets it into her head that her mistress has been murdered, and her dislike of Mr Strood suggests him as the guilty person. As soon as the notion presents itself to her, it becomes a conviction; and in the light of that conviction she begins to remember things. She remembers things that happened, and she thinks she remembers other things, things that in fact did not happen. I have already given you an example of that. And between the true and the false memories, she is unable—perhaps unwilling—to distinguish: they are all one to her and they 'll all help, she thinks, to hang that wicked Mr Strood. For my own part, members of the jury, I would not hang a dog or shoot a rat on the evidence of a woman like Mrs Tucker.

But when all is said, what does that evidence amount to? Even if one were so rash as to take it at its face-value, what does it amount to? It amounts to this: that here was a married couple who sometimes exchanged angry words—how unlike married couples, how extraordinary, how unheard-of! And here is a man, the husband, who had an opportunity, provided he had the means, an opportunity of doctoring his wife's malted milk. For two or three minutes — let us call it three minutes—the cup of malted milk was within his reach and he was unobserved: that is, if we take Mrs Tucker's evidence at its face-value. That, members of the jury, was the only opportunity he had. Now who else had such an opportunity? Who had a boundless opportunity? Clearly Mrs Tucker herself. At any time of the day or night Mrs Tucker could have given a drug to Mrs Strood. That she did so once, and without Mrs Strood's knowledge, she has told us herself in evidence. That was on Dr Cartwright's instructions. But what she did on Dr Cartwright's instructions she could do again without his instructions. What she did once legitimately she could do a second time and feloniously—or through some compound of ignorance and excessive zeal. Understand me, members of the jury, I am not accusing Mrs Tucker of murdering her mistress or even of causing her death. I am accusing nobody. I am merely putting forward an hypothesis that is every whit as credible and as probable as the one submitted to you by my learned friend. I go further and say it is *more* credible, it is *more* probable. On the question of the time of death the medical evidence does not help us much—there is a wide margin for conjecture—but Dr Cartwright, who saw the body at eight o'clock, judged that death had taken place some seven or eight hours earlier. That takes us back to midnight. Now we know that Strood left the house at twenty minutes to eight (we have the unimpeachable word of Mr Nix for that); so for over four hours, from seven-forty to midnight, Mrs Tucker had the free run of the house. Her husband wouldn't be keeping a watch on her actions—why should he? It is her right, it might even be her duty, to enter Mrs Strood's bedroom from time to time; and no question would be made of that. She had given Mrs Strood one dose of oscitalin by stealth; and if she chose she could give her another. But how would she get possession of the material for this second dose? I don't know; nobody knows. But, if it comes to that, how would Strood get possession of such materials? Again nobody knows. The Prosecution doesn't know and makes no pretence of knowing. No evidence, I repeat, has been brought to show that he possessed either the chloral itself or the means of obtaining it. He had at most a three minutes opportunity of administering the poison, while Mrs Tucker had at least four hours. I say emphatically that there is no more evidence against Strood than against Mrs Tucker. And I do not accuse Mrs Tucker. If there is insufficient evidence to support a charge of murder against Mrs Tucker—and certainly the evidence *is* insufficient —there is equally insufficient evidence against Roderick Strood.

Perhaps you noticed that a few moments ago, in dealing with that crucial matter of the cup of malted milk, I used the word 'doctoring'? I suggested that what the Prosecution alleges against my client is that he was guilty of 'doctoring' the malted milk. Now I chose that colloquial way of expressing the matter because it happens to be a very accurate way. You will hear, from Strood's own lips, that he added nothing whatever to that malted milk; you will hear that on no occasion has he given drugs to his wife. But even according to the theory of the Prosecution, which he will repudiate, the amount of chloral alleged to have been given was not a fatal dose, and could in fact have been given in innocence, as was the oscitalin given by Dr Cartwright. And now it is my duty to set before you another hypothesis, namely that Mrs Strood herself, for reasons which we shall never know, had taken something before the doctor's arrival. Her manner was strange, said Mrs Tucker. The doctor was sent for without her knowledge, and, as it turned out, against her will: the doctor himself told us that. She asserted that he had been brought on a fool's errand. All this may suggest to you that Mrs Strood had special reasons for not wanting the attentions of a medical man. I do not stress the theory; I do not stress my suggestion about Mrs Tucker; I offer them as alternatives to the theory advanced by the Prosecution, a theory which, I suggest, has nothing in logic, and little in probability, to recommend it. You may still think that the Prosecution's story is a little more probable than these alternatives I am offering you. You *may* think so, though I do not believe you will. But even though you do think so, that is not enough. If there is doubt in your minds, reasonable doubt, it is your duty to acquit. It is not for me to prove any alternative theory: it is for the Crown to prove, beyond reasonable doubt, that the story they advance is true in fact, that it really happened so. My lord will tell you the law in this matter, which is that the burden of proof rests upon the Crown, and that Roderick Strood is innocent unless and until he is *proved* guilty.

Now, members of the jury, if I have carried you with me thus far, if I have succeeded in showing you that the theory of the Prosecution is unsupported, or very dubiously supported, by the facts elicited in evidence, you will perhaps be inclined to wonder how that theory was ever arrived at. A moment's reflection will resolve the puzzle. At

the beginning of my speech I characterized the case
for the Prosecution as a tissue of suspicion, conjecture, and false inference. A good deal has been
said, and a good deal more has been hinted, about
a lady in this case, an Austrian lady who happens
to be a distinguished musician. That Strood is
deeply devoted to this lady is not in question; and,
as you will hear, he blames himself bitterly for those
indiscretions which have led to her being mentioned in this case. For that, I dare to say, he
will never forgive himself. Again and again he
has insisted that, whatever happens, Fräulein
Andersch must not be put into the witness-box.
I know you will agree that the sentiment does
him honour, and I think you will equally agree
that I am doing no more than my plain duty in over-
riding his wishes on this point. As you will presently hear from his own lips, it was precisely
because he desired to protect this lady's name from
the least breath of scandal that he was proposing
to travel under the name of Roderick Williams
instead of as Roderick William Strood. The
Crown asks you to believe that because Roderick
Strood and Fräulein Andersch were devoted friends,
and possibly lovers, they had planned to marry each
other, and that Strood killed his wife in order to
be free to carry out that plan. This, they tell you,
is the motive; and my learned friend the Attorney-
General, if I remember him aright, assured you
with great confidence and satisfaction that if you

were in search of a motive for this alleged murder here was motive enough and more than enough. As to that, I will make two observations. The first observation is this: just as it is not incumbent upon the Prosecution in a case of alleged murder to prove motive, so no amount of motive can prove a murder. If there is no murder proved against the prisoner, if the evidence is insufficient to support such a charge against him, all the talk in the world about motive makes not a pennyworth of difference. All that has been said and hinted about Strood's 'motive' can have no weight whatever (subject to what my lord will tell you) if you are not satisfied, beyond all reasonable doubt, that the Crown is right on the main issue. That is my first observation on the question of so-called motive. My second observation is that this same motive, when subjected to a searching examination, proves to be as dubious as everything else in this dubious case. You will notice that I am taking you through this case step by step, and that at every turn of the road we find new doubt awaiting us. You will hear in evidence that it was not the intention of these two people to marry each other. To my mind that is a conclusive answer. But I will add this: that if they had intended to marry each other, there would still have been no sort of reason why Strood should have felt it necessary to commit the dastardly and dangerous crime of which he is accused. Why should he perpetrate such an

atrocity? And why should he take such a risk?
He is not precisely a rich man, but he is a man
very comfortably off, and the payment of alimony,
had it come to divorce, would have been no very
great burden upon him. Incidentally, the late
Mrs Strood had a little money of her own. But
that is all hypothetical, for the reason that I have
already given you, namely that this plan of marriage
between them has never existed outside the imagination of the learned gentlemen who are conducting
the Prosecution.

Now I will come to the evidence of Detective-
Sergeant Bolton. That was the witness, you will
remember, who spoke to meeting Strood at Southampton and who claimed to be able to quote, with
precise accuracy, the words uttered by Strood.
I was able to test his accuracy here in court, by
asking him to write down, from memory, the alternative form of words that I had suggested to him a
few moments before. The result of my little experiment was very illuminating indeed; for the
witness, in trying to reproduce my words, made
precisely the same mistake which, in my belief, he
made when trying to write down in his note-book
the words spoken by the prisoner. I have no
doubt that Bolton is an experienced and able
officer; and experience is a very good thing, but it
sometimes leads to a rather excessive self-confidence.
It was a small mistake he made, but a significant
one. 'My God! So I killed her!' That was

what the witness understood me to say, and that was what he wrote down. What I did say, as my lord told you, was: 'My God! So I've killed her!' I do not believe, members of the jury, that you will fall into the error of thinking that the difference is a trifling one, and of small account. It is a very significant difference indeed. If you, any one of you, had murdered a woman, you might exclaim in a moment of agitation: 'I killed her!' You would certainly not say: 'I have killed her.' A foreigner might say that, being unfamiliar with ordinary English idiom; but no Englishman would. On the other hand, if one of you gentlemen of the jury were conscious of having caused a great deal of mental pain and distress to your wife, and if you were suddenly informed of your wife's death, what more natural than that you should imagine, in your remorse, that she had been driven by your conduct to take her own life? And what more natural than that you should exclaim: 'My God! So I've killed her!' There is another thing I would point out to you in this connexion. I fancy that the Prosecution regards this alleged remark of Strood's as a very important part of their case. Yet even in the form—as I suggest the inaccurate and misleading form—in which Bolton first gave it to us, it is open to more than one interpretation. What does the exclamation 'My God!' suggest to you? It suggests horror, yes—but does it not equally suggest astonishment? Now a murderer cannot be astonished to learn of his victim's death, and the astonishment displayed by Strood at Southampton must therefore tell in his favour. And if the Prosecution says that the astonishment was insincere, was put on, I answer that they cannot have it both ways. A man acting innocence is a man on his guard, and though such a man might exclaim 'My God!' with an eye to the effect on his audience, the very last thing he would say is 'I killed her' or 'I 've killed her.' With great respect to my learned friend, I do not think he has strengthened his case by laying so much stress on that unguarded exclamation of the prisoner's. Whichever way you look at it, whichever of the two versions you adopt, it strongly suggests innocence in the man who uttered it.

Members of the jury, I shall not at this stage trouble you with a long speech. I shall have an opportunity of addressing you later on, after the evidence is concluded, and then, of course, I shall have to deal rather exhaustively with the evidence and to put my client's case squarely and finally before you. My learned friend will reply, and, finally, my lord will sum up. But before I make an end of these few remarks I will say something about the evidence of House, the barman at the Zenith Hotel, Southampton. I do not know what impression that witness made on you, members of the jury, but I will say that during some twenty-five years' experience as an advocate in His Majesty's

Courts of Justice I have never listened to evidence so unsatisfactory, so unconvincing, never listened to so palpable a farrago of guesswork and fancy. I will put it more strongly than that and say that it will surprise me if you can persuade yourselves to believe a word of that evidence. This man House asserted . . . [*analysis of House's evidence omitted*]. Moreover, Fräulein Andersch, of her own free will, and to the neglect of her professional interests —for she has contracts in America which it will now be impossible for her to fulfil—this lady, I say, will go into the witness-box, and you will hear from her own lips. . . .

§ 27

THE WOMAN ANDERSCH

ELISABETH FRIEDA ANDERSCH, examined for the Defence by MR RONALD YOUNG: I am an Austrian subject, by profession a pianist. I first met the prisoner at Heidelberg, in the spring of this year. I came to England in July and have been here ever since. I do not speak English so very well, but I understand it without difficulty.

Can you recall the events of October the 31st?— Perfectly well.

On the evening of that day did you dine with Mr Strood at the Zenith Hotel, Southampton?—Yes.

When the meal was finished did he leave you for a moment or two?—Yes.

Will you tell us more about that?—He wished for some brandy and the waiter was gone away. If he ring the bell the waiter will come back, but he says No, he will himself go for the brandy. He asks me if he shall bring to me also some brandy, but I did not want some.

When he came back, had he the brandy with him?—Yes.

About what time was it when he rejoined you in the dining-room?—It was nine o'clock.

Exactly nine o'clock?—The clock in the dining-room sounded nine times. And my watch said also nine o'clock.

How long, after that, did you and Mr Strood remain in the dining-room?—A half-hour. A little more.

We know that at nine o'clock a message was broadcast by radio and received by a receiving-set that stood in the lounge-bar. Now a witness has declared that Mr Strood was standing in the bar when that message came over?—At nine o'clock he was with me in the dining-room.

When you are in the dining-room, is it possible to hear voices from the lounge-bar?—I think not.

Even when the door is open?—If the door is open, one should know that people are talking and laughing, yes. But what is said, no.

It would be impossible to distinguish words at

that distance?—If you listen very carefully, and the words are very loud, perhaps you hear a word or two. But I think not.

When Mr Strood rejoined you in the dining-room at nine o'clock, did you notice anything unusual in his manner?—No.

We have heard that when you and Mr Strood left the hotel, Mr Strood was accosted by a plain-clothes police officer. Did you hear the conversation that took place between them?—Yes.

Did you hear the officer say that Mrs Strood was dead?—Yes.

Did you hear your friend say 'My God!'?—Yes.

Did you hear him say 'My God! I 've killed her!' or anything like that?—No.

If you *had* heard him say such a thing, would it have greatly surprised you?—No.

Will you explain why?—He is a very good man, very strict. He has sometimes been afraid that his wife should injure herself or take her own life, in anger, you understand. He has said that if such a thing should happen, he should feel to blame himself, he should feel that he had killed her.

The police-officer has said that in his presence Mr Strood exchanged some words with you in a foreign language. Would you tell us the substance of what was said?—Mr Strood tells me not to wait, but to go to the ship. He was very anxious that I must go. But I said No. I wished to stay with him in his trouble. I said also that the man, the officer, was not a good friend.

One last question, Fräulein Andersch. Have you ever had the intention of marrying Mr Strood? —No.

Would you have married him if he had been free to marry?—No.

And had you made that clear to him?—Perfectly. He knows that I have no time for marriage.

Cross-examined by MR TUFNELL: You have told my learned friend that you have no time for marriage. What does that mean?—I am an artist. That is my career.

You have no time for marriage, but you have time to entice a married man from his duty?— Please?

I am suggesting that you have time to alienate a man's affections from his wife?—

MR HARCOMBE: I strongly object to that question. It is not an honest question.

MR TUFNELL: Am I to understand that my learned friend accuses me of dishonesty?

MR HARCOMBE: My learned friend may understand what he pleases. I submit, my lord, that insinuations against the moral character of this lady cannot help the case for the Prosecution. They are entirely gratuitous. The lady is a distinguished visitor to this country and has come forward, in the interests of justice, to give evidence. She is entitled——

Mr Justice Sarum: You will have an opportunity of making a speech later on, Mr Harcombe. [*To Mr Tufnell*] Do these questions you are putting bear upon the issue?

Mr Tufnell: I am attacking the witness's credibility, my lord.

Mr Justice Sarum: Members of the jury, you must be at great pains to remember that this is not a court of morals, and that you are not to allow any moral disapproval to colour your judgement on matters of fact. [*To Mr Tufnell*]: You may proceed.

Mr Tufnell: Thank you, my lord. I will not, however, press that particular question. Fräulein Andersch, am I right in saying that you are on terms of the greatest intimacy with the prisoner?—Of course.

And that you and he are in fact lovers?—Of course.

You are very fond of him?—Yes.

You would do anything to help him?—I would do anything I could. But I would not marry, no.

Short of marriage, you would do anything to help him?—If he needed my help, naturally. Is not that right? I do not understand.

Let me make myself clearer. The prisoner is in grave danger. He is in danger of his life. Now you, since you love him, would do anything, would you not, to protect him, to save his life?—I would do anything I could.

You would do or say anything?—It is not necessary to say anything except the truth.

But if you thought it necessary, would you hesitate to say what was not true, if your lover's life were in danger?—It is not necessary. I have told the truth.

MR JUSTICE SARUM: That is a proper answer. I do not think, Mr Tufnell, that I can say as much for the question. What the witness thinks she would do in hypothetical circumstances is altogether too remote a speculation.

MR TUFNELL: As your lordship pleases. [*Continuing cross-examination*] I suggest to you that at some time during your relationship with the prisoner you have allowed him to believe that you would be willing to marry him if he were free to marry?—It is not so.

There is such a thing as coquetry, is there not? I mean this: that though you may have told him that marriage was out of the question, you cannot be sure that he took your statement seriously?—We are serious people, both. He knew very well.

But may he not have thought that you would change your mind, once the obstacle to marriage was removed?—You must ask him. I do not think so.

As a married man, having to keep up appearances, he could not see you as often as he wished?—No.

Did he complain that the situation was a difficult one?—No.

Isn't that rather extraordinary?—We are not children. We had other things to talk about.

Did he not say that he wished to spend more time with you?—He has said so.

Did he ever say that he wished he need never leave you?—Of course.

Why 'of course'?—When one is in love one says such things, is it not so?

If he had been unmarried, he need never have left you. That is so, isn't it?—No.

What was there to prevent his being always with you except the existence of his wife?—There was his work.

Yes. You are right. But his work occupies him only so many hours a day. There was nothing to prevent his living with you continuously, was there?—Yes.

What was it?—My work. My temperament. I do not want a man always with me. I am not the good wife.

[Further evidence for the Defence showed that the mother of Daphne Strood had died of heart disease at the age of fifty-six, a sworn copy of the death-certificate being produced. The prisoner, RODERICK WILLIAM STROOD, was then called into the witness-box.]

§ 28

THE PRISONER'S STORY

RODERICK WILLIAM STROOD, prisoner, on oath, examined for the Defence by MR HARCOMBE: I am a member of a firm of architects. I am thirty-four years old. In 1914 I was a student at Heidelberg University. I was in England when the war broke out. In January 1915 I joined the army as a private and served with the Wessex Division. In November of the same year I was commissioned in the field. After my demobilization in May 1919, I went up to Cambridge, and in 1922 I took my degree. I was married in June 1924 and lived happily with my wife. There were no children of the marriage: this was a disappointment to me. In May of this present year I went on a visit to Heidelberg. There I met Fräulein Andersch, and fell in love with her. On returning to England I explained the situation to my wife, and our relations became very strained. We were both quick-tempered and on one or two occasions we lost our tempers and both of us said things we did not mean. We agreed that a temporary separation would be best for both of us.

Was there any question of divorce at that time?— No. I did not know whether I wanted a divorce, and my wife did not wish to divorce me. I was pulled both ways. I was in a state of indecision.

My wife naturally found that very exasperating. We exasperated each other. But I think we both hoped that a disaster might be avoided. We fancied that if we left the problem alone for a while, it would work itself out. That was why we agreed to a temporary separation.

During the period of separation did you lose touch with your wife?—Not at all. We were in constant communication.

Were you at all anxious about her?—In a way, yes. She was very much on my mind.

Was your wife an impetuous woman?—Yes.

Was she angry and distressed by what was happening?—Yes.

During those conversations you had with her on the subject, when (as you have told us) tempers were lost on both sides, did she ever threaten to take her own life?—Yes.

Were you alarmed by that threat?—That's not an easy question to answer. In a way I didn't take it seriously, because I knew she was speaking in anger. I thought she was trying to frighten me. But sometimes, when I remembered it afterwards, I had moments of great anxiety.

Did you ultimately return to your wife?—Yes.

There was a reconciliation?—Yes. That was early in September.

Now you have heard the evidence of Mrs Tucker, and you know that she claims to have overheard part of a conversation which she alleges took place between you and your wife at the breakfast-table, on the morning of October the 20th?—Yes.

Do you agree that Mrs Tucker's version of that conversation is correct?—No.

Will you tell the Court, in your own way, what did in fact occur?—We were at breakfast. Mrs Tucker was looking after us because Tucker was in bed with a cold. My wife had engaged herself to go to a theatre that evening with an old friend of ours. But she suddenly told me that she was going to cancel the engagement so that she and I could spend the evening at home. I was surprised, and, I suppose, rather nettled, because, supposing that she would be out, I had made another engagement for myself. We had some dispute about it and we were both out of temper. In the course of our argument—or quarrel, if you like—my wife suddenly said she was pregnant. This gave me a shock of surprise, because we had always wanted children and for years had failed to have any. We had been married eight years. Then my wife said she had deceived me all those years.

Will you state a little more precisely what she said?—Yes. When I say she told me she had deceived me, I mean that she gave me to understand that she had consistently taken steps, without my knowledge, to prevent our having a child. I was very angry and I said that she had cheated me. I remember using the word 'cheated'. But I certainly did not say what Mrs Tucker attributes to me. I don't remember exactly what Mrs Tucker's version was, but I know it was a damned lie.

Or shall we say 'a gross distortion'?—A very gross distortion. But I should like to explain further about this point. At the time I believed what my wife said, about cheating me, as I called it. But I very soon realized that she wasn't speaking the truth. She only said what she did because she was angry, and wanted to hurt me. I'm quite sure now that there was no more in it than that. We had always been good friends, and I know she was always loyal. All the disloyalty was on my side.

Before this dispute or quarrel reached its climax, did Mrs Tucker enter the room?—Yes. She came in answer to the bell. My wife asked her to bring some fresh coffee, and she answered my wife insolently, in my opinion. I told her as much.

You rebuked her?—Yes. Perhaps more harshly than the occasion warranted. I don't know.

Perhaps that did not make her like you any the better?—Probably not.

Now I will ask you to recall the events of October the 30th. You arrived home from your office that day at about half-past six, I believe?—About then, I suppose.

Your wife was not then downstairs, but you saw Mrs Tucker, did you not?—Yes.

And she told you?—She told me my wife was feeling a little feverish and had gone to bed.

Did you then go upstairs to see your wife?—Yes.

And did you remain with her till about a quarter-past seven?—No. Mrs Tucker is wrong there. What happened was that I spent five or six minutes with my wife and then went to my bedroom to pack a suitcase. When that job was finished I went back to my wife. I dare say it was a quarter-past seven when I finally left her. I don't remember.

What impression did you form of your wife's condition?—She said she wasn't at all ill, and I didn't think she looked ill. She was a little excited, I thought.

Had you already, at that time, formed the intention of going to America?—I had it in mind.

You knew that Fräulein Andersch was sailing on October the 31st, and you had conceived the notion of travelling with her?—Yes.

Did your wife know of this plan?—I told her about it that evening. I was still a little undecided, and her being not quite well made me more undecided.

Did your wife raise any objection to the plan? —No. She was very generous about it. She even urged me to go.

She urged you to go?—Yes.

Had you already obtained a passport in the name of Roderick Williams?—Yes.

Will you explain why you wished to travel as Roderick Williams instead of in your own name?— I thought it possible that my name had already been coupled with that of Fräulein Andersch. We had been as discreet as possible, but I couldn't be sure that we had succeeded in keeping our relationship a secret. And I thought that if it became known that we were on the boat together she would be refused admission by the American authorities.

Would such an event have meant a serious loss to her, both in money and reputation?—It would have been a disaster.

After leaving your wife, did you go down stairs and encounter Mrs Tucker on her way to your wife's bedroom with the malted milk?—Yes.

I do not wish my learned friend to say I am leading you, so will you tell the Court what occurred in connexion with this cup of malted milk?—When Mrs Tucker was passing through the hall, carrying the stuff on a tray, I encountered her and sent her back for biscuits. She left the tray on the hall-table.

Was that at your request? Or with your help?— No. It was the obvious thing to do. She put the tray down and went back to the kitchen. I did not touch the tray.

In order to save my learned friend trouble, I am going to ask you the crucial question in this case. Did you add chloral to that malted milk?—No.

Did you add anything whatever to it?—No.

Have you at any time, so far as your knowledge goes, administered chloral to your wife?—No.

On October the 31st you were in Southampton,

287

in the company of Fräulein Andersch, and you had dinner with her at the Zenith Hotel?—Yes.

You have heard that a certain message was broadcast at nine o'clock, and received by a receiving-set in the lounge-bar of that hotel. What can you tell us about that?—I know nothing about that but what I have heard in this court and in the coroner's court. I did not hear the message. I was not within hearing distance of the loudspeaker. I was with Fräulein Andersch in the dining-room.

Will you now tell us about your encounter with Detective - Sergeant Bolton outside the hotel?— What am I to tell you? His evidence was not far wrong. My first thought was that he was some kind of tout. Then the thought of blackmail crossed my mind. That is why my first answers to him were evasive. I was taken by surprise.

When he said he had news for you, did you say, as has been alleged: 'Is it about my wife?'— I believe so.

Was the possibility of blackmail in your mind when you said that?—Vaguely, yes. And also I had a sudden feeling of alarm about my wife.

Because you thought she was more ill than she had admitted, or for what reason?—It is difficult to say what I thought. I didn't formulate my thoughts. I merely felt uneasy. I think it was already in my mind that she might have taken something.

Taken something?—Yes, suicidally.

And when the officer said that she was dead, was that notion strengthened in your mind?—It was a horrible shock. I couldn't believe it, if you know what I mean. But yes, I thought it must be suicide. And everything seemed to fit in with suicide.

And did you——?

MR JUSTICE SARUM: Just a moment, Mr Harcombe. I should like to hear the prisoner amplify that remark: that everything seemed to fit in with suicide.

THE PRISONER: She had seemed a little excited, my lord. Almost gay. There was a—a sort of happiness, as though nothing could hurt her any more. And when I looked back I felt that it must have been a false gaiety, consistent with a resolve to commit suicide. I don't know if I can make myself clear.

MR HARCOMBE [*continuing examination*]: At this point you said something to the police-officer, did you not? Can you give us the exact words?—Not the exact words. I know what I meant. I know what I felt. I certainly didn't say: 'I killed her'. I may have said: 'So I 've killed her!' because that was exactly what I was feeling.

You must try to be a little more explicit. What were you feeling?—I was feeling guilty of her death. I felt like a murderer.

You are speaking in a metaphorical sense?—

Yes, of course. What I mean is that I thought I had asked too much of her, that she had broken down under the strain of those months and had taken her own life.

At the beginning of this examination, in answer to a question of mine, you said you had taken your degree at Cambridge. What was that degree?—The usual thing. An honours degree in arts.

That is to say, you are a Bachelor of Arts?—Yes.

In what subjects did you read, for the purposes of that degree?—History and modern languages.

Did you read any science?—No.

Have you any knowledge of science? Of physics or chemistry, for example?—No.

You learned some rudiments of those subjects at school, no doubt?—I learned very little of them.

And you have not studied them since?—No.

So far as you remember, when did you last have a textbook on chemistry in your hand?—I suppose about sixteen years ago, when I was last at school.

§ 29

THE PRISONER CROSS-EXAMINED

Roderick William Strood, cross-examined for the Crown by Sir John Buckhorn, His Majesty's Attorney-General: You have told my learned friend that you and your wife were reconciled early in September, and that you resumed your life with her?—Yes.

Are we to understand that the differences between you were settled?—Yes.

That means, presumably, that you had promised to discontinue your intrigue with Fräulein Andersch?—No.

That was one of the conditions of your agreement with your wife, was it not?—It was not.

During that period of separation from your wife, did you frequently visit Fräulein Andersch as her lover?—

MR JUSTICE SARUM [*to the* PRISONER]: You are not bound to answer that question, but you may do so if you wish.

THE PRISONER: I do not mind answering it, my lord. The answer is Yes.

ATTORNEY-GENERAL [*continuing cross-examination*]: And when you returned to your wife, to live with her as her husband, was it not understood that such visits would cease? Whether anything was said on the point or not, was it not understood?—No.

Was the contrary understood? Was it understood between your wife and you that you would continue to commit adultery with Fräulein Andersch, at your whim and pleasure?—Yes.

Are you asking my lord and the jury to believe that your wife condoned your misconduct, withdrew her objection to it?—I have answered the question. I have nothing to add to my answer.

Was it merely a tacit understanding between you and your wife that you should be free to continue in your adulterous courses, or was it explicitly agreed?—It was explicitly agreed.

Was your wife quite happy and friendly about it?—She was quite friendly.

And happy?—She did her best to make me believe so.

And did you believe so?—Does it matter?

You are to answer my questions, not to ask questions of me. Did you believe so?—Sometimes I believed so. Sometimes I doubted. It was a difficult situation.

Did this situation in fact exist, this fantastic situation in which a wife tolerates her husband's habitual infidelity? Did it in fact exist, or is it an invention of your fertile imagination?—I have already told you.

Will you nevertheless answer my question?—I cannot answer meaningless questions. If you are asking me whether I am a liar or not, I say I am not a liar. I have told you the truth.

You had a nice friendly arrangement with your wife whereby you were free to resort to your mistress as often as you pleased, and no questions asked?—If you choose to put it that way, yes.

Is it not an accurate way of putting it?—Oh, yes. Yes.

It was early in September that this arrangement was entered into?—Yes.

Did you know that your wife, during October, engaged a private detective to observe and report your movements?—No.

Are you aware of the fact now?—It may be so. I don't know.

Is that fact consistent with your story of this extraordinary toleration on your wife's part?—My lord, is it necessary for me to answer questions of that kind?

MR JUSTICE SARUM: It is not an unreasonable question. In your own interests I think you must answer it.

ATTORNEY-GENERAL [continuing cross-examination]: Let me help you, if I can, by altering the form of the question. If, as you have just told us, your wife was perfectly willing that you should visit Fräulein Andersch, is it not extraordinary that she should have caused you to be shadowed in this way?—Yes.

You see for yourself that it makes your story the harder to believe, don't you?—My story is true, all the same.

So you have said. But you will admit, perhaps, that it is an unlikely story?—

MR JUSTICE SARUM: That is surely a question for the jury, Sir John. Not for the prisoner.

ATTORNEY-GENERAL: Quite so, my lord. And I fancy they will know how to answer it. [Continuing cross-examination] Now you have admitted, in answer to my learned friend, that you exchanged angry words with your wife on the morning of October the 20th. The quarrel began by your wife telling you that she was with child, did it not?—No.

MR JUSTICE SARUM [*reading from his notes*]: 'In the course of our argument or quarrel my wife suddenly said she was pregnant.'

ATTORNEY-GENERAL: The mistake is mine. I am obliged to your lordship. [*Continuing cross-examination*] But I am right, am I not, in saying that you were displeased by this piece of information?—I was astonished.

I asked if you were not displeased?—There was no question of being pleased or not pleased. I was merely surprised.

Come, Mr Strood. You must surely know whether you were pleased or not by the information that you were likely to become a father?—I don't know. My emotions were mixed.

The remark with which you greeted the news hardly suggests acute pleasure, does it?—I don't know what you are alluding to.

When your wife confided that secret hope to you, your first words, I believe, were: 'Well, I'm damned!'?—Were they?

A witness has said so. Do you deny it?—If Mrs Tucker said so, it is more likely to be false than true.

Will you be good enough to answer the question?—I may have said: 'Well, I'm damned!' That only bears out what I have just told you. I was surprised.

But not pleased?—The information was blurted

out in the middle of a dispute about something quite different.

You were disconcerted?—Well, yes.

It was awkward that your wife should be an expectant mother when you were on the point of leaving her for another woman, was it not?—I was not on the point of leaving her.

It would have looked so bad, wouldn't it?—The question does not arise.

It would have made a disagreeable story in the Divorce Court, would it not? To say nothing of the extra provision that would have to be made on account of the child?—Those questions don't arise either.

Are you sure that in fact they did not arise in your own mind?—Quite sure.

That was October the 20th, ten days before your wife's death. Now it has been stated in evidence that on the 30th, the day on which you last saw her alive, she was suffering from lack of sleep. Were you aware of that sleeplessness?—Yes.

Do you know what caused it?—We were both of us worried and unhappy.

About what?—About the situation.

The matrimonial situation? Your personal relationship to each other?—Yes.

The question whether your marriage should go on or be brought to an end?—Not quite that.

The question of your relationship with Fräulein Andersch?—Yes. That of course was part of it.

But didn't that involve the other question, of your marriage, and whether it would survive or crash?—I suppose it did.

And therefore the possibility of a final break, and perhaps of divorce, must have entered your mind?—It wasn't so definite as that. It was just a general unhappiness and indecision.

Indecision as to what? As to whether to make a final break with your wife or not?—I felt a final break with my wife to be impossible.

There was no indecision on that score then. Was it perhaps the question of a final break with Fräulein Andersch that you were undecided about? —That seemed impossible too.

I see. There were two possible courses open to you, and both seemed impossible. Is that it? I am not being ironical; I am trying to understand you. Two courses were in fact possible, but you could not make up your mind to either. Is that a fair way of putting it?—Yes.

Did it never occur to you that the death of one of the two women concerned would solve the problem for you?—No.

Do not misunderstand me, Mr Strood. I am not suggesting that the idea of such an event was not painful to you. But it would, wouldn't it, have cut the Gordian knot for you?—The idea did not occur to me.

It never occurred to you to say to yourself: 'If I were a single man, or if I were a widower, I could marry the woman I love'?—There was no question of marriage.

There was, however, a question of your giving up either your wife or your mistress?—In a sense, yes. But the question wasn't definitely in my mind.

Whatever questions were in your mind, and in your wife's mind, I suppose you discussed them with her during those last ten days?—No.

Why was that?—We were unhappy. We talked very little.

Do you mean you were not on speaking terms?—We were not on comfortable terms.

The quarrel of October the 20th still rankled?—Yes.

There was, in fact, hostility between you?—Misery rather than hostility.

It was during those ten days that you planned to go to America with Fräulein Andersch, was it not?—I was contemplating the possibility.

Wouldn't it be fair to say you planned it?—It was hardly as definite as that.

But you don't deny that you applied for and obtained a passport in a false name during that period?—No.

That suggests planning, doesn't it?—I should call it providing for a contingency.

Did you also pack some clothes, mainly new clothes, into a new cabin-trunk, bought for the purpose, and did you deposit that trunk in the Left Luggage Office of a certain London railway terminus?—Yes.

And did you, in your agitation, or for some reason of your own, neglect to reclaim that trunk when, on October the 31st, you travelled to Southampton *en route* for America?—I forgot it, yes. But not because of agitation.

You were perfectly calm and collected, yet you forgot the main part of your luggage?—Yes. I often forget things. I 'm an absent-minded person.

You obtained a false passport, and you packed and deposited a trunk. Is that your idea of providing for a mere contingency?—Yes.

When you realized that your wife was suffering from insomnia, did you suggest a sleeping-draught? —I don't remember doing so.

It would have been a natural suggestion, wouldn't it?—I may have suggested it. I don't remember.

Did you suggest her consulting Dr Cartwright and getting a prescription from him?—I think not.

Try to remember. Perhaps on the morning of October the 30th, or perhaps on some previous day, did you not urge her to consult Dr Cartwright?— I can't remember doing so.

Were you indifferent to the state of your wife's health?—No.

You knew she was suffering from insomnia?— Yes.

Then I must ask you again: Did you not feel it your duty to urge her to consult her medical man, and did you not in fact do so?—No.

A moment ago, you couldn't remember?—I still can't remember.

You can't remember that you did?—No.

Can you swear that you didn't?—I swear that I can't remember doing so.

You knew that on a previous occasion Dr Cartwright had prescribed oscitalin for your wife?—No.

You didn't know he had given her a sleeping-draught on a previous occasion, when she was complaining of neuritis?—A sleeping-draught, yes. But I knew nothing about what it contained.

Do you not remember saying to your wife: 'Why not get Cartwright to give you another dose of oscitalin?' or words to that effect?—No. I couldn't have said that. I knew nothing about his having given her oscitalin.

I suggest to you that you knew perfectly well.—It is not so. And you have no evidence for your statement.

During those last ten days you and your wife were, to use your own phrase, on uncomfortable terms. May I take it that she was bitterly resenting your continued visits to Fräulein Andersch?—Yes.

Yet in answer to my learned friend you said that your wife made no objection to your going off to America with the lady, that in fact she urged you to do so?—Yes. That was on the last day. Her attitude had changed.

Are you asking us to believe that in the morning

she was bitterly resenting your adultery and in the evening was urging you to it?—In effect, yes.

What do you mean by 'in effect'?—I mean that there is more in it than what you are pleased to call 'adultery'.

Indeed?—Quite apart from all that, my wife thought it would be a good thing for us both if I went away for a while.

A good thing for whom?—For herself and me. For our future relationship. For our marriage.

She thought it would be good for your marriage for you to dishonour your marriage?—Oh, if you like.

It is not a question of what I like, Mr Strood. It is a question of what is true. Have you ever practised the art of fiction?—No.

But you are a pretty good actor, I believe?—Nothing of the kind.

When you were an undergraduate did you not distinguish yourself in amateur theatricals?—I took part in them.

I have here a copy of a Cambridge weekly journal of that time. Would you like me to read what is said about your abilities as a character-actor?—If it pleases you.

MR JUSTICE SARUM: It does not please *me*, Sir John.

ATTORNEY-GENERAL: Quite so, my lord. It is quite unnecessary, I agree. [*Continuing cross-examination*] You booked your passage to America on the morning of October the 31st?—Yes.

You do not deny that it was your intention to sail with the *Mercatoria*?—I do not deny it.

You had come to a definite decision on the point?—I definitely decided to go after that talk with my wife.

When you left your wife did you feel any sort of anxiety about her?—Yes.

You left her, however, to go to another woman that very night?—Yes. With her consent.

By next morning, I take it, your anxiety concerning your wife had magically disappeared?—No.

You still had her welfare at heart?—Yes.

Did you take any steps to communicate with her or with your household, in order to find out whether she had had a good night?—No.

Not so much as a telephone call?—No.

Did you inform your partner, Mr Cradock, that you were leaving that day for America?—I wired that I should not be coming that day and that a letter would follow.

Was it not very extraordinary behaviour on your part: to absent yourself for an indefinite period and without a word to your partner except this enigmatic telegram?—Very extraordinary.

You are content to leave it at that?—Yes.

There's one little point I want you to clear up for me concerning what happened at the hotel at Southampton. You said that at nine o'clock you were with Fräulein Andersch in the dining-room?—Yes.

What makes you so sure?—I don't understand.

You do not deny going into the lounge-bar that evening to get brandy?—No.

At what time was that?—It must have been a minute or two before nine, since the dining-room clock was striking nine when I got back to Fräulein Andersch.

You heard Fräulein Andersch say in evidence that the clock was striking nine?—Yes.

Until you heard what she had to say about it, you did not remember, did you, that the clock was striking at the very moment of your entry?—I really don't know.

Then you are unable to confirm her evidence on that point?—It really doesn't matter.

Very well. Now a moment or two ago you said that when you left your wife for the last time, on the fatal night, you were in a state of anxiety about her?—Yes.

Was that why you slammed the door when you left her?—I did not slam the door.

You have heard Mrs Tucker's evidence?—Yes.

You have heard her say that she heard the bedroom door slam?—Yes.

Do you tell us that she was lying?—Not exactly.

What do you mean by that?—Precisely what I say.

MR JUSTICE SARUM: You must refrain from giving pert answers to learned counsel's questions. You will gain nothing by heat.—I am sorry, my lord.

MR JUSTICE SARUM: I am speaking in your own interest. Now let us get this point clear. Did you slam the door of your wife's bedroom on leaving her?—Not intentionally.

MR JUSTICE SARUM: 'I slammed the door, but not intentionally.' Would that be a fair way of putting it?—Yes, my lord.

MR JUSTICE SARUM: Did the door slip out of your hand?—I don't think so.

MR JUSTICE SARUM: Then what happened? Give me your explanation in your own way.—I was disturbed. I was in an emotional state. Nervous, too. I tried to shut the door quietly. But I had a sort of nightmare feeling. It was like slow motion. It was as though I wasn't moving the door at all. And then I gave it a sort of jerk, and it slammed.

ATTORNEY-GENERAL [*continuing cross-examination*]: You have just told my lord that you were in a disturbed and nervous state. Can you account for that state?—I had just said good-bye to my wife. I was affected by her changed attitude.

Were you by any chance contemplating giving your wife something in her cup of malted milk, a sleeping-draught for example?—No.

Was that why you were agitated?—There is no sense in that question, since I have said No to the previous question.

You knew she was suffering from sleeplessness? —I have said so.

303

But the idea of a sleeping-draught never entered your head?—No.

Detective-Sergeant Bolton has told us that on hearing of your wife's death you said: 'Was it the sleeping-draught?' Did you say that?—Very possibly.

You did not know that a sleeping-draught had been given, yet almost your first words on hearing of the death were: 'The sleeping-draught'?—If you like.

You did not know that a sleeping-draught had been given?—No.

Nor prescribed?—No.

Mrs Tucker has sworn to having told you that the doctor had prescribed a sleeping-draught, has she not?—Has she?

You were present when she gave her evidence?— Yes. Now you mention it, I remember she said that in evidence.

You remember her evidence. Do you also remember her telling you on the evening of October the 30th, that the doctor had brought round a sleeping-draught?—No. If she said that, I could not have heard her.

She said it, but you did not hear her. Is that your answer?—She may have said it. I didn't hear her say it. I tell you I didn't hear her say it.

Why are you so emphatic on the point? If you are an innocent man it doesn't matter, does it, whether you knew or not?—Then why do you keep asking me about it?

Of course you could not have given chloral to your wife with an innocent intention if you had known that she was having oscitalin from another source, could you?—I did not give her chloral.

Is that why you are so emphatic on the point?— I am emphatic because you keep asking me the same question over and over again. That's all.

Re-examined by MR HARCOMBE: Was it a very unusual thing for you to be away from your office in November?—No.

Will you explain that?—I have made rather a habit of avoiding the beginning of the London winter. For the last few years I have taken holidays then either in the west of England, or in the south of France.

May we take it for granted that on previous occasions such holidays had been prearranged with Mr Cradock, your partner?—Yes.

Had you some special reason for not caring to broach the subject with Mr Cradock?—Yes, I was hideously self-conscious about the whole thing. I knew he would disapprove of what I was doing, and I couldn't bear the idea of discussing it with him. I was weak and cowardly.

You realize now that you acted unwisely and perhaps inconsiderately?—I acted like an hysterical fool. Like a baby.

Did you write a letter of explanation and apology to Mr Cradock?—Yes.

When my learned friend asked you if you were in a position to corroborate Fräulein Andersch's statement about the striking clock, you answered: 'It really doesn't matter'. I think it would be helpful to the jury if you explained what you meant by that answer. Will you try?—I meant this: that it really doesn't matter whether or not I noticed the clock striking, so long as Fräulein Andersch did.

You mean that the really material point is that you were not in the lounge-bar at nine o'clock, and therefore couldn't have heard the broadcast message concerning your wife?—Exactly.

And whether you could have or couldn't have, in point of plain fact you did *not* hear it. Is that so?—That is so.

My learned friend has been at pains to elicit from you (*a*) that you were anxious about your wife when you left her, (*b*) that you did not make any inquiry about her next morning. He did not, however, ask you to explain the superficial discrepancy. I think the jury would like to hear an explanation.—When I said I was anxious, I didn't mean anxious about her physical condition. I meant anxious about her state of mind, her happiness.

A happiness which, as I understood you, was a new-found happiness?—Yes.

A matter which could hardly be discussed very fruitfully on the telephone?—Exactly.

Again, my learned friend has professed to find

matter for wonder in the fact that though you knew your wife lacked sleep you never thought of suggesting a sleeping-draught?—She had been worrying and therefore couldn't sleep. But that day she seemed to be different. She seemed to have got rid of the burden. So I never doubted that she would get a good night's rest.

Further cross-examination by the ATTORNEY-GENERAL: You have said that you wrote a letter to Mr Cradock explaining and apologizing. Would it surprise you to learn that Mr Cradock has never received that letter?—No. I didn't post the letter.

You didn't post the letter?—I had it with me at Southampton. I intended to post it before we sailed.

Can you produce that letter?—No, I destroyed it.

Did you in fact ever write such a letter?—Yes.

Were you not in fact anxious that no one should know of your movements and your destination?—No.

Were you not in fact fleeing from justice?—No.

§ 30

MR JUSTICE SARUM

COUNSEL for the Defence and Counsel for the Prosecution having finally addressed the jury, after luncheon on the fourth day MR JUSTICE SARUM began his summing-up. After a detailed review of the evidence the learned Judge said:

Before leaving this grave matter in your hands, before sending you away to consider your verdict and to discharge the duty that rests upon you, I will recapitulate what I said to you at the beginning of this summing-up. The evidence in this case is what is known as circumstantial evidence. Now circumstantial evidence is not necessarily bad or inconclusive evidence. Many men have been convicted, and rightly convicted, on circumstantial evidence; indeed, in premeditated and carefully planned murder, direct evidence, such as that of an eye-witness, is more than we can reasonably expect. Circumstantial evidence may be good and sufficient, but it is so only if it is unequivocal: that is, if it points unmistakably to one conclusion, to the exclusion of others. It is not enough that it should establish a probability: it must also exclude alternative theories: by which I mean, of course, other reasonable theories. It would be wrong of you to take refuge in merely fantastic suppositions, on the grounds that all things are possible: it would be equally wrong of you to convict on the strength of a mere probability. No man should be convicted of murder, or indeed of any crime, merely on probabilities, unless they are so strong as to amount to a practical certainty. You cannot, in such a case as this, look for the kind of absolute proof that you get in the case of a mathematical proposition, such as the proposition that two and two make four. You cannot get mathematical certainty, and it would be weak and frivolous to expect it. What I call reasonable certainty, practical certainty, is another matter, and if that is lacking in your minds you cannot convict. You are the judges of the facts, not I: I am here only to give you the law, and to help you, if I can, to look fairly and squarely at all the evidence. It is for you to sift that evidence and to decide whether or not the case against the accused is proved beyond reasonable doubt. That, I must remind you, is the question, and ultimately it is the only question. Various considerations may enter in, but that alone is the question you must answer. Let me be more explicit on this point. It has been suggested to you by the Defence that this may be a case not of murder at all, that it may be a case either of suicide or of accidental death. I make no comment on that beyond saying that if, on the facts presented to you, you think there is reasonable warrant for such a doubt, you are entitled so to think, and the

case against the prisoner must break down: that is
obvious enough. If on the other hand you are
convinced that murder has been done, you will then
have to ask, not 'Who committed this murder?'
—that is not the question before you—but 'Did
the prisoner do it?' or rather, to put it more
accurately: 'Is it proved beyond reasonable doubt
that the prisoner did it?' The burden of proof
is upon the Prosecution. You may find it difficult
to think that the prisoner did not do it; you may,
at the same time, find it difficult to think that he
did do it; and if any reasonable doubt exists in
your minds the prisoner is entitled to the benefit
of it. You, I repeat, are the only judges of fact.
You have heard the evidence and you have heard
the speeches of learned counsel on both sides. It
is by the evidence that you must judge. If anything has been said by way of argument or exhortation which is not warranted by the evidence, you
must disregard it; and if I myself, in my survey
of the evidence, have in your view made too much
or too little of any matter, well, it is your view,
your considered view, that must prevail.

I have warned you, and I warn you again, that
you must be very much on your guard against
allowing moral considerations to affect your judgement on points of fact. I do not mean, however,
that the behaviour of the prisoner, in respect of
his wife and in respect of the other woman in the
case, is not to be taken into consideration in arriving

at your verdict. I have no doubt that some of you, perhaps all of you, feel very strongly indeed about those matters; it may be that I feel very strongly about them; but it is your duty, as it is mine, to put such feelings on one side. The prisoner is a confessed adulterer, and you may think that there was something uncommonly casual in his manner of confessing to that wickedness and in the manner in which the woman who was his paramour confessed to it. But adultery is not murder, and many a man has committed the one who would never dream of committing the other. Sexual licence, unfortunately, is no rare thing in our modern world; and a cynical disregard of sexual morality does not by any means involve a disregard of the sanctity of human life, still less a disposition to murder. On the other hand there is no doubt that a guilty sexual passion has time and again furnished a motive for murder, and it is for you to consider, quietly and dispassionately, as reasonable men and women, whether the prisoner's behaviour in respect of this woman does or does not suggest that he had a powerful interest in wishing his wife out of the way. If you decide that he had, if you decide in your own minds that he wished for his wife's death, that will not of course be the same as deciding that he actually encompassed his wish: nothing of the kind. But, for what it is worth, there it is.

I have no doubt that you will carefully consider

the prisoner's behaviour on October the 31st, his going to Southampton and his evident intention of sailing to America by the night boat. I won't go into that again beyond directing your earnest attention to it. On the one hand you have the view of the Prosecution, that the prisoner was fleeing from justice; and to set against that you have the prisoner's story, that he was going to America with his mistress with the full knowledge and consent of his wife. As to the flight-from-justice theory, you may think it odd that the prisoner, if indeed he was flying from justice, wasted so much time about it, first spending a night with his mistress at her London flat, and then, at his leisure, making for a boat that was not due to sail till five minutes before midnight of the following day. On the other hand, you will remember that criminals, even the cleverest among them, often do very foolish things, especially if they are in a state of amorous infatuation. As to the prisoner's story, you alone have the right to judge whether or not he was speaking the truth: it is not for me to instruct you on that point. You have seen and heard him giving evidence in his defence, and you will form your own conclusions of his veracity. You may think that in general he answered the questions put to him in a straightforward and candid manner, and you may nevertheless think that on one or two points he was a little evasive, or at least not quite convincing. You may think he is speaking the truth but not the

whole truth, and of course it is open to you to
think that he is lying. You may find it impossible
to believe, for example, that his wife's attitude to
his adulterous way of life miraculously changed
from one of anger and reprobation, with which all
must sympathize, to one of complaisance and con-
donation—and all within the space of a few hours.
In the morning, when he leaves her for his office,
she is still angry and disapproving, as any woman
might be reasonably supposed to be in the unhappy circumstances. In the evening, when he
returns, she was (in the prisoner's own words)
'very generous about it, she urged me to go'—
that is, to go to America with his mistress. You
are, most of you, men and women with some experience of life, and your knowledge of human
nature, and of your own natures in particular, will
help you to decide whether or not such a story is
the kind of story you feel justified in believing.
Now if the prisoner is lying, on that or on any
other point, it is because he has something to hide,
but can you be sure that what he has to hide—if
there is any such thing—amounts to murder? I do
not say that you can or that you cannot: I leave the
question with you. You may think murder has
been done; you may think the prisoner had both
motive and opportunity. It is not necessary for
the Prosecution to prove his manual possession of
the poison, but it is necessary, before you can be
justified in convicting, that you should be convinced

beyond reasonable doubt both that he administered the poison and administered it feloniously, that is, with murderous intent. That means you must be convinced that he gave it knowing that another dose had been, or was about to be, given. The prisoner denies both the one and the other; he denies giving the poison, he denies having heard Mrs Tucker say that a sleeping-draught had been supplied by the doctor, and he denies that he was aware that his wife had at any time been prescribed oscitalin. You may think it unlikely that the prisoner would know that the sleeping-draught prescribed on that previous occasion was oscitalin, or that he was familiar with the formula of that drug; but oscitalin, as we have heard, is a fashionable prescription, and in any case if you are convinced, on the evidence, that he gave his wife chloral, knowing that the other draught had been or would be given, you will be justified in presuming a murderous intention. It is not necessary that he should have known precisely what he was giving or precisely what else was being given, if you are satisfied that he believed both to be a fatal dose when taken in conjunction or in rapid succession. That two draughts were given, there can be no doubt; for the post-mortem examination revealed the presence of three substances—bromide, hyoscyamus, and cannabis indica—which are not accounted for by Dr Cartwright's prescription; and, as you will remember, the amount of chloral

found in the body exceeded the amount given on
Dr Cartwright's instructions. I went over that
ground very carefully at the beginning of this
summing-up: I needn't go over it again. You
have heard the prisoner's evidence, and you have
heard the evidence of the woman who was with him
at the hotel in Southampton on the evening of
October the 31st. Her evidence is in direct conflict with that of the barman, House; and the
conflict concerns a crucial point, whether or not
the prisoner was within hearing of a wireless
receiving-set when the appeal to him to return to
his wife was broadcast over the ether. It is for
you to decide which of the two is speaking the
truth. The woman may be lying; the man House
may be mistaken; that is a question for you. You
have seen them both and you must judge for yourselves without further help from me. But you must
allow no consideration whatever, no prejudice or
haste or impatience, to persuade you to return a
verdict of guilty unless you are satisfied beyond
reasonable doubt that it is a true verdict. If you
are not so satisfied, if the charge is not proved,
then whatever your surmises or suspicions may be,
whatever your mere feelings may be, it will be your
duty to find the prisoner not guilty. You will now
consider your verdict and say whether you find the
prisoner guilty or not guilty.

PART THREE

THE TWELVE DEBATING

RODERICK'S PEERS

To Charles Underhay, who had never seen the
inside of a criminal court before, the place was
agreeable, almost academic in atmosphere, emi-
nently safe. Here reason and law held absolute
sway. Here the established order was quietly and
elegantly sustained. A number of cultivated gentlemen were met together to discuss whether a man
should live or die, and it was all very reassuring to
Mr Underhay. In his hot youth he had gone
through a period of Dissent, and the varnished oak
in which the walls were half-panelled, and of which
dock and bench and jury-box were constructed,
reminded him—though he did not consciously
entertain the memory—of the Wesleyan Chapel
where his ecclesiastical wild oats had been sown.
He was not a religious man; of the supernatural
he was mildly and politely sceptical; but as a good
citizen, as a conscientious Second Division clerk, he
had a veneration, almost religious in temper, for
all national institutions. The court ceremonial profoundly impressed and satisfied him: the entry of the
Judge, the bowing, the archaic language of the
usher's exhortation and of the oath administered

to every several member of the jury. 'I swear by Almighty God that I will well and truly try and true deliverance make between our Sovereign Lord the King and the Prisoner at the Bar whom I shall have in charge, and a true verdict give, according to the evidence.' He did not know nor care whether that was good prose or bad: enough for him that it was archaic, traditional. It sounded a trifle odd on the lips of some of his fellow-jurors, Mr Bayfield for example; but he was quick to rebuke himself for the observation. It was a solemn moment, and the solemnity was very congenial to him: it touched a responsive chord. If he himself had had the misfortune to be sentenced to death, it would have greatly comforted him to have that sentence pronounced in cultured accents and by an elderly gentleman in grey wig and scarlet gown; and so long as the sentence was carried out in due form, with all the traditional routine, he would have died almost happy.

But though Nature might seem to have designed Charles Underhay to be a foreman of juries, she had spoiled her work at the last moment by endowing him with an uncommon degree of shyness. When, time and again during the summing-up, he met the patient fatherly gaze of Mr Justice Sarum, he was fluttered by a sense of the responsibility that rested on him; for he imagined that when the time came for the jury to retire and consider their verdict, he, the foreman, would be expected to

guide their deliberations. Being a man of sedentary and unsociable habit, a stranger to every kind
of board-room and committee-meeting, he had
never been in such a position before and he wished
himself well out of it. Why his name had been
called first, whether by accident or design, he did
not know; but he felt, especially during that
summing-up, that the judge was relying on him,
on him rather than the others, to search out and
deliver the truth of this matter. With the words
'you will now consider your verdict', the old gentleman had looked straight into his eyes, into his
mind, as if to say: 'We understand each other, you
and I. We know that society must be protected
from such passions as these.'

Charles had welcomed this chance of sitting on
a jury: it would provide distraction at a time when
he badly needed it. For the great decision had
been taken, and six-year-old Betty was now at
school. At school and away from home. Her
aunt, his late wife's eldest sister, had persuaded
him that the child needed the companionship of
other children and a well-planned mental dietary
such as school would provide. The thing had been
put to Betty in terms cunningly designed to excite
her curiosity; for though Charles was unconscious
of entertaining modern ideas about the relations
between parents and children, and would have
vigorously repudiated any such suggestion, he had
always treated the child with a certain courteous

consideration, and it was out of the question, for him, that she should be bundled out of the house without her own consent. So, with Aunt Ann as author and stage-manager, a drama was enacted in which Mrs Fairfax, who had a nursery school six miles away, played a decisive part. Invited to tea by Aunt Ann, she let fall, in Betty's presence, stray references to a family of white rabbits that lived with her, and to a tortoise that had the run of her large garden, and finally, as an afterthought, to sundry girls and boys with whom she passed her days. Each child, it appeared, had a tiny green-glazed toilet-set, a bedspread of its own choice, a book to read in and a book to write in, besides the use of other conveniences—such as swings and rocking-horses—which they held in common. The trouble was that they were all so busy learning things, and making things, and enjoying themselves, that they sometimes forgot to feed the rabbits; and Mrs Fairfax did so wish she could find a little girl who would come and stay with her and put that matter right, for if something of the sort didn't happen soon the rabbits would grow thin enough to escape through the bars of their hutch, when no one was looking, and then perhaps the cat would get them. Betty was sympathetic but cautious. She committed herself no further, at that interview, than to say that she wished she could see the rabbits. But very soon those celestial creatures, with the tortoise aiding, and the unknown children

adding relish to the glittering prospect, took possession of her heart. 'I wonder what the rabbits are
doing?' she asked Aunt Ann. Aunt Ann, seldom
at a loss, replied that they were doing this or that.
And, five minutes later: 'What are they doing *now*,
Auntie, those rabbits?' Whereat Aunt Ann gave
expression to her secret anxiety that they were very
likely waiting to be fed.

Before breakfast was over, next morning, the
die was cast and the day appointed. Betty was
going to school, school being, in her mind, a place
where, between intervals of washing oneself in a
tiny green basin and drawing pictures and being
read to, one indulged, with motherly solicitude,
the voracity of white rabbits. Charles, during
these delicate negotiations, had been racked with
anxiety, a torture which he strove to hide under a
demeanour laboriously normal. If these arts and
devices of Ann's should fail, what then? They
did not fail: Betty was going to school. It was
arranged and she was happy in the arrangement.
Then, just as in a dream one sees one's hopes and
fears magically transformed into fact in the very
moment of conceiving them, so poor Charles's
bogey, that Betty might change her mind, took
shape and substance before his eyes. In the
morning it was agreed that she should go tomorrow, and throughout the morning all the talk
was of rabbits. But during the afternoon she
became significantly quiet, and in the early

evening, when Charles arrived home, she had reached the point of confessing that she was undecided whether to go or not. 'Sometimes I think I will,' she remarked, her features screwed into that ultra-thoughtful frown which generally boded tears, 'and sometimes I think I 'll stay with you and Charlie.' And, having felt her way cautiously, she announced a moment later that she would certainly stay. A silent frenzy raged in Charles's heart: it was wretched enough to have to part with Betty, but if she too was going to feel the parting, it would be intolerable. How to persuade and not coerce: that was the problem.

'What about those rabbits?' he said.

No answer.

'I 'm worried about those rabbits, Betty.'

'Are you?' asked Betty politely.

'They 'll be awfully hungry, poor things, with no one to feed them.'

Aunt Ann intervened. 'Oh, they 'll be all right, Charlie.' Confound the woman's cheerfulness, he thought. 'It 's turned out very fortunately, as it happens,' said Aunt Ann.

'Indeed?' Charles could not follow his sister-in-law's gymnastics.

'Yes. Very fortunately. Mrs Fairfax rang up just now to say she wasn't sure whether she 'd got room for Betty after all.'

'No room, eh?' said Charles, with belated intelligence. 'The rabbits must go hungry then: that's all.'

Betty glanced from face to face. 'I want to go to Mrs Fairfax's *tonight*,' she said firmly.

'And stay?' asked Aunt Ann. 'And look after the rabbits for her?'

'Yes,' said Betty.

'There now!' exclaimed Aunt Ann. 'What a pity Mrs Fairfax hasn't room for you!' But she was cheerful even in face of that disaster. 'Perhaps if we asked her again . . .'

Charles convulsively swallowed his mouthful of buttered toast and rose from the table. 'That's right, Ann. You speak to her on the telephone, while Betty and I get the car out.' He left his second cup of tea untasted.

Sitting in his commanding corner of the jury-box, Charles recalled that drive to Mrs Fairfax's house, with Betty on the seat beside him dancing up and down and singing in her excitement. How long would that mood last? A most unwonted mood, for Betty was in general a silent child. Working hard, he kept up a flow of genial conversation, hoping against hope that the child could be handed over, the parting effected, before her ecstasy subsided. In every dull moment of the trial his thoughts returned to that drive—gratefully, wistfully. And dull moments were not lacking. At first a sense of the importance of the occasion kept his attention alert, but three days of it wore his patience rather thin and he was conscious of missing things. Was that what the judge meant by looking so intently at him?

And now he and his oddly assorted companions were to consider their verdict. The black-gowned usher, who had administered that resounding oath, was now doing a bit of swearing on his own account, to the effect that he would see the jury safely bestowed in the jury-room, and that he would neither speak with them nor allow others to do so. So, in single file, they passed out of the jury-box, down a corridor, and into a bare room containing twelve chairs ranged round a table. The door was locked behind them.

'It almost looks as though we were expected,' remarked one of the company, a long-faced, square-jawed man. There was a blueness about his chin. His black hair was plastered down close on his head. His nose was long and large and straight, a nose of character. His blue serge suit was indifferently cut. Not quite a gentleman, Charles decided, and flashed at the fellow a deprecating glance, for he suspected an attempt at jocularity which, to say the least, was ill-timed. But there was nothing in Bonaker's face to confirm the suspicion, no mischief in the dark eyes, no hint of a smile. Massive and matter-of-fact, he sat himself down.

His voice and his action disturbed the religious silence, dissipated the slight awkwardness created

among them by the sound of that key turning in
the lock. They took their places at the conference-
table.

'May I?' asked Major Forth gallantly, with his
hand on the back of the chair next to Clare Cranshaw's. A superfluous inquiry, for the lady had
already been his guest at luncheon and had heard
a good half of his life-story. But it was the Major's
way to err on the side of ceremony, and it was
Clare's way to like him the better for it. She
seemed to him a nice sensible little woman, and,
what was more, a lady. They saw eye to eye in
this matter of the murder.

Clare answered him with nothing but a smile,
but when he had sat down she said, with a quietness almost confidential: 'Why don't you smoke?'

'You permit?' he asked. He produced a
cigarette-case, with a glance of disapproval at the
plump person opposite who was filling a briar-pipe.
'Perhaps you . . .?' he suggested.

'No, thank you,' said Clare Cranshaw. It cost
her something, a little, to say that. But she judged
that the Major, though not quite old-world enough
to be censorious of a woman's smoking, would
think it more suitable for her, more feminine, to
refrain in this mixed and semi-public gathering.
And, while she had by no means made up her mind
what to do with him, she was conscious of desiring
his good opinion.

'Ah, no,' said the Major. And the satisfaction

327

in his tone rewarded her, told her that she had done the right thing. In a company anything but select she was behaving like the lady she un-questionably was. It might almost be said that she was keeping the flag flying. The white man's burden rested, for a moment, upon her elegant womanly shoulders.

'But I won't pretend I never do,' she added daringly. 'Do you disapprove, Major?'

Mr Bayfield, filling his pipe, had noticed the Major's scowl and ignored it with defiant ostenta-tion. If this military-looking gentleman, or any other gentleman, had dropped into the shop to buy an evening paper or a ball of string, he would have been received with a civility little short of obsequious by Mr Bayfield or Ernie (for even Ernie was beginning to learn, despite the time he wasted in the cinema). But out of the shop, and as a member of a jury, he was as good as the next man and probably a good deal better. Dragged away from one's business, and then, him a grown man, set a problem a child could solve, and have to listen day after day to question and answer, quibble and evasion, when the truth was as plain as the nose on your face! That was bad enough in all con-science, and Ernie and the wife probably ruining the business between them (Ernie with his cheek, which no amount of teaching could quite subdue, and the wife with her happy-go-lucky carelessness); a pretty fine thing it was, and if a man couldn't enjoy a pipe of tobacco in peace, after sitting all those hours, and it might just as well have been in church for all the comfort there was . . . and besides, there was Dolly on his mind still. Dolly would be bedridden for a long spell. Maybe she 'd never be really right again, for it had been touch and go. And that young fellow, George she called him, who was always hanging about and sending flowers and what not, but never came to the point. Nothing said about marriage—oh, dear, no! But I 'll see as my girl gets her rights, Master George: you see if I don't.

Next to Mr Bayfield, and looking her primmest in case he should speak to her, sat Lucy Prynne, with Blanche Izeley's moral power to protect her from the threat of mild Mr Arthur Cheed, who sat on Blanche's right. Lucy had found the trial at first dreadful and afterwards rather muddling and boring. Seeing the prisoner, who had done all those wicked things, she quite forgot to wonder how Poor Mother was getting on without her. Three days away from Mother!—Lucy couldn't remember when it had happened before. It certainly made a nice change to be seeing a bit of life for once, though hardly decent to have to listen to such things in mixed company. Lucy was frightened of the prisoner at his first appearance, and frightened for him. The way they brought him up into the dock—from underground it seemed—gave her a sense of nightmare. But when she knew how he had treated his wife, and his horrible behaviour with that fast foreign woman, she couldn't help seeing that he had a look of Father about him: in fact it was Father and the so-called Aunt Lena all over again, and it might have been Mother herself who was murdered, just fancy that! 'I wonder if Lucy would like sixpence to buy sweeties with?' Aunt Lena had said. Lucy remembered it perfectly: it all came back. Netherclift-next-the-Sea, and the dead rabbit dripping blood, and Father's wicked genial spell-binding gaze that had made her feel like a rabbit herself, helpless, fascinated, limp with docility. How was Mother managing in her absence? And how was Someone Else managing? He asked me to call him Edward, she said to herself. That was an old story: he had since said many things more daring and more loving than that. But somehow it was to that moment—'I wish you would call me Edward!'—that her thoughts continually reverted. For that had been in a sense the beginning of everything, hadn't it? Except for that little talk at the Literary Society, and the wonderful night when he had called at the house for her, ever so late it was, and lent her his piece about Wordsworth to read. But indeed her commerce with Edward Seagrave had been, from first to last, a series of beginnings. One day they were the merest acquaintances; the next they were friends; and then, suddenly, heaven knew how, they were dear friends. From being no one in particular he had become the most marvellous of living creatures—and this, not, as it seemed to Lucy, by stages, but with a blinding flash as from heaven itself. What are we going to do now? I hope they'll be quick. He asked me to call him Edward.

Lucy had learned something about herself as well as much about Edward. For it seemed that there was, after all, 'something about her'. Is it true that I am lovely? she asked herself: but not quite seriously, for she was not so simple-minded as to treat a lover's confession of faith as though it were evidence of fact. Yet it was evidence of something, and if one man had found her fair, so could another; and it more than ever behoved her, as a young woman already pledged, to keep herself unspotted from the roving glances of men. Arthur Cheed had looked more than once in her direction; he had even, she fancied, allowed the ghost of a greeting to hover on his lips. But in fact he was unaware of this, and unaware of cherishing any particular interest in this Miss What's-er-name. He was lonely, and, after hours of listening, he wanted to exchange a word or two with someone, anyone. His neighbour, Cyril Gaskin, who sat at the end of the table, six o'clock to the foreman's twelve o'clock (ex-Gunner Cheed remembered that much military technique), seemed to have such a conceit of himself as to repel advances before they were so much as offered; and Cheed had already been gently, oh so kindly and spiritually, snubbed by his other neighbour, Mrs Izeley. Small wonder, then, that his glance sometimes rested on Lucy. But he was thinking, if thinking at all, not of her but of his business, the precious garage, and of the young man Fred, left precariously in charge; and more particularly he was homesick for a sight of his Bessie and of Silas and Henry, the two cats.

Neither Cyril Gaskin nor Mrs Izeley would spare a glance for him; and that drab little creature two chairs away, whose name he had forgotten, seemed to think she was sitting in church yet surrounded by potential despoilers of her virtue. You 've nothing to hope from me, miss, said meek Mr Cheed, silently indulging a kind of humour of which only his wife knew him to be capable. Chilly you *may* be, my dear, but *I* 'm not warming you. Mrs Izeley—for he remembered most of the names, having heard them called several times by the usher—Mrs Izeley sat like a Buddha, with eyes turned inward; and Mr Cyril Gaskin, still glowing with self-satisfaction in having begotten Master Cyril Gaskin (aged three weeks), had eyes for no one but the gentleman at the opposite end of the table, Charles Underhay to wit, whom he recognized as a weak, diffident fellow, quite unfit for the office of foreman. At Gaskin's right sat Sidney H. Nywood, wondering, underneath the discomfort of having to vote for the death of that poor lying devil in the dock, whether Sir Godfrey

Bunce's little job up at The Grange, which promised to put a net profit of twenty-seven pounds into his pocket, would in his absence be snatched away from him by some other jobbing builder. Moreover, at this time of the year you never knew when a nice funeral mightn't fall into your mouth, as it were.

On Nywood's right, Roger Coates, still a youngish man (he told himself passionately) in spite of his forty-five years, was already beginning to plan what he should say, when he got home to Mother and the children, to impress them with a sense of his preternatural sagacity, his knowledge of human nature, his quickness in getting at the truth of a complicated affair. Behind his conscious thoughts, to be scornfully repelled whenever it threatened to push its way forward, lurked the uneasy suspicion that Marjorie and Vincent, who were too smart by half, were not as grieved by his absence as they ought to be, and that even Mother herself was perhaps managing to suffer it cheerfully. That Little Supper in Soho had been an eye-opener to Mr Coates—or would have been had his eyes been capable of opening in the presence of facts uncongenial to his view of himself. For the behaviour of Vincent had been blarsy, as our French cousins say, and Mr Coates had been constrained to tell him as much, with self-protective jocularity. 'Blarsy, my boy, that's you. I suppose you know what blarsy means, after the education I've given you?'

Of course there were things in this case that couldn't be mentioned in front of the children. Children knew a great deal too much nowadays, but there was no need to encourage them, and anyhow, if the shameful secret of their begetting couldn't ultimately be kept from them, he was at least resolved to say nothing that could possibly remind them of his own participation in 'that side of life'. But the wife was another matter. He could tell *her*, preferably in bed; and she, realizing what some men are like, and what running after women may lead to, would more clearly appreciate her luck in possessing such a husband as himself. She would be grateful—and why not?—for his twenty years of fidelity. There had been episodes; a bit of fun is a bit of fun; but since she didn't know about them it was as if they had never happened. It was sometimes dullish work being breadwinner for three hungry mouths besides one's own; but since Mr Coates had kept straight, and resisted temptation again and again (there was that little piece at Boulogne, for instance, when he 'd only four-and-six left in his pocket), he was damned if he could see why this architect fellow, with his university education and all, should carry on as he did and get away with it. It wasn't right or decent. And anyhow, murder was murder: you couldn't get away from that.

Between Roger Coates and Major Reginald Forth sat the sharp-featured red-faced auctioneer, George

Oliver Brackett. Alert and watchful, he sat still and said nothing; and no observer could have suspected that upon the stage of his soul, with himself the actor in every part, himself the fascinated audience, a tremendous drama was being enacted. He was the usher presenting the black cap; he was the judge invested with it. Roderick William Strood, you have been found guilty by a jury of your fellow-countrymen of the terrible crime of murder. You have had a fair trial and I am bound to say . . . oh, yes, Oliver knew how it went, and what he didn't know he could invent. If the phrases failed him he could eke it out with ample and dramatic gesture. He gripped the edge of the dock and gazed unflinchingly at the face of the Judge. My lord, I have nothing to say (how resonant the voice, how steady the eye!) except that I am innocent of this crime. My lord, I loved my wife, and now that this thing has come upon me I do not care whether I live or die. . . . Hanged by the neck till you be dead, and may the Lord have mercy on your soul. Very fine. Superb performance. But better still, or anyhow pleasanter, to set the prisoner free, with noble and charitable cadences ringing in his mind. Roderick William Strood, you are greatly indebted to your learned counsel, who has . . . after a terrible ordeal, in which you have borne yourself with dignity and fortitude, the jury has declared you innocent of the dreadful crime of which you were accused. With that verdict I heartily agree, and it is now my pleasure, as well as my duty . . . But, said Mr Brackett, with a shudder of pity, there's not much chance of that, poor swine. A nasty piece of work, if he did it. Must have planned the thing pretty carefully.

Some twenty-five seconds had passed since the shutting and locking of the jury-room door. Charles Underhay, very conscious of the sudden silence, interpreted it as a reminder that some sort of lead was expected of him. He supposed himself called upon to make a speech.

Fingering the sheets of paper that lay on the table before him, he cleared his throat and began.

'Well, ladies and gentlemen . . .'

It's no good, thought Cyril Gaskin. Having given a covert glance to see if the mauve silk handkerchief were still protruding from his outer breast-pocket by the requisite one and a half inches, he braced himself for action. It's no good: he's not the man for it.

'I fancy we're not in much doubt about our verdict, Mr Foreman.'

'What? Eh?' said Charles. 'No, I suppose not.'

'I don't want to butt in, sir,' fluted Cyril, with the charming laugh that little Stella so much adored. (And lucky for Agnes she did, for what would she and the baby have done without Stella's help?) 'But how would it be to start with a show of hands,

336

just to see where we are? What I mean is,' he went on, seeing that Charles was about to say something, 'it's an unpleasant business for everyone, especially, if I may say so, for the ladies—' he enveloped all three ladies in a bland, chivalrous, complacently deprecating smile—'and we want to get through with it as soon as possible. Consistently with justice, of course. Justice and fair play. We're all English here, I believe—or at least British, and—— Well, I don't want to make a speech, but I don't mind telling you, since frankness is my way, cards on the table and always has been, I don't mind telling you, ladies and gentlemen, that I don't think there's much room for what his lordship called reasonable doubt. Do you agree, sir?'

Charles Underhay wriggled unhappily in his chair. To hide his nervousness he put on a face of extreme boldness. His eyes dilated.

'I'm afraid you may be right, but we must talk it over, you know. We can't rush things.'

'Quite,' said Mr Gaskin. 'We won't rush the thing, but we'll keep moving, eh? Let's go round with the clock. Now, madam, Miss Cranshaw, I believe?' Clare Cranshaw was on Underhay's left. 'Perhaps you'll be good enough to tell us what *you* think.'

A loud report followed this request. It was the sound of Major Reginald Forth blowing his nose.

§ 32

A MEAL WITH THE MAJOR

THAT Major Forth and Mrs Cranshaw should have lunched together, on the strength of so slight an acquaintance, was almost a miracle. The Major was no longer precisely young; he had always been a stickler for the proprieties, and time had only confirmed him in the persuasion that unconventional people were not to be trusted. In the Major's philosophy there were two categories of women: nice women and fast women. There was also an abstraction or commodity called Woman, *tout court*, the first and most dangerous part of a trinity whose other components were Wine and Song. He had committed his follies, like other men; but that was long ago and he did not remember it against himself. Finding himself next to Clare Cranshaw, as a member of the same jury-in-waiting, he had been surprised and indignant that a so obviously 'nice' woman should be exposed to the kind of thing one heard in a criminal court. He wondered, as he had so often wondered before, what the world was coming to; but this wonder was lost in admiration of the clear, detached, and disdainful way in which she recited the oath. To have your name bawled out in court, to have to stand up and read the formula from a card, with a Bible held conspicuously in the right hand, that in itself was

338

a sufficient ordeal—not for an old soldier indeed, but for a delicately nurtured young woman (young? well, say thirty-five), and, by gad, she came through it with flying colours. Before this ceremony began, two prisoners, with the right to object to any member of the jury, were 'put up' into the dock. They stood stiffly, side by side, a fair-haired shifty-eyed rabbit of a man, and another, tall, severe, and self-controlled, in spite of his sensitive hands and suffering dark eyes. 'Put Strood back,' ordered the Clerk of the Court, when the jury had been sworn in. So Strood was put back, and the rabbit remained, with an uneasy half-smile on its pale pimply face, to plead guilty to an offence which no gentleman, thought the Major, should dream of even mentioning in the presence of ladies. The trial was mercifully brief; the jury listened but were not consulted; sentence was passed and . . . 'You will be back in your places at ten minutes to two,' said the Clerk.

The Major sat, eyes front, almost blushing with vicarious shame. Clare, suddenly noticing his confusion, liked him for it, and as they rose to file out of the box she put him miraculously at his ease by remarking firmly 'And he richly deserves it', suppressing, for the Major's benefit, her uneasy suspicion that, though eighteen months' hard labour would teach the wretch a lesson, it would perhaps have been better, kinder even, to shoot him out of hand.

'I agree with you, madam,' said the Major gratefully.

It was pleasant, after that disgusting story, to hear the Major's honest, educated, masculine voice. What a nice old gentleman! And on the way downstairs, to the street, she heard it again.

'Permit me to apologize, madam,' said the Major, raising his hat. 'On behalf of our so-called civilization, permit me to apologize for having brought you to this court.'

She smiled acknowledgment of his civility. 'We *were* rather unlucky this morning. But it's hardly your fault.'

'No, indeed!' said the Major. 'If I had my way you would have been spared all that. But you've the Suffragettes to thank for it, mind!' he added rather fiercely.

'Still,' objected Clare Cranshaw, 'we mustn't leave everything to the men to do, must we?'

A stalwart policeman opened the door and they passed through, to pause a moment on the topmost of the five steps before descending to the pavement.

'I mean,' she amplified, 'it's only right that we should take our share.'

'Of the privileges, yes,' said the Major. 'But not of the more disagreeable duties. That's man's work.' An audacious plan presented itself to him. 'Forgive me if I presume too far, but would you allow an old soldier to give you luncheon?'

It was the boldest speech he had ever uttered, and no one was more astonished than he to hear it issue from his lips. Astonished and alarmed. He could hardly believe his ears.

'That's very kind of you, but——'

'We'll take a taxi,' said the Major, with surprising promptitude, and Clare began to perceive that he was not so old after all.

The taxi took them, in seven minutes or so, to a 'little place' known to the Major. They were received, with delighted ceremony, by a gentleman whose beaming smiles and florid gestures and foreign accent, as he well knew, made the Major feel more English than ever: English and benevolent and confirmed in his conviction that these foreigners weren't bad fellows at all if only you knew how to treat them: like animals and children, they nearly always responded to kindness. This exuberant *maître d'hôtel* conducted them to a table which, with transparent and charming mendacity, he declared had been specially reserved for them; and there, illumined and heart-warmed by two pink-shaded electric candles, they advanced from acquaintanceship to something like friendship.

'We're lucky to have so long,' remarked the Major. 'Fellow at the Club was telling me, one often gets a bare three-quarters of an hour for luncheon. Wine all right? Not too dry for you? Splendid! Queer mixture, our fellow-jurors.'

'Indeed, yes,' agreed Clare.

'Excellent people, no doubt, in their way.'

But how different from us, thought Clare, her mind jumping with his.

The Major glanced at the clock. 'We must be back in forty minutes. Quite like old times to be under orders again.'

Clare smiled. He was more like a schoolboy than any other man she had ever met. This she found an engaging characteristic: it made her feel indulgent and maternal. And his grey hair, very thin on the crown, made her feel a girl again.

'But I expect you were in command, weren't you?' she objected.

'Ah,' he said sagely, 'but there's always a higher command.' He laughed, admiring his generalization. 'Yes, there's always a higher command.' He couldn't help feeling that to be a rather pregnant utterance.

'Colonel?' asked Clare, growing bolder.

'Acting colonel,' he answered. 'Never confirmed. But I don't complain. They call me Major now. Indiah. Retired these ten years. We'll have another half-bottle, I think. No? Come, change your mind. We shall be prisoners, you know, as soon as that murder trial comes on. Better make the most of our chance.'

'Prisoners? What do you mean?'

'Once you get on the jury in a murder trial, you're as good as a prisoner, fellow at the Club was telling me. They won't let us out of their

sight till it's over, in case, don't you see, we should
be got at in some way.' Her apparent surprise
made him cock a solicitous eye at her. 'Will they
be anxious at home about you?'

There was more than solicitude in the question,
as she was shrewd enough to see. 'You mean my
husband, don't you?' The wine was very good
and she felt serenely mistress of the situation, and
amused by it. 'No, Major, there's no one to
worry about me. My husband died five years ago.'

'Ah!' said the Major. 'Dear me!' He sipped
his wine and remarked in a tone that hardly
concealed his satisfaction: 'So we're both alone
in the world. Should give us a fellow-feeling,
what?'

'Don't you sometimes miss India—the sunshine
and the bugles?'

'Ah, yes,' he answered. 'You put it in a nut-
shell. The sunshine and the bugles. Quite a gift
of phrase, upon my word!'

Clare glowed with pleasure. 'There's something so terribly thrilling, I always think, about
The Last Post.'

For a moment their eyes met, intimately.

'I wonder,' he said. 'You won't mind my
asking? Was your late husband in the service,
by any chance?'

She shook her head, smiling inscrutably. 'Henry
was a clergyman. Do I look like a vicar's wife?'
Really, Clare! she admonished herself: what *are* you

343

saying! Before he could find an answer she added: 'But my father was a soldier, as it happens.'

'Of course!' said the Major. 'I ought to have known it. I felt at once, if I may say so, that there was, how shall I put it, a link, a bond . . .'

'Perhaps you knew my father? General Dyce.'

'No. I didn't have that pleasure.' The Major bowed. 'But I'm proud to know his daughter.' He smiled at her, being now at the top of his form. A clergyman's widow and a soldier's daughter —it was hard to believe that so much merit could be crammed into one small and comely person. A fine pair of eyebrows. A soft but confident voice. In short, breeding. 'Most courageous thing I ever did, asking you to luncheon. Proud of myself, upon my word!'

Clare laughed. 'I'm not sure whether to take that as a compliment or not.'

'Might easily have thought me a bounder,' mumbled the Major.

'Oh, come, Major!' she protested. 'I'm not so old as that!'

He was at a loss. 'So *old*, Mrs Cranshaw! What can you mean?'

'Well, I've still the use of my eyes, you know.'

He thought it out carefully, and, when he had at last got the point, a look of grave pleasure dawned in his eyes, making him, thought Clare, almost lovable while it lasted. 'The most charming thing that's ever been said to me,' he declared with a bow, of which, to hide a touch of shyness perhaps, the ceremony was a trifle exaggerated. 'And now that we *are* acquainted I hope you 'll do me the honour . . .' He eked out the sentence with a wave of the hand. 'Get too much of my own company. Dull old fellow, as I know to my cost. Mustn't let me bore you as I bore myself.'

In the taxi, on the way back, he pursued the theme of his dullness and loneliness, confessed that he had loved not wisely but too well, 'as the Bard has it'. To her look of sympathetic inquiry he answered: 'It 's not an amusing story. Some other time perhaps, if it won't bore you . . .'

'I 'm sure it won't.'

'I 'd like you to meet my children,' said the Major, a little dubiously. Well-washed insolent young persons, Evangeline and Edgar. Ten to one they 'd be smilingly disagreeable to the little woman. 'Well, here we are, back at the scene of action, what!'

He got himself carefully out of the cab and turned to place a hand at her elbow. How very old-world, she thought. But gratification mingled with her amusement. She felt like a precious piece of porcelain.

'Here we are, here we are,' he said again, as they mounted the steps to the Court. 'Moreover'— he consulted his watch — 'there 's exactly four minutes to go before we fall in. Good staff-work, Mrs Cranshaw. Good staff-work.'

As they passed into the great hall she placed a hand on his sleeve.

'We shall meet upstairs,' she said. 'And thank you, Major,' she recited, like a good little girl at the end of a party, 'thank you for a very nice lunch.'

§ 33

LUCY THINKS SO TOO

AND so when the Major heard Cyril Gaskin say 'Miss Cranshaw, I believe?' he experienced a spasm of indignation which in logic it would have been hard to justify. He thereafter blew his nose with peculiar emphasis, like a motorist sounding his horn at an impudent pedestrian. Who the deuce was he, this sleek young fellow, that he must needs take so much upon himself? The foreman was evidently a duffer, but he looked like a gentleman, not a shopwalker, snorted the Major under cover of his nasal performance. And for little Mrs Cranshaw to be singled out for this officious attention . . .

'*Mrs* Cranshaw, sir,' said the Major, in a gentle voice that did no sort of justice to his inward ferocity.

'Pardon, sir?' asked Cyril.

346

Pardon. Pardon. Just what he *would* say.
'The lady's name is *Mrs* Cranshaw.'

'I see,' said Gaskin. 'Well, Mrs Cranshaw,
what's the verdict?'

Ignoring Gaskin with a coolness that was nectar
to Major Forth, Clare turned to Charles Underhay.
'I don't think there's much doubt he did it,
Mr Chairman, do you?'

'Frankly, I don't,' answered Charles gravely. He
forgot his shyness. 'But we mustn't be hasty. We
must hear everyone's views. Don't you agree,
Major?'

'Most emphatically, sir. The way we have in
the service, in courts martial, you know, is to let
the youngest officer speak first. And so on, in
inverse order of seniority.'

Charles nodded. 'Quite so.' He had a profound respect for the army and all its ways.

'Well, there's no doubt who's the eldest here,'
went on the Major. 'My turn comes last. Mrs
Cranshaw has given us her opinion. So perhaps
one of the other ladies . . .' He sketched a
courteous bow in the direction of Lucy Prynne.

'If you ask me,' said Mr Bayfield, his impatience
boiling over, 'I'm of the young gent's way of
thinking. Surely to goodness we've heard enough
talk about the business.' Suppose it had been
Dolly and that George of hers. Dolly, who might
be crippled for life. Too many of these young
sparks in the world.

Blanche Izeley, staring at Bayfield with frightened eager eyes, leaned forward and opened her mouth to speak.

But the others were waiting for Lucy. Blanche was unnoticed.

He asked me to call him Edward. Fancy that. 'Did you know I worked in a shop, Mr Seagrave?' She burnt her boats, for he 'd not want her to call him Edward now he knew she worked in a shop. He himself was something very distinguished, she felt sure. He might even be an editor, or a poet. Anyhow something awfully nice. But all he did in answer to her confession about the shop was to stammer a repetition of his request.

'Well, I 'll try,' said Lucy. 'It 's very kind of you, I 'm sure.'

'It 's so absurdly formal, that other,' he explained. 'And you—are you always called Miss Prynne?'

She laughed happy confusion. 'Of course not. How absurd of you!'

'Isn't your first name Lucy?' he asked, pronouncing the name as though it had been a prayer.

'You *do* say funny things sometimes.'

'Really? What have I said funny?'

'About everybody calling me Miss Prynne. Mother, frinstance. Did you think Mother called me Miss Prynne?'

He ignored that. 'Lucy is a very beautiful name,' he solemnly announced.

'But *did* you know I worked in a shop?' Lucy insisted.

'I didn't, indeed. But I'm most interested to hear it. What sort of a shop is it?'

'I have to design things,' said Lucy, with her curious self-defensive trick of never giving a direct answer if she could avoid it.

'Then you must be very talented,' remarked Edward gravely, not quite keeping the surprise out of his voice. 'What sort of things do you design?'

'Of course I'm not always designing,' she explained. 'I sometimes help in the showroom.'

'Ah, the showroom. Dresses, perhaps?'

'Brenda's better in the showroom than I am. And I'm better at the designing part.'

'You'll think me very ignorant,' said Edward, with the blandest irony. 'But I don't even know who Brenda is.'

'Madame Brenda, she calls herself. But she's really Brenda Willingdon. I was at school with her sister Phyllis, but she's married.'

'Brenda is married?'

'No, Phyllis.'

'Then Miss Willingdon, Brenda, is your business partner. Have I got it right?'

'In a way.'

'And you design dresses?'

'Well,' said Lucy, 'I'm more successful with hats, in Brenda's opinion.'

349

'Dresses and hats,' said Edward, as though counting his spoils. From his smile you would have judged that the information was precious to him in proportion to the trouble he had had in extracting it.

What was there in this conversation that it should have changed the direction and quality of her life? The change was not pure happiness. The return of spring to a heart so long wintered, and so stubborn to resist the genial invasion, was at times exquisitely painful, like the return of sensation to frozen fingers. By incessant sacrifice at the altar of Father's Wickedness and Mother's Need she had trained herself to turn away from anything that might tempt her to a life of her own: she was as busy, almost as mindless, almost as neuter, as a worker-bee. These shafts of strange joy brought pain and confusion into her too-ordered life. And there were dire specific consequences. Edward and Mother were irreconcilable loyalties: the new image distracted her from the old. She was betrayed into what she could not but know was wickedness, for she began, with a cunning that appalled her, to deceive Mother, spinning tales about having a bit of supper with Brenda in town for a treat, when in fact she was to be Edward's alarmed delighted guest. Candour she had never had since that day, so many years ago, when Father and Aunt Lena had put an abrupt end to her childhood. She was incorrigibly secretive even about

matters of no importance. And this habit of
evasion, combined with an unsuspected talent for
plain lying, served her present ends well enough,
though at incalculable cost to her peace of mind.
She had told her mother nothing—nothing significant—about Edward Seagrave; and was resolved
to tell nothing. Sooner or later, if the thing went
on, it must all come out, she dimly supposed; but
she would not hasten the revelation by so much as
a word or a glance.

For if Mother were to learn the truth before
she, Lucy, was irreparably committed, Lucy, as
Lucy well knew, would be outmanœuvred in a
moment: at the first sighing breath, at the first
plaintive or reproachful word, she would capitulate,
her hatred of Father and her angry compassion for
Mother would gush out in passionate and final
re-surrender, and she would renew her lifelong
allegiance to this woman — once a young, gay,
affectionate mother—who demanded (believed Lucy)
not only her company and attention but her un-
divided heart. The lurking fear that 'something
might happen to Mother' sometimes presented
itself in smiling guise. She remembered that figure
at the stairhead on the night of Edward's first and
only visit to the house, and remembered her eager,
frightened, ashamed, involuntary thought: If Mother
were to lose her balance. . . . And throughout the
trial of Roderick Strood, while she listened to the
evidence in her meek, muddled fashion, somewhere

in the darkness of her being, only just below consciousness, floated images of what had been and what might have been in her own life: of Father, of Mother, of Edward, and of how the whole posture of things may be changed for one person by the death of another. This man Strood, with his eyes like Father's, dark and brilliant, had wanted, like Father, to be rid of his lawful wife. Supposing Father had done what this man did. . . . Lucy caught the merest glimpse of this theory and of what followed from it: that if Mother . . . if Father . . . if anything *had* happened to Mother, she and Edward . . . well, everything would be different and simple, there would be no problem left to solve.

But the surface of her mind was engaged, conscientiously enough, with the business of the moment. She quite believed herself to be absorbed in the dreadful story that Sir John Buckhorn so persuasively unfolded. She quite clearly saw the prisoner pouring poison into that cup of malted milk, which Mrs Tucker had unsuspectingly left on the hall-table. She quite clearly saw it, and seeing is believing. While Sir John was speaking it hardly occurred to her to doubt the prisoner's guilt. He had such a nice deep voice, Sir John; he was so confident and calm, and you could see that he was frightfully clever. But when Mr Harcombe held the floor, somehow it put a different complexion on things; for he too seemed fright-

fully clever, and just as confident as Sir John. Was
it possible that the prisoner hadn't done it after
all? But if he hadn't, how did the poison get into
the cup? Besides, he must have done it, because
he did, didn't he, want to get rid of his poor wife?
He must have done, because of that woman. That
woman who didn't seem to know the difference
between right and wrong. But these foreigners
are like that. Not all foreigners, because we must
be broadminded, but anyhow foreigners aren't the
same as English people: they're foreigners. Nice
to hear their funny way of talking; you had to
laugh; but you couldn't rely on what they said, and
of course that woman—for even a wicked woman
she supposed could be fond of a man in a sort of
way—of course that woman would try to save him if
she could, and you couldn't blame her for it. Not
blaming her wasn't the same thing as believing
her. Still Mr Harcombe spoke so awfully nicely,
and seemed so very sure, that it was difficult to
know *what* to believe. And the Judge's speech
was more muddling than ever. Lucy was ready
to do her duty if only someone would tell her what
her duty was; but from what the Judge said you
really couldn't make out what he thought. Had
the man done it or hadn't he? That was what
Lucy wanted to be told, and to have these important
and learned gentlemen in wigs telling you quite
different things made it very confusing indeed.

There was no doubt that Father would have been

M 353

glad enough to poison Mother, instead of having to pay her thirty shillings a week. And all men were like that, once they gave way to their evil passions. That woman was behind it all. All men, except Edward, were like that. That was the difference between love and lust. Real love was Edward's kind of love. Gentle and considerate, a nice warm friendly feeling. She knew quite well that Edward was as pure as pure. Everything he said and did showed that there was nothing *horrid* in his love. All that side of life was something he never so much as thought about. How different from this man in the dock! An educated man too. It was dreadful, dreadful and unfair. Unfair that she should be dragged into it. The thought of what would be done to him if they found him guilty was too hideous to be imagined, even for a moment. The Judge (or was it Sir John?) had said that the jury wasn't to consider that part of it; and Lucy was glad enough to obey the injunction. Her plan, if anything so vague can be called a plan, was to let the others decide and then agree with them. If they said he was guilty— well, she couldn't stand up against eleven of them, could she? And, indeed, that visual picture of the man pouring poison into a cup of milk had become firmly lodged in her imagination: there was no shifting it. It was as clear as that of King Alfred burning the cakes, which had been part of her mental furniture since childhood.

And now they had got her in a corner (ran her panic-stricken thought) and wanted to make her speak first, because she was the youngest. She saw the Major's inquiring glance, and the foreman's, and that Mrs Cranshaw's. They were all looking at her.

'What's your opinion, Miss Prynne? Guilty or not guilty?'

Harried and cornered, she shrank into herself. A look of mulish obstinacy, masking fear, settled on her face. Her reply was too indistinct to be heard.

'We didn't quite catch that,' said Charles Underhay kindly. 'It's a disagreeable business. We all feel that. But would you mind telling us . . .'

'What do you want to know for?' asked Lucy sullenly.

Poor girl, she's a cretin, said Charles to himself. He smiled encouragingly. 'Well, it's obvious, isn't it, we've all got to vote one way or the other.'

'Why do you have to ask me first?' insisted Lucy.

Blanche Izeley leaned forward again, and again she opened her mouth to speak.

'I want to say,' said Blanche Izeley, her voice harsh with effort, for she was not at home in this company, 'I want to say that I don't believe in capital punishment.'

Major Forth exclaimed 'Tchah!' and had manifest difficulty in leaving it at that. A murmur arose among the twelve. Tongues were loosed, and nervousness was forgotten.

355

'That's neither here nor there,' exclaimed Charles, almost testily. 'Quite right!' said Cyril Gaskin. 'Hear, hear! Hear, hear!' grumbled the Major. 'If that don't take the bun!' remarked Mr Bayfield despairingly. Even Arthur Cheed let fall an exclamation of protest. And Roger Coates uttered a snort of derision.

'You must see, Mrs Izeley,' explained Charles, remembering his manners, 'that it's far too late in the day to raise a question like that.'

'I have conscientious objections,' said Blanche, cold with hostility.

'If you have conscientious objections, madam,' put in the Major, 'you have no business on this jury at all. You should have raised your objection at the proper time, before the trial began. Since you didn't do so, it's your duty to help us.'

Blanche sat with a fixed uneasy smile, trying to feel superior to these crude men. But despite herself she recognized the force of the Major's argument. That shaft had gone home: she ought indeed to have refused to sit on this jury. What had tied her tongue at the critical moment? The severe impressive aspect of the Judge, the weight of ceremony and circumstance? Or had it been not so much timidity as a fantastic conceit, a proud persuasion that by sweet reason she would purge her fellow-jurors of their mortal error, their belief in sin and death, and win them for the Higher Truth? Some such ambition had lurked, perhaps unrecognized, in her mind; and it had the more prospered in that soil because, obedient to her inclination, she had taken it for granted, before a word of evidence had been offered, that the prisoner was innocent. But the story that had been told in court had shaken that conviction; she perceived the wretched man to be so sunk in error, so deeply wallowing in the illusion called sex, that anything, anything, might have emanated from him—not, of course, from his Real Self, but from the mortal appearance, the bodily illusion, in which the Principle of Goodness was so far from being reflected. As the trial proceeded, and the court-room filled with Bad Thoughts, she even found herself forgetting to translate the experience into terms of her peculiar philosophy, and gave herself up, from time to time, to the simple reactions of horror and loathing. This man had done what her own lost Paul had done. He had left his wife and gone in carnal wickedness to another woman, just as Paul had left Blanche. That he had added murder to his wickedness mattered little, the so-called death of the body being of no account in the light of Reality. Yet . . . murder . . . and it might have been me! No, Paul would never have done that. But what if he had wished it? She shut her eyes against the hideous supposition, and for a while the noises of the court, question and answer and measured speech, seemed like noises in a dream.

'Moreover,' said Charles, with an appreciative

nod to the Major, 'you 'll remember what we were told in court. We are not to concern ourselves with the question of punishment. That 's outside our province. Our job is to give a true verdict on the evidence before us. The consequences of that verdict have nothing to do with us. I think I 'm right, am I not, Major?'

'Certainly, you 're right, sir. Quite. Quite.' A deuced clear-headed fellow, this foreman: shaping much better than I thought he would.

A new voice joined the discussion. It came from that lean, dark, saturnine fellow in the blue serge suit, who sat on the foreman's right. By name Bonaker.

'We 're not concerned with the consequences,' remarked Bonaker, slowly and rather heavily. 'That 's right enough . . .'

'So perhaps . . .' said Charles, still intent on Blanche Izeley——

'All the same,' proceeded Bonaker, unhurrying, but in a suddenly raised voice that quite drowned the more cultured accents of the foreman, 'all the same we know what the consequences will be, don't we, if we find that fellow guilty?' No one contradicted him. 'And it 's no use pretending we don't.' He looked gloomily round the table, apparently unaware of being tedious. 'What I mean is,' he added, after a pause, 'that knowing the consequences, hanged by the neck and so on, we can't take chances.'

358

'You mean,' said Cyril Gaskin, witheringly, 'that we mustn't say he 's guilty if he isn't.'

'Precisely,' agreed Bonaker, seeing nothing amiss with the remark. 'That 's just what I do mean.'

'I 'm sure that 's very helpful,' said Mr Gaskin, distributing his famous smile round the table. 'That gets us on splendidly.'

Charles, ignoring Cyril's smile, and heartily disapproving of the smiling responses to it, returned to the attack on Blanche Izeley.

'So the question is, Mrs Izeley, did this man Strood, or did he not, give his wife poison?'

'I can't help thinking,' said Blanche—for there was no escape—'that he gave her what you call poison, but——'

'I think so, too,' interrupted Lucy Prynne, suddenly breaking out of her silence. 'In the malted milk,' she explained, looking round.

'Very well,' said Charles. He noted that there were now six votes for conviction, including his own, the Major's, and that nasty little ladies' man's at the opposite end of the table. The plump Bayfield had made no secret of how *he* would vote, and that made seven. No dissentients.

'And you, sir? What do you say?'

'Guilty,' said Arthur Cheed.

§ 34

HAPPY MARRIAGE

IT cost Arthur a pang to say that, but he had made up his mind and when it came to the point he did not hesitate. To have to send a fellow-creature to the gallows was the vilest compulsion that the fates had ever put upon him. He felt he would have given anything to get out of it, and his heart warmed to the illogical Mrs Izeley, with her absurd belated talk of conscientious objections. Up to a point he shared those objections, and in nine cases out of ten he wouldn't have scrupled to seize wilfully upon some fine-drawn sophistical doubt and argue himself into a state of believing the crime unproved, even though in his secret mind he had been convinced to the contrary. If the man in question were a murderer not by disposition, but, as it were, by accident, if you could be morally sure that he 'd never do it again, what good purpose was to be served by hanging him? So argued Arthur Cheed. But poisoning was in a class by itself; poisoning was all too apt to become a habit. If Strood had done what they said he had done, you couldn't think of him as a man at all: he was a subtle and dangerous beast, and the sooner the world was rid of him the easier we could sleep in our beds. Because, don't you see, he must have planned and timed the thing with extraordinary

care; quietly, in his mind, he condemned his poor
young wife to death, and smiled at her, and kept
up a pretence; kissed her as usual; made love to
her, perhaps, with murder in his heart. And,
whatever the Defending Counsel might say, the
case against Strood did carry conviction. It fitted
together; you could see it all happening; and you
couldn't, by any manner of means, miss seeing
that the prisoner's story was largely, and at all the
crucial points, a pack of lies. Either the man was
guilty, thought Arthur, or he was the most unfortu-
nate victim of coincidence that ever lived. Arthur
Cheed posed the alternative in a merely rhetorical
spirit, for in fact he had no doubt of Strood's
guilt. Had he powerfully wished to doubt, he
could have managed it; but the wish, inevitable
flower of a naturally gentle heart, was not strong
enough to contend against the counter-wish, rooted
in the same rich soil, that cruelty so vile in its
effects should be cut off from the body of mankind
like the malignant growth it was. This was his
reasoning, and, so far, he knew his mind. But
there were perhaps other things working in him
that he didn't know, or didn't notice. He didn't
notice, for example—why should he?—that up to a
certain point in the trial he was passionately with
the prisoner, pitying and understanding, and beyond
that point saw him with entirely different eyes and
could believe no good of him. COUNSEL: 'Now
tell us, Mrs Tucker, how did the prisoner receive

this piece of news?' MRS TUCKER: 'He flew into a temper.'

Arthur Cheed did not pause to recall the time of his own wife's pregnancy, but it lived in him, part of his intimate history, part of himself: like the first things of childhood, like sunlight and flowers dawning on a virgin mind, it was a cardinal event lending its own subtle colour to the window through which he saw the world. A golden age, anxious, hopeful, shot through with shafts of unimaginable excitement. In their first year of marriage he and Nellie had exercised a deliberate caution. His garage was then only a dream, scarcely that; and a cycle-dealer, running a small shop in an Essex town inconveniently far from London (but rents were the cheaper for that inconvenience), is not in a position to rush headlong into paternity. Arthur's little bit of capital—his mother's sixty-pound legacy, augmented by the army gratuity—had been quickly engulfed in the twin enterprises of commerce and marriage. One ambition he had realized promptly: ever since he had been old enough to think about such things he had wanted to own a bit of freehold, to stand on his own ground and know that every grass-blade that sprang up within given boundaries was his own. It was a blissful day when he fixed up with Hartop, a little eager speculative builder and a man after his own heart, to buy an acre in the middle of a field. Three months before the wedding he sprang it on Nellie, this blessed acre, as a surprise. They arrived, cold and hungry, in the dusk of a November day; having glanced benevolently at the exterior of the cycle-shop, they walked a mile or two into the country, and a further mile across sodden fields, and there it was, the acre, bare grass indeed, and to the unseeing eye no different from the land that environed it, but invested with rare beauty for these two people by the single strand of barbed wire that marked it off as their own.

'Something to show you,' said Arthur, desperately afraid now lest the long-prepared 'surprise' should fall flat. She waited, mystified. It was rather cold when you stood about. 'You see this bit of land, Nellie?'

'What bit of land, Arthur?'

'Well, this bit, this fenced-in bit.'

'You mean this what we 're standing on?'

'Yes. That 's right. Well—' his heart sank into his boots—'do you like it?'

She was almost afraid to guess what he was driving at. 'You don't mean——?'

'Yes, I do,' said Arthur. 'It 's ours.'

'Ours!'

'I 've bought it,' said Arthur. 'For us,' he added. He was beginning to feel better. Things were going to be all right after all.

Nellie had never seen anything so lovely in her life as that wire fence. Her eye, travelling round it, came incredulously to rest upon the vast extent of greenness that it enclosed.

'Go on,' she said. 'You're pulling my leg.'
But she believed no such thing. It couldn't be
true, but it *was* true. She was embarrassed with
so much happiness, and felt that she could never do
enough to deserve so wonderful a man as Arthur.
'You don't mean it, do you? Not really?'

Arthur was now himself again. 'Course not.
Just a little joke of mine. But Hartop doesn't
know that. He's been and spent the money by
now, I shouldn't wonder. Thought it was real
money, don't you see.'

'Oh, Arthur, what a tease you are!' said Nellie
blissfully. When she lifted her eyes to the hills,
the wooded hills of the horizon, she felt the tears
coming, because he was so good and she so happy,
because her love was more than she could bear,
because she couldn't begin at once, that very night,
to be a wife to him. All she could do was to
squeeze his hand and say: 'Who's Hartop? First
I've heard of him.'

'Hartop? He's the chap I bought it from.
I mean the chap I pretended to buy it from—he
don't know the difference.'

'He must be an awfully nice man,' said Nellie.

'Good as gold,' agreed Arthur. 'He's a sort of
builder in a small way. Takes an interest too.'

After a silence heavy with contentment Nellie
asked: 'Does anybody else know, besides Hartop?'

'No fear! Only you and me.'

'It's our secret,' said Nellie. 'Oh, Arthur!'

She looked at him, a lean sandy-complexioned young man in a somewhat grease-stained waterproof coat. He had recently lost a front tooth. 'I want to give you a hundred babies,' she said.

He smiled, with a mingling of happiness and irony that she found angelic. 'More the merrier. But one at a time, ducks, if it's all the same to you. Though of course,' he added, with an air of gravely pondering the question, 'they might come a bit cheaper if we had 'em in dozens.'

'Oh, Arthur, you *are* silly!'

'Well,' said Arthur, 'have to be getting back, I s'pose.' It wasn't much fun sending Nellie back to her mother after this. 'By the way,' he threw out casually, disguising his pride, 'it's an acre, in case you want to know.'

'Really!' cried Nellie. 'But it looks much more than that,' she added loyally.

'We'll have a few trees in, later on,' promised Arthur. 'Trees all the way round. How'd that be?'

'Are we going to make a nest in one of the trees, to live in?' asked Nellie.

'That's the idea,' said Arthur. 'You've got it. Just right. But we'll maybe have some sort of a wooden shack as well. You know,' he explained. 'Doors and windows and a chimney-pot.'

'What shall we want that for, if we live in the trees?'

'For the birds, of course,' said Arthur. 'They've got to live somewhere, poor little devils.'

After a silence, a silence big with the future, Nellie asked rather anxiously: 'Will it cost an awful lot, Arthur?'

'Not so bad,' said Arthur. 'My idea is, one of those wooden huts. Only for a time. Till we see a bit further ahead. You can get one ready-made and put it up yourself. They 're quite a decent size, you know. Easily fix up a couple of rooms inside. But of course,' he added, anxiously, 'it won't be a proper house like you 've been used to.'

'Aren't men stupid!' cooed Nellie softly. Darkness was coming on fast, but the light that shone from her was enough light for Arthur. 'Aren't they just!' Before he could say anything she went on in a dreaming voice: 'A tiny wooden house all to ourselves. And this enormous piece of land. You 're sure it 's really ours, Arthur?'

'More than if it was freehold,' he assured her. 'It 's better than freehold: it 's what they call fee-simple.'

'What 's fee-simple?'

'I don't exactly know,' confessed Arthur, 'but I do know it 's better than freehold. If the King himself wanted this bit of land off us he couldn't have it, not without paying. Couldn't turn us out, not the King himself.'

'Well, p'raps he won't try, dear,' said Nellie. 'Where shall we get our water from?'

'There 's to be a well dug. Hartop 's seeing to that.'

'I suppose there's plenty of farms near?'

'Expect so. Why?'

'Oh, nothing. But we might like a drop of milk with our tea sometimes.'

Arthur stared admiringly. 'Trust a woman to think of things.'

That piece of extraordinary foresight confirmed him in the conviction that Nellie was the best wife a man could have, as well as the most taking. Nor had he seriously doubted it since. There had been bursts of temper and disputes between them, but no full-dress quarrels; impatience and exasperation, but no radical unkindness. And if some of its features fell far short of the bliss that imagination had promised, this new life yielded other satisfactions that had been impossible to anticipate and remained impossible to define. There was something about the smell of the morning when you put your head out of the window to make sure that the acre was still there, and, for the eyes of a young husband ploughing his way home after a day's work, there was the sight of smoke curling from the chimney of a small wooden house in the green valley, three fields away.

Arthur and Nellie on Sundays, and Nellie alone in spare hours throughout the week, diligently dug into the acre and cultivated potatoes, cabbages, carrots, celery, beet, scarlet runners, gooseberries, and red currants. They also kept 'a few chicken', and later on they acquired a goat, a beast so active

and voracious that it had to be tethered on a stout
chain, which, at nicely chosen intervals through the
night, just when a fellow was dropping off again,
it rattled violently under the bedroom window. And
it was all very well to say move it (he said to Nellie,
damning her unreasonable reasonableness), but the
wretched animal had got to have some sort of shelter
from the wind, these cold nights, and they couldn't
afford to build a special place for her ladyship.
The goat, though with evident reluctance, yielded
enough milk for their needs and so spared Nellie a
daily expedition across fields—generally muddy—
to the nearest farm. And goat's milk, they had
heard, was good for babies, far better than cow's.

Soon, and sooner than they had at first intended
('for if we wait till we can afford it we shall die
waiting', said Arthur sagely), there was a baby in
prospect: no longer a mere dream, but a mysterious
entity giving definite signs of existence. Nellie
became afflicted with sick feelings, not only in the
mornings, but at intervals throughout the day; and
it was found by experiment that this meant hunger,
or anyhow that the taking of food, a little and
often, would ward it off. So nowadays they never
went for their long Sunday walks (for they refused
to be slaves to their acre, much as they delighted
in it) without taking sandwiches with them and a
thermos flask filled with hot milk. 'George hasn't
half got an appetite,' said Arthur, grinning. 'Eat
us out of house and home he will.' His fancy

raced ahead, to entertain pictures of the child
running about in the acre, shouting and laughing
with pleasure in precisely those things that gave
his father pleasure: the elastic quality of the turf,
the dew on the grass, the wooded hills of the
southern horizon, the vivid changing sky, and all
the intoxicating aliveness of nature. Nellie agreed
that you couldn't wish for a nicer name than George,
but sometimes in their fancy the child was a girl,
whom they called Vera, which was Nellie's second
name. Nellie always thought of George or Vera
as a tiny plump baby, delicious and helpless; but
Arthur's visions were of a five-year-old, someone
you could play with and hoist on your shoulder
without fear of breakages. Often, on his return
from the shop, he saw young George or little Vera
running across the field to meet him. It was going
to be a costly business, but who cared? The
months went slowly by; Arthur's pride and excitement grew; and towards the end he could think of
nothing but the coming baby, until one morning,
three weeks before the expected arrival, Nellie came
to him with grey face and limp hands and collapsed
into his arms.

When they told him that the baby was dead in
her womb, and she in danger, he spared no more
thought for George or Vera, though their ghosts
haunted the acre. Nor did he mention them when
at last, the day after the operation, he was allowed
to see Nellie. Instead, he gave her a circumstantial

account of the behaviour of Nancy the goat when he had tried to milk her. Nellie did not so much as smile at his nonsense, but she looked one degree less forlorn by the time he left her, and that, said Arthur to himself, that 's a start anyhow. After five weeks alone in the wooden hut he shut the place up and cleared out, to take possession of a four-roomed cottage on the outskirts of Whinley, within twenty minutes' walk of his shop. To this cottage Nellie came at last. She was not yet her old self. 'What do we want four rooms for?' was her first comment. And Arthur felt a blunderer, for he knew that now there could never be more than two in family. Swallowing his disappointment, for he had hoped to please her, he took her hand and drew her into the kitchen.

'See what 's here,' he said. 'The kitchen, see? A sink, what 's more. Two taps, hot and cold.' He watched her anxiously out of the corner of his eye, waiting for her to see something else than the sink.

'Why, what 's this?' asked Nellie. 'Oh, Arthur, isn't it pretty?'

'Oh, *that*,' said Arthur, cunningly. 'That 's only a kitten.' It was, however, the loveliest kitten that Nellie had ever seen, a golden tabby measuring about seven and a half inches from tip to tail.

'Like him?' said Arthur, with an air of indifference tempered by surprise. 'Well, he 's not a bad kitten, as kittens go. Nuisance about the house, rather. Doesn't know his manners.'

'But where did you get him, Arthur?'

Arthur had acquired the kitten by simple pur-
chase. 'Found him in the street, straying. Starved,
too, by the look of him. And he wasn't half
frightened,' added Arthur, with a brutal laugh.
'Of course we don't have to keep him. I dare say
one of my customers 'll give him a home.'

'What shall we call him?' asked Nellie. 'Silas,'
she answered herself quickly, picking on a name
at random, in her haste to avoid remembering
the name she must learn to forget. 'He's *alive*,'
said Nellie softly, renewing a forgotten moment,
twenty years away, when, as a child, she had held
a kitten in her arms for the first time, and found it
so much more lovely and exciting than even the
loveliest of dolls.

The Cheeds were childless. Whereas Roderick
Strood . . . how could Arthur feel pity for a man
like that? Pity he did feel, but horror and something like hatred were uppermost.

He scowled. He said: 'Guilty.'

Charles Underhay passed the question round
the table.

'Guilty.'

'Guilty.'

'Guilty.'

There were two more to vote. Bayfield was one
of them. The jury had been in conference for
precisely four minutes.

§ 35

CLEARING THE GROUND

THERE was a sudden silence in the jury-room, and a strong current of excitement began flowing among the twelve, an excitement born of a sense not so much of crisis as of solidarity and power. For a moment the jury was one: from the fusion of those separate psyches a new being had emerged, a group-spirit, an emotional monster in whose godlike power all personal inadequacies and impotencies were lost. Its eyes glittered, it breathed delight, it swelled and swelled until the whole earth was full of its glory. It gave itself with shuddering pleasure to the contemplation of the blood-rite, the sanctified vengeance, to which it was dedicated. In that moment the session became a love-feast, garnished with the intoxicating spices of cruelty. The jury, in all its members, felt the rising tide of a lust to which, as individuals, they believed themselves to be strangers. The mob-soul, seizing its brief chance, achieved definition. Humanity was eclipsed, civilization in abeyance.

But the moment passed. The monster disintegrated, as one by one the individuals composing it came back to life. With a sense of emerging from a strange orgy, of which the memory at once attracted and repelled them, they became conscious once more of where they were and what they were at: of the green-washed high walls and bare polished table of the jury-room, and of the task before them. Beginning more or less by chance at Lucy Prynne, who was situated at 9 on the clock-map, Charles had sent his question travelling anti-clockwise round the table, ending at Oliver Brackett (3 o'clock), Major Forth and Clare Cranshaw having already voiced their opinion. Bayfield and Bonaker to the right of him, sitting at 10 and 11 o'clock respectively, he had momentarily forgotten, and now, remembering them with a start, he deliberately refrained from repairing the omission. He was a little disconcerted by the result of his canvass, for it seemed to him unseemly that a decision, even though he agreed with it, should be so swiftly arrived at, without discussion and on a capital charge. He would never be able to face the Judge, and pronounce the verdict, after an interval so indecently brief. Indeed it was only Gaskin's importunity that had harried him into putting the question at all at this early stage.

'Well,' he remarked nervously, hardly daring to face the company, 'this unanimity is very surprising.'

'Very gratifying, I should say,' said Cyril Gaskin, with a meaning glance at Bayfield, followed by a winning smile for the ladies.

Oliver Brackett had already taken a dislike to Gaskin. The bland confidence of the fellow put his back up and provoked him to make difficulties.

'I suppose there 's no doubt about it, is there?'

he asked diffidently, addressing the company in general. His theatre was closed down for a while. He had just enacted the execution on that secret stage; had stood blindfold on the scaffold, listening to the voice of the chaplain and waiting for the drop; had adjusted the knot with his ready, hangman's fingers. And now there was a lump of nausea in his throat, and he was conscious of a foul contagion in the air about him.

'That's just the question, isn't it?' said his neighbour, Coates: rather cleverly, in his own opinion. 'I don't wish anyone any harm,' continued Mr Coates, 'but it's a clear enough case to me. And some of us have got businesses to attend to.'

'That's right,' said Mr Nywood. 'We can't do the poor chap any good by hanging about.'

'We've only got to use our common sense,' contributed Mr Bayfield.

'Good idea,' said Bonaker.

'Exactly,' cried Cyril Gaskin, taking possession of the floor. 'I'm sure,' he went on in a honeyed voice, 'I'm sure none of us like the job we're on. Speaking for myself, I know I'd give a lot to be relieved of it. But we've got our duty to society, and we must really make up our minds, ladies and gentlemen, to be a little, well, shall I say, *brave* about it. Yes, brave. The ladies, as we all know, have very tender hearts. We honour them for it. Personally speaking, and I think I shall carry the gentlemen with me in this, I very much wish this dreadful decision could have been left to what I may perhaps call the sterner sex. We've got our duty to society——'

'You've said that before,' said Bonaker, in a loud but not unfriendly voice.

Cyril turned to him with a sickly smile. 'Thank you, my friend. And I say it again.'

'Just as you please,' said Bonaker cheerfully. 'Thought you'd like to know though . . .'

'As I was saying——' Cyril went on.

'In case it was an accident,' explained Bonaker.

Cyril reddened. To be treated like this in the presence of the ladies! 'Will you allow me to speak, sir?'

'Go ahead,' said Bonaker. 'Society.'

'What do you mean by that?'

'Society,' repeated Bonaker. 'You were telling us about society.'

It was impossible to know whether the fellow was being deliberately rude, or merely clumsy. There was a massive simplicity about him that made the second theory the more probable. And yet . . .

'What I can't get over'—Sidney Nywood joined in—'is that wireless business.' He scratched his head thoughtfully: a trick his wife had often told him about. She didn't like the undertaking business and she didn't like to see a man scratching his head. A woman so full of well-off notions took a good deal of living up to, but Sidney didn't let it worry him. 'All right, old girl!' he would say. 'Have it your own way.' But she didn't like that either. 'Old girl,' it seemed, was a low way of speaking. 'Well, you know best,' said Sidney. And he meant it. He himself had no claim or aspirations to refinement: all he wanted was a steady comfortable income and no worry. But he respected such aspirations in others, and especially in Flo. He made no secret of his conviction—and hers— that Flo was a good cut above him. He was proud of her superiority; he boasted of it; it was almost his only point of vanity. 'Course, the wife, she 's a lady,' he told his friends. 'She 's too good for a chap like me, really. But she don't complain, not her. That 's where it comes in, don't you see? There 's some that *would* complain.' When neighbours dropped in for a chat (which was all too seldom nowadays, for there didn't seem to be time to be sociable as you got older), when for example Mr Cattel dropped in, there was nothing that pleased Sidney more than to set Flo at her piano-playing. 'P'raps Mr Cattel would like a tune, Flo,' Sidney would say, in a voice hesitating between heartiness and timidity. And then, if Flo felt in the mood, they would switch off the wireless, with its Bach and its Beethoven and its Herman Finck, and have either *List to the Convent Bells*, or *Melody in F*, and very often both. *Melody in F* was Sidney's favourite, and he never tired of hearing it, at least in Flo's rendering. After all, it wasn't everyone that possessed a piano; and fewer still possessed a wife who could play it so loud and fast. And you couldn't expect a woman like Flo to see eye to eye in everything with a man like himself. She was all for doing things on a grand scale, buying land and building rows of houses and feathering the nest in a dignified way. But Sidney's ventures in this line were seldom successful. 'There's no money in property,' he told her, again and again. 'That's because you're too soft with people,' Flo retorted. 'You seem to want to work for next to nothing.' But soft though he was, and proud though he was of Flo's gentility, it did not occur to him to change his ways in order to accommodate himself to her point of view. He was humbly unyielding when it came to a matter of business, holding, as he did, that just as it was part of a wife's office to nag a little, and especially a wife who was the daughter of a linen-draper in such a big way of business that he had ruined himself, so it was a good husband's job to listen patiently and take no further notice. It does her good to have her say, thought Sidney, but there are some things a man knows best about. 'Tell you what, Flo,' he said one day. 'You take over the business, fix up the contracts and all that, and I'll do the mending and cooking.' That was his sole excursion into irony, the nearest he ever got to 'answering her back'. But with all this he knew well enough that she was fond of him, and in that knowledge he was content.

And, now, what Sidney couldn't get over was that wireless business.

'You 'd be a clever man if you could,' commented Gaskin, recovering the poise that Bonaker had momentarily lost him.

Thus encouraged, Sidney plunged into superfluous explanations. 'That message, you know. He must have heard it. The man said he saw him listening.'

'Exactly,' said Cyril Gaskin. 'A message that his wife is dangerously ill, and what does his lordship do? Goes calmly off to America—or would have done.'

Bonaker raised a puzzled head. 'Do you mean the Judge?'

Everybody stared at him.

'We said nothing whatever about the Judge.' Gaskin tried to be patient, but really . . .!

'We 're speaking of the prisoner, don't you see!' said Nywood. 'And that business at the hotel.'

'*He* said something about "his lordship ",' objected Bonaker, jerking a shoulder towards Gaskin. 'The prisoner isn't a lordship, is he? First I 've heard of it.'

'Really!' exclaimed Gaskin. 'Don't you understand, it 's a way of speaking?'

'Silly way of speaking, don't you think?' asked Bonaker, as one friend to another. Gaskin opened his mouth to answer, but Bonaker's voice, dull and flat and loud, went heartily on: 'You know—confusing somehow. Doesn't make sense, to my mind.'

'It really doesn't seem to me,' said Gaskin, with dignity, 'a matter of very great importance——'

'Quite. Quite,' interrupted Bonaker. 'Thought I'd just mention it. No offence.'

What a common sort of man that is! thought Lucy. So unlike someone *I* know. He asked me to call him Edward.

'On the other hand,' said Charles Underhay, 'that particular bit of evidence was a good deal shaken by the Defence. It's only fair to remember that. That barman didn't seem to me a very trustworthy witness.'

'What the German woman said,' remarked Brackett, 'flatly contradicted his evidence. She said the prisoner was with her in the dining-room at nine o'clock. And we know that the message came over at nine o'clock.'

'And, pray, what does that mean?' cried Gaskin. 'It means that one of the two is lying. Come now, let's ask ourselves, let's face it: Which of them had the strongest motive for lying?'

'The woman,' said Roger Coates.

'Hear, hear!' said Bayfield. 'She didn't want to give him away.'

'I agree with you, gentlemen,' said Gaskin cordially. 'And personally speaking,' he added, with an air of courageously defying the whole world, 'I can't find it in my heart to blame her for it.

379

It was her that had got him into the mess, and it was up to her, perjury or no perjury, to get him out of it. Perjury or no perjury,' repeated Mr Gaskin, almost passionately. We 'll have no narrow-minded cant here, his flashing eyes declared.

He 's really rather splendid, thought Lucy. Now suppose Edward had committed a murder, and the only way I could save him was to tell an untruth . . .

'Of course,' said Charles Underhay, 'it 's not a vital point. The case doesn't by any means depend on it.'

'You mean, sir,' suggested the Major, 'that even if we reject the barman's evidence, that doesn't prove the prisoner's innocence.'

'Exactly, Major.'

'But we haven't got to prove the prisoner's innocence, have we?' Bonaker inquired. 'What I mean is, the boot 's on the other foot, isn't it? We 've got to make sure whether he 's guilty or not. Isn't that so?'

'That,' said Gaskin, 'if I may say so, my friend, is a distinction without a difference.'

'Well, you know best, I 'm sure,' said Bonaker. 'But there seems to *me* a sort of difference. Put it this way. Suppose I took it into my head that you were a dirty scoundrel. Nothing personal, of course—just an illustration. Well, I couldn't hang you for it, could I, till it had been *proved* that you were a dirty scoundrel. And if it wasn't proved,

I 'd have to let you go, wouldn't I? It stands
to sense.'

Gaskin agreed.

'Good,' said Bonaker. 'Now this is the point:
I shouldn't have to prove that you *weren't* a dirty
scoundrel, before letting you go, should I? As a
matter of fact, it might take a bit of doing. It
might be impossible.'

It appeared to Gaskin that he was being insulted.

'I beg your pardon!'

'Not at all,' said Bonaker.

'You mean,' Charles elucidated, 'that we 've got
to be satisfied of the fact of guilt, and that if we
aren't so satisfied, the contrary fact, of innocence,
has to be assumed, whether we find it easy to
believe or not?'

'That 's the idea,' agreed Bonaker.

'True enough,' said the Major. 'But isn't it
all rather hypothetical, rather in the air? Isn't it
painfully evident, from the facts before us, that the
fellow 's guilty? Here 's a husband with a very
good reason for wanting his wife out of the way.
The wife dies of poisoning, and meanwhile, between
the taking of the poison and the death, the husband
has fled, without a word to anybody, and under an
assumed name. Whether or not he listened in to
that wireless S O S is neither here nor there.'

'We 'll take it then that he didn't?' suggested
Bonaker.

'Take it so, by all means,' said the Major. 'But

381

I 'm afraid we shall also have to take it that he poisoned his wife.'

Roger Coates, leaning across the table towards Gaskin, raised a question which for a long while, too long for his comfort, he had been entertaining in silence.

'I say,' said Mr Coates. 'That woman of his. D' you think she knew he 'd done it?' He smiled knowingly at the company.

§ 36

PRISONER'S FRIENDS

MARK PERRYMAN glanced again at his watch. The jury had been away seven and a half minutes. He touched his neighbour's arm.

'Shall we wander outside for a bit?'

Elisabeth looked at him questioningly.

'They 'll be some time yet,' said Mark, his hand still resting on her sleeve.

She made a gesture of assent, and rose. Mark followed her out of the court-room. At the door he paused, to say to the constable on duty: 'We shall be just outside.' Though of that he was not sure. 'You 'll give me the tip when they come back?'

'Very good, sir.'

Mark overtook Elisabeth in the corridor. She smiled briefly as he fell into step by her side.

To Roderick, Elisabeth's quality was something infinitely subtle: subtle, lovely, elusive. It was his destiny, which he had passionately embraced, to adore her mystery and never possess it. Mark Perryman, to whom a shy faltering version of this conviction had been confided, did not see her so. His incorrigible bias towards realism, and his half-rueful persuasion that reality was essentially un-romantic, made him hazard to himself, though not to Roderick, the opinion that his friend was the victim of a purely visual and aural enchantment. The warm darkness of the woman and the cold blue of her eyes, the lithe figure suggesting swiftness and the soft contours suggesting languor, the young fragility of the flesh and the rich maturity and haunting overtones of the voice: this blend of physical delights, said Mark, was more than enough to fill a man's head with mystical notions, if the man happened to be old Roderick, who had some-how never outgrown the sublime folly of adolescence. Mark himself was not insensible to it, but for him, in spite of all that seemed to contradict it, her beauty was that of a child flowering luxuriously into womanhood. In Mark's estimation, she did not in the least tally with Roderick's account of her, except in the single point of beauty and charm. For all her intelligence, he found her simple *au fond*, and, for all her sophistication, primitive as

Eve. To Roderick she was timeless, a flower of paradise: of her past and her future he made no question. To Mark (who lacked Roderick's inches) she was a tall young woman in process of ripening into a maturity whose wonder would richly excel her present charms. Those charms, from a position of safe neutrality, he found no difficulty in admiring; but in five years' time, he thought . . . and was dazzled by the prospect, for he had, among other and contrary tastes, a predilection for amplitude in woman.

He glanced at her half-averted profile and asked tentatively: 'Would you care to go out into the street? Or stay here?'

In watchful solicitude for Elisabeth he found some distraction from the hideous anxiety in himself which, now that the crisis had come, could no longer be ignored. From the first moment of Roderick's danger he had laboured in his mind to make light of it. He made no pretence of denying that many a man had been hanged on such evidence as this, but after that his logic failed, and, though he distrusted mere hope, it was in a rationalization of hope that he took refuge. Since Roderick was palpably innocent, he argued, it was unthinkable that a British jury should find him guilty. And when the thought came, They don't know him as I do, he looked the other way, refusing to entertain it. But now, with only the verdict to wait for, all his inward resistances broke down. The case

against Roderick was infernally plausible; and, to
an outsider, was Roderick's story altogether convincing? Worse than that, Mark could not quite
suppress an uneasy suspicion that Roderick had
lied in one or two particulars. That S O S message
for instance—did he or didn't he hear it? He
might have heard it and disbelieved it, thinking it
a trick not uncharacteristic of poor Daphne in her
more desperate moods. He might have heard it
and ignored it for that reason. It wasn't like
Roderick, for that kind of ruthless determination
was something he conspicuously lacked: still, it
just might have happened so. As for the poisoning,
he could not have done that, except in madness; and
if he had done it in madness, he would certainly
have destroyed himself in the moment of returning
sanity. You had only to know Roderick to know
that. But what did the jury think? What were
they thinking and saying at this moment? Surely
they had enough common sense to see the kind of
man he was? In spirit, Mark too was in the jury-
room, flattering, cajoling, reasoning. In any group
of twelve persons you get a few good fellows, don't
you?

But while the uncontrolled part of his mind
moved with a feverish activity, his will was fixed
protectively on Elisabeth. To serve her was the
only service he could now render to his friend, and
in this he was single-minded and self-forgetful, so
that he did not even remember to play his usual

game of humorously deriding his own motives. To all appearance he was his ordinary urbane self serenely waiting upon events. There was a kind of suspended pain in his mind and body, but the voice that spoke to Elisabeth did not tremble or falter.

She smiled at him. She had heard his voice but not his question. He did not think it worth repeating, and they continued to pace slowly to and fro.

She turned to face him, taking him by both hands. 'The summing-up. What do you think, Mark?'

'We must be patient,' said Mark.

A veil came over her eyes. 'Yes, we must be patient. . . . It is not so very nice, this waiting,' she added, as if offering an explanation.

'It will be all right, of course,' said Mark smoothly. 'Even if they bring in the wrong verdict—you understand?—even then there's the appeal.'

'You think they will say he is guilty,' said Elisabeth. It was a statement, not a question.

'No,' said Mark. 'I don't know what they'll say. I'm in the dark, like you. I think what the Judge said was in Roderick's favour. A sensible jury would acquit him on that summing-up. But you can never tell with juries. But this is the point. Listen. If this jury turns out to be stupid, Harcombe will lodge an appeal. Now the appeal

will be heard without a jury, by three judges—
long-headed old buffers.'

'Long-headed? What is that?'

'Clever,' said Mark. 'Far-seeing. Clever enough
to see that Rod is an innocent man.' He abstained
from mentioning that in about ninety-eight of every
hundred cases the appeal was dismissed.

He went on talking. And while he talked he
had his eye on the door of the court-room. He
relied on the constable's promise. He went on
talking, in low tones, knowing well that Elisabeth,
though she seemed to listen, did not hear what he
said, and, though she stared at him with wide eyes,
did not see him. She 's seven years old, he said:
not a day more.

When he had run out of words it was as if a
spell had been broken. Elisabeth emerged from
her trance to say: 'Why did she die? It was so
foolish.'

The enigma of Daphne's death was something
for which Mark had no thought to spare at this
moment, and he felt that he could not help Elisabeth by discussing it. It had long been decided
between them that the theory they favoured was
that of suicide. But Mark had not been content
to let it rest there. Someone, chance-met in that
Fleet Street resort of his, mentioned having seen
the late Mrs Strood in the company of a pale young
man. 'I 'm not sure it wasn't the very day she
died,' said this crony. 'Funny, that.' And three

days after Roderick's committal for trial, recalling
this and that, adding two and two together and
getting for answer a fantastic incredible figure,
Mark jumped out of his fireside chair and went to
the telephone. After an industrious use of that
instrument he set out in search of Brian Goodeve.

§ 37

AN AFTERNOON IN OCTOBER

MEETING Daphne in Regent Street, Brian began
a hurried search among his attitudes, uncertain
which to assume.

The agony of that summer had left him weary
but not weary enough. That woman has destroyed
me, he said. But no, it's not true: she's left me
still alive in my shell, buried alive in my shell, and
to live is to suffer. October was as beautiful as
ever. Burnt ashes of summer, fragrant in the
nostrils: he tried the line over, hoping it might be
poetry, but did not get so far as writing it down,
for he found it on examination to be full of the
very quality he spent his life in denouncing. Every
word was wrong; every word was romantic and
banal; 'burnt ashes' was a vile cliché, 'summer'
dreadfully overdone, 'fragrant' unspeakably sentimental; and even 'nostrils' had probably been used
by the so-called poets of the nineteenth century.

388

Those impossible Romantics! He tried again: ochreous residue, heart's dregs. That was sufficiently unlike Tennyson, but it wouldn't do; 'dregs' was trite, and 'heart' was one of the bad old words, and anyhow the whole thing came perilously near being a statement. 'Excrement' would be better than 'dregs', for neither Keats nor Shelley would ever have said 'excrement'. But why write about autumn at all? 'Autumn' — another prohibited word. It only shows how frightfully second-rate I am, concluded Brian. He was self-contemptuous and enjoyed self-contempt. He took a sadistic pleasure in analysing his moods and disposing of his pretensions. Why pretend you 're a poet? Why pretend you *want* to be a poet? Ask Freud: he 'll tell you. Imperfectly sublimated sex, that 's what it is. And very imperfectly, by God. Hail, copulation, bird thou never wert! Poetic flights are not for you, my dear libido. And Daphne, who the hell 's Daphne? Is she the only woman, and aren't they all alike? There was a sort of pleasure in blaspheming his passion for Daphne, precisely because, despite his rantings, it retained a sacred quality and could not be reduced to a formula, whether bawdy or scientific. Having lost hope and sight of her, he saw his life as empty and aimless, and, obedient to his conception, it became so. He went on writing acid reviews as often as editors would let him, but the afternoon generally found him with nothing to do, nothing to think about, and then he would wander for hours about the streets of London, furtively glancing at the face of every young woman he saw, and sometimes turning on his heel and following one of them, for a hundred yards or so, feverishly, irresolutely, and to no ultimate purpose.

And then, suddenly, on the last day of her life, he saw Daphne coming towards him. She had not seen him: there was time to dodge. Alternatively, he could pass her by without a word, without a sign. Would that be effective or merely theatrical? Would it make her reluctantly admire him, make her feel humble and unworthy, make her think wistfully of all she had lost in him? Or would she merely smile to herself, derisively, saying: Poor Brian! What a pity he isn't even a gentleman! Worst of all, she might fail altogether to see him, and then a chance of being in her thoughts, somehow, anyhow, it didn't matter how, would have been lost for ever.

And now she had seen him. What should he say, and do? He would not avoid her: the prospect of pain was too enticing.

'Hullo, Daphne!'

He had decided to be casual, genial, man-of-the world. Polite he would be, but not frigid; friendly, but quite independent. He would say 'Yes?' and 'Well, well!' and things like that, all in a vein of irony so delicate as to leave her quite baffled. After all, he said to himself, one does not wear one's broken heart on one's sleeve: already he was feeling his way into his role.

'Hullo!' said Daphne. 'What are *you* doing in Regent Street?'

'Just walking about,' said Brian, with an air of humour. 'And you 're shopping, I suppose.'

'In a way,' admitted Daphne.

'Oh, I wasn't accusing you,' returned the genial fellow. 'Shopping 's an innocent occupation. I 'm all for it.' My God, he thought, I sound like a muscular Christian. Or a hearty schoolmaster. Or a fatuous young man trying not to be sheepish.

'What a lovely day!' said Daphne, and the way she said it, alas, made the day still lovelier. Before he could answer she asked, in a rather different tone: 'How are you, Brian?'

In another moment she would offer him her hand and say good-bye. He didn't want that yet. Forgetting to be casual he asked quickly: 'Are you in a hurry?'

'Well . . .' She hesitated. 'Not for a minute or two.'

'Couldn't we have a cup of tea?'

'Yes, I 'd like to. But it 'll have to be a hurried one, I 'm afraid.'

'Oh,' said Brian airily, 'I haven't much time myself. Day's work to do yet. There 's a place down here on the left. . . .'

She supplied the name. 'That 'll do quite well.'

'Now I come to think of it,' said Brian, 'I believe we went there once before, didn't we?'

This was dangerous ground, and it would have pleased him to explore it further while they sat facing each other over the teacups. To talk of the past with friendly indifference, with bland unconcern, what a triumph that would be, and how oddly disconcerting for Daphne! 'How young I was then!' he might say, with a carefree laugh. But the conversation did not take that turn, for Daphne, who had quickly thrown off the moment's confusion, now plied him with questions about himself.

'How are you, Brian? You don't look very well.'

'Don't I?'

'Thinner than ever,' said Daphne. 'And tired. Are you tired?'

He shrugged his shoulders, and smiled. On reflection he feared it must have looked like a 'brave' smile.

'You ought to take care of yourself,' she admonished him. 'Two lumps, isn't it, and not much milk? There's a lot of illness about at this time of the year.'

'So I've heard.'

'Are you still in the same rooms?' she asked. He nodded. 'Why don't you find somewhere else? The rooms are nice enough. Very nice indeed. But the district is so cheerless, don't you think?' Detecting a hint of bitterness in his smile she withdrew her eyes from his and added self-consciously: 'I know it's not my business, but . . .'

'It might have been,' said Brian. He couldn't resist it, though it spoilt his high resolve to maintain an inscrutable front. 'Anyhow there's no need to apologize for taking a benevolent interest in me.' His voice took on an edge, half sarcastic, half self-pitying. 'I'm in no danger of misunderstanding it.'

'Thank you for snubbing me,' said Daphne.

There was no resentment in her tone, and for that reason he was instantly ashamed of his wish to hurt her. Yet he could not let her get off so lightly. 'The truth is, Daphne, you'd like to be a sister to me, wouldn't you? You've got the traditional good woman's passion for collecting brothers.'

'Dear me!' She laughed. 'That sounds more like Mark than you.'

'Mark?' Brian's heart leapt. His jealousy began smelling out the offal it would feast upon.

'Mark Perryman,' said Daphne. 'I thought you knew him. Didn't you meet him at our house?'

'Oh, Perryman. Yes, I know Perryman. Great friend of yours, isn't he?'

'Yes. Roderick's known him ever since Cambridge days.'

Clever, thought Brian. But not clever enough. He stared at her. 'I didn't mean he was a great friend of your husband's.'

She met his stare blankly. 'But he is, all the same.'

'I meant of yours,' insisted Brian. His mouth began to twitch.

'Of mine too,' she agreed. She looked at him steadily, not liking what she saw. 'What did you have for lunch today, Brian?'

He uttered a short theatrical laugh. 'Two double whiskies.'

'Anything else?'

'Food is bad for the stomach,' said Brian.

'Do you mean you're living on whisky?'

'Good old whisky. Bad for the memory. That's why I like it.' He was not drunk, nor even shamming drunk. He was merely wretched, and eager, in his wretchedness, to say anything that would draw her attention to himself. 'Food bad for the stomach. Whisky bad for the memory. That's how it goes.'

She looked away from him, embarrassed and unhappy. 'Is this your way of punishing me?'

Out of the corner of her eye she saw him put two fingers into his waistcoat pocket and bring out a white tablet, which he dropped into his tea.

'What's that?' she asked, with nervous suddenness.

'The innocent aspirin,' said Brian jauntily. 'I'm not proposing to die at your feet. Have no fear.'

Daphne began pulling on her gloves. 'I must go.' She smiled rather sadly. 'This meeting hasn't been quite a success, has it?'

Brian watched her with a sick smile. 'Yes, hurry up. You mustn't keep Perryman waiting.'

She was already on her feet, but at that she sat down again, and faced him intently. 'Listen, Brian. You 're talking the most terrible nonsense. You don't believe what you 're saying or hinting: you only want to make me unhappy. But no one can make me unhappy today . . .'

'Of course not,' said Brian quickly. 'Your heart is filled with Perryman. The manly Perryman. Though I speak with the tongues of men and of angels and have not Perryman, it profiteth me nothing.'

Ignoring his words, she went on. 'Something 's happened to me today. Inside me. And I shan't be unhappy any more. . . . If only you 'd stop thinking about yourself, Brian.' The smile with which he greeted this piece of counsel made her flinch. But she persisted. 'I know I 'm a funny one to preach. I 'm desperately sorry about— about us. I treated you shamefully. But a lot of things have happened to me since then. I feel about ten years older . . . and ten years happier. Things have come straight somehow. And . . .' Laughing, she ended on an anticlimax: 'I feel as though I were going to have flu.' She rose from her chair. 'Good-bye. Do come and see us if you 'd like to. Ring up some time.'

For a moment she stood smiling down at him, visibly the same Daphne, yet different, remote, beyond reach both of his malice and his desire.

395

§ 38

MARK INQUISITIVE

CLIMBING the stairs to Goodeve's top-floor flat, Mark Perryman was accompanied by the ghost of a younger Mark, the man who had occupied his skin ten years ago. For in those days he too had lived on a top floor in a mean street, and he too, for a brief and callow season, had subjected the weekly papers to a fusillade of lyrics. Just the kind of lyrics, moreover, that were nowadays contemptuously derided by angry young gentlemen like Brian Goodeve. Fortunately, very few of Mark's poems had been printed, and he soon became engaged in pursuits of a more remunerative kind, special reporting, personal paragraphing, stunt articles, editorial activities, and the writing of slick copy for the Dexter Shirt or the Quantum Fountain-pen. But it was the lyrics that completed the parallel with Brian Goodeve, whom one thought of first as a poet, though one hadn't read his poetry, and indeed there was precious little of it to read. Forgetting his immediate errand for the space of half a second, Mark renewed the sensation of that bygone age when he had been twenty-five. So much had happened in those ten years, he was now so mellow and disillusioned and age-encrusted, that he was constrained to smile at that former ingenuous self. How young I was then!

he thought, with a sentiment hovering between envy and derision. In the very moment of enjoying the sentiment he was able to observe himself enjoying it, and to observe himself observing himself. He perceived that the experience was spiced with self-complacency, and, mocking himself for that, found further occasion for self-complacency in the fact that he mocked himself. This too he perceived, recognizing with a grin the recurring decimal of vanity. But, though the process was endless, he had other things to do than observe it. He passed the shut doors that were ranged round the first and the second landing, with only a moment's idle speculation about the lives they were hiding from him, and so came, a little out of breath, to the self-contained flat at the top, where, as he had begun to believe, a secret that more nearly concerned him awaited discovery.

He seized the knocker and knocked with unusual decision. By the flutter of his pulse he knew himself to be a little excited. Listening with an intentness that made him feel theatrical, and rather self-conscious, he heard an inner door open and footsteps approaching.

The door was flung open. With his untidy head resting against its edge lolled the lean young man, Brian Goodeve.

'I don't know if you remember me?' said Mark.

'Eh? Of course I do. Perryman.'

'Thought I'd look you up. Hope you don't mind.'

Brian laughed, as though laughing himself out of a dream. He appeared to be in an advanced stage of spiritual dilapidation. 'Good old Perryman!' he said, with some difficulty. 'Come and have a drink, Perryman old boy. Jolly nice to see you. Jolly nice. Jolly.' He opened the door wider and waved his guest into the room at his back. 'Sit down, old boy. Cigarette. Hoping you'd come. Tha''s right.'

Mark, lighting a cigarette, took in the whole scene at a glance. The half-empty whisky-bottle and the untouched siphon of soda-water were superfluous hints of the difficulties he anticipated. The gas fire was at the point of death. 'Gas running out, old boy,' said Brian, noticing his glance. 'No shillings.' Confound the fellow, thought Mark: he's quick enough, in spite of the whisky. He produced a shilling, saying 'Catch!', and the young man left the room and went into the kitchen, whence Mark could hear him coming to terms with the meter.

Returning he said: 'Have a whisky and soda, Perryman.' Thoughtfully, he had brought a tumbler with him.

Mark was already at the table. 'Thanks very much. May I help myself?' He helped himself. 'You're not looking awfully fit, Goodeve.' Seeing the beginning of his host's movement towards the bottle he added quickly: 'I'll do that for you. You sit down.' He poured a sprinkle of whisky into

Brian's glass and filled up to the brim with soda-water. 'Here you are, my son. Too much spoils the taste.'

'Generous fellow,' said Brian. 'You think I'm drunk. That's what it is.' Mark took the opposite chair in silence. '*Do* you think I'm drunk, Perryman?'

'All gentlemen are drunk at ten o'clock,' said Mark blandly. 'It'd distress me if you were sober.'

'Ah, that's where I've got you,' answered Brian. 'I'm not a gentleman, see? Nearly, but not quite. Tha''s where I've got you, Mr Bloody Periwinkle. No gentleman.'

Mark raised his glass. 'Well, whatever you are, here's to you!'

Having taken a sip of his scarcely discoloured soda-water, Brian sank back into his chair, and the silence, to Perryman's sense, became full of his despair. The artificial gaiety was already sponged from his face, which, hollow-cheeked and puffy-eyed, haggard and inattentive, had lapsed into an expression of infinite wretchedness. Mark restrained an impulse to ask him if he had slept in his clothes. The silence went on and on, every moment of it adding to the tale of Brian's misery. With a preconceived idea of the answer, Mark asked himself: What has brought him to this?

'So you were hoping I'd come, were you?' said Mark.

Brian roused himself, as though surprised to find that he was not alone. 'What?'

Mark tried another gambit. 'It was at the Roderick Stroods' house that we first met, wasn't it?'

Brian started, scowling. 'Was it?'

'Bad business about them,' said Mark. No answer. Mark felt that he was wasting his time and making a fool of himself. In desperation he changed his tone somewhat. 'Listen, Goodeve. I want to talk to you. . . . Are you listening?'

'What d' you want? Have another drink.'

Mark got out of his chair and placed himself in front of the gas-fire, bestriding what should have been the hearth. 'Look here. You knew Daphne Strood pretty well, didn't you?'

'What about it?' said Brian. The question angered and tortured him. 'Have you come here to crow over me, you bastard?' For the moment he had forgotten that he no longer, after Daphne's express denial, believed in his theory that Perryman had been her lover. He hated the fellow, wished him dead.

'My dear chap,' said Mark patiently, 'I haven't the least idea what you mean. I thought you were a great friend of hers: that's all. As a matter of fact I had the honour of her friendship too.'

'Yes, you did, didn't you!' The sneer was painfully apparent.

'I've just said so,' answered Mark. He was

making no headway, but for Roderick's sake he
went stubbornly on, according to plan. 'Do you
happen to remember when you last saw her?'

'Perfectly.'

'Oh, you do?'

Yes, I do. How d'you like my cigarettes?
Have another. Special line. Ten for sixpence.'

Mark smiled. 'Quite so. You're telling me
to mind my own business. But don't bother to
pretend you're drunk. It's too thin.'

'Really?'

'You're as sober as I am, fundamentally, And
even more unhappy—which is saying a good deal.
Roderick Strood is one of my oldest friends.' He
spoke simply, without anger or guile. 'You know
they've charged him with the murder?'

Brian nodded without speaking.

'Yes,' said Mark. 'They're trying to make out
he poisoned her. Will you tell me this, Goodeve:
is it true that you were with Daphne on the day of
her death?'

'Yes. Do you mind?'

'Have you told the police that?' asked Mark,
rather sharply.

Brian began laughing, and having begun he
exhibited a disposition to go on endlessly. Laughter
turned to coughing, and coughing seemed to jerk
him out of his chair. He stood facing Perryman
with a satirical grin. 'No, Perryman,' he said,
gasping for breath, 'I haven't told the police. But

you 're welcome to, Perryman. Look'—he darted
to the table—'first I 'll have a little drink.' He
poured out his drink. 'Come and help yourself,
Perryman. First a little drink, and then I 'll get
'em for you.' Gulping down his drink he went
out of the room, leaving the door open. Mark
heard him lift the receiver from the telephone and
ask, after a pause, for Whitehall 1212.

Mark strolled into the passage. 'Why be a
fool, Goodeve?'

'Is that Scotland Yard?' said Brian, into the
telephone. 'Mr Perryman wants to speak to you.
He 's found the Strood murderer. No, not the man
they 're charging—the real murderer. Mr Perryman will tell you all about it.' Grinning maliciously
at Mark, he recited the address. 'Send one of
your best men, won't you? Someone who can read
and write, if possible.' Coughing again seized him
and he slammed the receiver down and gave himself
up to a paroxysm. . . .

Pacing up and down the corridor with Elisabeth
Andersch, Mark confessed to himself that Goodeve
had made him feel a little silly that night, though
he was too old a hand to be betrayed into looking
so. The story of the young man's meeting with
Daphne in Regent Street had not visibly interested
the two officers sent round from the local station;
nor had Roderick's advisers been able to turn it to
any good account.

'Why did she die?' asked Elisabeth again, touching Mark's hand appealingly. 'Do you think it was because of me, Mark?'

Mark shrugged his shoulders. 'We shall never know.'

She did not hear his answer, for her mind, as he saw, had suddenly dropped Daphne and had seized again, desperately, upon Roderick. Out of the tail of his eye he saw the door of the court-room opening. The friendly constable stepped into the corridor.

Mark took a step towards him. 'They're coming back?'

'Not yet, sir. Sorry, sir. His lordship's gone to his tea.'

§ 39

BONAKER DISSENTS

BLANCHE IZELEY, tormented by anxiety and indecision, searched the faces of her fellow-jurors. The three days of the trial, and the two nights spent in a strange hotel under the surveillance of the court, had wrought drastic changes in her. The bland fiction in which her psyche had sheltered for the past five years had gradually yielded under the pressure of an ugly reality. Roderick and Daphne, Paul and Blanche, she could not avoid seeing the parallel, and once seen it loomed larger and larger in her imagination. She remembered, with

particularity, that day on which Paul had decided
to leave her and go to his new love. 'What is it you
think you see in her?' she asked him. 'Well, for
one thing,' said Paul, 'she happens to be beautiful.'
To which Blanche answered, gently, patronizingly:
'But there is beauty in everyone, my dear. Do
try to be clear about what you 're doing. There
is true beauty, and there is an illusion of the so-
called senses. . . .' He interrupted: 'I 've heard
that record, Blanche. Try another one, if you must
talk.' 'But listen, Paul,' she said sweetly reasoning,
'if you can't see beauty in me any more, it 's
because . . .' 'It 's because you bore me,' he
broke out passionately. 'I 'm so bored I can hardly
breathe.' That was virtually his last word to her,
and it was something which, since it could not be
forgiven, had to be explained away as an aberration,
an illusion, a sickness, a what-you-will—anything
rather than face it as a plain fact. There was a
moment when Blanche saw herself visiting Paul and
his woman with death in her hand, confronting them
in their guilt and slaying them with one blast of her
mighty thought: a fantasy born of the feeling that
she could never breathe again so long as those two
lived to shame her. A moment only, quickly buried
under the mountain of her desperately induced persuasion that their so-called love for each other was
merely a gross error of a kind from which she herself, having Truth to guide and sustain her, was
gloriously immune. She trained herself to think of

them, not with kindness or charity (though she called it that), but with a falsely-pitying smile. But the impact with this other story, the contagion of these other lives into which the trial of Roderick Strood had plunged her, had quickened that buried moment: the mountain heaved, the bitterness erupted. And, power being given into her hands, she saw a chance, at last, of taking vengeance against her former impotence, of getting even with the fate that had humiliated her, by cleansing the world of this Roderick-Paul. Such a plan could not be entertained in her consciousness: to recognize it made it impossible of fulfilment. In the instant that she caught herself wishing for the prisoner's death, she knew that only by saving him could she rid herself of guilt.

So, anxiously, almost with despair, she searched the faces of her fellow-jurors.

They had just been refreshing themselves with tea and toast, which had been brought into the conference-room by two solemn silent policemen, with the black-gowned usher as invigilator. The pale-faced little miss on her left, as Blanche noticed with vague disapproval, had consumed, with a furtive efficiency, as many as three fingers of buttered toast. Mr Bayfield's vigorous work with a hand-kerchief had failed to dislodge a crumb that had taken refuge in his moustache. Almost every face wore an expression that hovered between shame and defiance. To admit to hunger at such a time

seemed somehow indecent; and to eat in stolid
silence—for the debate was suspended by tacit
consent during the munching period—was an embarrassment. Blanche herself took nothing: it was
the only way in which she could gain, in her mind,
an ascendency over these other and grosser mortals.
She felt, moreover, incapable of swallowing. It
was almost as if there were a rope round her neck.
She wondered what sort of a tea the prisoner was
having.

'Well,' said Mr Gaskin, 'what about getting on
with the job?'

In a voice harsh and dry with effort Blanche said
abruptly: 'I'm very unhappy about this case.
I . . . I don't think we've considered all the
difficulties.'

'No?' said Charles Underhay.

Bayfield muttered impatiently, but the foreman
quelled him with a gesture.

'I feel,' said Blanche, taking courage, 'that we've
no right to condemn this man to death.'

The Major intervened. 'But that isn't quite the
point, is it? You've told us that you have conscientious objections to capital punishment. Quite
entitled to your opinion, Mrs Izeley. Respect you
for it. But that's a question we can't consider
now. If I may say so?' he added, with a bow
to the foreman.

'Well,' remarked Bonaker, 'if no one else'll have
the last bit of toast, I *will*.' He gave the impression

of a man thinking aloud at the top of his voice.
'We shan't get another meal for a long time, by
the look of it.'

Blanche, in her terror, looked like a small stubborn
child. She trembled with nervous hatred of these
men who were forcing a sin upon her. She felt
that the whole burden of decision was hers. If
the prisoner were condemned it would be she, not
these others, who would have condemned him,
because in her heart she had already condemned him.

'I still object,' she said weakly.

The silence of consternation fell upon the company. Charles Underhay broke it at last. 'Are
we to understand that you refuse to serve?'

Blanche nodded. It would be murder, she said
to herself. Whether the prisoner lived or died was
of no consequence to her. But she must save herself from the guilt of taking vengeance on Paul.

'Do you realize the consequences of that?' asked
Underhay in a shocked voice.

Blanche did not answer, and suddenly Bonaker
took up the tale. He had swallowed his mouthful
of toast, and his speech had its usual ponderous
clarity. 'It's like this,' he said, leaning towards
Blanche, to the great inconvenience and indignation of Mr Bayfield. 'If anyone drops out now,
they'll have to get a new jury and start the trial
all over again. Three days of it, don't you see?
Everything all over again. Not very pleasant for
the prisoner, that. Bit of an ordeal, I mean. It

must be a worrying business for him. Stands to reason.' Blanche buried her face in her hands. Bonaker's voice went imperturbably on. 'Now, you object to capital punishment, don't you?'

Blanche, uncovering her face, said firmly: 'Yes, I do.'

'Very well,' said Bonaker. 'Now look at it like this. The question of punishment doesn't arise unless we find this chap guilty. Do you follow me?'

Blanche nodded.

'Very well,' said Bonaker again. 'Then you 've no need to worry about that.'

Blanche frowned. 'I don't quite see what you mean.'

'Simple enough,' Bonaker assured her. 'If we don't find him guilty, the question of punishment needn't trouble you. And, don't you see, we 're not going to find him guilty.'

'Oh, aren't we?' asked Blanche meekly.

'Speak for yourself, sir,' admonished Cyril Gaskin.

Bonaker, still addressing Blanche, went on to amplify his statement. He was evidently a man who liked to make everything clear. 'This jury won't find him guilty. But some other jury might, don't you see?' Having satisfied Blanche Izeley he turned to the company in general. 'May as well tell you, gentlemen, before we go any further. I don't agree with you.'

'You seem to be in a minority of one,' said Underhay. 'Perhaps you 'll give us your reasons.'

'The evidence isn't good enough.'

'Many a man has been hanged on no better,' remarked Mr Coates.

'Quite agree,' said Bonaker. 'Time we stopped doing that sort of thing, in my opinion. It gave me the surprise of my life to hear you ladies and gentlemen saying the fellow was guilty. I won't say I don't think he did it——'

'But,' said Gaskin, 'if you think he did it——'

'I won't say I don't think he did it,' repeated Bonaker heavily, 'because that would be putting it too mildly. I 'm quite sure he didn't do it. You 've only got to look at him, the way he gave evidence and all that. He 's not the murdering kind.'

'Surely it 's a mistake,' suggested Underhay, 'to think that a murderer is necessarily a different kind of person from the rest of us. Some are, of course,' he added hastily, conscious of a stir of protest among his audience. 'There *is* such a thing, no doubt, as a murderous type. But there 's a sense, isn't there, in which every one of us is a potential murderer? Given, I mean, a sufficiently powerful motive, such as Strood had?' He glanced round the table for support. At the back of his mind was a picture of his daughter Betty, growing up in a world where murderers went unpunished, undeterred. 'And opportunity, such as Strood had.'

'And a good nerve,' said Bonaker, 'which Strood hasn't.'

'Personally speaking,' put in Gaskin, 'I think

he 's got a wonderful nerve. Pretty cool customer, if you ask me.'

'That 's because you 've made up your mind he 's guilty,' said Bonaker.

'Look at the way he behaved in the witness-box,' urged Clare Cranshaw. 'The calm, collected way he spoke. The *careful* way.'

'That 's because you 've made up your mind he 's guilty,' said Bonaker again. 'If he murdered his wife, his composure was remarkable. But if he didn't, it was quite natural that he should be self-controlled and careful in his answers. Fact is, once a man 's charged with murder nothing he does is right, in some people's eyes. If he gibbers with funk, that shows he 's guilty. If he doesn't gibber with funk, he 's guilty just the same, and a cool customer into the bargain.'

'I agree with you there,' said Major Forth, un-expectedly. 'A gentleman,' he explained, with a side-glance at Gaskin and apparently for his in-formation, 'knows how to keep his nerve when under fire. All the same,' he went on, addressing Bonaker, 'I got the impression the fellow was lying.'

'I got the impression he was telling the truth,' said Bonaker.

'But, my dear sir,' cried Underhay, excitedly, 'what a tale he told!'

'What was wrong with it?' asked Bonaker.

'Everything was wrong with it.'

'Hear, hear!' Chorus of voices.

'Everything's too much,'said Bonaker stubbornly.
'I'm waiting to hear what was wrong with his story.'

Everyone looked at the foreman. But Charles
was now beyond feeling diffidence. 'Here's a
married man of the upper middle class. His wife,
by all accounts, is young and beautiful. Nevertheless he carries on an intrigue with another woman.
Well, I dare say we oughtn't to make too much of
that. The man's not being tried for his morals.
The wife resented his infidelity, as any wife would.
There were quarrels about it, and ultimately a
separation. A temporary separation, if you like,
but enough to show that there was no question of
her condoning his behaviour. As I say, she resented it. The prisoner admits as much, and even
if he didn't there's plenty of evidence on that
point. However, he does admit it. He admits
that ten days before her death she was still bitterly
conscious of her grievance against him. Yet he
asks us to believe that at their last interview, a few
hours before she died, she freely and deliberately
sent him to his mistress. With her blessing,' said
Charles, indignantly sarcastic. 'Now that's what
I call a tall story. In fact I call it an impudent lie.'

When the murmur of approval had subsided, a
new voice spoke. 'I don't think you're necessarily
right there,' said Oliver Brackett.

His neighbour, Major Forth, turned on him
fiercely. 'You mean to say you believe that
nonsense?'

'I didn't say that,' answered Oliver cautiously. 'I say it's not necessarily nonsense.'

'You admit it's an unlikely tale?' suggested Charles.

'Yes,' said Oliver, 'it *is* an unlikely tale. And, now I come to think of it, that makes it all the more believable.'

The Major shrugged his shoulder in despair. 'I don't follow your logic.'

'What I mean is this,' said Oliver. 'If a man's making up a tale, and his life depends on its being believed, he takes pretty good care to see that it's a likely tale. Strood's no fool: we're all agreed about that. Why should he pitch us such an improbable yarn? What's he got to gain by it?'

'Surely,' said Charles Underhay, 'he wanted us to believe that he was on good terms with his wife, and that he wasn't playing her false by going off with his mistress.'

'I don't see why,' said Oliver. 'He's on trial for murder, not for being a bad husband. He knows that as well as we do. His only hope of escaping the gallows is to convince us he's speaking the truth. Now I could invent half a dozen likelier tales than the one he told. So why did he hit on that one? Because it happened to be the truth. There's no other conceivable reason.'

'It's the truth,' sneered Gaskin, 'because it's unlikely?'

'You've got it.'

'Something in that,' muttered Cheed. 'I see what you mean.'

'Well, for my part,' said Gaskin, 'that tale's not merely unlikely. It's impossible.' He tried to picture his own Agnes encouraging him to run off to Brighton with, say, little sister Stella. The idea filled him with excitement and despair. He swallowed convulsively and declared: 'It's against human nature!'

'I *know* you're wrong there,' said Oliver, with a slightly embarrassed smile.

'Really,' exclaimed Clare impatiently, 'how *can* you know?'

'Well, I do know: that's all,' said Oliver. 'I know from my own experience.'

§ 40

OLIVER REMEMBERS

IT had happened just after the war, when Oliver was thirty-three. And it would perhaps never have happened but for Molly's long, tiresome, undangerous illness, and the fortnight in Cornwall which she spent, convalescent, with her mother. For her maiden home was in Cornwall: Oliver had found her there, a simple comely young woman, and, on the eve of his going to France as a soldier, had married her. It had seemed the obvious, the only thing to do. The war over, he found himself the husband of a wife and the father of a three-year-old boy; and, though he could not pretend to be surprised at his situation, it was vaguely disconcerting at a time when, newly released from the mechanical thraldom of the army, he felt in the mood to begin his own life in his own way, making an entirely new start. But the lines were already laid down for him and he must follow them willy-nilly. A disappointing prospect, and he couldn't resist glancing wistfully at what might have been. He was fond of Molly and the child, but sometimes, in unguarded moments, he wanted adventure: not the kind of adventure, so called and so absurdly miscalled, that military service had offered, for there was no pleasure in being part of a blundering machine with every minute of one's life ordered, but the adventure of following, after four years of frustration, one's own bent, particularly (for such is the nature of man) one's own amorous bent. Particularly but not solely. Brackett senior, having shouted himself nearly hoarse during his forty years of auctioneering, was more than glad to take Oliver into the firm; and Oliver, having no practical alternative in mind (for the footlights were of fairyland), was constrained to agree. He settled down, and his father, when the time came, died happy in the knowledge that the voice of a Brackett, when his own was silenced, would continue to call for bids in the auction-rooms of East Farringay.

If Molly had enjoyed better health, if Molly hadn't had a mother in Cornwall to whom she could go for a change from the January bleakness of London, if Molly hadn't sent him to buy wool, and if an electric spark had not flashed from the warm brown eyes of the shop-girl to his own, Oliver would not have found himself gazing thoughtfully at the sea one cold clear evening in 1920. It was a night of many stars, and the moon was on the water. The amplitude and the intimacy of sea and sky made a perfect setting for what promised to be, in its way, a perfect experience. He felt as though he were living beyond time and space, in a moment that had no beginning and could have no end. He felt, in fact, as though he were living in a sentimental song. Deliberately he had put out of mind the extravagance, the danger, the dubious ethics of this adventure; had forgotten the hotel, the furtively-purchased and somewhat ill-fitting wedding-ring, the scheming and the secrecy; and he contrived, by an act of will, abetted by imagination, to think of nothing but the beauty in which he was now enclosed. Standing on the balcony of this too-expensive hotel, with the star-tingling sky above him and the lithe sea shimmering below, he almost forgot the bedroom at his back and the joy that awaited him there; and at this moment, to add the last impossible touch of perfection, he suddenly caught sight of the winking lanterns of three fishing-smacks on the far horizon. Mingling with his rapture, however, was a sub-mood of ironical self-protective humour. This is quite a Nefarious Enterprise, he thought. I've taken to lying, and I'm leading a young girl astray, or she's leading me astray. Bit of both perhaps: which is as it should be. But a child like her, she knows nothing of life. I'm twelve years older than she is. Am I a blackguard? Taking his cue from that word, he began to see himself as something rather sinister, the Cynical Seducer, the prowling Lothario. It's a shame; I can't do it; I'll have to send her home before it's too late. Too late, too late—ominous phrase. For a moment he was the anxious father, horsewhip in hand, confronting the ravisher of his daughter. You cur, you cad! Speak, child, speak! Am I indeed already too late? It is your old father who asks. All the same, said Oliver self-reprovingly, I *ought* to send her home; and true to his prevailing histrionic passion he dramatized the scene in which he explained to her that for her own sake she must forget him and go back to her mother's care. (No, that wouldn't do: her mother had been dead three years.) Then a few tears, a gentle kiss of parting, and . . . and what? Nothing would then remain but a very awkward interview with the manageress of the hotel, a taxi-ride to the station, a midnight journey, and an ignominious arrival at a London terminus in the small hours of a desolate morning. It's too late to retreat now, he said, and his heart leaped with happiness.

Stepping through the french windows into the
bedroom, he perceived, shyly, that Jane was
already in bed. The bedside reading-lamp shed
a soft pink glow on her pillowed face. Himself
and his histrionics forgotten, he stood at the
bedside, looking down at her. A slight frown
puckered his forehead. 'Are you quite sure,
Jane?' Touched by her childish appearance, he
was in the mood for renunciation: the idea
positively allured him.

She smiled reassuringly. 'Of course.' Seeing
him still dubious she added mischief to her smile.
'You don't seriously imagine you're seducing me,
do you? It's quite the other way round, I assure
you.'

He laughed. 'But you're so young,' he protested, 'so ridiculously young. You've no experience of . . . of situations like this.'

She countered, with a celestial grin: 'It's not
fair to blame me for that, darling. Everyone has
to begin some time.' He began kissing her, and
between the kisses she remarked: 'I doubt whether
you're such a hardened sinner either.'

'You're an innocent child,' he said, 'in spite of
your impudence. I feel I ought to——'

She kissed him again. 'I know. You feel you
ought to save me from myself. Poor fun for me,
that would be.' It seemed to him that he had
never known such kisses as these. 'If you start
being chivalrous, darling, I shall make a scene,

I warn you. . . . Isn't it time you undressed?' she
asked lightly. 'It's past eleven.' He gave her
a grateful glance, and her eyes, friendly and untroubled, regarded him with sober pleasure. . . .

Sitting in the jury-room with eleven pairs of
inquiring eyes turned towards him, he spared one
glance for that blissful night. By moral canons
which he hardly thought of questioning, he should
have felt guilt and shame. But in fact he felt
neither. That there was something shabby and
mean in the preliminary secrecies had been apparent
to him, but in the sequel, in the warm dark night
of love and friendliness, he had found nothing but
happiness, a happiness sharpened to pain by the
glancing shadow of tomorrow's farewell. Morning
found him neither ashamed nor defiant. He was
grateful, not only to Jane, but to something less
personal, some vaguely apprehended beauty of
which she was a vital flower. He was proud and
humble; contented and a little anxious; aware of
being permanently the richer for what had happened; aware too, with a twinge of dismay, of having
given a new hostage to fortune. He was also, at
this pre-breakfast hour, a little dispirited, and
inclined to take refuge in ironic humour. In the
cold morning light, and with an empty belly, it
was easy to hold the balance between the sentimental
and the practical; but he dimly foresaw that as the
day mellowed the magic would begin to return,
and that with the first feather of dusk his memory

of Jane would quicken, made poignant by her absence, would quicken and stir and become a voice crying in the heart. Returning from his luxurious bath he talked to her with forced gaiety, but in his mind was the uneasy question: When shall we be together again like this? We 'll manage it somehow, he answered himself. But he couldn't silence the other answers that crowded in on him. She 's young and high-spirited: why should she hang about for me? She 'll want marriage and children and I 'm not in a position to give her either. The end 's inevitable: she 'll find someone else, someone who 's free, and marry him and be happy. Well, it 's only right that she should. I mustn't get too fond of her, that 's all.

But he was already too fond of her.

It was rather of Molly, however, that he was thinking now, with the eyes of his fellow-jurors upon him. Molly came back looking much the better for her holiday. The sight of her gave him a shock of pleasure, and of surprise. It was a home-coming in a double sense, for he felt that with Molly's return he too had come home. To find himself so fond of Molly was disconcerting, for it did not, as by the laws of arithmetic it should have done, make the idea of Jane any the less alluring. He had parted from that young woman on the expressed understanding that they were not to meet again—except by chance and as mere nodding acquaintances—until another adventure like the first

could be arranged. To be seen together in Farringay, or near it, was too dangerous: on this point
they were heartily agreed. But after three days of
loneliness Oliver had persuaded himself that such
caution was unnecessary. They met, talked, and
vainly desired, on five occasions during the last
five days of Molly's absence; and after her return,
though with less frequency and with a more
elaborate stealth, they continued to meet. It was
nervous work, like tight-rope walking, and the
danger was not of a kind that Oliver found exhila-
rating. In moments when he yielded to his fear
of being found out he saw the situation as intolerable
and himself as a cad. He thought at first that he
hated deceiving Molly, but in the course of repeated self-examinations he discovered that what he
hated was not the deception but the idea of its failure and Molly's inevitable pain. Could everlasting
success have been guaranteed his conscience would
have ceased to trouble him, for so long as Molly was
happy all was well. But, as things inexorably were,
he began to realize that his passion for Jane was
in danger of being dissolved in nervous anxiety
and irritation.

It was Molly herself who averted that danger, by
remarking, at the end of the midday meal one
Sunday, after her young son had escaped to his
nursery: 'She's a nice girl, Olly, your little friend
Jane. I've asked her to tea this afternoon.'

Oliver blinked. 'You've done *what?*'

'She's coming to tea. We had quite a nice talk together.'

'Oh, you did, did you?' Profoundly embarrassed, he half-smiled at her, searching her face for the reproach he thought he must find there. 'All the same, she can't come here.' The proposal shocked him.

'Why not, pray?'

And this was the woman he had thought simple! 'Look here, Molly. How much do you know?'

'Quite enough,' said Molly, with a touch of grim humour. Husband and wife stared at each other appraisingly. 'I must say, Olly, you might have been a bit cleverer about it.'

'Cleverer?' He was baffled, confused, put to shame. 'What d' you mean, cleverer?'

'Everybody knows, it seems, except me,' said Molly. 'And now *I* know. I've known since Wednesday. But you needn't look so miserable about it,' she added briskly. 'No bones broken. I'd sooner you'd told me yourself than have kind friends tell me. But never mind. You'll know better next time.'

Oliver stared at his boots. 'It's no use saying I'm sorry . . .' He broke off. 'But *how* much do you know about this?' It was inconceivable, in view of her good temper, that she could know everything.

'She didn't keep anything back,' said Molly. 'That's one thing I liked about her.'

Oliver shrugged his shoulders in bewilderment.

'This beats everything.' He tried to puzzle it out. 'What did you want to go and see her for? What was the idea?'

'I didn't much like it at first,' said Molly, musingly. 'It's no good pretending I did. But when I'd had a look at her——'

'But *why* did you have a look at her?'

'To see if she was the right sort, of course,' said Molly, rather indignantly. 'I couldn't have you taking up with some nasty piece of goods. I had to see for myself. And a great relief it was, I can tell you. Quite took my fancy from the first, she did.'

Oliver got up from the table. 'And so she told you everything, did she?'

'All she knew,' said Molly, with a hint of mischief.

'She told you we went away together?'

'Well, naturally. She seemed to think I ought to know,' said Molly, with dangerous innocence.

He struggled to explain. 'Of course I oughtn't to have done it. I was carried away.' Recognizing the falsity of that, he withdrew it. 'No, I wasn't. I walked right into it with my eyes open. There's no excuse. I was bored and lonely, but——'

'You were fond of her,' said Molly. 'And still are, I should hope. Well, that's natural enough. Now I've had a talk with her it makes all the difference. So long as you don't go getting her into trouble, Olly. That *would* be a shame, poor little thing!'

He moved nearer to her, and put out a tentative hand. Meeting him half-way, she took hold of his arm and gave it a reassuring squeeze. '*We're* all right, aren't we, Olly?'

'You do know,' he said, 'that I feel just the same to you?'

She nodded. 'When I came back from Mother's you were glad to see me. You weren't pretending. You couldn't. When I remembered that . . . well, it made everything all right again.'

Oliver had nothing to say. Nothing he could say would be adequate to this astonishing occasion, and he had the sense to know it. . . . And, all these years later, in the jury-room, he found it impossible to embark on the story: not merely because it would have been an uncomfortable story in the telling, but because he read clearly, in the faces of his fellow-jurors, something that made him despair of its being believed.

§ 41

MRS HENSTROKE PAYS A CALL

MARRIAGE is what you make of it, thought Mrs Henstroke, as she approached her daughter's house. What you make of *him*, she corrected herself. Poor Gertie, on the whole, had done pretty well with the material that God had rather thoughtlessly provided. She's her mother's daughter in some things, bless her, said Mrs Henstroke: not many could have made a better job of that Roger. The Coates family lived in one of a row of villas designed and built in the eighteen-eighties. It had steps leading up to the front door, steps leading down to the basement-kitchen, and railings in front. Though still respectable, it was a street that had seen better days, and these better days were with Mrs Henstroke as she picked her way neatly along.

She was a small slight woman, very active and serene, her step light and unhurried, her complexion rosy. She wore a mackintosh coat and carried a tightly-rolled umbrella, which she used as a walking-stick; her white hair, bobbed and fringed in the style of a Tudor page, and not entirely hidden by her small close-fitting hat, gave her an appearance rather of youth than of age; and her expression of blue-eyed resolution, emphasized by a slight pursing of the lips, had been as characteristic of her at seven years old as it was now, at seventy-three. In this street, and in the very house now occupied by Roger and Gertie and the two children, she had lived the nineteen years of her married life and the first five of her widowhood. Then gracefully, and in her heart almost gleefully, she had cleared out, to begin a new life for herself elsewhere, in two comfortable rooms, managing very nicely, as she said, on what little her husband had left her, augmented by the rent that Roger paid— and punctually, she *would* say that for him—for

this house in Prince Albert Avenue. 'Why don't
you have a room with us, Mother?' Gertie had said
anxiously. 'It's all right, my dear,' answered Mrs
Henstroke soothingly. 'You needn't be afraid
I'll say yes.' There were a hundred reasons why
she should not say yes, and Roger was ninety-five
of them. Not that she thought so ill of Roger:
he was steady and solid and meant well by his wife.
But she wasn't so fond of Roger as Roger was, and
she had no intention of putting Gertie under an
obligation to him. But, beyond all that, she wanted
a quiet life, a quiet and busy life, chewing the cud
of her many memories, making new friends here
and there, doing things (concerts and theatres) that
she had never been able to do before, and finding
out much that she had always wanted to know.
I'm an ignorant woman, she said to herself at fifty-
six: time I went to school a bit. Of family problems
she had had her fill for the time being. Tom Henstroke had been a problem, and two sons killed in
the war had been another. This new loneliness was
a problem too, but it was also a challenge and she
went gladly to meet it. I've had a good life all
said; and I've time for another yet. . . . And here
she was, detached, affectionate, pleasantly warmed
and excited, knocking like any stranger at the door
of her daughter's house.

'Why, Mother!' exclaimed Gertie. 'Now isn't
that nice!' She opened the door wider and drew
back to let her mother pass in. As they leaned

forward to kiss, the younger woman said: 'I mustn't come too near, darling. I 'm all pastry.' She was wearing a blue print apron; her cheeks were flushed; looking much younger than her forty-one years, in Mrs Henstroke's eyes she was still the large romping daughter struggling out of her teens. There 's more of Tom in her than of me, after all, she thought.

'Well, Gertie, how are you?'

'I 'm all right, Mother. How are you? Quite a stranger you are.'

'Just what I was saying to myself as I came along,' said Mrs Henstroke equably.

'Were you? How funny!'

'A stranger to my daughter. It 's rather nice, don't you think?'

'Nice, Mother? That 's a funny way to look at it.' Gertie laughed uncertainly. You never did know quite how to take Mother.

'Nice when we do meet, I mean. Makes it more fun.'

Gertie's brow cleared. 'Oh, I see what you mean. Well, shall we go downstairs? I 'm in the kitchen. Do you mind?'

'I 'm interrupting your bit of cooking,' said Mrs Henstroke. 'But the pastry 's in the oven, I hope?'

She followed Gertie down the dark stairs, into the kitchen that for so long had been her own, and for a moment it was as though she had never left it.

Though she and Gertie had exchanged visits with reasonable frequency—reasonable when a journey of an hour and a half was taken into account—not for many years had she penetrated into this semi-subterranean region. It was like stepping back into the past. As she stood for a moment at the window peering up into what they used to call 'the area', she caught herself listening for her husband's cough as he turned in at the gate, or for the sound of a child whimpering into wakefulness in the room behind her.

She turned round, and saw at the table, with her hands in the mixing-bowl, an ample, middle-aged, aproned woman.

'You haven't made many changes in the kitchen, my dear.'

Gertie gave her a placid smile. 'Time we lighted up, almost. How short the days are now. You're staying the night, aren't you, Mother?'

'I haven't brought anything with me.'

'That doesn't matter. It won't take a minute to get the spare room ready.'

'We'll see,' said Mrs Henstroke.

After a pause Gertie remarked: 'Quite like old times for you, Mother.' She suddenly saw what Mrs Henstroke had meant about the kitchen. 'Wouldn't you like to take a peep at the smoking-room? It's just as it was, you know. And seldom used, I must say. Wouldn't you like to?'

'Time enough,' said Mrs Henstroke. She spoke

427

rather briskly, a little nettled to find her moment's sanctuary so easily invaded.

'Just as you like,' said Gertie unnecessarily.

I hope you 're cleverer than this with Roger, my girl, thought Mrs Henstroke. 'Of course,' she said, 'I could sleep naked.'

Gertie laughed. 'Mother! What extraordinary things you say! You 're just the same, only younger.'

'It wouldn't be the first time,' said Mrs Henstroke.

'As if I couldn't provide my own mother with a nightdress!' cried Gertie, indignantly hospitable. 'So you *will* stay. That 's lovely. . . .'

And presently, when Gertie's attention was on her oven, Mrs Henstroke slipped away for a moment and opened the door of the room where Tom's billiard-table and Tom's inherited unread books went on existing, curiously, almost incredibly, in the absence of Tom. It was a place now of silence and shadows. Beyond the window was an asphalted gully enclosed by a wall shoring up the little back-garden, which stood level with the half-way line of the window; and beyond the garden, invisible now except to the eye of memory, was the railway-line, at which Maurice and Eric, and Gertie too, had once loved to stare. The handful of westering daylight that came in through that window served only to lend phantasmal existence to the book-case and table and chairs. One somehow could not think of Tom Henstroke as a ghost haunting

the room: there had been too much flesh on him
for that, and he had been heartily fond of his victuals.
But she found it easy, before going back to the
kitchen (which Gertie had lighted in her absence),
to call back the past itself for one strange instant,
and see Tom himself, in an atmosphere pungent
with masculinity and tobacco-smoke, dealing out
the cards to his dubious cronies. Where did he
pick such people up? She had often asked herself the question, but it no longer troubled her
that it would never be answered. Gertie's right,
she thought: I'm younger than I was then. I
could manage things better if I'd my time over
again. Though I didn't manage so badly, she
added, with a self-appreciation by no means diminished by her ironical recognition of it.

It was pleasant to be back with Gertie.

'Oh, I wrote to you yesterday, Mother.'

'Yes, dear. A very nice letter, too.'

'Did I tell you Roger was away?' asked Gertie
hypocritically.

Bless you, my child, why else am I here? 'Yes,
I think you did. Something about a jury, wasn't it?'

'Yes. Awkward for him at this time of the year.'

'Why's that?' asked Mrs Henstroke. ''Tisn't
his own business after all.'

'No, but it puts them out at the office, Roger
says.'

'I've no doubt they miss him,' said Mrs Henstroke politely.

'Well,' remarked Gertie, with disarming candour, 'all men seem to think themselves indispensable, don't they?'

Mrs Henstroke laughed softly. 'So they do, my dear.' There followed a warm comfortable silence. 'Where's Marjorie and Master Vincent?' asked their grandmother. 'The schools have broken up, surely?'

'Three days since,' said Gertie. 'Vincent's at business of course.' She spoke with careful casualness, thinking that her mother had forgotten this vital fact, and anxious not to ruffle her by seeming to think so. 'Marjorie's out doing a bit of shopping. And a long time she is.'

Mrs Henstroke had always had difficulty in remembering what was told her about Vincent. 'How's Vincent getting on?' she asked.

'Quite nicely,' said Gertie. 'Early days yet, you know. He's only been at it four months. But he seems to like it. He's got a lot of ambition, that boy has. That's why Roger put him to the rag trade.'

Mrs Henstroke smiled. How sweet Gertie is! she thought, with indulgent irony. 'When d' you expect Roger back home?'

'Well . . . any time now,' admitted Gertie, almost defensively. 'But you can never tell with these juries, Vincent says. We rather think he must be on that awful murder case. You know, the Merrion Square Murder. Of course we don't know. We hear nothing. But it's the right court and everything.'

'You haven't heard?' Mrs Henstroke was surprised.

'Not a word,' declared Gertie, enjoying the importance of the situation. 'They're frightfully strict, Vincent says, in a murder trial. They lock the jury up, and no one's allowed to speak to them. Once the case has started, there they are, practically prisoners, no matter how many days it lasts, Vincent says. He's a wonderful boy for knowing things, Mother.'

'I'm sure he is, dear,' said Mrs Henstroke.

'They have to sleep all together, at an hotel.' Seeing a gleam in Mrs Henstroke's eye, Gertie added, uncertainly: 'You know what I mean . . .'

'I know. Not all in one bed. But at the same hotel. I suppose it's only right, when you come to think of it.'

Having finished her cooking, Mrs Coates was now able to give more of her mind to wondering what had become of Marjorie. 'It *makes* you wonder, with the streets so dangerous. I don't like her being out like this.' But, in the midst of the wondering, Marjorie arrived, an overgrown buxom creature of sixteen. She was flushed, and secretly smiling. She saluted her grandmother with an air of thinking about something else, and answered her mother's questions with the lofty assurance: 'I ran across someone I knew, and we

431

got talking.' She was adept at wheedling people into a state of fond indulgence of her, but seldom troubled to exercise her arts on her mother. Among males, Vincent was her one failure in this department, and Roger her conspicuous success. As for Granny, she was a more or less unknown quantity, and for that reason might be worth taking into account. Feeling the old lady's appreciative smile upon her she bounced to the dresser, fished out a tablecloth, and began busily laying the table for tea. 'Is the kettle boiling, Mum? No, I'll do it. You sit down a bit.' With a comfortable smile Gertie obeyed, wishing Mother would come to see them every day.

'Did you get a paper, dear?' she asked Marjorie. To Mrs Henstroke she explained: 'We quite miss Roger's evening paper, you know.'

'There!' exclaimed Marjorie. 'I left it in the hall. I'll fetch it.'

'After tea'll do,' said her mother. 'Granny's staying the night with us. Isn't it nice?'

'Lovely,' agreed Marjorie. She moved towards the door. 'I'd better get the paper. There's something about the trial in it.' She disappeared. A peal of thunder announced that she was leaping upstairs, and a second peal advertised her descent. 'Here we are. Judge's summing-up.'

'Not a very nice case for *you* to read, I must say,' said Mrs Coates primly.

'Do they give the verdict?' asked Mrs Henstroke.

'No,' said Marjorie. 'Nothing in the Stop Press about it. But the summing-up's over, it seems. It took an hour and fifty minutes.'

'That means . . .' began Mrs Coates. But she stopped herself. That means that Roger 'll be home tonight. Any time now.

Mrs Henstroke, visited by precisely the same thought, began wondering how she could excuse herself from staying the night.

§ 42

BONAKER CROSS-EXAMINES

OLIVER's memory of that golden episode, now ten years or more away, was not unmixed with pain. For his prediction had been fulfilled: Jane in due time had dissolved the alliance in order to become the wife of a young man in Huddersfield, and while recognizing the inevitable, and for Jane's sake rejoicing in it, there still occurred moments, fugitive feather-weight moments, when she came, wantonly, unexpectedly, to haunt his imagination. If at such times he was tempted to self-pity, he hastened to remind himself that everything has its price, and that the sensible thing to do is to pay up and look pleasant. There was no question about its having been worth the price. It was worth it for its own sake, and worth it for the sake of what it had done

433

for his marriage. And now, glancing at the surprised expectant faces of his fellow-jurors, he was wondering how he could reveal Molly to them, how convince them that what they were calling impossible had occurred in his own life.

'When I say my own experience,' he said, with an apologetic smile, 'I mean it. There *are* women capable of that. And . . . well . . . my wife is one of them.'

The confession was greeted with an embarrassed silence, punctuated by a deprecating cough from the Major and an indeterminate noise from Charles Underhay. Each one of the eleven was conscious of an eagerness to hear more, though in Clare and Blanche a strong disapproval was at war with that eagerness; and as for poor Lucy, she couldn't bring herself to look at the man who could talk calmly about such wickedness as that. How different from her Edward! For Edward would never, no never . . . it was not to be thought of. On the heels of this reflection came the odd notion that if Mother had been wicked enough to put up with Father's wickedness, the Prynnes would now perhaps have been a happy and united family. But that was absurd, because you couldn't be happy and wicked too, or if you could it was a different sort of happiness, in fact a wicked sort.

For the first time during this discussion something like warmth had come into the appraising eyes of Bonaker. 'Now that's very interesting,' he said.

'The Judge dropped a pretty broad hint about that point,' remarked Roger Coates. 'He as good as said, in the summing-up, that the prisoner was a liar.'

'Very interesting indeed,' said Bonaker, with an appreciative nod at Oliver. 'Perhaps you agree with me, sir, that there's a good deal of doubt in this case after all?'

'I believe you're right,' answered Oliver, emerging from his personal embarrassment. 'Evidence isn't good enough.'

'Too risky,' said Arthur Cheed. A great load slipped from his mind. He was exultant. 'A damned sight too risky,' he exclaimed exuberantly. Conscious of indignant stares, he changed colour and murmured confusedly: 'Beg pardon. Ladies present.'

Bonaker attacked the foreman. 'Point is, don't you see, there's *doubt*.' He leaned on the table and gazed fixedly at Charles, awaiting his answer. 'Never mind whether he wanted to get rid of the poor woman or not. That's neither here nor there. Point is, did he put poison in that stuff? And if you think he did, can you be *sure* he did?'

Charles stared at distance, the fingers of his right hand playing a tattoo on the shining surface of the table. 'One can't of course be positively sure, in a case like this.'

'Put it this way,' said Bonaker, speaking with irritating slowness and still gazing with rapt and sympathetic attention at the foreman. 'Is it out of the question for you . . . *on* the evidence . . . *on* the evidence,' he repeated thoughtfully. 'Is it out of the question for you, *on* the evidence, that the late Mrs Strood met her death some other way?'

Deeply as he resented being put on the defensive like this, Charles saw no way of escape. And he was honest enough not to let resentment colour his answer. 'Well, no. I couldn't say that. There *are* other possibilities, one must confess. Nevertheless——'

'Then there's doubt,' concluded Bonaker. 'If you can't be sure he did it, if it's not out of the question for you—*on* the evidence, mind—that she met her death some other way, from some other hand, then I say there's doubt. And reasonable doubt.'

Major Forth, opening his mouth to speak, got as far as his preliminary 'Er . . . um . . .' when Bonaker's voice, gathering volume but no speed, went over him like a steamroller. 'Now you, sir! Mr Coates, I believe?'

'That's my name,' agreed Mr Coates defiantly.

'Well, Mr Coates, let me ask you this. Can you be sure—sure, mind you! . . . *on* the evidence . . . that the prisoner . . . put poison . . . into that stuff? And, *on* the evidence, is it quite out of the question for you, is it quite out of the question, that the late Mrs Strood . . .' The sentence moved massively to its long-awaited conclusion. Roger Coates sat in sulky silence for a moment, and, just as he was beginning his answer, 'Don't hurry yourself, Mr Coates,' said Bonaker kindly. 'We 've plenty of time. No hurry at all. For my part,' he announced, with a cheerful glance at the company, 'I don't mind staying here all night. Not the least objection in the world.'

§ 43

A TELEPHONE MESSAGE

THE young fellow of forty-five who attended Mr Strood during his last illness was a new-comer to Budleigh Parva, and, knowing himself capable of better things, he had no intention of staying there longer than he could help. The villagers didn't take to him, because he was always in a hurry and would never stay chatting with them about this and that (as old Dr Welch had been wont to do), and therefore, though he had several times heard of 'the Vicar's trouble' from some of his humbler patients, he was content to invest the phrase with a vaguely medical connotation and leave it at that. Time enough to inquire about the Vicar's trouble when he was summoned, in his professional capacity, to the Vicarage: to which summons, when it came, he responded with no quickening of curiosity, innocent of the knowledge that his prospective patient was the father of that Roderick Strood who

437

was on the point of being convicted for poisoning his wife. He found the old gentleman in bed, weak but resolute, and sustained by a patience which the medical man, who had a pigeon-hole for every phenomenon, attributed to the mental vagueness of senility. A careful examination made it clear to him that the mechanism was running down. He made a silent calculation: If I can get him through the winter. . . . Delivering a guarded verdict, he detected the first gleam of anxiety in his patient's eyes. Poor old chap: he 's afraid. In spite of his precious Kingdom of Heaven. Doesn't want to go there: they never do, poor devils.

'Yes, you 've had a bad little turn, Mr Strood. But you 've come through it very well for a man of your age.'

'When can I get up?'

The doctor shook his head, smiling to hide both his compassion and his astonishment. 'You mustn't dream of such a thing. We 've got to take things slowly, very slowly.'

'But the telephone 's downstairs,' said Mr Strood. 'If I can't get up . . .'

'Please understand,' said the doctor earnestly (for this babble about telephones suggested a wandering mind), 'you mustn't get out of bed on any pretext whatever. We 'll make you as comfortable as possible. I 'll send a nurse along——'

'Nonsense,' said Mr Strood. 'My old servant 's the only nurse I want.'

Science shrugged its shoulders. 'As you wish. But I would advise a nurse. However, we'll see how you are in a day or two.'

'And I can't get up?'

'On no account. Perhaps when the warm weather comes . . .'

'Ah,' sighed Mr Strood. He smiled benevolently on his adviser. 'But I needn't last so long as that. A few days more, and I shall be ready.' He closed his eyes, saying: 'It won't be more than a few days now, please God.' And when next he opened his eyes he was alone again, and the last light of a December day was fading from the room. How long is it since they began? It's three days, or is it four? He seemed to have lost count, and with that realization his anxiety returned, and his hand, stealing out of bed, groped for the bell-rope. He heard the distant sound of the bell, and set himself to the task of waiting. Was it three days or four? And how long now . . .? He must not get out of bed. That would never do. But his fingers, prying under the pillow, counted Perryman's letters. There were three of them, and the first had said (he had them all by heart): The trial began today. Two more since then, one every day, that meant . . . what did it mean? Ah, here was Sarah at last.

'Sarah my dear, which day is this?'

'Thursday, sir.'

'Yes, yes. But which day . . . how many days . . .?'

'It's the fourth day, sir. Won't be long now.'
Sarah came close to the bedside. 'Everything 'll
be all right. Don't you make no mistake about that.'

'I've been asleep, Sarah.'

'Have you, dearie?'

'Yes,' he said proudly. 'Ever since the doctor
went.' That's ten minutes ago, thought Sarah.
'I suppose you didn't hear anything while I was
asleep?'

'Hear anything? What should I hear?' She
was wilfully obtuse.

'No, I expect not,' said Mr Strood. He smiled
at Sarah, with the submissive patience of a child.
She, eleven years his junior, suddenly saw him as a
little boy. And him seventy-five, she said, startled
by her strange fancy.

Presently he spoke again. 'And you didn't hear
anything just now . . . the telephone?'

'I heard your bell ring,' said Sarah firmly.
'That's all I heard.'

'Yes, it must have been that.' Suddenly he
longed to be alone. 'I think perhaps I shall sleep
a little more.'

With Sarah gone, he lapsed again into daydreaming, to be roused from time to time, jerked
into trembling wakefulness, by the master-thought
which he was labouring to avoid. He listened to
his heart-beats, saying persuasively: A little longer,
a little longer. Four days: I can't leave him yet.
The third day he rose again from the dead. But

this is the fourth day, and Perryman said . . . The thought of Perryman, whom he had never seen, was a benediction buoying him up. Perryman, invisible as God himself, had been a voice speaking in his inward ear. Perryman had promised to tell him at once, whatever happened; and in the arms of that promise he now fell asleep, to dream that he was walking alone in a large city. One of the houses suddenly burst into flames, and there, straight in front of him, planted in the middle of the pavement, was a scarlet fire-alarm box. He smashed the glass with his hand, a bell began ringing, and with that sound in his ears he pitched forward into consciousness of the bed, the bedroom, and the telephone-bell.

Hearing at last the sound for which she had been waiting all day, Sarah felt a sickness rise in her throat. Days before, and on her own initiative (for she was determined not to endure a crisis every time the butcher or the baker chose to ring up), she had given instructions that only London calls were to be put through. This, then, could have only one meaning: it was something about Master Roderick at last. If those lawyer people in London hadn't been so stupid as to pretend he 'd poisoned his poor young wife, Sarah could have hardened her heart against Master Roderick, who, if half what the papers said was true, had been a very naughty boy, such as you couldn't hardly believe. But as it was . . .

As she lifted the receiver from the telephone she became aware of Mr Strood standing at the head of the stairs.

'Oh, sir, you didn't ought . . .' This 'll be his death, she said. 'Yes, this is the Vicarage. Is that Mr Perryman? Yes. Yes. . . .'

§ 44

RETURN OF A HERO

WHILE Mark's call was being put through to Budleigh Parva, Mr A. J. K. Simpson, whose exposition of the New Physics had so greatly interested the Vicar of that parish, sat in a teashop near Blackfriars, wondering whether he should wait any longer for his friend Bonaker. It was something too indefinite to be called an appointment, for his expectation was founded on nothing more solid than a postcard, written in his own spider-crawling calligraphy, to the effect that if Bonaker had time and inclination to look in at such and such a teashop next Thursday afternoon, between five and five-thirty, he and Simpson could have a cup of tea together. Answer had been neither expected nor received, Simpson's habit of scribbling invitations at the last moment having accustomed him to their being ignored. Since that chance encounter in the

442

train, which for an hour had so luminously re-
created his boyhood, he had told himself at intervals
that he really must fix up something with old
Bonaker, a lunch, a dinner, anything, so that they
could have the long eager talk, crammed with
reminiscence, which they had oddly failed to have
on that summer morning six months ago. Simpson
did not remember that it was so long as six months
ago, and would anyhow have shrunk from taking
so exact a measure of his negligence. He fancied
it was some time in the summer, and hastily left it
at that. But six months it was, and during the
first of them, when (if ever) he should have renewed
contact with Bonaker, there had been a tide in the
affairs of Simpson, which Simpson, rather to his
own astonishment, had taken at the full. Gilian
had brought matters to a head by calmly announcing
that she was going to set about having some
children. Not marriage necessarily: that was a
minor point. But children she would have, and
marriage was probably, on the whole, the tidiest
arrangement. Simpson recognized the remark as
an ultimatum. He and she had been secret lovers
for eighteen months, and only his infantile loyalty
to sister Eleanor, who kept house for him, had
prevented his consolidating the alliance. To put
her meaning beyond doubt, Gilian added that
since there were at least ten million potential fathers
in Great Britain, she anticipated no difficulty in
realizing her wish. She was married within three

weeks, and to Simpson. And Eleanor, with a smile of disdain for such conventional behaviour, made the best of it in her own fashion.

Simpson, consulting his watch, decided that Bonaker would not be coming. A newsboy with evening papers approaching his table, he bought one and glanced incuriously at the headlines relating to the Strood trial: ELOQUENT APPEAL BY STROOD'S COUNSEL—JUDGE SUMS UP—WOMAN FAINTS IN COURT. While Simpson turned the pages in search of something more interesting, Roger Coates strode majestically past the teashop on his way to Black-friars Underground Station. As he joined the queue at the booking-office, as he flowed into the lift, as he entered his train and stood in considerable physical discomfort hanging to a strap, the hint of a smile played about his plump lips. For he had the advantage of his fellow-passengers. He was a man of destiny, an arbiter of fate. He had a secret of which these others—good people in their simple way, no doubt—were ignorant. Many of them were reading their evening papers, and some were almost certainly engrossed in the report of the trial, *the* trial. It was a profoundly satisfying thought. They were reading the summing-up: that is to say, such little miserable scraps of the summing-up as had been reported in the press. They were wondering, calculating, guessing (poor things!) what the verdict would be. But Mr Coates was in the know. He was the power behind the scenes. He knew something that wasn't in the papers, something that couldn't be in the papers since it had only happened fifteen minutes ago, something in which he himself had had a part. A part? Indeed yes. And a decisive part, what's more. They couldn't have done anything without him, his experience, his sagacity, his gift of seeing into the heart of a problem. After all the hard work he had put in on the case, four days of conscientious duty, it was strange to think that there would be no mention of *him* in the papers. But he didn't complain of that: not he. It was enough that he knew what these others did not know. He knew, and if he so chose he could tell them. If you want to know the verdict, my friends, ask me: I was on the jury. But he did not so choose, for there was equal gratification in keeping them in the dark: it made him serenely master of the situation, a strong silent man who knew how to keep his own counsel. I should have made a pretty good barrister, thought Mr Coates, adjusting his wig, fingering the ribbons of his gown. Or a judge, for the matter of that: a bit of scarlet sets a man off. But one can't be everything, he concluded with a sigh: I 've got responsibilities enough as it is. The thought of those responsibilities, that buying and selling in the city, made him thrust the proposal aside. No, he wouldn't be a judge: they must manage without him.

Roger Coates could see a joke as well as another,

provided it was a reasonably broad one; but no inconvenient sense of the ludicrous lurked in the sanctuary of his secret mind (secret even from himself) where raged, perpetually, a hunger to believe that he was not the stupid, lying, ineffectual nobody that his parents and schoolmasters had too often, in the intervals of ignoring him altogether, declared him to be. The large self-confident gesture of his body, as he sailed along the road to his house, gave the lie to that long-buried slander. He was eager to be home and tell his tale, eager to see the faces of his wife and children and to breathe the incense of their astonishment and admiration. As he pushed open the gate and ascended the steps to the front door, latchkey already in his hand, he remembered, only just in time, that he was tired, a sensitive man much tried by a long nervous ordeal, a giant exhausted by prodigious and triumphant labours. But having stepped into the house and shut the door behind him he found weariness to be superfluous, for there was no one to witness it. No one, as he took his overcoat off and hung it on the hall-stand, came running to greet him; no voice called out: 'Is that you, Father?' Disconsolate, he peered into the dining-room. No one. There was a light in the hall (wasting good current), but no fire in the dining-room, no other sign of habitation. A pretty fine thing, he said to himself, and at that moment (within twenty seconds of his arrival, though to him it seemed as many minutes)

446

he heard a sound of movement below stairs. So
that 's where they are, he said grimly. Living like
a pack of servants as soon as my back 's turned.

The sound he had heard was made by Marjorie
dancing up the stairs from the basement. She now
burst upon him. He suffered her embrace with
dignity, and she led the way down to the warm
kitchen, calling: 'It 's Daddy, Mother!' He followed in his own time, and paused in the doorway,
merely to show that he was not to be hurried. He
took in the scene at a glance—and the situation.
So the wife's mother had turned up. I might have
known! he thought bitterly. She 'll be staying the
night, no doubt. Very jolly, I *must* say. And on
my first night home! He returned his wife's peck
and stepped forward to greet the intruder.

'Well, Mother! How are you?'

'There 's never much wrong with me, thank
God,' said Mrs Henstroke. 'You 're looking well,
Roger.'

Roger's smile made it plain that she had said the
wrong thing and that he forgave her. He put a
hand to his weary brow. 'A little tired. Nothing
more.'

'And hungry too, I expect,' said his wife
placatingly. 'I 've got a nice supper for you,
dear.' Awkward about Mother. But it can't be
helped. He 'll feel better after his meal.

'Have you?' said Roger. A shade too eagerly.
'Well,' he sighed, 'I 'm not sure I shall be able to

447

do justice to it.' They all looked at him. He read solicitude on every face, except young Vincent's, which was hidden by the newspaper he was reading. It seemed the right moment for his piece of news. 'Four days of it. Rather wearing.' He paused before saying casually: 'It was a murder case. The Strood case.'

'There!' cried his wife brightly. 'We thought it must be that case you were on. Didn't we, Marjorie?'

'Oh, you did, did you?' said Roger. He felt deflated. His effect was ruined.

Young Vincent had pricked up his ears. 'What's the verdict, Dad? Is he for the long jump?'

'He is not,' said Roger icily. 'And that's not the way for my son to speak either. As a matter of fact we acquitted him.'

'Kind of you,' remarked Vincent coolly. 'Especially as he probably did it.'

'Be quiet, Vincent!' snapped Vincent's mother. It was her constant endeavour to keep Roger in a good humour. Nor was it a difficult task. Treat him the right way and he was the kindest of men. But Vincent, she sometimes thought, did everything he could to frustrate her wifely endeavour. 'Can't you see poor Father's tired? . . . How horrid for you, Roger! Such an unsavoury case, too. You must have hated it, dear.'

'Unsavoury, yes,' agreed Mr Coates. 'But we won't talk of that now,' he said, silkily discreet.

'You needn't mind Sis and me, Dad,' remarked Vincent cheerfully, 'and our young minds. We 've been reading it every day. Funny sort of chap, Strood. Look at the way——'

'Ah,' interrupted his father, 'that 's just where you go wrong, my boy.' In his eagerness for the ultimate triumph he forgot his resolve not to discuss dubious matters in front of the children. 'I don't defend the man's morals, mind you. The least said about that the better. And it 's a disgrace that children of mine should read such things. But that man wasn't being tried for his morals: he was being tried for murder. And you 'd be surprised, Gertie,' he said, turning to his wife. 'it 's cost me the best part of a day's work to make 'em see that.'

'Make who see it?' asked Vincent.

'The jury, boy. Who else? Time and again I said to them: we mustn't allow ourselves to be prejudiced, I said. The question for us is, Did he or did he not poison his wife? Can we be sure, I said, that the poor woman didn't meet her death some other way? On the evidence before us, I said, can we be sure beyond all reasonable doubt? I put it to them one by one. People won't think clearly. They jump to conclusions. It was my conviction, right from the first, that the evidence wasn't good enough. And I told them so, straight from the shoulder.' Carried away by his story, for the moment, like the artist he was, Mr Coates believed what he said.

P 449

Gertie gazed at him with pride. She too had thought Strood guilty, but was instantly converted by her husband's eloquence. And it was nice to know that the poor young fellow wasn't to be hanged after all.

'On the first show of hands they were all for conviction,' said Mr Coates, after a moment's rapid thought.

'Oh, Roger!' said Gertie fondly. 'And if it hadn't been for you . . .'

Mr Coates shrugged his shoulders, and smiled deprecatingly, disclaiming all merit. 'Well,' he said modestly, 'someone had to see fair play.' Glancing from face to face he encountered the strangely innocent gaze of Mrs Henstroke and was vaguely disquieted. But never mind her. 'Well, Gert, what about this nice bit of supper you've kept for me? I believe I could manage a mouthful, after all.'

§ 45

AN EVENING IN OCTOBER

At six o'clock, on the thirtieth of October, Roderick Strood had said to himself: Yes, I *will* go. All day, and for five previous days, he had debated the question. The idea, the fantastic idea, had been his heart's audacious answer to Elisabeth's announcement that on the thirty-first she must sail for

America. She had sprung it on him very quietly and casually, with an air that gave him no excuse for protestations. Nor in fact were protestations reasonable. He had always vaguely known that her sojourn in England must come to an end some time. The fact had been too obvious to need stating: it had been implicit in everything she did and said. But Roderick, having diligently ignored the spectre, found himself unprepared for its sudden appearance, and bitterly resentful of the lumbering impersonal forces that were about to divide him from his hope of happiness. 'But *of course* we shall meet again,' Elisabeth assured him, in answer to his agonized questions. In his heart he did not believe it. She is saying that to comfort me, as she would comfort a child. If she escapes me now, new interests will claim her—yes, and new lovers perhaps—and all that has been between us will remain with her only as a dream. Music is her first love. She had left him in no doubt of that, and because he too had an almost religious feeling for music he was content to have it so, knowing, or half-knowing, that this high impersonal devotion which was the light of her being, and which made her ultimately independent of himself, was part of the very quality he adored in her: had she lost it, to lose herself in him, he and she both would have been the poorer, and the end of his passion for her would have been already in sight. Music was her first, her dominant love; and it would have caused him an agony of jealousy to believe that any new lover, superseding himself, could make her faithless to that.

Nevertheless she would go and she would forget. Not literally forget, but forget in the lover's sense: for a year or two her mind would retain a blurred picture of him, but her pulse would beat with emotions in which he had no part, her self would move exultantly into a strange future. To Roderick's romantic sense the tragedy of parting was not so much that it hurt as that it did not go on hurting for ever: better a hell of desire and regret, his heart cried, than craven submission to the medicine of time, that crowning insult to the human spirit! They would meet again, she said. But when? And where? In sober fact it was not impossible, nor even unlikely, that a meeting, somewhere in Europe, some time next year, could be brought about. But that prospect was all too remote to comfort him, though he clung to it for comfort. By next year, so much would have happened to her, so much would her stream of experience have broadened, that the love joining them now might seem to her no longer significant. She would be kind—but how terrible if she were no more than kind! How dreary if a miracle and a tragedy ended in the emptiness of anticlimax! So he began playing with the absurd notion of sailing with her. Absurd, because it would only postpone the parting by a few weeks, since he couldn't expatriate himself permanently. He refused, how-

ever, to look so far ahead; wilfully he allowed himself
to drift with his irrational impulse.

And in time he succeeded in making it seem
less irrational. If Elisabeth left him now, with this
ache in his heart, the possibility of achieving a
modus vivendi with Daphne would be infinitely
small. Since that breakfast-table quarrel the situation at home had been intolerable, and he knew no
way of mending it short of an hypocrisy, a carefully
staged reconciliation garnished with comfortable
lies, of which he knew himself to be incapable. He
had lost heart for even a friendly approach: while
Daphne's present mood endured, and while he was
unable to translate his obscure sense of guilt into
an active repentance, it was hopeless to make any
sort of appeal to her. Any such appeal must be
based on the memory of old times, and even to
hint of old times was something that she would
resent as a cruel mockery, a driving of the knife
deeper into her heart. Nowadays she moved about
the house locked in her anger. With his child in
her womb she fended off his attempts at conversation, with a studied politeness that was almost worse
than the quarrel that had initiated it. He tried in
his heart to meet anger with anger, telling himself
that she had gone back on her agreement and that
her infidelity cut deeper than his at the roots of
their comradeship; but when he glanced at her cold
shut face, which masked an hostility that owed
much of its force to the affection it was bent on

disavowing, he knew that self-justification was not enough, and that unless he could release her from her misery he had no alternative but to share it. Unless—and here his reasoning played into the hands of his impulse—unless he could get right away, beyond sight and knowledge of her. Perhaps, after all, a final breach was the only solution of the problem, the only honest and courageous way out. Perhaps only a moral weakness in himself, of which he was all too sharply aware, had blinded him to the obvious. And perhaps only that same weakness, with a pinch of egregious vanity added, had allowed him to persuade himself that he and Daphne could succeed (where so many others had failed) in keeping the ship afloat in these dangerous waters. Perhaps the crude common sense of mankind, with its insistence on a monogamy mitigated only by bland deceit, was right, and he, with his high-flown but dubiously disinterested idealism, a fool blundering after a false gleam.

The notion of sailing with Elisabeth for America grew insensibly into a plan. By his constant dwelling on it, it became real, practicable, even wise. He made tentative preparations, ever and again reminding himself that he was not yet committed to the choice towards which he was drifting. Meanwhile his partner, Cradock, was being kept in the dark. Old Cradock had always been a good friend, benevolently interested in Daphne, and because Roderick knew that he would strongly disapprove of the whole situation he felt a kind of guilt towards Cradock. For Roderick to be away from the office during November was no new thing: for years it had been his whim, a convenient one for Cradock, to stay in London throughout August, when Cradock went fishing in Scotland, and go in search of a second summer at the end of the English autumn. There was no reason why he should not have discussed his impending departure with Cradock, except his invincible aversion to stuffing the old man with lies. For if Cradock once got an inkling of the truth, that all was not well between Roderick and Daphne, nothing could prevent a painful scene, fatherly exhortation rising to anger and culminating perhaps in interference and obstruction. Cradock had given him more than one opening. 'You 're looking rather run-down these days, Roderick. Time you had your holiday, my boy.' But Roderick had studiously ignored them, saying to himself: It 's no good speaking yet. I haven't made up my mind. He didn't in fact make up his mind until six o'clock on the thirtieth of October, and by that time Cradock was on his way home. I can't tell him now, that 's obvious. Telephone? He won't be there yet. And besides . . . It would sound so feeble a story over the telephone: 'Oh, I forgot to mention—I shan't be coming tomorrow. Going away for a few weeks.' No: it would be better to telegraph in the morning, and then write a letter.

His decision filled him with energy and agitation. Too impatient to wait for a bus, he walked home, reaching Merrion Square inside the half - hour. Letting himself in with his latchkey, he was greeted portentously by Mrs Tucker, who trotted into the hall while he was taking his overcoat off.

She addressed his back. 'Beg pardon, sir!'

'Yes, Mrs Tucker?'

'Madam's gone to bed.' He wheeled round: she faced him triumphantly. It's you that's brought her to this, with your goings-on, she seemed to be saying.

'Gone to bed! Do you mean she's ill?'

'She's not so well,' asserted Mrs Tucker firmly.

'Has the doctor been sent for?'

'Indeed he has. He's been and gone.'

'Well?'

'No cause for alarm, he said. They always do. Better after a night's sleep. The same as they said about my poor mother. But she never got out of her bed again except to ride to her grave. The doctor gave me . . .'

Roderick stood rigid. He was listening, but no longer to Mrs Tucker. In moments of excitement Mrs Tucker, ordinarily rather sullen, was a garrulous woman, and Roderick had evolved a technique for not hearing what she said. The same technique had come in useful in his dealings with Daphne on the two or three occasions when her grievance or her enthusiasm had found vent in loquacity. When a spate of words threatened, his mind instinctively closed against it, and he was attentive now, not to Mrs Tucker, but to his own mental conflict. Daphne ill! Was she really ill? How could he leave her then? How could he tell her? Was he, having screwed his courage up, to be beaten after all?

Mrs Tucker went on chattering, till he said abruptly, unhearing: 'Yes, yes. I see. I 'll go and speak to her.'

'I 'm getting madam a nice cup of malted milk,' remarked Mrs Tucker, offended by the interruption.

He was already on his way upstairs. A painful self-consciousness was at war with his anxiety. The situation between himself and Daphne being what it was, their friendship suspended and her heart bitter against him, he would have given a lot to avoid the coming interview. His solicitude was genuine enough, but Daphne, he feared, would take angry pleasure in dismissing it as the merest civility, and hypocritical at that.

He tapped diffidently on the bedroom door, and after a moment's pause, hearing no response, he tiptoed in, thinking she must be asleep. But she was not asleep. Propped against three pillows, she was sitting up in bed, a book lying unregarded in her lap.

'Hullo!' said Roderick. He was nervous. If she chose to treat him as an intruder, he could do nothing.

She glanced up. She was a little flushed, but looked anything but ill. Roderick noted with surprise how extraordinarily pretty she was, and his heart lightened, for hers was a prettiness that could not co-exist with anger or unhappiness. 'Oh, it 's you,' she said.

'What 's wrong?' You 're not going to be ill?'

She smiled, rather shyly, and held out a hand to him. 'Come and talk to me, Rod.' He took the hand gratefully and sat down on the side of the bed.

'Are you in pain?' he asked.

'No,' she said softly. 'That 's just it. I 'm not in pain any more. Don't be polite to me, Rod. Let 's be . . .' She left the sentence unfinished, her meaning sufficiently apparent. 'I 'm not ill, don't worry,' she said, reading his face. 'I 'm well again.'

He smiled. 'That 's why you 've come to bed, I suppose?'

'Yes.' She laughed, enjoying the absurdity, but added with grave happiness: 'It 's true all the same. I 've come to bed to think. It was so unexpected, and so wonderful.'

It crossed his mind that perhaps she was light-headed. 'I 'm not sure I quite understand,' he confessed. 'What has happened?'

'I suddenly got well: that 's what happened. Well in my mind, I mean.'

He gazed at her in concern, but with a flutter of marvellous hope in his heart. 'Do you mean——?'

'Yes. Don't ask me how. I don't know. But I suddenly knew that I didn't mind any more.'

'Didn't mind about . . .?' But that was something he dared not put into words, lest he should be deluding himself.

'About you and Elisabeth,' she explained.

Her use of that name, which she had never uttered before, told him everything and more than everything. He was in the presence of a miracle, something he had absurdly entertained in his wilder imaginings, but had never quite believed in or confidently looked for. It was utopian, impossible, like heaven itself. Yet it had happened. Here was Daphne unmistakably telling him so. In a flash he recalled that other reconciliation, away back in the summer when they had walked together along the cliffs at Widdicot. But that had been more than half hysterical, a grudging surrender, product of sheer exhaustion. This was different: the difference shone clearly in Daphne's eyes, ran warmly in Daphne's fingers, which he was still holding. Something indeed had happened to her.

He bent over her hand, feeling humbled and unworthy. Now that Daphne was restored to him his first impulse was to give up everything that had made her unhappy. He laid his head in her lap, and after a long silence he said self-accusingly: 'I had planned to go away with her tonight.'

Daphne's hand still rested in his hair. 'Had you?' Her voice was still rich and warm.

He looked up, half-smiling, half-ashamed. 'Yes. And to America tomorrow. She's got engagements there.'

Daphne met him with unflinching affection. 'I think it will do you good.'

'But of course,' he said, 'this alters everything.' She agreed. 'It makes everything happy.'

'I mean,' he explained, 'I shan't go now.'

'Oh, but you must,' she said quickly. 'I want you to go. And *now* above all times. It will be lovely for you—yes, and for me too.'

'But don't you see,' he protested, 'I don't think I——'

'You don't think you want to go,' she said. 'I know, darling. I know how you feel. But that's only for the moment. You do really want to go, I'm sure. And you'll be sure presently. And I'm quite quite sure *I* want you to go.'

It was unbelievable. 'You *want* me to go!' Yet he believed it.

'It will be lovely for you,' said Daphne, glowing. 'Just the sort of change you need.' He gazed with rapt attention: she had never looked so beautiful before. 'And such fun for me when you come back,' she ended, with a sigh of content.

'I shall love coming back,' he said simply. The profound truth of the statement surprised him. He perceived, too, that by these words he was already committed to going. A ghost of his old doubt

assailed him. Was it fair, was it safe, to count so
much on this newborn Daphne? Was it perhaps
only a mood in her, an ecstasy, doomed to short
life, and to be followed by a reaction of misery?
Or was it, again he asked, was this lightheartedness
the effect of a temporary lightheadedness, a golden
confusion of the mind due to want of sleep? 'You 've
been having bad nights, haven't you?'

She nodded. 'But I shall sleep tonight.'

'Very likely,' he answered. 'But we must make
sure of that. Are you *sure* you don't feel ill? No
pain anywhere? No fever?'

'No. Only happiness. It 's too much for me.
I 'm almost limp with it.'

'What did Cartwright say?'

Daphne frowned and laughed, indignation
mingling with amusement. 'My dear, it was too
absurd, her sending for poor Dr Cartwright!
I *told* her I wasn't ill.'

'But what did he say, nevertheless?' persisted
Roderick.

'Oh, he tried to let me down lightly. Didn't
call me a humbug to my face. Said a night's rest
would do me good. You know. And that 'll cost
you half a guinea, Rod. What a shame! But
tell me about this trip to America. Does Elisabeth
know you 're going with her?'

What a shrewd question! he thought. How
well she knows me! 'No, darling. I wanted to
talk to you first.'

With unaffected pleasure she exclaimed: 'How lovely! And what a lovely surprise for her!'

Moved beyond speech he put his arms round her, and for a while they held each other in silence, perfectly at rest. Roderick felt this to be the most intimate moment of their marriage, and with an instinct not to impair its bloom by trying to express the inexpressible, he shied away from his emotion and sought refuge in practicalities. 'I think you ought to have some sleep,' he said, gently releasing her. Twenty-six hours later, outside a Southampton hotel, he was to be confronted by a plump bowler - hatted stranger with words of hideous import in his mouth; and then, then only, he was to recall a phrase of Mrs Tucker's which he had never consciously heard: 'The doctor gave me some medicine to make her sleep.' From that moment, realizing how incredible the truth must sound in the face of what Mrs Tucker would testify against him, he must put his trust in lying, and with the less reluctance because he knew himself innocent not only of what they would charge him with, but of anything but grief for the Daphne he had so newly found and so quickly lost. In the long ordeal that was to follow, many hearts would beat for him. His father, his friend Mark Perryman, Elisabeth herself: he was aware, almost continuously, of these presences about him. But most of all it was the memory of Daphne that sustained him, of Daphne as he had last seen her: it was for

Daphne's love and with Daphne's courage that he schemed and fought to save a life which, but for this menace to it, would perhaps have seemed hardly worth the saving.

But into this moment there came no premonition of what the future held. 'I think you ought to try to get some sleep,' he said, and he remembered, suddenly, nights of sleeplessness he had suffered during his last visit to Heidelberg, when the excitement of a dawning new delight had kept the wished-for sleep away. He remembered the pleasant little German doctor he had resorted to, and he remembered . . . 'I 've got the very thing for you,' he said, exultantly. 'I got it in Heidelberg. Wait a minute.' After rummaging for a while in his own bedroom he returned with a celluloid pill-box in his hand. 'This is good stuff. It gave me fifteen hours of perfect sleep and left not a wrack behind,' explained Roderick gaily. 'But I got hold of a second dose, for emergencies.' On the bedside table was a glass of water which Mrs Tucker had placed there three minutes before his arrival home. 'Is this water fresh?'

He dropped a white tablet into the water, crushed it with a teaspoon, and stood watching it dissolve.'

'I say, Daffy!'

'Yes?'

'Wouldn't you rather I didn't go tonight? It 's not a bit necessary.'

He handed her the tumbler, and she took a sip.

'It doesn't taste *too* nasty. No, I'd like you to do as you had planned. Say good-bye now, at once, and leave me to have my sleep.'

He bent over to kiss her, but his eyes were troubled. 'It seems so ... unfriendly,' he complained.

'Silly,' said Daphne, smiling with a child's candour. 'Don't you see, Rod, it's just perfect, this moment, this good-bye. It wouldn't be quite the same tomorrow. Happy, but not the same.'

He was persuaded. He was almost happy. 'I shan't be away long, you know.' He stood hovering, about to go. 'Mrs Tucker said something about malted milk. I shall send up a biscuit or two with it, in case you're woken by hunger.'

She drank her potion. 'Kiss me again.' He kissed her, and wished he need not go. 'Good-bye!'

When he reached the door she called to him. 'Roddy!'

'Yes?'

'You'll give my love to Elisabeth, won't you?'

He delivered the message at eight o'clock that same evening: by which hour Daphne was already lost in dreams, adrift on a dark hurrying tide.

Fifty Classics of Crime Fiction, 1900-1950

With prefaces by
Jacques Barzun and Wendell Hertig Taylor

1. *Classic Stories of Crime and Detection**
2. Allingham, Margery. *Dancers in Mourning*
3. Bailey, H.C. *Mr. Fortune: Eight of His Adventures*
4. Bentley, E.C. *Trent's Last Case*
5. Blake, Nicholas. *Minute for Murder*
6. Bramah, Ernest. *Max Carrados*
7. Bullett, Gerald. *The Jury*
8. Burton, Miles. *The Secret of High Eldersham*
9. Chandler, Raymond. *The Lady in the Lake*
10. Chesterton, G.K. *The Innocence of Father Brown*
11. Christie, Agatha. *The Murder of Roger Ackroyd*
12. Cole, G.D.H. and Margaret. *The Murder at Crome House*
13. Crispin, Edmund. *Buried for Pleasure*
14. Crofts, Freeman Wills. *The Box Office Murders*
15. Doyle, Arthur Conan. *The Hound of the Baskervilles*
16. Eustis, Helen. *The Horizontal Man*
17. Fearing, Kenneth. *The Big Clock*
18. Freeman, R. Austin. *The Singing Bone*
19. Gardner, Erle Stanley. *The Case of the Crooked Candle*
20. Garve, Andrew. *No Tears for Hilda*
21. Gilbert, Michael. *Smallbone Deceased*
22. Grafton, C.W. *Beyond a Reasonable Doubt*
23. Green, Anna Katherine. *The Circular Study*
24. Hare, Cyril. *When the Wind Blows*

*Includes a General Introduction to the entire set.